To the Public

CC Anderson
4/26/15

THE FARM

Charles C. Anderson

outskirtspress

DENVER, COLORADO

The Farm
All Rights Reserved.
Copyright © 2012 Charles C. Anderson
v2.0

Cover Photo © 2012 JupiterImages Corporation. All rights reserved - used with permission.

Outskirts Press, Inc.
http://www.outskirtspress.com

ISBN PB: 978-1-4327-8860-5
ISBN HB: 978-1-4327-9093-6

Outskirts Press and the "OP" logo are trademarks belonging to Outskirts Press, Inc.

PRINTED IN THE UNITED STATES OF AMERICA

1

Lieutenant Commander Andrew Carlson, U.S. Navy SEAL, stared from the crest of a 900 foot sand dune at the smoldering hulk that had been an HH-60H Seahawk helicopter only fifteen minutes ago. If he had not been the first one down the rope, he would have been included in the twisted metal and fireball. Just as he had been trained to ignore physical pain, he would postpone his grief for the other member of his recon team, Petty Officer Josiah Chambers, not to mention the nameless pilot and copilot. The bottle would be there waiting for him when the mission was over.

The pilots were new to the Navy base at Bahrain. They would be easier to forget. But Josiah had been his closest friend for the last five years. They were more like brothers than partners. They had endured thirty months of SEAL training together. This was their sixth covert insertion into Saudi Arabia.

Covert was really not an accurate term, since a member of the Saudi royal family not only knew when Andy was coming, he had picked out Andy's targets and arranged for camels and water to be near the insertion site. A typical sniper mission took out a financial supporter of Al Qaeda or Hamas or some other terrorist faction. Other targets were simply identified to Andy as team leader, and no explanation given for their elimination.

This mission was a rush job from the get-go. A curt phone call from his CIA contact, Harrison, gave Andy and Joe thirty minutes to gear up and report to the helicopter tarmac. There were no written orders. Andy was informed by Harrison that the royal family had approved the mission. He wrote the GPS coordinates for the insertion site and recon target on his paper map.

Satellite intel had noted that a Russian freighter had delivered a shipping container to the port of Al Jubayl, in the Persian Gulf, west of the island of Bahrain. This container was transported by truck to the remote desert palace of a Saudi prince named Khalid. Their mission was to investigate the contents of the container, avoid capture or identification at all costs, and leave no witnesses to their presence. Andy completed his GPS and map work en route to the insertion site.

Andy and Joe had encountered blinding sandstorms before. It would not have mattered if the pilot were a rookie to desert flying or a veteran. No pilot could control a chopper that was sucking hundreds of pounds of sand per second into its engines. Andy dropped most of his gear the forty feet to the desert before sliding down the rope. He planned to stabilize the rope in the wind for Joe while the chopper hovered.

As he descended the rope, he heard the engines coughing. Their steady whine dramatically decreased, accompanied by his free fall the last six feet to the sand. Instinctively he rolled out from under the helicopter, which keeled over, dug its rotors into the sand, and blew up. Andy's pack was blown off of his back, but it absorbed much of the blast as he was catapulted away from the inferno. He had crawled, clawed, and run up the sand dune to escape the heat of the burning JP-5 fuel.

Andy took stock of his physical condition and gear from atop the sand dune. He stood up and checked his boots. He felt sore all over, but could find no injuries. He still had his dust goggles. His binoculars hung around his neck, held against his chest by an elastic apparatus. A bota bag of water was slung by leather straps across each shoulder to his hips.

The handheld GPS receiver and the short-burst radio that he had attached to his combat jacket had been blown away, along with his desert hat. He had programmed his entire mission, including his maps, onto the missing GPS unit. From his backpack he had lost his camera, his secure long distance radio, a tool kit, a tent, a blanket, and all of his food.

Andy checked his paper map and compass in the inside pocket of his combat jacket. He was dressed in desert camo. Bedouin robes were supposed to be with the camels. He checked his knife, always attached to his left thigh. His SIG Sauer nine mm pistol had grown to his right thigh during his SEAL career. His M110 sniper rifle was rarely off of his shoulder unless he was shooting or spotting. Inside one cargo pocket he carried desert camouflage netting. Extra twenty round clips of 7.62 mm ammo were in his combat jacket.

Andy reminded himself of his current position. The southern fifth of Saudi Arabia is called the Empty Quarter. This is the world's largest sandy desert. It is almost waterless, 250,000 square miles, and uninhabitable except for nomadic Bedouin tribes and their camels and sheep. His insertion site was 128 miles into the windswept, rippling sand dunes, which stretched as far as he could see in any direction.

The sandstorm had passed, leaving an orange sunset. Within minutes, the sky turned blood red. The temperature would soon plunge a staggering seventy degrees. But he had planned to travel during the night, to avoid the 120 degree heat of midday.

His first priority was to find the camels. Lowering his dust goggles, he checked his compass and focused his binoculars north. The camels were a small mound out of place compared to the sand dunes around them. If he had not seen camels huddled for a sandstorm before, he would probably have missed them.

There was never any consideration in his mind that he would not complete his mission. The whole process of choosing the right candidates for SEAL training is to identify persons who never give up. An excerpt from the philosophy of the U.S. Navy SEALs states, "I will never quit. I persevere and thrive on adversity. My Nation expects me to be physically harder and mentally stronger than my enemies. If knocked down, I will get back up, every time. I will draw on every remaining ounce of strength to protect my teammates and to accomplish our mission. I am never out of the fight."

Like every other SEAL, Andy was trained in the expert use of weapons, explosives, underwater and parachute insertions into hostile territory, land combat in any terrain, and close quarters combat with and without weapons. He was the top sniper in his class. He was a communications and navigation expert. He was fluent in Arabic. He considered himself a patriot and a warrior, an American who would come out fighting on behalf of the U.S. government and his commander-in-chief, the President of the United States. Andy was a fully-trained emergency physician and a binge drinker.

Being an emergency physician and an officer had no meaning during his SEAL training. The Navy was glad to have a SEAL with extra skills, but they would never compromise their training to accommodate anyone. Team leaders earned their position and respect by out-performing their peers. Each of the 160 potential SEALs who started in Andy's class had to complete stringent physical and mental screening tests just to qualify as candidates. They were all volunteers.

Most rang the bell on the beach and gave up on their own. The rest were dismissed because their performance in any area was merely good, not outstanding. They simply could not swim well enough, run fast enough, or lift enough. Some lacked confidence in one terrain. Some were unwilling to punish themselves. Some had no fire in their gut or were not suited for difficult decisions under pressure.

Most who survived the training were college graduates. Only four of the twelve commissioned officers in Andy's class earned their trident patch as a SEAL, and only twenty-eight enlisted men graduated. Once the right thirty-two men were identified, they trained for another thirty months.

A SEAL believes that there are few problems he cannot solve with explosives or a well-aimed bullet. In his mind, he is invincible. SEALs gladly go in teams of two, or six, or sixteen into any battlefield. They expect to be outnumbered. They take for granted that they may be wounded, soaking wet, trapped, deprived of food and water, fighting for their lives in freezing cold or searing desert heat. Most of their work is done in darkness, in two to six man teams. They do not complain. This is what they signed up for. They do not seek rewards or medals.

So how did a fully trained emergency physician end up in SEAL training? Andy blamed it on the kids of active duty personnel. He had gone to medical school on a Navy scholarship. After four more years of internship and residency training in emergency medicine, he owed the Navy four years of payback. The choice was to be a general medical officer in the Navy or do something that suited his personal skills.

Andy loved kids, but he had come to believe that they did not like him. Those little Navy brats who whined about their sore throats wouldn't even open their mouths unless he drew blood from their gums with his tongue blade. If he got the blade inside their mouths, the little hellions would chomp down and commence kicking, spitting, or blowing snot out their noses. Deployments to forward areas did not come along often enough between the months of working in the Navy clinics scattered around Norfolk, Virginia Beach, Portsmouth, and Newport News, Virginia. Thus, a SEAL was born.

The desert insertion site had been chosen by Harrison. There are few places in the Empty Quarter where camels could be bought like used cars and delivered within an hour. After all, a camel only walks two and a half miles per hour. A Bedouin oasis, two miles to the south, was such a place.

The Bedouins were the idealized version of the American cowboy. They were tough, self-reliant, and fiercely independent. These noble loners didn't become involved in Sunni and Shiite disputes. They wanted no part of terrorist organizations. They didn't look to Riyadh for financial or political support. Camels, sheep, gold, and goats were their money. They knew every blade of grass and teaspoonful of water in their ancestral territory.

Andy and Joe had been inserted near this oasis twice before. They had never had a reason to kill Bedouins. Andy didn't like the idea of using a repeat insertion site, but those were his orders. The camel trader at the Bedouin oasis was not Bedouin but traded with them. Andy didn't know his name but had seen his eyes, the only part of him left uncovered by his pale robes and headdress.

Harrison always arranged for the camel trader to be paid. Andy had only one contact within the Saudi royal family, Prince Salmon Abdullah Akbar, who had the ear of the king. The prince knew Andy as "R.E. Lee," his code name. They had never met in person, but had talked over a secure radio many times. Andy trusted Prince Akbar, as much as he trusted anyone in the Middle East.

Andy checked his compass and walked toward the camels at his desert pace of four and a half miles per hour. From a hundred yards away he could see that something was wrong. The two camels were not watching his approach. They sat perfectly still, their forelegs folded underneath them, staring across the empty desert with indifference.

He pulled up on the nose rope of the closest camel. Its head lifted and stretched out, but it would not get up. This was a new experience for Andy, but he had watched Bedouin shepherds deal with stubborn animals. There was an old saying that the Bedouins loved their camels as much as a man could love a camel, which meant they only hated them a little bit.

No matter how stubborn they were, camels were a necessity in the desert. They were also a disguise for Andy and Joe, so they could move unmolested in the desert. A man could not survive for more than a few days in the desert without a camel because he could not carry enough water to sustain himself.

He walked around to the camel's rump and kicked it. The camel didn't seem to notice. More kicks, gradually increasing in severity, produced no response in either camel. He tried pricking the camel's rumps with the point of his knife, but neither camel cared. Andy had seen Bedouins build a fire under a camel's hindquarters to get it moving, or pour water into its nostrils.

There was no point torturing these camels. He noted that their pupils were dilated. They had been poisoned. It didn't make sense that they were dehydrated. They could not have been at this location more than an hour. Their mucous membranes and mouth were not parched.

Two goatskin bags of water were tied to each animal. Andy estimated each bag held five gallons. He would need at least three quarts a day if he were riding, more if he were walking. Each gallon of water weighed over eight pounds.

But if the camels were poisoned, the water might also be poisoned. Hurriedly he removed the stopper of the nearest goatskin bag, pushed his finger into the spout, closed his eyes, and brought his finger to his nose. The smell was fetid. Camel dung had likely been mixed with the water. He checked each goatskin bag. They all stank. Vomiting, diarrhea, and dehydration from drinking contaminated water were not options on this mission.

The loss of the water and the camels was a disappointment, but unexpected hardship was not a source of fear to a SEAL. He processed the information. Someone had made a connection between his past insertions near the oasis and the subsequent death of a prince or a terrorist supporter. Such a person would likely be following his tracks in the sand.

But this new enemy would likely travel like everyone else in the desert, on camels. Andy knew that he could easily walk faster than a camel. There would not be enough light tonight for a man on a camel to see his boot tracks in the sand without a light or night vision goggles. A moving light in the desert could be seen from miles away. He would push on. Even with night goggles, few men could match his pace up and down the sand dunes.

He felt the two leather bota bags on either side of his waist. Unlike canteens, they made no noise from sloshing water. As water was removed, the bags collapsed. Each held two quarts.

He would have to change his course to Prince Khalid's palace. Under normal conditions Andy could use his handheld GPS display to watch himself move through the desert toward his target. He could make random movements and still arrive at his target. Now he had only a compass and his map. And the red glow of daylight was almost gone.

Andy opened his map on the back of a somnolent camel and placed his compass on it. He would navigate by dead reckoning. If he could maintain a course of seventy-eight degrees NE for thirty-nine and a half miles, he should see the palace or intersect the concrete road that ran from northwest to southeast toward the palace.

He must follow the compass wherever it pointed, never giving in to the temptation to skirt a high sand dune. Even a fractional error in course could result in missing the palace entirely, and continuing on into the desert. The ground would become more firm as he moved northeast toward the coast. The moon was only one quarter, but would offer some light. His compass used LED lighting, only visible to the person holding it. The stars were beginning to appear. The temperature was falling off a cliff. He wanted to identify the north star before he left, and confirm his course relative to it.

Whoever poisoned the camels and the water did leave a Bedouin robe and headdress tied to each camel's saddle. He covered himself from head to foot in the traditional dress, except for the slit in the howli which accommodated his sand goggles. Andy had been encouraged to grow a full beard, like a Bedouin. This meant he had to dye his sandy hair and beard once a month.

From his left hip pocket he retrieved a small GPS receiver/transmitter with a safety pin attached to it. He activated the lithium battery and pinned the device to the left shoulder of his robe. The battery would only last three days in the desert heat. The device would give him no information, but he could be tracked by satellite.

He looked at the camels. He would not leave them suffering in the desert. With a quick slash of his knife across each neck, they lay their heads in the sand. If those camels were rentals, he thought, Harrison had lost his deposit.

Andy thought of Harrison. He had never even met the guy, who had a squeaky voice on a secure phone. He was apparently the CIA's point man in the Middle East. Harrison's intel was never as good as that of his Saudi royal family contact, Mr. Akbar. Akbar did not seem to hold Harrison in high regard.

Harrison would know about the helicopter crash by now, from an AWACS plane or a satellite. Now that the GPS homing device on Andy's shoulder was activated, Harrison would know that at least one person had survived the crash. He would be following Andy's course across the desert.

At 2000 Andy strode briskly into the desert night air. He calculated that it would take nine hours for him to reach Prince Khalid's palace. Marching all night was as much a mental exercise as a physical one. Most important, he was not afraid of the desert. At this point in his career he had marched hundreds of miles at night in the desert with only a compass for navigation. He usually carried a forty-five pound pack.

Another man might be complaining about the cold night air. Andy was grateful to be marching at night because he knew what it was like to march in the heat of mid-day. The M110 rifle on his right shoulder no longer felt like extra weight. It had become part of his body.

One sand dune led to another, and to another. He thought of his father, who was currently visiting Andy's two brothers in Uganda, where they were missionaries. He looked forward to the report from his dad. They had always been close, especially since his mother's death. Andy had been sixteen years old when his mother had died of breast cancer. She was only thirty-nine. The miles in the sand passed quickly as he thought of his mother. His family was always praying for him, but he was not religious. He had never forgiven God. His comfort was Southern Comfort.

Abruptly, there was a faint light in the distance. It appeared as he reached the top of another sand dune. He stopped and lifted his binoculars. The light was perhaps two miles away. It didn't flicker like a campfire or twinkle like a star. He was confident that it was Prince Khalid's palace.

He looked at his watch. It was 0415. He sat down and studied his back trail with the binoculars. Nothing. It was time to rest. No man or beast could catch up to him for the next three or four hours. He would not need to worry about oversleeping. The heat would wake him up. His last thoughts were of camping overnight with his mom and dad at age ten. They had slept on the sandbar in the middle of the Appomattox River, on his family farm in Virginia.

Andy awakened at 0710 and quickly scanned his back trail with the binoculars. He had chosen a good spot to stop. The crest of the nearest dune behind him was over 800 yards away. He preferred to shoot at this range. The M110 sniper rifle had a sound suppressor which muffled everything but the sonic boom of the bullet. At 800 yards, even the sonic boom was undetectable.

His bullet could arrive at the top of the other sand dune in less than one second. The M110 was just as accurate as the bolt action M24 he had initially been trained with. Unlike the M24, the M110 was fed by the spring in the magazine. He could make one carefully aimed shot per second until his twenty round clip was empty. Within three seconds he could remove the empty clip and insert another from his combat jacket.

Andy drank the remainder of the water from the first bota bag and unstrapped the second, placing it in front of him as he lay prone on the sand dune. The barrel of the M110 rested across the bota bag. He removed the plastic lens covers of the telescopic sight. The sun was on his left. It would not create glare or give away his position by reflection on the lens. He dozed off again.

By 0900 the temperature was already ninety. He sat up and rested the binoculars on his knees, looking toward the palace. He could see two buildings, one with a dome, inside a solid wall compound. The Bedouin robes provided some protection from the heat, which had begun to radiate off of the sand, producing a rippling effect in his vision.

He turned 180 degrees to scan his back trail. A speck was moving toward him. It was 0930. The speck disappeared behind another sand dune. Within an hour he could make out a lone traveler on a camel. There was no point in shooting too soon. He would allow this man to bring his camel, water, and provisions closer.

At 1012 the lone rider stopped his camel at the top of the sand dune in front of Andy and lifted his binoculars. The 7.62 mm bullet passed through the center of his chest. The camel heard nothing and was unconcerned as his rider dismounted into the sand.

Andy walked the 850 yards back to the camel, which had folded his forelegs underneath himself and lowered his rump to the sand. This camel watched Andy's approach.

He pulled back the headdress and stared at the man's face. He knew those eyes. It was the Arab camel trader from the Bedouin oasis. The man had a curved Bedouin knife in a sheath underneath his robes, along with an antique pistol. The Chinese-made AK-47 tied to the saddle was not antique, nor was his M24 sniper rifle. If the M24 had come from a SEAL, Andy was glad to recover it. The rightful owner could be identified from its serial number.

A pocket inside the man's robe held two grainy pictures. Andy recognized himself and Joe. The pictures had been taken at an earlier visit to the oasis. He looked at Joe's picture and reminded himself that it was not time to mourn.

What kind of a man would poison his own camels and contaminate another man's water supply? The answer was in two hefty bags of coins, tied together and slung over the saddle. The coins were gold, but Andy didn't recognize the language or picture on the coins. He took one coin and put it in his hip pocket. Harrison would have to figure it out.

The camel was loaded with almost everything Andy needed. There was plenty of uncontaminated water in twin goatskin bags. He helped himself to all he could drink and poured a quart over his own headdress before refilling his bota bags. The camel was stocked with a tent, a cooking bowl, a tin cup, a teapot, tea, and some desiccated goat's meat. A bag of mixed grain and hay was apparently for the camel. A smaller bag contained German night vision goggles and extra ammo for the rifles.

Andy grabbed the nose rope and pulled the camel to its feet. This camel walked obediently behind him for four hundred yards. They stopped between the two towering sand dunes. It would make a nice base camp. He needed the tent for shelter. The camel was tired from its night journey. He would watch the palace during the day and recon it tonight. Harrison should be able to figure out what he was doing from the GPS receiver/transmitter on his shoulder.

He left the camel at base camp, content with a second bowl of water and a small pile of grain and grass mix poured from the bag onto a leather roll. It was not much, but enough to make a new friend. Friends were important in the desert.

Andy untied the tent roll and stuffed it underneath his left arm. The leather bag with the night vision goggles and the goat meat fit nicely across the left shoulder and rested on his bota bag. He slung the AK-47 on his left shoulder and his own M110 on his right shoulder. With this gear he climbed the sand dune toward Prince Khalid's palace. When the palace came within sight, he pushed the barrel of the AK-47 into the sand and fashioned the tent overtop. The camo netting from his cargo pocket disguised the tent. He backed into his day bed and lay prone, facing the palace. The sand would soon be hot enough to burn uncovered skin.

The day was bearable due to his lack of activity and the tent to block the sun's rays. He drank frequently from one bota bag, knowing that he had plenty of water at his base camp. He rested his chin on the other bota bag and watched the compound below with his binoculars.

The palace was typical for a wealthy prince, of which there were between 4000 and 5000 in Saudi Arabia. Each had one or more vacation palaces which sported concrete roads into the desert, underground water pipes, and utility poles made of steel. This palace had a pale blue concrete dome and a water fountain. The walls surrounding the compound were solid, but only six feet high. He made a note of the electric transformer on a steel pole inside the compound and the satellite dish on the roof, facing almost straight up.

The concrete road and the splendor of the palace were out of place in the desert. What he had thought was a second building inside the compound was actually the shipping container still atop its tractor-trailer. This was encouraging. If he could get a good look at the contents of that container without having to kill anybody else, he would be even more encouraged.

This thought seemed strange to Andy. He had never been concerned before about avoiding casualties. Enemies were enemies.

No traffic came or went during the day. No one ventured outside, at least as far as he could see above the compound walls. As the sun dipped to the horizon on his left, he inspected his M110 rifle. After removing the lens covers he used the telescopic sight to take a closer look at the palace's vulnerable points. He checked his watch. It would be dark in thirty minutes. He needed enough light to hit the transformer and the communications lines and to see who would exit the compound.

Andy's first shot disintegrated the telephone line at its attachment to the pole in the compound. One second later the satellite dish that had been pointed up was pointed down. The third shot caused a minor explosion at the transformer. Three people ran out of the door and

down the steps out of sight. Within a minute a large dark sedan burst
out of the compound and accelerated down the concrete road. A second vehicle soon made its exit, a white sports car. These people were
unwilling to give their lives for whatever was in the container.

Andy checked the gear he would need to recon the palace. He
replaced the lens cover on his M110 telescopic sight and used its quick-
disconnect feature to remove it from the rifle. He left the sight in the
tent and picked up the leather bag with the goat meat and the night
vision goggles. He methodically touched his binoculars, his knife, and
his SIG Sauer pistol. The people in the two vehicles had made the right
decision, he thought, as he slung the M110 over his right shoulder.

He walked toward the palace until it was dark enough to put on
the night vision goggles. They were fourth generation, state of the art.
If there was anyone left at the compound they would probably not expect trouble from the south, from the Empty Quarter. Nevertheless,
he kept his gaze on the widows and walls of the compound. When he
reached the wall, he sat down and leaned against it. He listened for
thirty minutes. There was no sound.

He got up and pulled the SIG Sauer from its holster. The gate,
which faced west, was wide open. Andy circled the palace inside the
wall and peered into every opening. He noted no movement or light.
The palace was silent, except for the water in the fountain. Returning
to the front of the palace, he walked through the open door into an
empty room underneath the blue dome.

The rooms of the palace were spacious but easy to distinguish with the
night vision goggles. The sand from his boots grated on the marble floor.
He stopped to listen. He heard the sound of bare feet running on the floor
in a bedroom to his left. A child? The unmistakable click of a lock.

Andy entered the room with his pistol out in front, quickly scanning from left to right in a crouched position. There was only one
closed door in the room, which featured a large Jacuzzi built into the
floor and a massive round bed.

He walked to the locked door and stepped to the right side. Whoever was behind the door was breathing rapidly. He spoke softly in Arabic. "You don't want to see my face and I don't want to see your face. Tell me what I need to know and I won't harm you."

After a brief pause, a young woman's voice answered in Arabic, "I'm just a girl. They don't care what happens to me."

"Is there anyone else here? You must be truthful."

"I'm the only one left, and I'm at your service."

"I don't need anything from you, young woman, except for you to stay where you are for an hour. I ask you again: Is there anyone left at this palace that will die because you have not told me about them?"

"No."

"Then stay where you are."

"I understand. What you're looking for is in the shipping container. I heard the prince talking about weapons that were very valuable."

"Thank you."

Andy checked every other room to confirm the girl's story. Satisfied, he holstered his pistol and pulled his gloves from the cargo pocket on his thigh as he walked back outside toward the shipping container.

The international shipping lock on the container doors had already been broken. Andy pulled a pen from the inside of his combat jacket and wrote the unique shipping container number and GTIN number on his sleeve. Adjusting the focal length of the night goggles, he crawled underneath the container looking for trip wires and explosives. He found none.

From underneath the rear of the trailer he lifted the handle of the right rear door with the barrel of his M110 rifle. He pushed the door open with the rifle before crawling out from under the trailer. Standing behind the trailer, he noted two tarps covering two wooden crates with built-in fork lift openings in their bases.

He opened the second door and climbed inside the trailer. Removing the tarp from the first crate, he stared at a device he had only seen in pictures. It looked somewhat like a generator with hand rails. He squatted and peered through the openings in the wooden crate. He recognized a new keyboard and battery, which was disconnected. The center of the device was a basketball sized mass of molded metal with dozens of wires protruding, each connected to a box under the keyboard. Russian lettering was on several metal parts. In the side of the basketball he found the female threads for the tritium reservoir.

The reservoir itself was shielded in a smaller lead box attached to the inside corner of the crate using brackets. The second crate proved to be exactly like the first. He covered the crates again, closed the doors of the shipping container, and pulled down on the handle on the right side door.

Some faction in Saudi Arabia now had Soviet-made Cold War era tactical nuclear weapons in the ten to fifteen kiloton size.

Andy re-entered the house and walked into the bedroom. The door was still locked. Technically, he was not authorized to leave anyone alive who knew that he had been at the palace. He was not authorized to take any prisoners.

He again took a position to the side of the door. "Are you still there?"

"I'm still here. You can speak English. My father sent me to a good school."

"I must go," Andy said.

"Will you take me with you?" she asked.

"Why would you want to go with me?"

"Prince Khalid's men took me from my school two months ago. They've done things to me. Now my family won't take me back. If the prince returns and I'm here, he'll torture me until I tell him about you."

Andy took off his night vision goggles and pulled a mini Mag-lite from the inside pocket of his combat jacket. He turned the light on and said, "Come on out."

She unlocked the door and walked into the bedroom. She was wearing her abaya. He studied her eyes. They were young eyes. She was five foot four, he thought, and slim, maybe sixteen years old.

"What do you know about the shipping container on the truck outside?" he asked.

"The container has powerful weapons that Prince Khalid expected to sell," she said.

"Who would buy these weapons?" Andy asked.

"A man named Harrison."

"This man named Harrison--what do you know about him?"

"He was here at this palace for three days, two weeks ago."

"Tell me what you remember."

"He is a small man for an American. He has a high pitched voice and wears his dark hair and beard like a small animal in the zoo at Riyadh," she said. "His friends call him Weasel."

"Tell me what you heard from this Weasel."

"No one here knew that I could speak or understand English," she said. "The Weasel's voice is so unusual that I could hear him whispering. He secretly buys weapons for the CIA. He and Prince Khalid have done business before, but they don't trust each other. The Weasel hurt me in bed. More than once."

"I'm sorry," he said. "Would you be willing to leave with me tonight, on a camel ride?"

"I have no future in Saudi Arabia. Where would we go?"

"First we would go to a helicopter crash, and then a Navy base, and then to America, I hope."

"I have prayed for this day," she said.

Andy asked, "Did Harrison ever see your face?"

"That was the only part of me he was never interested in. I doubt it."

"Does he know your name?"

"Not unless the prince told him."

"We need to give you a new name before we get to Bahrain."

"My name was all I had left."

"Do you carry any weapons?" he asked.

"Only my brain. It's a very good weapon because no one expects me to have one."

This girl had spunk. He liked that.

She followed him into the domed room.

Andy asked, "Did Prince Khalid have a radio or a satellite phone?"

She walked to a table and Andy followed her with the flashlight. She handed him a satellite phone, which was sitting in a charger on the table. "They left in a hurry when the lights went out."

"What should I call you?" he asked.

"Sahar. It means dawn in English."

"I don't understand what's going on here," he said. "You and I have apparently stumbled into an extraordinary circumstance. I don't know who to trust anymore."

"You can trust me," she said.

"I believe you," he said. "My name is Andy. While you find some shoes for the desert, I'm going to try to make a phone call."

Andy considered the reasons that Harrison might have for buying nuclear warheads. He could think of no justification for CIA trafficking in such weapons on the soil of an ally of the United States. The whole thing didn't pass the smell test. There was no honor in it. He would not be defending the United States or its allies if he assisted Harrison.

Sahar opened a cabinet in the domed room, lit a lantern, and brought it to Andy.

He examined the phone carefully. The battery was fully charged. He considered the risks of using the phone, knowing that the United States listened to many calls. He concluded that the risks were worth the possible benefits and dialed a number.

"Mr. Akbar, this is R. E. Lee. I am calling from the palace of Prince Khalid, south of Harad."

"But I have heard nothing from Harrison. You are not authorized to enter my country without my consent. I am the Saudi Ambassador to the United States."

"I know that, Mr. Akbar, and I apologize. Harrison told me that my mission had been authorized by you."

"I'm not surprised, but why are you calling my secure line?"

"I've found something here that requires your immediate attention. You must come at once by helicopter and bring a tractor-trailer driver. I won't be here when you arrive. I must cross the desert to my extraction point. This will give you enough time to come and remove the tractor-trailer. Harrison will send a team to remove the trailer as soon as I tell him what's in it."

"What was your mission?"

"Apparently Harrison didn't trust Khalid. I was sent to confirm the contents of the trailer. I'll not mention our conversation to Harrison. When you see what's in the trailer, you'll understand why I'm giving you this information first. I hope that I'm not being a traitor to my own country."

"You are a reliable man, Mr. Lee. The king will call you an honest man. We have been suspicious of Harrison for some time. He's helped us maintain stability. Both of you have solved problems for us, but we didn't know that Harrison was in the arms business."

"It doesn't make sense for Harrison to buy what I'm looking at," Andy said. "We have plenty of our own. The Russians are already allowing us to dismantle their weapons of this type. Terrorists would not sell such weapons to the United States. They would want these for themselves. If Harrison wanted these weapons destroyed or removed from the reach of terrorists, he could destroy them at any time. My sources tell me he is trying to buy these weapons for the CIA."

"And on Saudi soil," Akbar said. "Most disturbing."

"This will likely be my last trip into your country," Andy said. "Whatever Harrison is up to, I want no part of it."

"May Allah go with you."

"And with you, Mr. Akbar." He turned off the phone and stuck it inside his combat jacket.

"We have something in common, Mr. Lee," she said. "Both of us dislike Harrison. Both of us feel betrayed by our own country."

She was wearing a yellow scarf with her abaya, and sandals.

"You're a very good listener."

He took her hand at the gate of Khalid's palace. He could tell that she had never held hands. He showed her how to lock fingers. They walked silently as he looked down at his compass.

Within an hour they were back at his recon site. He picked up the tent and the AK-47. He reattached the telescopic sight to the M110 rifle. The camel appeared to be glad to see them approach, standing up as soon as he spotted them. Andy repacked the equipment on the camel and allowed Sahar to use his hands to step into the saddle. He took the nose rope and set their course into the darkness, toward the burned-out helicopter.

After a few hours of silence, Andy said, "We must invent a story about how I found you in the desert. You must forget that you know English. You have never heard of Prince Khalid or weapons. You must request asylum in the United States because you were raped, and your family left you in the desert."

"That will be an easy story to tell," she said. "How many wives do you have?"

As the helicopter lifted off out of the sand, tears trickled down Andy's cheeks. Grief can only be shoved into the back of your brain for so long. His partner, his confidant, his best friend, was gone forever. He didn't regret his SEAL career. But there were so few opportunities to save lives as a SEAL, and so many opportunities to take lives. The day had finally come. He didn't want to take any more lives. Once such a thought enters your head, you have no business being a SEAL.

Andy had long since repaid his debt to the Navy. It was time to save lives for a living. Harrison would find someone else to kill people for him. The steady drone of the engines and rhythmic vibration of the rotors had rocked Sahar to sleep. He looked down at the girl who leaned against him. He had forgotten how good it felt to save one life, to free one person from a miserable existence. He would have to stay sober until she was safe.

2

Eighteen Months Later

Dr. Andy Carlson applied a dressing of four by four gauze and wrapped the stab wound to the left hand of a twenty-three year old intoxicated woman. She had been trying to separate frozen hamburger patties with a butcher knife and had managed to shove the knife up to the hilt into the palm of her left hand.

Carlson had no emotional response to the girl. She was a bread-and-butter night shift patient. His mind was on other things.

"In this case, we shouldn't sew up the holes on either side of your hand," Andy said. "When the knife went in, it brought germs and hamburger. When I pulled the knife out, some germs and hamburger were probably wiped off inside your hand."

"What's going to happen?" she slurred.

"You didn't damage any tendons or nerves," he said. "The latex drain that I left in the wound tract will allow the infection to come out of each side while you take oral antibiotics and keep your hand in a splint and an arm sling."

"How long does that drain stay in?"

"When you come back to the wound clinic in two days, we'll take the drain out. Hopefully you won't have any infection. The worst thing that could happen is that your hand would need to be opened up in the operating room to drain a pocket of pus, an abscess. I'm optimistic that this won't be necessary. Penny is going to give you written instructions and prescriptions."

"Thanks, Doc."

"One more thing," he said. "If you will put those frozen patties in the microwave for about forty-five seconds you won't need a knife."

Upon entering the exam room, Andy had detected alcohol, marijuana, raw hamburger, spearmint gum, and too much perfume.

While un-wrapping the bloody towel from her left hand, he had noted the pattern of blood spattering on the patient's upper chest and left arm as well as the lack of blood on the bathrobe she currently had on. She had not been wearing clothes at the time of this accident, and did not put on the bathrobe until after wrapping her left hand and the knife with the towel.

The lipstick underneath her left ear and the frantic girl who accompanied her to the ED suggested that the patient was gay. The angle of the knife confirmed that this was indeed an accidental stabbing, not an injury sustained in self-defense. There would be no need to notify the police. Certain antibiotics could safely be used with little risk that the patient could be pregnant without knowing it.

"Dr. Carlson?" The triage nurse approached him.

"Penny," Andy said, "How's your leg?"

"Getting better."

Penny was a petite equestrian with short brown hair. She loved her horse so much that she didn't seem to tire of the continuous stream of injuries the animal inflicted upon her. Her latest trauma was a kick to her right thigh, from which she was still limping ten days later. It was never the horse's fault. Andy thought that if her husband had caused the same injuries, he would have been locked up by now.

"These two guys the paramedics brought in are interesting," Penny said. "They're brothers, medical students at Eastern Virginia Medical School. They're real Saudi princes, members of the Saudi Arabian royal family. Their demographic page says to send the bill to the Saudi Arabian embassy in Washington. Apparently they were walking outside their home in Ghent, where they live together, and two men assaulted them with baseball bats."

Andy looked toward exam rooms four and five.

"One has a nasty forehead laceration over his right eye with a big hematoma, but it's no longer bleeding," Penny said. "He had no loss of consciousness. The other got hit across his left knee and can't walk. Other than that, it looks like minor bruises. Neither patient had been drinking. The prince with the head injury has a sore neck. Neither has back pain. Both have stable vital signs and are alert."

"Send the guy with the head injury over to CT to get a head and neck study," Andy said. "When he gets back, do a visual acuity. Send the other prince for a left knee film. Check on their tetanus status and I'll get to them as soon as I can. Do they speak good English?"

"Better than that Southern twang of yours," Lindsey Baker, the night shift charge nurse, said from behind him.

Andy Carlson was now a thirty-four year old bachelor. His thick brown hair was bleached from outdoor work on his farm. It flopped across his forehead when he lowered his head. All Carlson men had prominent cheekbones and noses, with midline dimples in their chins.

Physically, the most impressive thing about Andy was his upper body. His neck, shoulders, chest, and forearms were massive. Perhaps the size of his upper body was more noticeable because he spent most of each shift in the ED leaning over stretchers, his neck flexed and forearms extended. Chronic neck pain is an occupational hazard for emergency physicians, especially tall ones.

"Dr. Carlson," Lindsey said, "the chronic lunger in room twelve has had three nebulizer treatments and oral steroids. He feels better and wants to go home."

The typical chronic lunger is a middle-aged to elderly patient who has destroyed his lungs by smoking, yet continues to smoke, even after requiring oxygen at home, or having a hole cut in his neck to breathe through, or having been placed on a mechanical ventilator in the past. Any respiratory infection is life-threatening to these patients.

"Get a room-air oxygen saturation and bring me his vital signs," Andy said. "What about his chest X-ray?"

"It was read negative by the radiology resident," Lindsey said. "The guy with the kidney stone in room six says his pain is coming back."

Andy reviewed his evaluation and treatment of the kidney stone so far. "He has a three millimeter stone in the middle of his left ureter on CT. He's had thirty milligrams of Toradol , four milligrams of Zofran, and two milligrams of Dilaudid IV about two hours ago."

"Correct," Lindsey said.

"Give him another milligram of Dilaudid IV," Andy said. "He should be able to go home soon with a prescription for Percocet and a referral to urology. A stone that size will pass on its own. I'll go in and explain it to him. Make sure he has somebody to drive him home."

Lindsey stepped closer and whispered, "You're not going to cancel out on me this weekend, are you?"

"Not on your life. I'm having trouble thinking of anything else."

Lindsey Baker had only worked at DePaul for three months. She had a lot of ED experience and had applied for the job of night charge nurse. She said that she was twenty-eight. Her nose was subtly turned up. She wore her thick auburn hair short and, so far as Andy could tell, never wore the same ear rings twice. She was five foot three inches tall and weighed less than 110 pounds. Her eyes sparkled when she laughed. Andy felt overwhelmed when she was close to him.

Andy worked all night shifts, partly because he had no family to go home to and partly because they paid him ten dollars per hour more for a night shift. He noted that the male interns and residents often hung around when Lindsey worked nights with him. She appeared to enjoy ignoring them.

"Dr. Carlson," Lindsey called. "The heroin overdose left A.M.A. He ripped out his IV and ran out the ambulance entrance shortly after we gave him Narcan."

Andy nodded. "Too bad we never had a chance to tell him he almost killed himself. Leave the chart on the counter and I'll sign it."

"I'll check for him outside," Lindsey said.

She placed the patient's chart on the doctor's side of the long desk at the nurse's station and walked out of the ambulance entrance into the parking lot.

Once outside, she looked around and took a cell phone out of her pocket. "Harrison, it's me. The Saudi princes are here. I was worried that the EMS crew would take them to Sentara. ...They'll survive... We leave in the morning. Make sure everybody is in the right place... Dr. Carlson is thinking about getting lucky... See you tomorrow afternoon."

She closed the phone, walked back into the emergency department, and said to Andy, "The eloper isn't in the parking lot."

Andy's thoughts shifted to his family farm as he completed his chart work. The Carlson farm in Farmville, Virginia had been purchased from King George II in 1743 and the 3400 acres had never passed out of the family. Ten generations of Carlsons were buried there. Most of the property was encircled by the Appomattox River, resulting in unusual privacy. Since his father had been killed in a light plane crash a year ago and his brothers were still doing mission work in Uganda, Andy owned and operated "The Farm."

Andy had completed a one year fellowship in trauma at Sentara Norfolk General following his retirement from the Navy. He scheduled himself for four twelve-hour ED shifts in four days, twelve-on, twelve-off. That left him four consecutive days off, time that he used to do those things that were in his blood—farming, building, and hunting with primitive weapons.

Such a routine also allowed him to schedule his binge drinking. He didn't drink in Norfolk. He looked forward to getting drunk during his first two days at the Farm, using the next two days to sober up. This had been his habit since his dad's death.

Up until a month ago the only woman in his life had been Sahar, whom he had enrolled in Old Dominion University in Norfolk. She was majoring in computer science, but her primary interest was Andy. The fact that he was twice her age did not deter her. Despite his reassurances that she would soon find the right man, Sahar stalked him like a panther. They met regularly for dinner, but Sahar refused to accept him as a father figure.

Sahar had abandoned her abaya. She was a lovely eighteen year old woman now, integrating rapidly into America. Andy felt guilty whenever he thought about her. To give in to his physical attraction for her would be dishonorable. He didn't save her life to take advantage of her.

Andy classified himself as an amorous drunk, as opposed to a mean drunk, a fightin' drunk, a sleepy drunk, a crying drunk, or a giggling drunk. As a teenager, alcohol had helped him dull the pain of losing his mother. He hadn't grown up with a sister. Approaching any woman who wasn't a patient without the help of alcohol was a steep mountain to climb.

On the other hand, once he had a few drinks Andy tended to be amorous with whatever was available, especially during his Navy career. On more than one occasion he had left a bar with a sure number ten, only to wake up with a number two. He could attest that such things happened in the real world outside of country music. The experience had scared him sober for more than a month on two occasions, during which time he treated himself for imaginary STDs that might have gotten through imaginary holes in his condom. In the Navy, he had solved the problem by taking Josiah with him to serve as an advisor in bars. Joe had a steady girl back in Virginia Beach and seemed content in this role.

Since his retirement from the Navy, Andy had come to worry that he could not have sex without alcohol. Sahar aroused feelings in him, but she was out-of-bounds. He vowed to abstain from drinking around her. Without alcohol, no other woman evoked sexual desire in him.

Until Lindsey had appeared in his life. While they had never actually had sex, there was clearly no lack of motivation on his part. Curiously, since Lindsey took over his thoughts, he had lost his desire to drink. He had never even discussed his drinking problem with her.

The abrupt end of his need to binge had set off a round of introspection over the preceding weeks. What had he been seeking in his binges, in exchange for the hangovers and self-loathing the following days? How had booze and loss and sex become so entangled? The answers were coming into focus. He had been seeking love. The love he had lost from his parents and from Joe.

For him, even those mindless one night stands were about love, the only cure for loneliness and emotional pain. Alcohol had become his only access to love. For this love he had been willing to crawl on the floor to empty his stomach in the toilet, over and over. Lindsey was going to change all this.

Lindsey had all of the physical attributes that Andy admired in a woman. As a lad he had an aunt who tried to suffocate him with her gigantic breasts every Sunday after church, using the guise of a hug. He tried to hide from her, but she would not be denied. He traced his love for small breasts back to this frightful period in his life. Drunk or sober, petite women were his first choice.

"Excuse me, Dr. Carlson."

Lindsey had silently walked up behind him while he was suturing a wound. She leaned forward with her mouth next to his left ear. He could feel her breath. Her perfume locked-on. Her right hand lingered on his shoulder. She spoke softly, updating him on the status of several patients. When she finished, he wished he had paid more attention.

Andy knew that other people who worked in the ED had picked up on the sparks between him and Lindsey. It was impossible to keep any secret for long in the ED.

They planned to have three days and three nights together on the Farm. He had invited Lindsey once before, but she had a schedule conflict. Things had fallen into place. They were planning to leave at the end of their shift at seven in the morning for Farmville, Virginia, a two and a half hour drive.

Lindsey returned to give more follow-up information and Andy tried harder to pay attention to what she was saying this time.

"Your head CT on the Saudi prince is on the PAX machine. The radiologist has already read it negative."

"I'll take a peek at the CT and go see him."

A computerized axial tomography study, or CT scan, allows the physician to take X-ray slices through any part of the human body, and then reassemble those slices in any plane. It is difficult to hide injury and disease from a CT scan.

The prince's CT showed only soft tissue swelling outside the skull with no intracranial injury. The CT of the neck was normal.

Andy picked up the prince's chart and walked into exam room number four. "I'm Dr. Carlson."

He shook the patient's hand. The prince listed his age as twenty-three. He was dressed as an American, with short dark hair, clean shaven, polite.

"I understand that you're a medical student at EVMS," Andy said.

"I am Muhammad Abdullah. My brother is also a student at EVMS, only he is one year ahead of me. This is my first year."

"What happened tonight?"

"We were walking near our apartment, not far from here, when two men jumped out of a car and beat us with baseball bats."

"Did you know either of these men?"

"We didn't know them or why they would want to beat us up."

"Were you robbed?"

"No."

"And you reported this to the police?"

"The paramedic said that the police would come to the emergency department to interview us. My head was bleeding."

Andy asked, "Have you been the target of a hate crime before?"

"We have been treated very well in the United States," the prince said. "We are so busy studying and going to classes that we don't travel much. No one has ever tried to harm us."

"Your wound needs to be cleaned out a bit and I need to remove some of the clotted blood under the skin," Andy said. "Are you allergic to local anesthetics?"

"No, sir."

"Have you ever had sutures before?"

"Once, in my foot, in Saudi Arabia, at King Faisal Hospital."

"Then I'm going to open up a suture tray and anesthetize your wound with a small needle and one percent lidocaine," Andy said.

He prepared the tray with non-sterile gloves, anesthetized the wound, and then switched to sterile gloves. He painted the area around the wound with Betadine, an antiseptic. The laceration was just above the right eyebrow, horizontal, seven centimeters long, but did not involve the right orbit. Swelling had already extended to the soft tissue around the right eye. Andy placed sterile drapes around the wound and began to remove the hematoma with his index finger.

"You'll have a black eye from this wound," Andy said. "The blood gravitates to the loose skin around your eye, and it takes about ten days for all of the breakdown products of blood to be absorbed. There's nothing wrong with your vision and you don't have any broken bones in your face."

Andy cleaned the skin around the wound with Shur-Clens and irrigated the wound with a syringe of saline. He repaired the wound using individual nylon sutures and gave his standard speech about wound care.

"Lindsey, could you give this gentleman a wrap-around pressure dressing for his forehead, with an ace bandage to top it off?"

She nodded. "Mr. Abdullah, I have some written instructions for you. Your tetanus status is up to date. Your sutures will need to be removed in seven days. We can do it here in the ED."

"They will have to be taken out in Saudi Arabia," replied the prince. "Our school year has ended and my brother and I will be traveling home on Sunday."

Lindsey looked up. Two Norfolk police officers were walking toward them. "The police are here to interview you, Mr. Abdullah."

Andy moved on to prince number two in the next room, Fahd Abdullah, age twenty-four. They looked like brothers.

"How is my brother Muhammad?" asked Fahd.

"He'll be fine," Andy said. "The police are talking to him. I'm Dr. Carlson. Tell me about your injury."

The prince extended his hand. Prince number two seemed as amicable as prince number one. He told essentially the same story as his brother.

Both princes spoke the King's English--the king of England, that is. Since Andy could not discuss his SEAL career, he didn't mention that he spoke Arabic or that he had been to Saudi Arabia many times.

"They were white males," Fahd said, "about our age. They didn't say anything or ask for our wallets. One of them hit me on the left knee. Now I can't stand up."

"Please excuse me while I look at your X-ray," Andy said.

After a few minutes, Andy returned. "There're no broken bones in your knee." Andy tested the ligaments of the knee and found them intact.

"The swelling is caused by a bruise over your kneecap, or patella. I don't see any fluid inside your knee joint. That means that this is not a serious knee injury, but a bruise."

The prince nodded.

"The reason that you can't bear weight is that the kneecap is part of the system that locks your knee when you stand," Andy said. "Any bruise from the quadriceps muscles in your thigh to the patellar tendon in your lower leg will result in a feeling of giving out if you try to stand. It's a reflex that warns you that locking your knee will be painful."

"What do I need?"

"A good splint and a pair of crutches for about a week," Andy said. "I would recommend an ice pack, a knee immobilizer, elevation of your knee above heart level during the next couple of days, and some short-term pain medication. If you don't try to bear weight, the bleeding around your kneecap will stop."

Lindsey moved in on cue, with a knee immobilizer and crutches.

Andy went back to the main counter and leaned against it as he completed the two records. *Haven't seen any Saudis lately*, he thought. Lindsey really looked nice with those pearl earrings.

The night wound down with coughs, sore throats, vomiting and diarrhea, allergic reactions, and alcohol-related trauma and illness. Andy's only real challenge was a sixty-seven year old female patient in congestive heart failure. By 7:10 in the morning he was searching for the day shift doctor. One of his best friends, George "Tank" Hedley, was looking over the patient tracker on the wall.

Tank asked, "Bad night?"

"Not really. I have one lady, Ms. Bailey, who was in respiratory distress from CHF, but I think she's going to make it. The guy with the kidney stone has a prescription on his chart, an instruction sheet, and a urology referral. He can go. He's been waiting on his ride. I'm going to finish up my paperwork while I wait to see if Ms. Bailey can grab the brass ring of life."

"All we can do is dangle it over the bed," Tank said. "They got to reach up and grab it."

"Dr. Hedley has the con," Andy said as he saluted him.

"Dr. Hedley has the con. Aye, sir." Andy loved to work with another former Navy doctor, who understood the proper way to change command.

Dr. George "Tank" Hedley was a talented career emergency physician whose life-long obsession was to stay in top physical condition. He signed his emails "Fitness is a journey, not a destination." He belonged to three health clubs in Hampton Roads, in case he got the urge to pump iron at odd hours or from remote locations. Unwilling to compromise with his thinning hair, Dr. Hedley shaved his entire head, hence the nickname.

Andy looked up Ms. Bailey's medical records on the hospital computer. She had a history of congestive heart failure, which had worsened several times due to non-compliance with her medications.

Walking back into room two, he found Lindsey adjusting the frequency of blood pressure measurements on the monitor over the patient's left shoulder.

"I haven't heard any screams from this room, so things must be looking up," he said.

Lindsey whispered, "You're good at what you do, Dr. Carlson."

"But we haven't done anything yet," he whispered back.

"I'll meet you at your truck."

The patient smiled.

"You didn't by any chance stop taking your medication did you?" Andy asked Ms. Bailey.

"I wanted to give it one more try," she said. "My pastor told me that all things were possible for those who believed. I believe now that he doesn't know anything about my heart."

"That's a fair assumption," Andy replied. "But you should be good to go in a couple of days."

She said, "I hope that you and Miss Lindsey have a nice weekend."

Lindsey looked at Andy and raised an eyebrow.

3

Andy pulled out of the ED parking lot, then headed north on Granby Street toward I-64. "Have you ever been across the Hampton Bridge-Tunnel?"

"I flew here from Denver and bought my little car. The traffic is so bad that I've been afraid to do much sight-seeing."

"The piece of real estate that we're now on is called Willoughby Spit," he said. "It was formed by a hurricane sometime in the 1800s. The Chesapeake Bay is on your right and the Navy base is on your left."

The sea gulls danced around in front of them as they moved slowly through Saturday morning traffic onto the bridge. It was the last weekend in May. The weatherman had promised a pleasant seventy degree high for the entire weekend.

"Can we stop at that new restaurant on the other side of the bridge tunnel and get a bagel or something?" she asked. "I saw an advertisement in the paper."

After arriving on the Hampton shore of the bridge tunnel, Andy took the first exit. They arrived at the gate of Fort Monroe. A security officer checked identification and then passed them through.

The food at *Thumpers* was not as spectacular as the view, but you can just do so much with a ham and egg sandwich on a bagel. They watched a dozen civilians preparing their sailboats for a day sail and admired ships moving in and out of Hampton Roads.

"You can see people on the decks of the ships," Lindsey said. "Could we drive over there to the seawall for a minute? My camera and binoculars are in your truck."

Andy drove over to the sea wall and parked the truck. On the opposite side of the seawall, fifty yards away and ten feet below them, were two young men sitting on the rocks with a fishing pole. Two familiar looking young men.

"I don't believe this," he said. "Look to your left at those two people fishing from the rocks."

Lindsey leaned forward. "It's those two Saudi princes from the ED. Hand me the binoculars in the back." She put the binoculars to her eyes.

"It's them, all right. The one with the head laceration still has the wrap-around dressing on, but he has a clean shirt on now. The other guy has the knee immobilizer on, but I don't see any crutches."

"They told me that they were going home to Saudi Arabia on Sunday," Andy said. "I guess they wanted to get in some fishing first. They aren't exactly sticking to my follow-up directions, though."

"That's their problem now," Lindsey said.

"If you were assaulted last night," he asked, "and probably had a terrific headache, or say, you couldn't walk without pain, why would you be fishing in the hot sun a few hours later?"

She laughed. "I'm sure that this isn't your first encounter with a con-compliant patient. You'll learn not to take it personally."

Andy reached for the binoculars. "The guy with the knee immobilizer must have crawled over that wall and dropped five feet to the rocks. He had a huge hematoma on his left knee. It must have really hurt to land on that leg."

"Look, there's a big ship coming," Lindsey said.

From the left a huge container ship plowed its way between the channel markers, only a 150 yards away.

Andy said, "That ship could be going to Norfolk International Terminals, over there behind the aircraft carriers. Or it could be going to the Newport News terminal, over there past the second island of the bridge-tunnel, or to Portsmouth Marine terminal, which is out of sight."

He handed the binoculars to Lindsey.

Lindsey looked at the container ship as it neared the gap in the Hampton Bridge-Tunnel. "I can read the names on the sides of the containers. Lots of different languages."

She swept the binoculars back to her left. "The Saudis are taking pictures of that ship."

Andy reached for the binoculars and adjusted the eyepieces. "That's not a camera."

He straightened up in his seat.

"Is something wrong?" she asked.

"That Saudi prince has a sophisticated laser rangefinder," Andy said. "It's made by LaserTech. It can range for miles. I know that model because I worked as a surveyor's assistant in high school. You hold it like a pistol and look through a telescopic sight. When you press the button, it sends a laser beam out to whatever object you're focused on. You get a digital readout."

He studied the pair and let out a long breath. "I don't know what's going on here. Get your camera and take a few pictures of these clowns."

"Why would two Saudi princes be under the seawall with a rangefinder?" she asked.

Andy peered through the binoculars. The rangefinder must have come out of that cooler on the rocks between them. The prince put it back into the cooler. The guy next to him appeared to be writing on something. His fishing pole was propped up between two rocks. There was only one pole. The prince next to the cooler pulled a real camera out with a zoom lens.

"Take a picture of the guy with the real camera. Get the guy who's writing, too," Andy said.

The container ship glided past. Andy took a deep breath and let out another long sigh. The Saudi prince continued to take pictures, and Lindsey continued to take pictures. Several more ships entered and exited the channel.

"He's not just taking pictures of ships," Andy said. "He's taking photos of those carriers at the Navy piers. See him shoot the Newport News Marine Terminal? Try to get him pointing his camera at several angles. Let's just sit here for a few more minutes and see what happens. Maybe they're just rich idiots."

Lindsey said, "He's got something else in his hand now, and he's looking down at it and turning from side to side."

"It's a GPS unit," Andy said. "Zoom in on his right hand."

"Why do Saudi princes care about the distances between ships and terminals at this spot?" she asked.

"I don't know yet, but I do see a pattern. He's used the rangefinder on four consecutive container ships entering the channel, but has ignored the three ships exiting the channel and heading out to sea."

"Why do we care, Andy?"

"He's taking something else out of the cooler," Andy said. "It looks like a windicator. It measures wind speed and direction. Take a picture. This isn't encouraging. He's dictating to the prince with the bad leg. Wasn't his name Fahd?"

"It looks like they're packing up," she said. "What do you think?"

"Take a look at the fishing pole he just pulled out," Andy said. "There's nothing on the end of the line except a sinker. No lure. No bait."

"So they weren't here to fish. What do we do now?"

"I don't know," he said. "People do strange things. Let's give them the benefit of doubt for a few minutes."

The prince with the injured leg struggled to his feet and slowly navigated the rocks back to the seawall, crawling on his hands and toes. The prince with the forehead dressing carried the cooler to the seawall and set it down. Then he stepped on top and was able to jump up and get his palms on the concrete wall, lifting himself up. The crippled Saudi prince handed up the cooler.

"Keep taking pictures," Andy said. "And start taking notes to time your pictures. There's a notepad and pen in the glove box I use to keep mileage."

Lying on his stomach, the prince on the sea wall extended his arm to the prince below. Using his good right leg to push off, the prince on the rocks swung his injured leg up onto the top of the seawall while holding onto the arms of the prince lying prone above.

The two loaded the cooler in the back seat of a black Nissan sedan.

"I'm going to drive out of this lot," Andy said. "As we circle around them, I want you to take a picture of their license plate. Can you do that by shooting behind my head?"

"I'm going to set my camera on very high speed."

As Lindsey prepared her camera for the shot, Andy backed up. He turned left toward the Nissan.

As they passed the Nissan, Lindsey said, "Got it."

"They left the fishing pole on the rocks," Andy said.

Circling around the lot in front of the Chamberlain Hotel, Andy continued back toward the Marina.

"I'm going to pull into the Marina where we parked before until they go past us," he said. "Then I'm going to follow them until I have a better feeling in my gut."

"This isn't going to interfere with our weekend, is it?" she asked.

"We can report them to the security guard when we go out," he said.

They watched as the black Nissan drove past them toward the gate.

After waiting for the Nissan to get a hundred yards ahead, Andy turned left out of the lot and followed. The Nissan was waved on by the security guard.

"If we stop to talk to the guard, they're going to get away," he said. "We won't know where they went. Where they go could be important."

As they reached the gatehouse, the officer looked at the visitor's pass on the dashboard and waved them through as well.

The black Nissan continued on South Mallory Street and turned west on I-64.

"Hey, they're going our way," Lindsey said.

Andy kept a safe distance. "It'll be easier to follow them on I-64. We can hide behind other cars."

Lindsey followed the Nissan with the binoculars. "I hope this isn't going to cost us a lot of time."

He looked at her and smiled. "I'm sorry. It may not take long."

She said, "They're taking an exit up ahead. It says Highway 134, Armistead Ave. and LaSalle Ave, Exit 265B."

"Then that's where we're going," he said.

Andy exited at 265B. "Langley Air Force Base is just ahead on your right."

She put her hand on his right knee. "Does that mean we can go on to Farmville?"

"It could mean they're stupid," he said. "It could mean they're indiscreet. It's too soon."

The black Nissan continued past the gate of Langley AFB and then turned right on 172 North.

"They're stopping at a parking lot just ahead, on the right, in the last row," she said.

"It's outside the gate of NASA Langley Research Center," Andy said. "I'm going to try to pull in toward the left with a couple of rows of cars between us. Get your camera ready."

Andy found a spot in the first row, facing away from the Nissan.

"I'll watch them in the mirrors," he said. "You get ready to take pictures."

The Saudi princes got out of the car and sat on the hood, looking around.

The prince with the knee injury had changed to some kind of T-shirt. They both had on baseball caps now, although Muhammad couldn't snap his Atlanta Braves cap in the back because of his wrap-around dressing.

"They're getting out the cooler and putting it in the grass in front of the car," Andy said. "We know what's in that cooler, and it isn't fish or sandwiches. They're smack in between Langley and NASA."

"What's here?"

"Langley is the Air Force's largest command," he said. "It's where the F-22A Raptors are based. They also have the 9th Air Force Fighter Wing here. NASA Research Center has all sorts of classified functions, but one of them is satellite communications. The prince with the head injury, Muhammad, has his GPS out again. The other guy is a lookout. Take a picture."

"Got it."

They watched the pair do their routine again with each instrument. Lindsey continued taking pictures and making notes.

Andy said, "No one notices behavior like this because everybody carries Blackberries and cell phones and lots of electronic stuff. But tourists don't need a lookout or a long-distance rangefinder or a wind instrument. If a tourist had a GPS unit he would be using it to navigate with, on the dashboard of his vehicle, not locking-in military bases.

The pair put the cooler back into their car.

After the Nissan pulled out of the lot in front of NASA, Andy followed it back to Armistead Avenue, where it turned left.

"They're heading back the way they came." Lindsey looked through the binoculars. "No, they're turning right on Mercury Boulevard."

Andy groaned.

"They are still going west on Mercury Boulevard," she said. "What's on Mercury Boulevard?"

"About three miles from here Mercury Boulevard crosses New Market Drive, and just beyond that is the James River Bridge."

"What's there?" she asked.

"Newport News Ship Building," he said. "All the Nimitz class carriers were built there. It's the only shipyard capable of building a nuclear carrier. They also build nuclear submarines."

At New Market Drive, the Nissan pulled into a Taco Bell. A horizontal crane from the shipyard towered just over the hill. Andy found a spot in the parking lot. The Saudi princes repeated their now familiar behavior. Lindsey zoomed in and got more pictures.

Andy slumped in his seat. "I don't think that following these guys any more is worthwhile. It doesn't matter what they do now. They've already done enough suspicious things that we have to report them. I have a contact in the CIA who deals with the Saudis. I don't like him, but he should know about this."

Lindsey smiled at him. "You're right. It's not our job to chase suspicious people around Hampton Roads. Let's report what we've seen and offer our pictures. Let the professionals take over. I'd rather spend the rest of the weekend getting to know you better and visiting the Farm than chasing Saudi princes."

"I hope you mean to encourage me," Andy said.

4

A ndy turned the wheel toward Farmville. "Would you mind getting my cell phone out of the briefcase in the back and asking the operator for a number for the CIA?" he asked.

Lindsey located the briefcase on the jump seat of the extended cab. "Is it locked?"

"It has a combination lock but it's too much of a hassle to use. I just keep it on 000. My phone should be clipped on one of the dividers inside."

Lindsey clicked the two locks and opened the briefcase on the jump seat. "I don't see a phone."

Andy's lips tightened. "I'm sure I packed it before going to work last night. Maybe it's in my travel bag. If you don't mind picking through my underwear and socks, would you look? The bag is behind me in the floor."

Lindsey closed the briefcase, pushed it to the left, and picked up Andy's leather bag and put it on the jump seat. She rummaged around in the bag while Andy frowned.

"I can't find it," she said.

"When we get to the Farm, I'll look for the phone again," he said. "I can use the land line in the farmhouse. How about your cell phone?"

"I didn't bring my cell phone," she said. "If I brought it, then I would be called to come in and help out in the ED at some point over the next three days. I just wanted to spend this time with you. Why don't we call DePaul when we get to the Farm and ask Delores to pull the ED records for our Saudi princes? Delores can be very discreet. She could fax us the records or email them to your computer. It may save time."

"Good thinking."

She asked, "Why couldn't these Saudi princes have gotten the information they wanted from a map of Hampton Roads? A good map would show where all the military stuff is."

"Some of it, but not the critical stuff," he said. "They couldn't know how many carriers were in port from a map. They couldn't know prevailing wind directions and speed from a map. Without coming to Old Point Comfort, those Saudis wouldn't know that almost anyone can get within a few hundred yards of the Hampton Bay-Bridge tunnel shipping channel, perhaps the most vulnerable spot in America. It's within spitting distance of NOB, the largest Navy base in the world."

Andy motioned toward the marina. "There are lots of private ships over there to hide a weapon in."

"If you're thinking nuclear, why not park a truck with the thing in it near the sea wall," she asked.

"That would require smuggling a nuclear weapon into the country by some means," he said. "There are radiation detectors at border crossing points. A container ship would be much easier, because those ships pass right through that channel every day with containers from all over the world."

"Doesn't somebody inspect all of those containers?" Lindsey asked. "They probably have radiation detectors at all of the international ports in Hampton Roads."

"Only a small fraction of containers are actually inspected once they get here," Andy said. "But who says that the ship ever has to reach one of the ports? You brought up the nuclear threat. A nuclear weapon would do the most damage to Hampton Roads if it went off on a container ship in the channel next to Old Point Comfort, before it ever reached a port...." He put his foot on the brake, checked the rear view mirror, and pulled off onto the shoulder of the highway.

"What's wrong, Andy?"

"There's one possibility that just occurred to me."

She smiled. "Go ahead."

"Part of my military training was to doubt the obvious."

She shifted in her seat. "What do you mean?"

"What if somebody wanted us to see the Saudis at the seawall?"

"Don't you think that's a little far-fetched? We just stopped for breakfast."

"But we stopped at your suggestion," he said slowly. "When you don't know what's going on, it's important to consider even the ridiculous."

"I'm glad to hear you use the term ridiculous." She looked away.

"Maybe I should be praising God that you were hungry, and because of that hunger we stumbled onto something important. It bothers me that someone of my background would have two encounters with a pair of Saudi princes within one day and that you were present on both occasions. Hampton Roads is a big place. That's a lot of circumstance."

"I didn't schedule your shift last night," she said. "And I couldn't have assaulted two princes while we were working together. What possible motive could I have for bringing you here?"

Her voice was shaking. "I don't like the way you're attacking me. Maybe this weekend was a mistake."

He saw the tears out of the corner of his eye.

"I'm sorry," he said. "You're right. I'm reading too much into this. You were asking about how we know what's in the containers before they arrive."

She sniffed. "We don't have to talk about it, okay?"

"No, it was a good question. Each ship has to radio their manifest to the terminal in the U.S. long before they get here. So there is some opportunity to identify cargo that sounds suspicious. Unfortunately, what's on the manifest for a container may have little to do with what's inside. Most containers are sealed at the company that manufactured the contents and are never seen by anyone until they reach their destination in another country."

"Then how do we know that somebody doesn't tamper with a container after it has been inspected and locked?" she asked. She was wiping her eyes with a tissue.

"We don't," he said. "We're still depending on the good will of our trading partners for an awful lot. And the world is not so full of good will these days."

"What did you mean about someone with your background? Do you know any Saudis?" she asked.

"The ones I know I can't talk about," he said.

"You don't trust me anymore, do you?"

"It has nothing to do with trust. I worked for the military and I took an oath not to talk about individuals and places. I'm still in the Reserves."

"Then tell me something about Saudi Arabia."

"The Saudis supply the lion's share of all the Islamic terrorists. They supply most of the cash to fund terrorism. Unfortunately, they also own much of the world's oil reserves. We can't get along without their oil. It would be an understatement to say that the U.S. relationship with the Saudis is complex."

"I think it's a little convenient that those two princes will soon be on their way back home," she said. "Maybe that means that something will happen soon."

"That's a possibility," he said, "but the key to what they're up to may be the places they visited."

"They covered a lot of ground."

"That's true. But it would be nearly impossible to attack all of those targets individually. There's only one type of weapon that would be sure to damage everything they scouted. Now that I've considered everything, there's no way for you to know what previous contact I've had with the Saudis or with nuclear weapons."

"Would you take a good look at me and ask yourself if I resemble any nuclear terrorists you've ever seen?"

He glanced at her and laughed. "To be honest, I haven't really seen enough of you to make a definitive determination."

"I've heard that Saudi women are not sexually aggressive," she said. "Perhaps before the day is over, you'll feel more comfortable which side I'm on."

Andy groaned.

"So tell me what a nuclear explosion would do to Hampton Roads while you're waiting to learn about sexual aggression in American ED nurses," she said.

"Hampton Roads would be put out of business just like Nagasaki and Hiroshima," he said. "It would take years to decontaminate and years to replace everything here. Who would want to work in an area that caused cancer? Thousands of people would be killed."

They rode in silence.

She touched his shoulder. "What are you thinking? I hope I'm not a suspect anymore."

"If there is a plot here, and it's successful, the United States could not rebuild four nuclear carriers," he said. "The only shipyard capable of building those Nimitz class carriers would be too contaminated to use. The last time I heard, each carrier cost five billion dollars and took five years to build."

"I've had enough of this, Andy. Let's call your CIA contact as soon as we get there. You're not in the military anymore, at least not active duty. You've got other duties this weekend."

"My driveway is coming up."

"I'll show you everything if you show me everything," she said.

5

The Farm had formidable natural boundaries. Thirty-four hundred acres lay inside a sharp turn of the Appomattox River northwest of Farmville. To the east of the Farm was Plank Road, and to the north, Airport Road. Only one gravel road led into the Farm, from South Airport Road. The River protected the backside and left flank of the Farm.

Since the two asphalt roads were lined with mature trees and barbed-wire fences and had no entrances to the Farm, the result was an unusual amount of privacy for Andy. No one lived on the Farm when he wasn't there. Only one neighbor across South Airport Road, Charlie Dodd, knew the combination to Andy's gate. There were no neighbors within two miles of Andy's home in the woods.

Andy got out of the car, opened the gate lock, and swung the door wide open. After driving in a couple of car lengths, he got out of the truck again and locked the gate behind him.

"Get ready to step back in time," he said.

The gravel road had one wide lane. A thick stand of twenty year old pines lined the road for the first 150 yards. Then the road narrowed, with mature hardwoods on either side. Just before the last gentle right turn down to the covered bridge over Dry Creek, a massive hill rose on the left side of the road.

"That's Little Round Top," Andy pointed to the hill. "It's shaped like a giant Hershey's Kiss."

Dry Creek was an additional barrier to the outside world. This bridge was the only way to get across Dry Creek, which wasn't dry. With the exception of the point where Andy's covered bridge spanned the creek, several hundred yards of swampland obscured the creek banks from the time the creek entered his property at South Airport Road until it emptied into the Appomattox River. This swamp barrier was the work of local beavers, who had created a maze of stick dams, ponds, and hutches to obscure the true depth of the water. Andy considered the beavers his allies, helping to hold off the modern world.

To get to Andy's farmhouse a person had to either cross the covered bridge, swim a major river, or cross a swamp. Only the beavers, the deer, and Andy knew how to cross the swamp without becoming disoriented or ending up in muck up to the eyeballs. Poachers had given up trying to hunt the Farm centuries ago.

As the truck reached the center of the wooden-covered bridge, Andy stopped to let Lindsey look out of the two windows on each side at the water below. The tin roof crackled as it heated up from the sunlight. They opened the windows of the truck to enjoy the breeze.

Andy put the vehicle in park and leaned toward Lindsey. The kiss started out soft and tender.

He disengaged. "I think I could be getting ahead of myself."

They both sat up straight, giggling.

"You built this bridge, didn't you, Andy?"

"Yes, I did," he said, putting the truck back in gear and moving forward up the hill. "It took me almost two years to finish. My ancestors have been building bridges across Dry Creek since 1743."

"It's gorgeous, and romantic."

"Look at the 1860 smooth bore cannon at the top of that alfalfa field to the left. We have three cannon that were left here by the Confederate army during the retreat to Appomattox."

"What do you raise on the Farm?"

"Twenty-four hundred acres of pine trees. Seven hundred fifty acres of hardwood. I have about fifty acres of alfalfa, scattered around in eight small fields. I sell it to my neighbors, who raise horses. That's my barn and shop on the right."

At the top of the hill the farm road came to a T.

"To your left is the original plantation house, about a quarter mile." He pointed. "We'll go down there and explore tomorrow. It's been restored."

He turned right at the T and then left into his driveway.

Andy's farmhouse was a long one-story ranch style with cedar siding and a central brick chimney.

When the truck came to a stop in front of the farmhouse, Lindsey stared at an eighteenth century grist mill only forty yards to the right of the farmhouse. Water splashed over the top of a huge wheel into a pond below.

He got out of the truck. "At night I turn on a light at ground level and it shines on the waterwheel. It's a unique sight. We could sit in the grass when it gets dark and enjoy it."

"Those gears inside look like a giant old watch," she said.

"We're going to have plenty of time to look at the mill and my still, which occupies an entire building behind the mill," he said. "But I've got to make that call before I can relax."

They unloaded the truck into the floor of the great room. Andy found Harrison's number in a file in his office.

"Harrison, this is R. E. Lee."

"What can I do for you?"

Andy explained the bizarre behavior of the Saudi princes and admitted that he did not know what it meant.

Harrison responded with a chilling observation. "You are the only person who can verify that Saudi extremists have the nuclear capability to hurt us in Hampton Roads."

Andy played dumb. "You never recovered what I found in that container in the desert?"

"The truck and the container were gone when we got there," he said. "I'm going to send a couple of FBI agents to talk to you. I need details now, and you're good at details. They may remind you of something you saw. Give me your location."

Andy was reluctant to give Harrison his address but complied. He informed Harrison that the Farmville Municipal Airport was next to his farm. The agents could get there quickly by helicopter. Andy got up to unlock his gate on South Airport Road. They would likely use the only rental car at the Farmville airport.

"They say that they can be here in one hour. I hope this won't take long," he said to Lindsey.

6

"Let me show you around my house while we're waiting on those two agents," Andy said. "This is my favorite room."

A single giant four-inch by fourteen-inch ridge beam in the center of the room supported vaulted white ceilings descending on each side of the beam to real vertical knotty pine plank walls. A unique crown molding fit the juncture of the sloped ceiling with the walls. A chimney anchored the ridge beam in the front of the great room, with an old brick fireplace at floor level. The other end of the beam disappeared into a wall that separated the great room from the dining room.

The oak floor of the great room had a thick Persian rug. Animal heads with gigantic antlers extended above the walls into the space normally occupied by a square ceiling or ceiling joists. Each wall had four heads, their antlers highlighted against the slanted white ceiling by lighting from table lamps. Each gabled end of the room held a collection of other mounted heads, with shelves for smaller animals built into the brick or pine.

A huge six by six elk was mounted over the fireplace and faced a caribou on the opposite wall. There were mule deer and white tail deer, each with massive antlers. A full body stuffed mountain lion crouched high on top of an entertainment center. Its teeth were bared menacingly.

Lindsey stepped back when she saw it. "It could have jumped on me when I walked into this room. I never even saw it until I was in the center of the room."

"Most people never see a cat like that alive," he said.

A full body mounted bobcat prowled inside the built-in bookcase on the wall facing opposite the fireplace. A black bear's head guarded the door to the master bedroom, on the left side of the great room. The wooden coffee table was handmade. The easy chair and couch had brown leather coverings with wooden forearm rests carved to match the coffee table.

"You built all of this?" She turned around 360 degrees.

"I enjoy building."

There was only one picture in the great room, an original post-war oil painting of Robert E. Lee. It was Andy's prize possession, and occupied a cherished spot on the mantel, just below the six by six elk.

"This picture was painted in May of 1869, while General Lee was being photographed by Matthew Brady," he said. "It was the only time that the General put his Confederate uniform on after the war. He died in 1870."

"How did you end up with it?" she asked.

"That's one of those family secrets," he said. "It's a one-of-a-kind painting that most of the world doesn't know exists. If you will look closely at his beard you can see the stain of tobacco juice on the right side. He had likely suffered a stroke and had right sided facial weakness."

"You have a passion for history, don't you?"

"Upstairs in the plantation house are two barrel-top trunks with leather hinges. These were brought by my ancestor to America in 1635. The barrel top allowed the trunk to lie on its side and fit up against the curved hold of the ship he arrived on, "The Bountiful Hope." I have a copy of the manifest of this ship which lists Richard Carlson as a passenger, and a family Bible that records marriages and births and deaths back to 1624, when my family lived in England. This kind of documentation doesn't make me any better than anybody else, but it does make me a historian by default."

"It sounds like your family has had a fifty-yard line seat at the history of the United States," she said.

"No ma'am, my family has played in every game."

Lindsey nodded and continued walking through the house. Andy picked up the groceries and walked into the kitchen. The sound of kitchen cabinet doors and the refrigerator door reverberated through the house. Andy noted that Lindsey had left two bottles of red wine on the kitchen counter next to the double sink. He would tell her this weekend.

The phone on the coffee table in the great room rang. Lindsey picked it up before Andy could get to it.

"Yes, he's here. Just a minute. May I ask who's calling?"

Lindsey handed the receiver to Andy. "It's a girl named Sahar," she said.

Andy winced and sat down in his La-Z-Boy. Lindsey sat down on the couch next to his chair and smiled at him.

"Hello," he said. "She's a friend, Sahar...Yes, she's very pretty... All weekend, I hope...Next Tuesday night...How's school?... Meet any interesting boys yet?... Okay, I won't ask that question again... Thank you for calling. Goodnight."

"She's Arabic, but speaks very good English," Lindsey said.

"A foreign exchange student. Right now I'm her only friend."

"She sounds a little possessive of you."

"That's insightful, but nothing to be concerned about."

"I wasn't concerned. Is she pretty?"

"Don't jerk me around, Miss Baker," he said, springing out of his chair.

He straddled her legs and pinned her arms against the back of the couch. "You could force me to take aggressive action."

It was an aggressive kiss.

She moaned, but wiggled out from under him and stood up.

"Do you get inspiration from all these animal heads mounted on the walls?" she asked. "The ones with horns?"

"Sometimes."

"I don't even recognize some of your animals," she said, walking into the master bedroom. "Are those sheep or goats?"

"A couple of each."

"And you shot all of these with a gun?" she asked.

"I never shoot animals with guns. No challenge. Most of these were killed with a handmade bow and arrow. Some were killed with a knife. Some with a spear. That's what I did when I was on leave in the Navy. Stalking animals teaches stealth."

He pointed toward a tall, slender wooden barrel in the corner of the room which had four spears. The spear tips pointed toward the ceiling.

"Where are the knives?"

"I have to keep the knives locked in the gun closet downstairs," he said. "When I left them in the great room on the mantel or on the coffee table, people were always cutting themselves."

He pointed to a black ram on the wall in the dining room. "I once spent a week in Hawaii hunting black rams and wild boar with a spear. A native there named Pablo taught me to hunt with only a loincloth, a spear, and mud on my body."

"Could I cook you a real meal for dinner tonight, not involving the imminent death of an animal, perhaps with a bottle of wine?" she asked.

"I would love that," he said.

"You said we had something to do before the FBI gets here," she said.

"Get your camera."

She opened her pocketbook and handed the camera to him.

He walked into his office to the right of the great room. Lindsey followed.

He inserted the memory card into the printer. "I want to download all of the pictures you took today into a file, make copies on plain paper, and then burn a CD with all of the pictures on it."

"Would this be for the FBI?" Lindsey asked.

"Maybe it will shorten their time here."

Andy sat in front of his computer and turned on the master switch. After booting, he clicked on the photo software on his computer desktop and inserted the memory card in the printer. Lindsey stood in the doorway and watched.

"Why don't you change clothes?" Andy asked. "You can use the master bedroom on the other side of the great room. Put on some jeans and you won't get mosquito bites when we go out for a walk tonight."

Andy dialed the number at the registration desk at the DePaul ED from his computer desk, and was connected to the ED at DePaul. "I need a favor, Delores. I need for you to be discreet about it."

"You know me."

"Last night I saw two Arab patients in the ED who claimed to be members of the royal family of Saudi Arabia," he said. "Their names were Muhammad Abdullah and Fahd Abdullah. I need for you to find their charts, scan them including all of the demographic information, and email them to me. Could you do that?"

"Not without committing several HIPAA privacy violations. Give me about fifteen minutes."

Andy put down the phone and looked at the pictures. They were exceptionally good, almost professional looking. Even the Nissan license plate was easy to read.

He made a new file to include all of the pictures and printed all twenty-six color pictures on letter-sized white paper. When the prints were almost completed, Lindsey returned. She stood in the door of the study, smiling, radiating her signature perfume. The jeans were tight.

"Did you get everything you needed downloaded?" She moved her hand across the back of his neck.

"Just about." He smiled up at her. He stacked the pictures on the desk next to the printer.

"You're quite a photographer," he said. "Would you write down the time and place of each photograph at the bottom of each photo, using your notes?"

Andy checked his email. The charts from Delores were already there. He forwarded the file to his computer at the Cow Palace, attaching the file of pictures. He placed a blank disc into his DVD burner and copied the same files of pictures and ED records to the disc. The ED records from Delores were printed onto letter-sized paper.

In the emergency department Andy had learned a hard lesson. When something goes wrong or occurs unexpectedly, it is important to gather all pertinent information, make copies of documents, and secure them. No two people remember the same event quite the same way. Something important had happened today. Why had it happened to him? And what role, if any, did Lindsey play in it?

7

Car wheels rattled over the heavy planks of the covered bridge. Andy looked out the window and recognized the grey Crown Victoria rental car from the airport pulling into the driveway. He met two gentlemen at the door.

"I'm Sid Bennett and this is Brandon McNeil. We're from the Richmond office, FBI."

Both men held up authentic-looking identification badges and photo IDs. They wore dark business suits and both had short dark hair. Bennett sported a short handle-bar mustache. McNeil once had his nose broken. They were approximately the same height, but Bennett had fifteen to twenty pounds on McNeil. They wore shoulder harnesses but no body armor. Bennett was about forty years old and McNeil a few years younger. Bennett's accent identified him as a Yankee, probably a Bostonian.

"This is Lindsey Baker, who was with me this morning when we had the encounter with the two Saudi princes." Andy said. "We work together at DePaul Hospital Emergency Department."

Mr. Bennett clearly was the man in charge. His aftershave was designed to disguise the alcohol on his breath.

"Brandon has a camcorder and a tripod in the car," Agent Bennett said. "Do you mind if we tape this interview?"

Andy and Lindsey looked at each other and shrugged.

Agent McNeil got up to get his equipment from the Crown Victoria.

"I'm going to comb my hair and put on some lipstick, if I'm going to be in the movies," Lindsey stated, returning to the master bedroom.

Special Agent McNeil set up the tripod and camera. Lindsey returned in her tight jeans, fresh makeup, and pink T-shirt.

Bennett began by stepping into view of the camera. "This is Special Agent Sid Bennett of the Richmond FBI office and Special Agent Brandon McNeil is behind the camera. This interview is conducted at the home of Dr. Andy Carlson in Farmville, Virginia on Saturday, May twenty-eighth. Dr. Carlson is seated to the right of Ms. Lindsey Baker, a nurse who works at DePaul Hospital Emergency Department in Norfolk, Virginia. Dr. Carlson is an emergency physician in the same department. The time is 3:42 in the afternoon. Dr. Carlson, could you describe the events which prompted you to call the FBI at approximately 2:25 this afternoon?"

Andy described his encounter with the Saudi princes in the ED the previous night and handed the two ED records to Agent Bennett. "I think national security trumps HIPAA," he said.

Then he described the drive to the Old Point Comfort Marina and the subsequent sighting of the same two princes below the sea wall in front of the Chamberlain Hotel.

"Ms. Baker," Agent Bennett said, "how can you be sure that these two Arab men below the seawall are the same two Arab gentlemen you saw in the ED?"

"I applied the dressing to the one with the head injury who called himself Muhammad Abdullah," she said. "I also applied a knee immobilizer to the second prince, who had a knee contusion and called himself Fahd Abdullah. I taught him how to use crutches. I got a really good look at both of them. Muhammad still had my wrap-around dressing at the seawall, and Fahd still had the knee immobilizer."

Andy said, "I also got a good look at both gentlemen. I believe that they are the same. Because of their suspicious activities, Lindsey took pictures. The problem is, I can't understand why this happened to me."

"You don't think you were a casual observer?" Bennett asked.

"I'm perplexed that someone with my background could be confronted with two Saudi princes twice in a single day."

Bennett and McNeil looked at each other. Andy sensed that they were surprised at his response to the events he had observed.

Andy handed the twenty-six color images from the coffee table to Bennett. "We took these at the seawall at Old Point Comfort, at Langley AFB and NASA, and near Newport News Ship Building. You can see in these pictures the dressing and splint Lindsey applied. Both of us observed that Mr. Fahd Abdullah could barely walk due to his injury. Mr. Muhammad Abdullah had a cooler in many of these pictures. He uses multiple instruments from this cooler to measure distance, wind speed and direction, and GPS position."

"Is this the picture that you think shows a rangefinder?" Bennett pointed to the picture in his hand.

Andy looked carefully at the photograph. "I'm certain that this is a LaserTech long distance rangefinder because I have used one like it before. It can range accurately for five-ten miles. It costs $5000. It's not a tourist toy."

Mr. Bennett looked at Agent McNeil and then back to Andy. "Why did you follow these two alleged princes?"

"We were minding our own business," Andy said. "We didn't want to follow them. Tourists might take pictures of maritime facilities and military bases, but they shouldn't be using a long distance range finder, a handheld GPS unit, a windicator, and a sophisticated camera at all of these sensitive locations. One of them acted as a lookout."

Andy looked at Lindsey. "Lindsey has written the time and place that each picture was taken on the pictures. Also, I copied both the ED records and the pictures onto this CD." Andy handed over the CD to McNeil.

Bennett rapidly sifted through the stack of prints and ED records, and then looked up. "Dr. Carlson, you mentioned your background. What did you mean?"

"Harrison can give you all the information about me that you are entitled to. I can only give you general information."

"But we are here from Harrison. I need to know what previous contact, if any, you have had with the Saudis."

"You need to ask Harrison that question." Andy said.

Bennett ground his teeth. "What experience do you have in Hampton Roads?"

"I served as an intern at Portsmouth Naval Hospital and briefly as a general Navy medical officer in Hampton Roads. I have been deployed on several aircraft carriers out of Norfolk. I've worked at medical clinics at most of the Navy's military bases in Hampton Roads. I've been to Langley AFB and NASA. I was assigned to the SEAL command at Little Creek Amphibious Base most of the time. I'm on the HAZMAT committee of Tidewater Emergency Medical Services and have studied possible terrorist threats to Hampton Roads."

"Given the broad knowledge and expertise you claim, what are your conclusions about this incident?" Bennett asked.

"Bennett, I didn't claim to be an expert in anything. I'm on a weekend holiday and this whole thing is getting in my way. I told you what I saw. Your boss invited you to my house. I didn't."

"I'm sorry, Dr. Carlson, I didn't mean to show any disrespect."

"I don't know what happened today," he said, glancing toward Lindsey.

Lindsey raised her eyebrows and crossed her legs.

"We observed some strange behavior that needs further evaluation," Andy said. "Would you settle for my worst fears?"

"Go ahead."

"If these two princes were planning a terrorist attack, they have found the most vulnerable spot on the east coast, the channel at the Hampton Bridge Tunnel. The distance between the sensitive sites they visited suggests a powerful weapon, perhaps a nuclear weapon."

"Do you claim to be an expert in nuclear weapons also, Dr. Carlson?" Bennett asked.

"Your aftershave doesn't do a good job covering up the alcohol on your breath, Bennett," Andy said slowly, "and the alcohol is bringing out your asshole personality. If there are no more questions, then I suggest that you and your partner go back to checking parking meters." He stood up.

"Please forgive us for this intrusion, doctor," Bennett said. "And it's cold medicine, not alcohol."

"I smell alcohol for a living, Bennett. If Jim Beam made a cold medicine, I would have had a sip of it myself by now."

"All right. Tell us the rest of your worst fears and we'll get out of your hair."

Andy sat back down. "None of the sites visited by these Saudi princes would be significantly affected in the long run by a dirty bomb. But a real nuclear warhead detonated at the bridge tunnel would render much of the military in Hampton Roads destroyed or so contaminated that it would be unusable for an indeterminate period of time."

"How do you think such an attack could be carried out?"

"Their behavior at the seawall suggests detonation of a weapon near the channel, possibly a weapon in a container ship. This is just speculation."

Agent Bennett stood up. "The ED records that you obtained and the pictures need to be analyzed by FBI and CIA. Somebody more important than us needs to decide what to do with this."

McNeil finally opened his mouth. "We should be able to obtain good passport pictures of the princes."

Another Yankee accent. Maybe he didn't like to open his mouth because his teeth were bad.

"We would like to take the CD with the pictures on it, as well as the photographs and ED records you have," McNeil said.

Bennett said, "We will be back by daylight with passport pictures for you to identify and probably more questions. I would like to caution both of you not to call anyone, not even family members, until we return. And please do not go anywhere."

"You're inviting yourselves back?" Andy asked, "And you're telling me what I can do on my own property?"

Agent McNeil disconnected the microphone and removed the camcorder from the tripod without saying anything.

Bennett looked up at the walls and said, "You like killing things, don't you Carlson?"

"Yankees most of all," he answered with a thousand-yard stare.

They took the camcorder, the ED records, the prints, and the CD. The grey Crown Victoria churned up gravel in the driveway.

"I feel like I'm trying to get tar off of my hands," Andy said. "Those two were idiots."

"You'll feel better after you get in bed," she called from the kitchen.

8

Andy walked into the dining room and sat down where he could watch Lindsey prepare spaghetti.

"You don't talk much about yourself," he said.

"Why should that bother you?"

"I'm hoping that you will learn to trust me."

"Are you a therapist?" she asked, laughing.

"I feel a kinship with you and I'm trying to figure out why."

"Is there something that I should confess to?"

"Yes, there is. You are deflecting my questions. That makes me want to know even more."

"I don't know what to say," she said.

"My mom and dad loved and trusted each other completely. It was a great education for me. She died at thirty-nine of breast cancer. I was sixteen. Dad died in a light plane crash in Uganda a year ago."

"I'm sorry. I didn't mean to make light of ...I didn't know."

"It's all right," he said. "Since Dad died, I've found it hard to confide in anybody. I don't date much. I drink too much."

"How did you get over your tragedies?"

"I'll never completely get over them," he said. "I'm learning to concentrate on all of the good things that I enjoyed with my parents when they were alive."

"You're more resilient than I am," she said.

"I doubt it, but talking about my losses does me a lot of good. It's hard to find anyone trustworthy to talk to. You are not required to tell me anything about yourself. I didn't mean to pry. I was just following my heart."

"This information that you get from your heart is probably suspect," Lindsey said. "The heart is a pump in the center of the chest. You should know this, being a physician. It's not a romantic body part that has feelings and hands out love."

"I disagree," he said. "I think that hearts are the center of our feelings, and they can talk to other hearts."

"What medical school did you say you attended?"

"Your heart is really part of your brain," he said. "We have conscious and subconscious thoughts. We don't have much control over either. What comes out of your mouth is a tiny fraction of what is going on in your heart. Hearts can sense attraction for each other, even when there is no audible exchange. I did not fully appreciate this myself until recently."

She looked down. "How can you possibly know that?"

He reached gently for her chin and forced eye contact. "I believe that your heart has already heard what my heart is thinking and it has already responded, whether you choose to recognize it or not."

She quickly pulled her head back and swallowed hard. Andy noted her eyes darting about.

"Andy, would you open a bottle of red wine on the counter and pour us a glass?"

He opened the bottle, poured two glasses, and placed one in front of her.

"I heard something on the deck," she said. "It's too dark now to see anything."

Andy opened the left French door, stepped out on the deck, and closed the door behind him. An internal alarm was screaming in his head. Why did she want him outside? If there were a noise on his deck, he would be the first to notice it. He didn't turn on the light on the deck, which extended around the rear of the house.

Instead he walked immediately to his extreme left and looked through the kitchen window, through the opening between the kitchen and the dining room, to the dining room table. He watched Lindsey emptying a syringe into his glass of wine. She stirred the mixture with a spoon.

9

ndy slowly walked back through the French door and sat at the
table. Disappointment welled over him. He fought to maintain
composure. She was an amateur at killing, if that were her intent, but
how could his heart have been so wrong? His discomfort with the
events of the day escalated. What could possibly be her motive? And
why did he feel that she cared about him anyway?

"I don't see anything," he said. "Bears sometimes come down the
river in the spring. It could have been a raccoon looking for a handout.
Don't worry about it. I can understand your being a little jumpy after
the kind of day we've had."

"It's time to eat," she said as she brought the spaghetti to the dining
room table. "And I do think we both need a drink."

They clicked glasses and Lindsey took a swallow.

"What we need is some music," he said. "Can you turn on the iPod
stereo on the kitchen counter?"

As she turned her back to walk into the kitchen, Andy poured half
his glass of wine into the antique cream separator behind his chair.

Lindsey returned to the table. The first song from the iPod was
"Strawberry Wine."

"Somehow, I just knew that there would be country music on your
iPod."

She was looking at his half-empty glass.

"Is that the bread I smell?" he asked.

"Oh no," she said, jumping up and returning to the kitchen. "I hope
it's not burned."

Andy poured the remainder of his wine into the cream separator
as soon as her back was turned.

"Have you looked at my grandfather's cream separator?" He pointed toward the contraption behind him and held his empty glass to his lips.

Lindsey turned her head as she removed the bread from the oven.

"Granddad would pour whole milk from the cows into the mouth of the machine while he turned this crank with his hand. Each of these arms that extend from the separator would hold a bucket, instead of a family picture. The cream went to one side and the skim milk to the other."

"That's pretty cool," she said.

Lindsey returned to the table and placed the garlic bread between their plates. She looked at the empty glass in his hand.

After eating for a while in silence, Lindsey reached over and put her arm around Andy's neck and hugged him.

"Can I show you the walnut bed I made recently?" he asked.

Andy got up and walked through the great room into the master bedroom. Holding onto the bed, he pointed out the features of the headboard, the four giant tapered posts, and the side rails.

"Andy," she called to him from the doorway.

He turned to see her smiling, wine glass in hand, leaning against the doorframe, her clothes in a pile at her feet.

"Oh my." He slurred his speech and slowly moved toward her.

"Let me help you with those hunting boots," she said, easing him backwards to a sitting position on the bed.

She removed his boots and socks. She lifted his legs and carried them around as his chest and torso collapsed on the bed.

"Andy?" she whispered.

His eyes were closed.

She leaned closer to his face. "Andy?"

He did not respond. She leaned over and whispered in his ear, "I apologize for never telling you that I love you."

She walked into the great room.

Andy opened his eyes.

10

Lindsey stood naked in the center of the great room and punched the speed dial on her cell phone. "It's me, Harrison. Everything went well...Yeah, he's out, but he's not convinced yet...He'll be unconscious for about eight hours, anyway...He'll be more convinced of the Saudi royal family's involvement once the bomb goes off...You're going to have to edit the interview a bit. Bennett pissed him off...Are we ready to grab the Saudi princes tomorrow?...And the ship is on schedule?...Have Sid knock on the door here at sunup. I want Carlson to identify both princes from their passport photos, and I want him to do it on tape tomorrow morning...One more thing. Dr. Carlson has an Arabic female friend named Sahar...Yes, I'm sure...No, I don't know where she lives. You think it's important?...She called here today, so I can probably get her number from his phone...I'll be sure."

Lindsey walked back through the doorway of the master bedroom. She stared at the empty bed. Her jaw sagged.

From behind the bedroom door, Andy brought a heavy flashlight down on the back of her head. She crumpled to the floor. He kicked the broken glass from the flashlight lens under the bed.

Andy stared down at her, shaking his head. Then he got down on his knees and carefully picked her up and placed her on the bed. Whatever was happening here, he felt that he needed his socks and shoes back on.

The occipital scalp wound appeared to be more of a bruise. A large hematoma was developing underneath the scalp. Beginning with the head, Andy meticulously examined every detail of her body. He picked up the bedside lamp with his right hand and opened her eyes with the thumb and index finger of his left hand. The pupils were three millimeters and equally reactive to the light. There was no blood coming from her ears or mouth. Her breathing was regular and her color good. He rolled her over on her stomach to get a better look at her back.

The tattoo was symmetrical and located in the midline, extending from the level of the iliac crest almost to the coccyx. It looked like an eagle with its wings spread about four inches on each side and its chest thrust out. Andy had seen part of it before when Lindsey applied splints to sprained ankles. The words underneath the bird were small enough that he could not read them unless he was less than two feet away.

"Make My Day" he read. There was no sign of Clint Eastwood or his .44 Magnum.

Andy palpated her posterior cervical spine. At the base of the left side of her neck, at the level of the first thoracic vertebrae, his fingers ran into a firm, metallic-feeling subcutaneous object. It was much like the device he wore on the shoulder of his robes in the desert. A GPS receiver/transmitter had been fitted with a pacemaker battery so that its signals could be amplified enough for a satellite to see her location even inside a house. But who was watching?

He walked into the kitchen and picked out a steak knife. In the bedroom closet was a roll of heavy nylon cord. After cutting four three-foot lengths of cord from the roll, he used a BIC lighter to prevent the strands from unwinding.

Andy retrieved Lindsey's camera from the great room. He took pictures of her tattoo, then rolled her over again and took pictures of her face from several angles. He propped open her mouth with a highlighter from the bedside table and took pictures of her dental work. Satisfied with his pictures, Andy secured her wrists and ankles to the bedposts and covered her with a sheet.

He walked into the kitchen and emptied the icemaker box into a large bowl. He filled the bowl with tap water and placed the bowl of ice water on the night stand in the bedroom.

Andy stood over Lindsey and wondered what he might be missing. He walked back into the great room and emptied her pocketbook and bags on the couch. There were two cell phones, his and hers, both turned off. He put his in his pocket. Her billfold had a notable lack of pictures.

In his study, Andy took the driver's license out of Lindsey's billfold and enlarged it on his scanner. He attached the enlarged driver's license to an email. He took the memory card out of Lindsey's camera and copied the photographs he had taken of her face, dental work, and tattoo to a file in his photo software. After attaching the new file to the same email, he sent this email to the Cow Palace on the Farm.

It was time for a wakeup call.

11

H e picked up the bowl of ice water and threw it onto her face.
"Aaaaagh."

Andy had observed many patients recover consciousness after a
concussion. He knew that the key to determining the patient's level of
consciousness was the face.

Lindsey's eyebrows began to twitch. They drew together as she became aware that she was in pain. The moan and the movement of her
head indicated that she had localized her pain to the back of her head.
She was trying to locate a spot on her occipital scalp that did not hurt
from the weight of her head on the pillow. Her eyelashes trembled as
she fought to open her eyes.

She stared at the ceiling. Her pupils dilated, then constricted
as she attempted to focus on some object that she recognized. Her
gaze fell on Andy's face. There was no smile or frown of familiarity.
This was retrograde amnesia, something most concussion patients
experience to some degree. The horizontal wrinkles in her brow
and tight lips indicated that she was attempting to sort out where
she was, what she had been doing, and who this person was standing
over her.

The maximum opening of her eyes, the elevation of her eyebrows,
and her open mouth meant that parts of the puzzle were falling into
place. Her lips stretched horizontally and her nostrils flared as she
struggled against the four restraints. She looked down at the sheet.
Epinephrine was surging from her adrenal glands to initiate a "fight
or flight response." She now appeared to fully appreciate that she was
naked under the sheet, restrained at each extremity, spread-eagled on
the bed, and under the scrutiny of Andy Carlson.

"That ice water always works on TV," he said, "but I never had a chance to try it out myself."

Her rapid eye movements probably meant that she had sorted out events almost to the moment that her lights went out.

"I'm sorry that I had to hit you on the head, but you had to be stopped," he said.

"What are you doing to me?" She yanked at her arm restraints and kicked at her leg restraints. "I came here for a nice weekend and you're trying to take advantage of me."

"I came here for a nice weekend and you and your FBI friends tried to use me in some kind of conspiracy."

"I don't understand."

He said. "You put a drug in my wine glass. I didn't drink it. I listened to every word of your conversation with Harrison after you thought I passed out."

She closed her eyes.

"Try to focus," he said. "I have a feeling that time is important."

"You heard everything?" Her voice sank to a whisper. Sweat appeared on her forehead and upper lip. Her rate and depth of breathing were increasing, but the color was draining out of her face. A fine tremor appeared in her hands.

"You have no idea what you are getting into," she said. "You would have been better off drinking the wine."

"Your moral compass is currently not reliable," he said.

"I work for the CIA. This weekend was an assignment for me. I like you. Now untie me."

Andy reached for the stool next to the bedside table and sat down. "I feel better already. You say that you plan and execute nuclear terrorist attacks on places like Hampton Roads for the good of the country?"

"It's not like it sounds. Can you please untie me? I can explain everything."

"I need a few more details." He looked at his watch. "Your friends are coming back here in the morning. You have a lot of explaining to do."

"There is no going back on this," she said. "The plan is too far along. Besides, we already have enough video of you confirming the involvement of the Saudi princes. Either you go along with the plan or Harrison will hunt you down and kill you."

"And what about you?" he asked. "Do you think that you will be left alive with all of the details you know? How long have you been with the CIA?"

"I was recruited about nine months ago. I spent six months training for this job. I can understand why you can't see the big picture."

"Does your family know that you hang out with CIA and FBI agents?"

"I had a brother who was killed in Iraq. There is no one else."

"Don't you think it's a coincidence that the CIA chose someone with no family and personal reasons to hate Islamic terrorists?" he asked. "You are a low-level operative in a gigantic conspiracy. There is no way that you will be left alive. At least Jack Ruby didn't have a GPS tracker sewn underneath his skin."

"You found that?"

"Don't you see? The U.S. military could unload a GPS-guided bomb on your head at any time. You're expendable. They can track your general movements with your cell phone. You might not always have your cell phone with you, but you can't forget that homing beacon sewn in your shoulder. Did you think that was for your protection?"

She turned her head away from him.

"It's time for you to do us both--and our country--a favor. I want the truth from you, probably for the first time."

"Then will you let me go?"

"I think we are both dead in twelve hours unless you come clean with me," he said.

She pursed her lips.

"I can offer you some Tylenol for your headache," he said. "And I'm sorry about the ice water. It was kinder than slapping you. But get on with your explanation. Somewhere a clock is ticking and a ship is apparently carrying a frightful cargo."

"We are at war with Islamic terrorists," she said. "Trying to be politically correct and dancing around this fact has cost America dearly."

"What does this have to do with your conspiracy?"

"I am part of a CIA operation to turn the tables in the Middle East. Our orders came from the top of the U. S. government."

"How could exploding a nuclear weapon be a good thing for peace and prosperity?"

"Arab countries like Saudi Arabia and Iran are supporting Islamic fundamentalists who want to kill Americans," she said. "You told me this yourself on the way here."

"I'm not putting this together yet."

"Listen carefully to me," she said. "The nuclear weapon will be exploded before the container ship gets close enough to Hampton Roads to do any real harm. The bomb has to explode somewhere in order to demonstrate the seriousness of the threat. Americans need to be outraged against the Saudis, the way Pearl Harbor galvanized us to fight the Japanese."

"But the Japanese actually attacked us," he said. "Your conspiracy is not analogous to Pearl Harbor."

"You haven't heard me out," she said. "The CIA knew that some terrorist organization would eventually get their hands on a nuclear weapon. That has happened. We now have moral justification for taking the oil we need. The CIA has discovered a bona fide al Qaeda plot financed by the Saudis. We didn't put that nuclear weapon on that container ship. Al Qaeda did. We are only using it to our advantage. We are going to see that it explodes before it can do any real harm to America."

"But you can't explode a nuclear weapon in the atmosphere without radiation contamination being blown all around the world," he said. "There is no such thing as a harmless nuclear weapon."

"The tides and prevailing winds have all been taken into consideration," she said. "The radiation damage will be minimal. Almost all of it will be scattered over northern Europe and Russia. That minimal radiation contamination you are worried about is part of the plan to unite our NATO countries against the Saudis. Do you think the Brits and the French or the Russians will cry about the Saudis losing their oil when they have radiation contamination raining down on their heads thanks to the Saudis?"

"How did you get talked into this bullshit?" he asked.

"I'm not a monster," she yelled. "I work for the CIA. We have to do things that no other part of the U.S. government can accomplish, and we act under the authority of the president. What you saw Saturday morning is your opportunity to be a hero. You discovered the plot in time to prevent the ship from reaching America. Harrison says that you are a critical witness because of something you saw in Saudi Arabia, something no one else can verify. The FBI and CIA are using the information that you have provided to look for a ship that is, at this moment, closing in on our East Coast."

"But you have already said that the CIA knows which ship the bomb is on," he said. "I'm just a prop in your scheme. Why did you have to poison me?"

"The syringe was only chloral hydrate," she said. "If I had wanted to kill you, I would have used something more deadly. I didn't know if you would start making phone calls or asking the wrong questions. Since you seem to have a talent for putting things together quickly, I thought that putting you to sleep for awhile was prudent."

Andy got up from his stool next to the bed.

"It's important that you weigh all of the facts before you attempt to interfere with a mission that comes from the top of our government," Lindsey said. "War was declared on us."

"You really believe in what you are doing, don't you?"

"Absolutely."

Andy left the room and returned with a glass of Coke and a straw. He held the glass for her and put the straw in her mouth. She took two swallows and shook her head.

She lifted her head up and the sheet began to slip below her nipples. Andy adjusted it immediately.

He sat back down on his stool. "Let me get this straight. The two Arab men we saw today at the military bases--were they real Saudi princes or actors?"

"Andy, we needed those pictures I took to leave no doubt in the minds of the world," she said. "We needed you to connect the dots for everybody. Are you going to stand up for your country, or what?"

"They were actors, then."

"They were actors," she said. "You saw the real Saudi Princes in the ED. We plan to grab them tomorrow as they are leaving town."

"According to U.S. law it is illegal to plant evidence on someone, even if you know that they are guilty of a crime," he said.

"But the Saudis have participated in the purchase of this nuclear weapon," she said. "We have solid evidence to back it up."

"This is because of your brother, isn't it?"

"Andy, you appear to be attracted to war heroes. The books and pictures in your house indicate that you admire men of action. If your heroes had been alive in the twenty-first century, there would not have been any Fallujahs in Iraq, financed by Saudis," she said.

He leaned back and frowned.

"If a city resists," she continued, "then it must be destroyed, like we annihilated German cities and Japanese cities in WWII. This type of action saves American blood. My brother died in Fallujah. And for what? He was the only family I had left."

She strained against the rope that held her wrists and looked at him with righteous anger.

"Tell me what happened to your parents," he said.

"They worked in the World Trade Center before they were chopped up into unrecognizable pieces by the people you want to protect," she said.

"Your campaign will not bring your family back."

"If we take over Saudi Arabia, other Islamic countries will think twice before supporting terrorism," she said. "The price of oil will fall dramatically. The economies of the West will recover. America will survive."

"Lindsey, it's not your job to punish countries that support terrorism. America has supported many terrorist regimes. We have practiced our own brand of terrorism whenever it suited our interests. Regrettably, I have participated in some of those efforts."

Her voice turned to ice. "There is a practical matter that you need to think about. Just whom do you plan to notify? Aircraft carriers and submarines are already moving toward the Middle East. Army and Marine units in Afghanistan and Iraq are already geared up and ready to go. We already have the Abrams tanks and the smart bombs in theater to do the job."

"That's not encouraging."

"And we don't call it a conspiracy," she said. "We call it a plan of action. You're smart enough to know who had to approve this plan of action. I don't suggest that you call the President, or the FBI, or the CIA, or the military."

"I'll think of somebody."

"No matter who you call, you'll never leave the Farm alive," she said. "We can't allow you to retract the evidence that you have already given regarding the Saudi princes."

"I don't want any part of this," he said.

"Do you understand the term redundancy?" she asked.

"Yes."

"It means that other credible witnesses have been identified and carefully supplied with information just like you," she said. "If you object at this point, we will both be killed for nothing. The operation will go forward with or without us."

He stood up and circled the room.

"You may have forgotten the security guard at Fort Monroe," she said. "He works for me. He will document that those two Saudi princes were at Old Point Comfort Saturday morning. He can identify both of them, just like you."

Andy pulled the sheet up around her neck again and then turned his back to her.

"Your feelings toward me were all an act," he said.

"Don't sell yourself short," she said. "I have very strong feelings for you. You are kind and sensitive. Everybody knows it. Do you think that nobody notices when you slip fifty dollar bills to moms who can't afford antibiotics for their babies?"

"It's just a few dollars."

"Do you know why we haven't had sex yet?" she asked.

The question caused him to turn around.

"I knew that there would be no hope for me to deceive you afterward. I was falling for you so fast that I was losing perspective. I was forgetting why I had been sent to Hampton Roads and why we had a relationship. One week ago you pushed me over the top. You did something so amazing that I had to admit that I loved you."

"I don't understand what you're talking about," he said. "I haven't done anything."

"That's the whole point," she said. "You did something that came naturally for you, something that no one else would have done, and you sought no credit for it."

"I still don't get it," he said, sitting back down.

"I know that you haven't forgotten Elizabeth Jacobs, because I'll never forget her."

Elizabeth Jacobs was a skinny sixteen year old girl with stringy blond hair and the hollow eyes of malnutrition. Her life had ended in the emergency department at DePaul one week earlier. Liz was unlucky enough to be born with an aggressive form of cystic fibrosis, a chronic terminal disease. A defective gene and its protein product caused the body to produce unusually thick, sticky mucous that clogged the lungs and led to life-threatening lung infections. Cystic fibrosis also obstructed the pancreas, stopping the flow of natural enzymes necessary to break down and absorb food.

Modern antibiotics and pancreatic enzymes had extended the lives of many children well past age sixteen, but Liz's disease overcame her body's defenses rapidly. She had suffered so many episodes of pneumonia that her lungs were mostly scar tissue. Every day was a struggle to cough up secretions just to continue breathing. At fourteen she had been placed on home oxygen permanently by nasal cannula. The Pseudomonas organism that grew chronically in her lungs was now resistant to any drug.

Andy had recognized about six months earlier that Liz only came to the hospital on the night shift and only when he was on duty, no matter how sick she was. She would arrive pale and cyanotic, hungry for air, yet she always managed to smile. She kidded him about Lindsey, having picked up on their courtship just by watching the two of them work together.

Liz's mom would usually follow along behind the ambulance within an hour because her dad worked nights and her mother would have to find a baby-sitter in the middle of the night for Liz's younger siblings, who were all healthy.

Liz knew that she was going to die that night. She and her parents had already signed the papers that instructed her doctors not to put her on the ventilator again. She was already on a non-rebreather mask at one hundred percent oxygen when she arrived at 2:15 in the morning. Andy had glanced at her vital signs and oxygen SAT of seventy-eight percent and realized that he had nothing medical to offer. She had been placed in a private room that was reserved for families to say goodbye to relatives.

The ED was packed with the usual mix, and the resident had called in sick. Fifteen minutes after Liz arrived, Lindsey had come to him and whispered. "Liz is frightened and she wants you."

Andy's recollections of that night were interrupted by Lindsey's voice.

"I saw what you did for that girl," Lindsey said. "I was hiding outside the door because I was a coward. I watched through the venetian blinds as you moved the foot of her bed away from the wall and got down on your knees between the bed and the wall. You took her hand and put your face on her pillow. You whispered into her ear. I saw the gratitude on her face when she turned her head to meet yours. Her monitor showed deterioration of every vital sign, but the fear left her. She knew you were not going to leave her alone in that room to die."

"She was very brave," Andy said.

"When she no longer had the energy to breathe," Lindsey said, "I saw you put both your arms around her and pull her up to you. She was looking straight toward me through those venetian blinds. You held her chin on your shoulder and her cheek against your face until the monitor flat-lined. She died smiling."

"It was a tough night," he said. He wiped his nose on his forearm.

"That's when I was sure that I was in love with you."

He ran his right hand through his sandy hair from front to back, and the locks immediately returned to their original position.

"I can't begin to deal with us until you give up this insane conspiracy," he said.

"I'm trying so hard to do something that counts," she said, "something that would give my parents' and my brother's deaths some meaning. My country asked me to do this. I didn't apply for the job."

"I understand your motives now," he said. "Those two guys who came here, Bennett and McNeil--were they even FBI agents?"

"CIA agents Bennett and McNeil are sitting in their car at the Farmville airport, about two miles from where we are. The leader of our task force is Harrison. I'm second in command. Now you know everything."

Andy stood up from the stool and looked down at her.

"Would you sit beside me on the bed?"

Andy sat down next to Lindsey and brushed her auburn hair out of her eyes.

She looked up to him and spoke softly.

"I want you to do what we both want," she said. "You can leave the restraints on. We may never have another chance."

She lifted her head up to him and pulled the ropes tightly with her arms. Her jaw was fixed. Her eyes projected sincerity. The sheet slipped down.

"Please excuse me for a moment," Andy said as he left the room.

He returned with the steak knife. "I don't want you tied up."

He leaned over and cut the rope between her ankles and the foot posts and her wrists and the head posts of the bed.

"I'll help you every way that I can," he said. "You don't have to offer yourself to me."

She sat up and swung her legs around to the floor. She reached up and began to unbutton his shirt. She did not break eye contact with him as she removed his pants.

He placed the knife on the nightstand next to the bed and helped her with the shoes and socks. Face to face in bed, he searched for truth until urgency overcame him.

Their eyes were locked when her pupils dilated and the muscles in her abdomen pulled her legs up around his chest. They trembled together until he collapsed on her chest.

He held on until the muscle tremors died down. After several minutes, they were breathing in unison.

He rested his right cheek between her breasts. When he lifted his head to look in her face, she said, "There's no reason for us to hide from each other anymore. We can't be enemies."

He lifted himself from her and stood by the bed.

"I would say that we have come to an understanding," she said, "We can figure a way out of this."

He leaned down and kissed her on the lips.

"Thank you for trusting me," she said.

Andy sat down on the bed and began to put his clothes on while Lindsey worked to untie the knots in the pieces of rope left on her extremities. The knots were stubborn. Andy handed her the knife. She inserted the knife between the rope and her skin. With a few strokes, the pieces of rope fell away.

Finished dressing, Andy started out of the room. Lindsey fell back on the bed, pulled the sheet up to her chin, and closed her eyes.

"You forgot your knife, darling," she called to him.

He returned to the bed and she handed him the knife.

"You don't think I would hurt anyone who could love me like that, do you?"

12

"Why don't you make us some coffee?" Lindsey called from the bedroom. "Then you can explain to me exactly how we can get out of this mess. Would you mind bringing my pocketbook? I'd like to take a shower."

Andy found Lindsey's purse in the great room and tossed it on the bed. Lindsey sat on the side of the bed, holding the sheet up to her chest.

In the kitchen, Andy slapped a coffee filter into the coffee maker and measured out three scoops of coffee. After filling up the coffee pot with tap water, he poured the water through the top of the coffee brewer and turned it on. He could hear the shower running in the bathroom of the master bedroom. He let the first cup of steaming coffee drain into his mug. The kitchen clock said 2:05 in the morning.

"I'm going to need a lot of coffee in the few hours I have left to live," he said aloud.

He sat down in a chair at the table in the dining room and looked out at the night through the French doors. The coffee was too hot to sip.

His coffee cup was appropriate for this occasion. The Gary Larsen cartoon on the side showed two deer bucks talking in the woods. One buck had a bull's eye target on his side. The other buck commented, "Bummer of a birthmark, Hal."

He watched her come out of the master bedroom toward him in the glass of the landscape picture on the wall next to the French doors of the dining room. She was coming for her coffee. He didn't mind that she was still naked.

He didn't anticipate the knife. She must have had it curled behind her wrist, making it invisible in the reflection. Within an instant it was between his ribs on the left side, halfway between his armpit and his waistline.

"I do love you," she said, "but you would never make a convincing liar."

He lunged counterclockwise, bringing the cup around with his right hand. The hot coffee splashed across her face. Her hands rose to protect herself. He smashed the coffee cup on the top of her head, leaving only the handle in his right index finger. She fell backward, moaning. He grabbed the handle of the left French door and ran out on the deck. In the darkness, he jumped the steps of the deck and ran toward his shed.

Within a few steps, Andy felt a twinge in his left chest. He slowed to a fast walk. The twinge became a catch in each breath. Reaching around with his right hand, he could feel the handle of the knife. He decided not to pull it out.

He must get to the Cow Palace. Everything he needed was in the Cow Palace. She didn't even know what the Cow Palace was. He quickly surveyed the farm equipment in the shed. Two tractors. A zero-turn radius lawn mower. The Kubota Diesel RTV.

He pulled a key off of the ceiling joist, and put it in the ignition of the Kubota.

Then he sat down in the golf cart parked next to the Kubota. It was quiet. It was on a battery-tender, so it was ready to go. He had to get away before she found a flashlight or a weapon.

Andy unplugged the cart and threw the battery-tender into the back, where golf clubs were supposed to be carried. Because any movement of his left arm caused sharp left chest pain, he turned the key and put the cart in reverse with his right hand. The cart jumped backwards when he stepped on the accelerator. Leaning forward to avoid pushing the knife in further, he switched from reverse to forward.

Lindsey was looking out the open back door while talking on her cell phone. She hoped that she would never have to look at his body.

"Sid, Carlson's on the loose. He's smarter than Harrison figured. And he hasn't been drinking. He knows the Saudi Princes are fake. He didn't leave me any choice. I stuck a knife in his chest. Until we find his body, he's a major threat to our mission. Forget the pictures. Forget the video camera. Call for a chopper in case we can't find his body by morning. He doesn't have any weapons. He can't go far. Send somebody to the local hospital to hang out, just in case. I need for both of you to get over here with your guns right now. And bring me a damn flashlight."

Lindsey closed the phone, then ran out to Andy's truck in front of the farmhouse and removed the keys from the ignition. She returned to the bedroom and put her clothes back on. She looked at her trembling hands and walked to the mirror. The blisters covered her forehead, nose, and cheeks. It was not supposed to be like this. But he had forced her to choose between him and her mission. She had thought that if she didn't bring a weapon, she could not harm Andy. He must have forgotten about the dagger in the closet.

13

The Cow Palace was an old dairy barn on the opposite side of Dry Creek from the farmhouse. The roof had deteriorated and Andy had rehabilitated the barn for storage. The building was stuffed with medical supplies scavenged from many hospitals. It had an apartment for hunters. Andy collected medical supplies for his two brothers, who were missionaries in Uganda. He also collected medications donated from drug companies. Much of the stuff was technically out of date, but it was useful in a country that had nothing.

Driving down the gravel road toward the covered bridge, Andy felt an urgency to breathe more rapidly. Each inspiration seemed more difficult and ended with a sharp pain. He smelled the blood dripping down his left side.

Guiding the cart with his right hand, he drove without the lights across the covered bridge. He turned immediately into the woods. He had navigated these trails in the dark hundreds of times on his way to a morning deer stand, carrying his bow and quiver of arrows. The thought of carrying a flashlight had not occurred to him since he was about five years old. Why use something you don't need that gives away your position? The Cow Palace was just ahead. Sharp chest pain and shortness of breath had kindled his anxiety, but the onset of dizziness and blurred vision within sight of the Cow Palace triggered an emotion he had not felt in years—fear.

He could not afford to panic. He had managed many penetrating wounds to the chest in other soldiers, including several in the field as a SEAL. He had the Cow Palace to work with.

Andy knew that the knife had caused a left sided hemopneumothorax. Blood and air were collecting in the left side of his chest from the knife wound to his lung. If the knife had reached his heart, he would already be dead.

When a lung suffers a puncture wound, the hole in the outside of the lung acts like a one-way valve. Normally the pleural space, between the outside of the lung and the inside of the chest wall, is only a potential space. When the diaphragm descends with each breath, the lung expands to fill the pleural space. But a hole in the lung allows air from inside the lung to escape into the pleural space without allowing any air to return to the airways through the same hole.

As air pressure increased in Andy's left pleural space, the left lung would collapse. The heart would be forced to the right side of his chest by the increased air pressure in the left chest. This shifting would cause kinking of the large veins returning blood to the heart, interfering with its filling between contractions. If the heart is unable to fill, it cannot pump blood to any organs.

Andy had good reason to fear this complication of a hemopneumothorax—a tension pneumothorax. Left untreated, a tension pneumothorax alone, without bleeding, followed an inevitable course: increasing shortness of breath, loss of blood pressure, loss of blood flow to the head, unconsciousness, and death. Andy knew that he must act quickly to release the air pressure on the left side of his chest.

He walked unsteadily from the golf cart to a nearby power pole, where he kept a spare key underneath a rock. He fumbled with the key at the deadbolt to the metal door on the left side of the building. Once inside, he flipped the lights on. After two steps to his left, he was overcome by nausea. He vomited spaghetti into the floor. The room went black. He fell to the concrete floor, gasping, and crawled through his vomitus toward the stainless steel medicine cabinet. His vision slowly returned due to an improvement in blood flow to his head in the horizontal position.

There was no time for sterile gloves or antiseptics. His chest felt as if it were about to explode. He was unable to lift his head without losing his vision. He couldn't get off his hands and knees without passing out. He fumbled with the drawers in the cabinet. The fingers of his right hand found the hollow needles in the top drawer. Ripping open the wrapper with his teeth, he plunged the needle into his left anterior chest. The room went black.

He awakened face down in a pool of blood, his chest heaving. A loud hiss of trapped air exited the left chest through the needle. When the hiss subsided, he reestablished his knees underneath him, and climbed the rungs of the stool next to the cabinet with his hands. When his face reached the height of the seat of the stool, he was glad that his vision did not betray him again. Using the side rails of the medicine cabinet, he pulled himself erect and positioned his butt on the seat of the stool. He put his forehead down on the counter. His right hand searched the top drawer until he found the bandage scissors.

Despite his respiratory distress and pain, Andy willed himself to sit up straight. He cut his shirt up the front, and then cut the left sleeve of the shirt from cuff to neck. Most of the shirt fell away.

The needle was only a temporizing maneuver. His left lung would not expand much by itself. The needle did nothing about the bleeding in his left pleural space and it was not large enough to release enough air. The blood had to go somewhere or it would also mash his left lung. He needed a chest tube to remove the excess air and blood in the pleural space. He needed massive intravenous fluids and blood transfusions.

Pulling out the knife at this point could be like pulling a cork out of the bottom of a bucket. Any clots would be disrupted. Blood would be released too rapidly. He might lose consciousness again before he could get the chest tube in. His dizziness correlated with a loss of at least one fourth of his blood volume. He would use his pain to stay awake and focused.

Andy had never heard of anyone inserting a chest tube into his own chest. Who better to try than an emergency physician with trauma training and field experience?

He was grateful that Lindsey had stabbed him in the left chest, instead of the right. That would make chest tube insertion more feasible, since he was right-handed.

Although his breathing remained rapid and shallow, the catch in inspiration was worsening. That meant the left lung had expanded enough to reach the point of the knife again. He was grateful for this, too. Was he thinking straight?

In combat and in his residency training in emergency medicine, he had learned to do things automatically, without thinking. He grabbed four plastic bags of normal saline from a box next to the cabinet and arranged them on the counter. He spiked two of the bags with a five-foot section of plastic IV tubing and ran the saline down until it dripped out of the end of the tubing, then clamped both lines.

He swabbed his left forearm using four-by-four-inch sterile gauze soaked in Betadine. Like all athletes who exercised their arm muscles regularly, Andy had large arm veins to drain blood from the muscles in his forearms. These veins were now smaller, but still visible. That was a good sign. These veins would have collapsed if he were about to bleed to death. He would not need a tourniquet.

He inserted two sixteen-gauge angiocaths into different veins in his left forearm and attached five-inch saline locks to each needle. He taped the saline locks to the skin in his left forearm. The nausea was coming back.

A hollow sixteen-gauge needle was attached to the end of each section of tubing coming from the plastic bags of normal saline. These needles were inserted into the saline locks. He hung the bags overhead on a hook on the left side of the cabinet, and then opened the clamps on the two lines so that the saline could run wide open into his veins. Seated on the stool, he watched the saline pour steadily into his left arm from both bags, making his arm feel cold. The dizziness improved as the saline rolled in. His mind sharpened.

After each bag had infused, Andy disconnected both lines. He held onto the cabinet and stood up. As the dizziness returned, he spread his legs.

With short steps and a broad-based gait, he moved toward the bear head on the wall. He kept the apartment key in the bear's ear. Once inside the apartment, he turned on the light and found the bedside table. From the top drawer he removed a single Trojan condom in its foil lubricated pack.

He staggered back toward the medicine cabinet on the left wall of the Cow Palace. Almost to the stool, he could not continue. He reached for a pole that supported the giant beams and trusses overhead and held on until his respiratory rate decreased.

Two more bags of saline were spiked and the plastic tubing clamps released to allow the fluid to run wide open. He sat on the stool and placed four more one liter bags of saline in front of him.

He hoped that his diminished blood pressure would slow the bleeding inside his chest, promoting blood clotting. But normal saline could not substitute for red blood cells. Saline carries no oxygen. Ultimately, he would need blood. For now, his heart would have to beat faster to get the most out of the red blood cells he had left.

Andy knew that stab wounds to the chest often stop bleeding on their own. Normal saline often sufficed to maintain reasonable blood pressure. A surprising number of stabbing victims never require transfusion. He believed that he would have a fair chance of survival if he could get the chest tube in before passing out.

Andy finished removing his shirt with the bandage scissors. He ripped sterile gloves open with his teeth and slipped them on. After squirting Betadine onto an open pack of sterile four by four inch gauze, he used the gauze to scrub the entire left side of his chest around to the knife below the armpit.

His dizziness was replaced with weakness. His rapid breathing was consuming more energy than his body could supply. He reached for the one percent lidocaine with epinephrine on the counter of the cabinet. A ten milliliter syringe was used to draw up the local anesthetic.

He anesthetized a silver dollar–sized area of skin under the left armpit at the level of his nipple using a thin one and a half inch needle. Then he gradually pushed the needle deeper into the thick muscles between his ribs and emptied the syringe. From the second shelf of the cabinet he removed a tray labeled "chest tube".

It had been sterilized fourteen months ago. He cut open the plastic wrapping to the tray and spread out the drapes to locate everything he needed. A metal screw-clamp large enough to fit around the chest tube was retrieved from the top drawer. He squirted Betadine into a small bowl in the tray, and then tossed the clamp into the Betadine. The condom was opened and placed on the chest tube tray.

No matter how much local anesthetic is used in the skin and subcutaneous tissues of the chest, insertion of a chest tube hurts. A railroad spike would be kinder than a chest tube. Unlike a chest tube, the railroad spike is generally sharp and tapered. The correct chest tube diameter for a trauma patient is at least as wide as the patient's middle finger. The more chest wall muscle the patient has, the greater force is necessary to force the chest tube inside. Without his shirt Andy looked like a linebacker who forgot to take off his shoulder pads.

Andy knew that an incision in the muscles between the ribs was hazardous. If the intercostal artery, the artery between the ribs, is severed, it will rapidly become another significant source of blood loss.

Chest tubes are inserted for life-threatening problems. The need for speed often makes the insertion brutal. The tube without the metal trocar inside is clear and flexible, blunt as a finger, with holes near the tip to drain blood and air. The metal trocar allows enough stiffness in the tube for the physician to force it between the ribs, hopefully with just enough effort to get inside the chest but not enough to push the chest tube and trocar into the lung or heart, creating another injury. The same trocar allows the emergency physician to direct the tip of the tube once it penetrates the chest wall inside. After the tube is correctly positioned in both depth and direction, the trocar is removed and discarded.

Andy's chest tube tray had a sterile retractable scalpel, which he used to make a skin incision in the area that he had anesthetized in his left lateral chest wall. Using a large curved hemostat, he spread the edges of the incision and the subcutaneous tissues by opening and closing the tip of the hemostat. The pain of tearing his oversized intercostal muscles made him nauseated again. When the curved hemostat struck the sixth rib, he retched. There was no time to stop. He was being suffocated by the blood collecting in the left pleural space.

Clamping the jaws of the curved hemostat, he directed the blunt tip just over the top of the sixth rib. Gritting his teeth, he shoved this blunt tip through the inside wall of the chest. Penetration of the pleura, the inside wall of the chest, brought tears and loss of vision. He fell backwards on the stool against the metal cabinet and turned his head so that the vomitus would not contaminate his chest wall. Holding onto the cabinet, Andy spit spaghetti onto the floor until his vision began to clear again.

Dark blood squirted around the tip of the hemostat, accompanied by bubbles. He wanted to rest, but he knew better. As soon as he could see clearly, he began to open and close the tip of the curved hemostat to widen the hole in his chest wall. Releasing the hemostat from his thumb and index finger, he shoved his right index finger next to the hemostat and into his chest. Once his index finger was inside the chest, he leaned forward to allow the hemostat to fall to the floor.

Andy's right index finger confirmed good positioning and an adequately sized opening in his intercostal muscles. He picked up the plastic chest tube with the metal trocar inside and directed the blunt tip into the opening with his right hand. Once he was certain that the tube was correctly positioned in the opening, he took a deep breath and shoved the tip into the left side of his chest cavity using the strength in his right arm, directing it toward his head and back.

After he removed the trocar, a flood of dark blood ran through the tube and onto the floor. He retched again and waited for the dizziness to pass. He was grateful that the spaghetti was gone and was not coming out of the chest tube. He knew that a collapsed left lung would cause the left side of the diaphragm to rise, making it very easy to ram a chest tube into the stomach.

Andy fumbled to advance the screw clamp over the external end of the chest tube. He began to feel intense air-hunger. Fighting panic, he slid the clamp five inches up the tube and turned the screw until the blood stopped at the level of the clamp. Once the screw was tight, he recalculated his chance for survival. Unless he bled to death, the worst might be over.

He picked up the condom and unrolled it onto the external end of the chest tube, using half of its length on the tube itself. The condom was taped airtight with adhesive tape. Surgical scissors were used to cut off the tip of the condom.

When he opened the screw clamp, approximately 300 more milliliters of blood came through the tube immediately to add to the volume already on the floor. When he took a breath, the condom collapsed, preventing any outside air from entering the chest. This arrangement was called a Heimlich valve. The condom would make a fine one-way valve for his chest tube. Using a curved needle with nylon thread attached, he sewed around the chest tube at the point where it entered the chest wall, creating an even tighter seal.

Andy covered the entry site of the chest tube with a Vaseline gauze dressing, half a pack of four-by-four inch gauze, and several rows of overlapping two-inch tape. He taped the chest tube to drain down his left side to the floor, then opened the screw clamp on the chest tube to allow as much air and blood as possible to escape.

There were still two extra pieces of metal in his chest. The needle he had used to release air pressure came out easily. It was no longer needed. He tried to pull the knife out along the track it had entered, without doing any additional damage. In a few seconds he was free of it. He stared at the five inch blade, which had a serrated cutting edge on both sides. This knife was made for killing. He knew where it came from. His friend Pablo in Hawaii had given it to him after showing him how to jump from a tree onto the back of a wild hog, plunging it into the hog's neck. He found it difficult to imagine such a thing in Lindsey's hand.

Now that the blood in the chest had a larger opening to go through, there was no significant blood loss from the knife wound. He cleaned the wound with Betadine and sutured it with a running silk stitch.

The sixth bag of saline was empty, completing 6000 milliliters of resuscitation fluid. He felt better, although he knew that he would have to move slowly. Ideally, the chest tube should be attached to negative pressure to help expand the lung and drain the blood. But Andy decided that there was a better use for the remainder of the blood in his chest. He tightened the screw clamp on the chest tube.

14

It was 4:59 in the morning. They would come looking for him soon. He did not want to be caught inside the Cow Palace. He walked to the twenty-foot high automatic roll-back door that faced the road. He pushed the up button, and then punched the stop button immediately, halting the door at only four inches' elevation. Then he inserted a wooden peg in a hole in the roller track on the right side of the door. Now the door could not be moved up or down, but the light inside would be visible.

There were no guns at the Cow Palace. He returned to the apartment and reached up on the far wall of the combination living room-bedroom, where one of his homemade hunting bows was hanging on a peg. Reaching made him wince. He counted the arrows in his quiver. All four arrows had three-blade, razor-sharp one and a quarter inch diameter hunting broad heads.

Andy had hoped that his days of killing other human beings were over, that he could live out his life in peace, saving other people's lives. The knife had changed everything. Lindsey had changed everything. He was once again a warrior. Anyone who attacked him on his own property should expect no mercy. Not even her. But much more was at stake here than what happened on the Farm.

Andy pulled out a fresh camouflage shirt and pants from the closet of the apartment and put them on. He blackened his face and hands with camo paint from plastic tubes. A black watch cap covered his sandy hair. After retying his boots, he lifted a leather belt from a deer's antler on the wall and strapped on one of his hunting knives. He inserted the belt in the loops of his camo pants and strapped the ten-inch knife in its sheath to his left thigh. He stuffed binoculars and parachute cord into his right cargo pocket.

From the refrigerator, he picked up a one liter bottle of Gatorade, which he slid into his left cargo pocket. He turned out the light, locked the door, and returned the key to the apartment to the bear's ear. As he prepared himself for the upcoming fight, he was already tuning out his pain. The prey would very soon assume its rightful place as the hunter.

Leaving the light on inside the rest of the Cow Palace, Andy stepped out of the small door of the left side into the night. He locked the deadbolt and put the key in the slash pocket of his pants. Walking slowly, with small steps, he reached his first line of defense, a bushy cedar tree on the edge of a large pine forest. Easing to his knees, he broke off several small limbs between him and the side door of the Cow Palace.

He confirmed that he had a clear shot to the left side of the building. After nocking an arrow, he attempted to pull back the string. Halfway to full draw, the muscles in his left chest wall screamed in protest. He commanded his brain to ignore the pain. He knew that drawing the bow would take a maximum effort. He decided to conserve his energy until a killing shot presented itself.

Waiting for dawn, Andy recalled a practical method of improving survival in a patient suffering a penetrating wound to one side of the chest. From his SEAL training he knew that lying on his right side would diminish his shortness of breath. With the right lung dependent, more blood would flow to this normal expanded lung due to gravity and increased resistance to blood flow in the partially collapsed left lung.

The result was that the best blood perfusion, in the normal right lung, was matched with the best ventilation, also in the right lung. The right lateral decubitus position would hopefully allow his heart rate to decrease. It would also keep the left side of his chest, with the chest tube, away from the hard ground and the dirt.

In the starlight he could see the dark liquid backing up behind the clamp on the chest tube. He was still bleeding.

15

Minutes after first light, Andy heard the Kubota RTV climb the hill just past his pond, half a mile away. They were on his back trail. Feeling stiff, he rolled onto his stomach behind the thick cedar tree and watched.

The orange RTV stopped as soon as the occupants saw the golf cart. The driver shut down the engine. It was Bennett and McNeil, still in business suits. They were not wearing body armor. They were armed only with their .45s, unless there was something else in the bed of the Kubota that he could not see.

"I can't believe he made it all the way over here," McNeil said.

"How many times did we have to get out of this thing to look for blood?" Bennett asked.

"Only twice, when he cut through the woods," McNeil said. "Better call this in."

"Lindsey, this is Sid," Bennett said. "I think we've located the subject."

"Is he alive?"

"Can't tell yet. It looks like he's in a metal barn. Golf cart's outside. Blood trail was easy. "

"Don't underestimate this man, Sid. He could have a weapon in that building."

"Send the chopper toward us to cut off any exits," he said. "This is a huge cream-colored building with a tin roof. It's east of the covered bridge, at least a mile from the house."

"Copy that, Sid. Advise when subject is accounted for."

Bennett and McNeil drew their pistols and approached the building from Andy's right.

"Sid, look at the door in the front," said McNeil.

Sid motioned for McNeil to approach from the right front of the roll-back door while he approached from the left. They flattened themselves against the wall of the corners of the building in front, their guns held high.

"Dr. Carlson, this is Sid Bennett," he called. "We can work this out. We can get some medical attention for you. Can you hear us?"

Sid motioned for McNeil to look under the door.

McNeil dropped to the prone position. "Don't see anybody moving."

"Then raise the door," Bennett said.

McNeil was unable to lift the door. "It's blocked in the track. Shooting the lock won't open the door. It must weigh three hundred pounds."

Bennett moved to the left of the building opposite Andy. He tried the door knob. The knob turned but there was a deadbolt. He moved to the rear of the building. This roll-back door was also locked.

Bennett called. "Meet me around the left side, at the small door."

Standing in front of the metal door, both agents had their backs to Andy.

"I'm going to shoot the deadbolt," Bennett said. "I'll go in first and move right. You follow me in and move left."

Andy spread his knees apart for balance.

Both men stepped back, and Bennett blew up the deadbolt with a .45 slug. Leaning forward from the left side of the door, Bennett turned the door knob and pulled the door wide open toward him. A dart board target was on the inside of the door.

McNeil flattened himself against the doorway, his gun held high, head turned toward the door, body facing Andy. Andy drew his bow slowly, negotiating with the torn muscles in his left chest wall. He held at full draw, his lips tight, fighting to keep the muscles in his left forearm from quivering.

When Bennett disappeared into the open door, the arrow struck McNeil in the epigastrium, a triangular space below the sternum. It lodged in his lower thoracic spine. He slid to a sitting position against the building.

McNeil looked down at the arrow. He shook his head slowly before losing consciousness. The target in the epigastrium is softball-sized and contains the aorta and the vena cava, the largest artery and vein in the body. It's not a survivable wound.

Andy nocked a second arrow and waited for Bennett to realize that McNeil was not behind him.

"Brandon," he called. "There's blood all over the place in here, but I don't see Carlson. There's some sort of apartment in here. Brandon?"

Bennett appeared in the doorway as Andy clenched his teeth and brought his bow to full draw again. When Bennett saw McNeil slumped against the building with an arrow sticking out of his upper abdomen, his mouth dropped open. He checked McNeil's carotid pulse.

Bennett had likely never seen an arrow wound before, but the wheels were probably turning in his head. Andy waited for him to put the location of the wound together with the direction of the arrow.

Bennett faced Andy's position, his gun held in front of him with both hands. The second arrow slipped silently into the triangle formed by the gun, his forearms, and his belly button. He, too, slumped backwards against the building, sliding to the ground next to McNeil. Andy lay down on his right side immediately, trying to rest everything in his body except his ears.

At 6:16 in the morning he heard the helicopter lift off from the airport and begin a methodical grid search of the Farm. They would probably find the Cow Palace, the Kubota, and the golf cart quickly. There was only one place near the Cow Palace where a helicopter could safely land, in a field next to the river, appropriately known as Riverbend field. This field was 200 yards away. The road that brought Bennett and McNeil continued past the Cow Palace to Riverbend field. After landing, it would likely take ten minutes for them to walk back to the Cow Palace.

The pine trees behind him were eleven years old. The branches were thick and close to the ground. This tract was a quarter of a mile deep and a mile long, sprinkled with a few tall hardwood trees. After the helicopter passed over, Andy pulled himself to his feet using the branches of the cedar tree and unscrewed the clamp from his chest tube. He held the end of the tube with the condom Heimlich valve away from his body and allowed the blood to drip on the ground. He set a course for one of the remaining hardwood trees, 120 yards into the forest.

Along a path known only to him and the local deer, Andy sprinkled a generous blood trail. The agents from the helicopter would note the trajectory of the arrows. They would find the blood trail that started under the cedar tree. Andy arrived breathless at the deer stand in the hardwood tree, called Longstreet stand, and continued to trickle blood along the deer path for another twenty yards, tightening the clamp on the chest tube at a point where the ground sloped downward and away from the tree stand. He looked up at the tree stand and broke off a few branches to ensure a clear shooting lane. Then he stepped sideways off of the deer trail and circled around in the pines to the hardwood tree, a fat willow oak with plenty of cover at the stand level. He couldn't help recalling the fourteen point buck he had arrowed from this tree stand when he was fifteen. His mom and dad had been more excited than he was.

Andy tied one end of the parachute cord around his bow and held the other end of the cord in his teeth. Longstreet stand had screw-in tree steps, which led to a platform and seat twenty-two feet above ground level. He would take one step at a time, resting after each step.

Climbing a tree requires pulling up with both arms. The arms are attached to the chest wall by the pectoralis muscles. Andy's well-developed left-side pectoralis muscles were torn and a chest tube protruded through his chest wall. Each pull left him shuddering with pain and more breathless. He feared that he would not be able to reach the platform before his enemies arrived.

He could be shot like a raccoon, halfway up a tree. There was no more time to rest. As his head reached platform level, he could hear footsteps and voices coming toward him. He jerked himself onto the platform and flopped into the seat, suppressing the urge to cry out. He tried to calm the noise of his breathing while he pulled up the bow with the parachute cord.

A good blood trail is exhilarating to most hunters. He expected these agents to be hurrying along the trail with their heads down, making no attempt to be silent, oblivious to General Longstreet twenty feet above them.

Andy was seated with his bow resting on his left knee when the two agents with business suits and .45 automatics stomped past the willow oak, pointing and grunting "blood" each time they saw a spatter. When they were ten yards past him, Andy silently clawed the string of his bow to full draw. Steadying his extended left arm, he wondered if this next shot would be his last. As the two men reached the end of the blood trail, they were in single file, with the agent in front slightly below the agent in the back.

Andy aimed just to the left of the spine of the agent in the back. At the critical moment of alignment, he released the string. The three-blade hunting broad head ripped through both chests. As their feet collapsed, they pitched forward and planted their faces in the leaves.

Andy lowered his bow with the parachute cord. Descending the tree was much easier than climbing, but still too painful to do rapidly. He walked around the two dead agents, and then reopened the screw clamp of his chest tube. This took away some of his breathlessness and reestablished the blood trail. He turned north on another deer trail. Following this trail into the thickest pines, he knew that he could not be seen. The pine needles would silence his steps.

A faint conversation was coming from his back-trail, at least a hundred yards away. He needed a way to way to eliminate this threat without having to pull on the string of his bow. Uncle Frank might be able to help.

He continued laying his blood trail until he reached a clearing eighty-five yards from Longstreet stand. Two large cedar logs were lying parallel on the ground. Sitting down, Andy pushed the logs apart with his feet on one end, and then pushed the logs apart from the opposite end. Moss, vines, pine needles, and leaves covered the ground in the center. Andy made sure that the blood trail led to the center of the new clearing. Then he closed the clamp on the chest tube. The two logs now formed a "V", with an eight-foot wide opening facing the blood trail and a two-foot opening at the end of the "V".

Andy took up position about twenty yards on the far side of the trap. Resting on his knees, he nocked another arrow, hoping it would not be required.

"Shit!" Andy heard someone cry from Longstreet stand.

Their approach was noisy. There were two voices. When they were opposite the well, Andy picked up a stick and struck the ground.

He heard the crash he had hoped for, then two men screaming, a series of thunking noises, and then moaning.

Uncle Frank's well was made of stones stacked in a circle. To Andy's best recollection, this well was twenty feet deep and six feet in diameter. Originally the well had been covered with tin sheets and logs, but the tin had mostly rusted out now.

Andy yelled into the hole, "I don't shoot injured soldiers. I'll send somebody to help you get out if I make it myself."

He lay on his right side on the ground and scanned underneath the pine branches as far as he could with his binoculars. The Gatorade was too sweet, but it provided much needed energy.

After fifteen minutes, he began the circle back to the Cow Palace. He opened the screw clamp on his chest tube. The blood in his chest tube was dark, but had slowed to a trickle. He hoped that this meant the blood in his chest was clotting. Even moving slowly, pain surged up and down his left side with each step. After every four or five steps, he was forced to pause and catch his breath. He had a new appreciation for why wounded deer that lie down do not get back up unless they are being pursued.

Andy again positioned himself behind the cedar tree to the left of the Cow Palace and lay down on his right side. He fought off the desire to sleep. Having been awake now for thirty-six hours, he quickly lost this battle.

The sound of a vehicle approaching from his right dragged him back to consciousness. He knew that sound. It was his S-10 Chevy truck. The driver stopped behind the Kubota RTV and surveyed the scene. The golf cart. The two men seated, leaning against the left side of the building.

Lindsey bolted out of the driver's door and ran for the building. She held a Glock .45 in front of her as she ran. Andy was unprepared to see her again. Enemy identification is the first rule of combat. Once the enemy is identified, there can be no hesitation. Hesitation makes your worst fears come true. He confirmed to himself that she was his enemy.

Andy spread his knees apart and nocked his last arrow. Lindsey flattened herself against the left front corner of the Cow Palace, and then peeked around the corner toward the two men. Her face was swollen and covered with a greasy cream. The cream could not hide the horror in her face as she processed the meaning of the arrows.

She ran to the bodies. Andy watched her examine the position and direction from which the arrow had come. She turned toward the pine thicket, arms extended, and made a quick sweep of the woods with her Glock. Seeing nothing, she squatted to check carotid pulses. Her back was toward Andy. The time had come. He could not allow her to get inside the apartment in the Cow Palace. Without the computer inside, he would be unable to warn the Saudis. He would be unable to stop a nuclear attack on America.

He steadied himself on his knees and began the excruciating seventy-pound pull on the string of his bow. At full draw, he released the string and arrow and fell forward to the ground. The arrow struck the bull's eye of the target hanging on the inside of the open door to Lindsey's left. The broad head penetrated the target and both metal panels of the door. The entire door was now stapled open to the outside wall of the Cow Palace. Only half the arrow shaft and its fletching were visible.

At the sound of metal tearing metal, Lindsey jerked her head toward the target and fell backward. Rolling into a prone position on her stomach, she emptied the Glock's thirteen rounds into the trees around Andy. She continued to pull the trigger after the clip was empty.

She rolled onto her back again and stared at the arrow and the target for several seconds. He watched her arms go slack. She did not reload. She stood up deliberately, stuffed the Glock inside the front of her jeans, and faced the woods.

She stood motionless, as if at attention. "Even if you kill me, you can't stop this. Make your best shot."

She unbuttoned the top two buttons and held her shirt apart with both hands. Andy could see no tears on her blistered cheeks nor fear in her eyes as she faced the pine thicket and waited for him to shoot. When he did not, she dropped her head and arms and walked slowly back to the truck.

She opened the driver's door but did not get inside. Instead of reloading a fresh clip, she threw the Glock into the passenger seat. She reached for a radio in the driver's seat.

"Harrison," she said, staring toward the pine thicket. "Bennett and McNeil are dead from arrow wounds. Subject is not dead. I saw Carlson cross the river south of my position. Couldn't get a good shot. He appeared to be moving slowly and bleeding. I don't hear the helicopter. I don't see anyone from the helicopter. Recommend you concentrate on the Prince Edward County side of the river."

Andy heard the response. "We copy. Return to the house. We'll get another chopper right on it. It's open farm land. He can't get away."

She faced the pine thicket one more time. She opened her mouth several times to speak, but nothing came out. She cleared her throat and choked the words out.

"I'm sorry."

She got into the driver's seat, closed the door, and started the engine. He watched her turn the S-10 around and drive back toward the covered bridge and the farmhouse.

16

After the S-10 disappeared over the hill, Andy stumbled toward the open door of the Cow Palace, dragging his bow. The dizziness returned. He feared that if he fell, he might never be able to get back up. The pain in his chest was keeping him awake. He stepped over Bennett's legs. He used the bow to keep himself erect until he reached the stool next to the medicine cabinet.

The smell of blood in the Cow Palace brought back his nausea, but he had nothing left to throw up. Seated on the stool, he looked down at the clotted blood in pools around him and tried to calm his breathing. He knew he was looking at half his normal blood volume in the floor. To maintain consciousness, he would have to dilute his red blood cells even further.

He spiked two more bags of normal saline and attached the two lines to the saline locks in his left forearm. After opening the clamps, he confirmed that the resuscitation fluid was pouring into his body. He lowered his head to the counter and considered what he should do with the computer.

After retrieving the apartment key from the bear's ear, he opened the door, sat down in the chair at the desk, and booted up the computer system. The satellite dish was mounted underneath the apex of the overhang of the roof on the far side of the Palace and faced south. It would be invisible to anyone who approached the building from the main farm road. Bennett did not live long enough to report it, even if he had seen it and understood its significance.

After booting up, Andy searched for the Saudi Arabian Embassy in Washington for his old friend Prince Salmon Akbar. He would remember Andy's code name. He began to type his message:

From: R. E. Lee
To: Salmon Akbar, Ambassador to the United States
Re: Plot to invade your country and requisition your oil fields.

I have recently become aware of a plot within the highest levels of the U.S. government to invade your country and requisition your oil fields for American consumption. The justification for such action is to implicate members of the royal family in a nuclear terrorist explosion at the mouth of Hampton Roads in Virginia. The nuclear weapon is on a container ship that is at this moment on its way to Hampton Roads.

The first attachment shows photographs of alleged members of your family using a rangefinder, a GPS unit, a windicator, and a camera at multiple Hampton Roads military installations and private marine terminals in Hampton Roads.

The second attachment shows photos of U.S. Government agent Lindsey Baker, apparently a key operative in this conspiracy.

After making contact with the president, you should be on the alert for the sinking of a container ship on its way to Hampton Roads, probably a ship that was recently at a port in the Middle East. The U.S. has the means to sink that ship before the bomb is detonated. I believe that the president will do so if you demonstrate knowledge of this conspiracy. The destruction of this ship will confirm my allegation that the plot came from the president. There is something that you can do for both of us. The CIA operatives in this conspiracy are currently trying to kill me on my farm in Farmville, Virginia. I am your best hope to document the intention of the United States government to steal your oil fields. If you could arrange an aircraft to land at Farmville Municipal Airport in central Virginia as soon as possible, I would greatly appreciate it. You may contact me by cell phone when you get here. I will be on a tractor next to the runway.

I have suffered a stab wound to the chest and I am in need of a physician familiar with chest tubes. Please have your doctor bring several plastic bags of normal saline, four units of O negative blood, and a portable source of suction and oxygen. Your physician will understand these requests. I would also recommend that you send a security detail to Norfolk to protect your family members. I am in some distress at this time and respectfully request your help.

Cell phone 804-390-9082
Attachment number 1. Actors impersonating members of the royal family
Attachment number 2. Pictures of Lindsey Baker, U.S. Government Agent.

Completing the attachments, Andy pressed "Send".

17

A ndy looked at his watch: 6:50 in the morning. It would take fifteen minutes for this message to be read and understood. And
another fifteen minutes for Akbar to confer with the royal family and
to contact the president. Then it would take about thirty minutes for
the president to scramble a Raptor out of Langley. The Air Force would
have to program the GPS bomb. He had at least an hour to depart
the Farm. Once the president was aware that his plan was unraveling,
Lindsey would be a liability to him and to the CIA. He calculated that
she had an hour to live.

He watched his stream of urine in the toilet of the apartment in
the Cow Palace and confirmed that it was adequate in volume and did
not appear too concentrated. These were good signs. He had replaced
enough intravascular volume to perfuse his kidneys. He changed into a
clean camo shirt and pants. Using his hunting knife, he made a walking
stick out of a push broom.

He stood at the corner of the Cow Palace and listened for several
minutes. It would be important to pace himself. He had one lung and
half his normal complement of red blood cells. He was short of breath
standing still. At best, walking would be a step-by-step fight against
pain, exhaustion, and breathlessness. He made sure that the clamp on
his chest tube was wide open. A trickle of blood and bubbles escaped
from the condom on the end of the tube. Unless they had a blood-
tracking dog, no one could follow him where he was going.

Andy wanted to take advantage of Lindsey's misdirection by entering the swamp next to Dry Creek. There was no time to speculate over
her behavior. She wouldn't survive anyway.

Urging his body forward, he followed the trails of the deer that traveled in the ditches of the swamp. The knife on his left thigh had never felt heavy before, but now it was a burden for each step. He unbuckled the belt at his waist, untied the sheath from his thigh, and dropped the knife in the mud.

The swamp grass was already six feet high at the end of May. He picked his way through the muddy ditches in the swamp grass until he could see the covered bridge ahead. His chest was heaving again. If he could reach the underside of the bridge, he could lie down on his right side among the rocks, shunting the precious blood he had to the only functional lung he had. Fighting the growing dizziness and blurred vision, he urged his legs to function without oxygen. They protested. His thighs burned and his calves cramped as he plodded forward.

Lying under the bridge, he looked at his watch. 7:20. From his knees he climbed the walking stick. A vehicle was approaching the bridge from South Airport Road. He felt naked without a weapon, but could not think of a weapon he had the strength to use. The vehicle rattled across the planks overhead and the driver gunned the engine up the hill toward the farmhouse. Time was running out, along with the blood from his chest tube.

He continued to stumble along the deep banks of Dry Creek to South Airport Road, where he again stopped underneath the highway bridge and lay down on his right side. After a few minutes, the dizziness passed. He heard a helicopter making passes over the farm on the opposite side of the river, almost a mile from him. Again he climbed the walking stick.

On the far side of the Dry Creek bridge on South Airport Road was the property of his friend and neighbor, Charlie Dodd. Vehicles crossed the bridge every few minutes, mostly from the airport. He waited until he could not hear any vehicle approaching, and then followed Dry Creek north as it wound around behind Dodd's house toward Pleasant Valley Road. At 7:48 he pounded on the back door of Charlie's house.

Charlie looked out the window of the door and jerked his head back. Hurriedly he opened the door.

"Andy, you look awful. What happened?"

"I got stabbed," he said, leaning on his walking stick.

"Let me take you to the hospital."

"No time for that now. I must get to the airport."

"But you look grey. You're not breathing right. You've got blood all over yourself."

"Trust me, Charlie. The Farm is full of people who want to kill me. I'm sure they're searching every car at the intersection of South Airport Road and Plank Road. Could I have a drink of water?"

"I saw the helicopters and all those cars on the road this morning," he said. "There is a government car at Pleasant Valley Road and South Airport Road. Please sit down."

"Can't get back up if I sit down."

Charlie handed him a glass of water, which Andy gulped.

Charlie was a retired police detective, a Viet Nam veteran who relished his new life as a horse rancher. He was in his mid-sixties, with white hair and beard, weathered face, slight build, and penetrating blue eyes. He made it a point to shave at least once weekly, but not in several days. Andy had never seen him in any outfit except jeans, boots, flannel shirt, and cowboy hat.

"I don't have time to explain it all, but I need to borrow that tractor in the front yard, the John Deere with the cab and the seven-foot mower."

"No problem, but what can I do?"

"You could drive back and forth between here and the airport while I'm mowing and bring a few guns with you. If somebody attacks me on the tractor, send them to hell."

"Then what?"

"Someone is going to pick me up in an airplane and take care of me," Andy said. "Get Jeanne to drive you down to the airport in about an hour to pick up the tractor."

"You look like we need to move fast." Charlie put his arm around Andy and helped him through the house to the front door.

Andy could reach the first step of the tractor's cab, but Charlie had to boost his butt the rest of the way. Before backing out of the driveway, Andy looked backed at his neighbor. "You might read about me in the newspaper. Don't believe everything you read and forget you saw me today."

"Good luck."

"Could I borrow that straw hat of yours and a towel? I'll leave them in the cab."

Andy turned right out of Charlie Dodd's driveway onto South Airport Road, and then engaged the power-take-off and began to mow the right side of the road toward the airport, about two miles away. He could feel his brain slowing down. He wiped the camo paint from his face with the towel. Bubbly blood continued to drip from his chest tube into the floor of Charlie's cab. He turned the vent of the air conditioner toward his face as he mowed past the thick stands of pine on the Farm to his left.

Several vehicles with extra antennas drove past Andy in each direction as he mowed toward the airport, but no one stopped him. From the height of the cab of the tractor he looked down into the front seat of Charlie Dodd's car as it passed him. He saw two automatic shotguns, a .45 pistol, boxes of shotgun shells, and extra clips for his Colt .45 semi-automatic. Charlie was wearing his green combat jacket.

The terminal at Farmville Municipal Airport would be empty this hour of the day. There were no private jets in sight, just the same five or six Cessnas that were always parked near the terminal.

He stopped near the center of the runway, forty feet from the blacktop, and shut off the engine. He opened the cab door and tried to descend the three steps to the grass, but his vision was fading in and out, forcing him to hold onto the hand rails with both hands. A sharp pain from his left chest wall shot up his left arm. He lost his grip on the left rail and fell backwards onto his buttocks.

Rolling over on his right side next to the rear tire of the tractor, he remained flat in the grass, trying to get control of his breathing. He wanted to make a phone call.

When her cell phone rang at 8:06, Lindsey was expecting a call from Harrison, who was in the helicopter now circling the farm on the south side of the Appomattox River, where Lindsey had reported sighting Dr. Carlson. She paced in the great room of Andy's house.

Flipping open the phone, she noted the display: "Andy is calling."

He said, "I can't tell you how sorry I am that things have worked out like this. Are you outside?"

"No," she said.

He spoke in short bursts, almost whispering. "Other people have been using your pain to manipulate you. There are some things you need to know."

"Go ahead."

"Two of your agents are in a well… in the pine thicket west of the Cow Palace. Their legs are probably broken."

"I've got that."

He stopped talking to take a few breaths. "You need to know that I've sent an e-mail to the Saudis… regarding your plan. The president of the United States… knows your name… and he knows that you failed with your mission to use me."

"I didn't see you carrying a computer when you ran out of the farmhouse."

"The Cow Palace is the only dairy barn… in Cumberland County… with a computer and an Internet connection."

She did not reply.

Andy said, "Your friends are about to kill you… the president will not want anyone around who can refute his version of what happened…There's a bomb with your name on it…Trust me… It's already on its way… Get a knife out of the kitchen. Cut the GPS tracker out of your shoulder… Run out into the alfalfa field next to the barn and throw it as far as you can in the field. Please don't give up Sahar to Harrison. I beg you. He'll kill her."

Her cell phone disconnected.

Andy slipped into unconsciousness leaning against the tractor wheel. He was awakened by the sonic boom of a military jet. The subsequent explosion shook the ground at the airport. He rolled onto his back and looked at the fire, smoke, and debris boiling up above the pine trees of the Farm.

When the private jet lined up with the runway from the northeast, he was unconscious.

At 9:00 Saturday morning, the Los Angeles class submarine Kingfish received an emergency action message. The message was authenticated by the executive officer and the captain using the unique security codes that accompanied each EAM. The captain was directed to proceed at flank speed to intercept the container ship that they had been assigned to trail across the Atlantic to Newport News Marine Terminal in Hampton Roads. The EAM confirmed that this container ship contained a nuclear threat to the U.S. The captain was ordered to confirm the ship's identity visually, sink it with a torpedo, confirm that it was sunk, and advise Atlantic Fleet Headquarters in Norfolk afterward. No survivors were to be picked up and the submarine was instructed not to surface at any time.

18

O nboard the private jet, Andy awakened to men in white robes. He considered that air conditioning would make sense in Heaven. He did feel like he was floating on air. But what was the purpose of the chest tube? And why was he in pain? This couldn't be Heaven.

Someone had attached his chest tube to a Pleurovac suction chamber, half-filled with water. He breathed deeply. He felt his left lung expanding normally. There was only about a hundred milliliters of thin blood in the Pleurovac. A blood transfusion was running into his left arm.

Two Arab men in traditional dress approached him from the front of the jet.

"Mr. Lee, are you well enough to talk?" the first one asked.

Andy answered, "I must have passed out at the airport. My real name is Dr. Andy Carlson."

"You were unconscious when we found you, and barely alive," said the man next to his bed.

"And whom do I have to thank for the blood and the suction for my chest tube?"

"I am Salman Abdullah Akbar. We have talked on the phone many times in the past. This is Ahmed Abdullah Al-Zahrani," he said. Mr. Akbar had a mole on his left cheek, bushy eyebrows, and perfect teeth.

Andy extended his hand to Akbar, who grasped it. "Finally we meet, old friend."

Mr. Al-Zahrani wore a full length robe and headdress. His thin face made his nose more prominent. He was the more anxious of the two. They were shorter than Andy and did not need to lean over as they moved around the white interior of the jet.

"I hope that you have also sent someone to protect your young princes in Norfolk," Andy said.

"It has been done. We're happy to report that they are safe and doing well," said Mr. Akbar. "As you know, they were attacked two days ago in Norfolk."

"What did you think of the pictures?"

"The persons in the pictures are not our princes," Akbar said. "Our princes have never been fishing anywhere in the United States. They did not leave their apartment yesterday. They were recuperating from their injuries."

Al-Zahrani added, "No one in Saudi Arabia paid for a nuclear weapon or put a bomb on a ship bound for America."

"Is it possible that a terrorist organization in the Middle East could have done this?" Andy asked.

"No Arab country or terrorist organization did this," Al-Zahrani said. "It is unlikely that such a thing could be done without our knowledge. The king is most upset. He wants to show the world that we're innocent. We do not want war."

"Did he contact our president?" Andy asked.

"King Fahd called your president on a diplomatic line immediately," Mr. Akbar said. "Your president promised to find out who was responsible for this. He promised to locate the container ship and prevent it from reaching Virginia."

"I suspect," Andy said, "that this ship has already been sunk. The president would not want anyone to identify the unexploded warhead aboard. If it exploded over open water, it would be difficult to identify where it came from. But an unexploded bomb would have the markings and technology of the bomb maker."

Akbar cleared his throat and sat down across from Andy's cot in the plane. "Are you saying that if the ship is sunk, your president could be personally involved in this conspiracy against Saudi Arabia?"

"That is exactly what I am saying, sir," Andy said.

"I don't understand," Akbar said.

"Your president has told us many times that he is our friend," said Mr. Al-Zahrani.

"Sir," Andy said, "in your country and in my country, there are crazy people. You have people in your country who want to kill Americans because Allah or Mohammad told them to. We have people in our country who want to kill Arabs and take their oil. I'm sure this is no surprise to you. What is different now is that unscrupulous people are in power in America, and they value foreign oil over honesty and friendship."

"The royal family understands that being rich in oil is not the same as being strong, and that being rich in dollars is not the same as being secure," Akbar said.

"But you do have one certain power over the president," Andy said. "And it would be wise to use it now. Demonstrate your displeasure by cutting back on America's share of Saudi oil, at least long enough to get his attention. You could help me by informing the president that if something happens to me, the United States will get even less oil."

"We are grateful to you, Dr. Carlson. This is the second time you have protected us from your own country. Why do you do this?"

"I would die for my country if necessary, but I will not dishonor myself or violate my oath as a SEAL by robbing other nations. I'm under no obligation to carry out immoral orders or assist politicians in illegal schemes."

"The king will not forget what you have done," Akbar said.

"Dr. Carlson," Mr. Zahrani said, "where would you like for us to take you in Washington?"

"Please take me to the emergency department at the George Washington University Medical Center. That is where I studied emergency medicine. And it's right down the street from somebody I need to talk to."

19

Monday morning Andy woke up in his room at George Washington University Medical Center. The unit of blood dripping into his arm had "#4" written on it with a black magic marker. He recounted the events of the past three days.

Since waking up in the hospital, he had called Sahar repeatedly. Her phone never rang. He picked up the Washington Post from the bedside table.

In the left-hand column, halfway down the page, he found what he was looking for. "Container Ship Capsizes in Heavy Seas. All Hands Lost". He read:

U.S. Maritime officials announced at noon Saturday that they had received an emergency message from a Middle Eastern container ship, the Abdullah Aziz, at 9:05 yesterday morning. The ship had encountered heavy seas and was taking on water rapidly. The U.S. Weather Service confirmed a freak storm in the area where the ship apparently went down with all hands aboard. After docking briefly in Saudi Arabia and Dubai, the ship was headed for Hampton Roads, Virginia. The U.S. Navy has sent a salvage ship to investigate the sinking. Multiple Navy ships are in the area looking for survivors. No further information is available at this time.

Andy immediately placed an order at the campus bookstore. After the package arrived, he dialed the hospital operator and requested to be connected to the White House switchboard.

"White House Switchboard," a female voice said. "Where may I direct your call?"

"This is Dr. Andy Carlson," he said. "The president should recognize my name by now. I'm currently a patient at George Washington

University Medical Center. I need to have a conversation with the president immediately."

"Sir," the lady said, "I must warn you that this conversation is taped and that we have caller ID. You are committing a crime."

"I'm counting on this call being taped, lady," he said. "Contact Harrison at the CIA and he will confirm that I have business with the president."

"Don't hang up, Dr. Carlson," she said. "This may take as long as ten minutes. Several people must approve this call before we can connect you to the president."

After six minutes, the operator returned. "Please continue to hold, Dr. Carlson."

After eight more minutes a familiar voice came on the line.

"Dr. Carlson, this is President Marshall. I'm so glad that you're alive. We didn't know what happened to you. Were you injured badly?"

"I have a chest wound, sir, but I'm feeling much better after receiving several units of blood."

"I'm looking forward to reviewing the events of the last couple of days with you when you are able," the president said.

"I'm okay to talk now, sir."

"I'd come to the medical center myself, but the subject matter we need to discuss is too sensitive to be addressed at a hospital," he said.

"I could go through the tunnel between GW and the White House, sir," Andy said.

"I wasn't aware that the tunnel was common knowledge, Dr. Carlson."

"Why don't you send a couple of Secret Service agents over with one of those golf carts with the flat bed for stretchers?" Andy asked.

"My God, you are well-informed, Dr. Carlson."

"The next time you want to keep something secret," Andy said, "I would suggest that you not connect it to an emergency department. There are no secrets in an emergency department."

"I'll send for you."

The President hung up and Andy pressed the nurse-call button on his bed.

"Ms. Rodriguez, a Secret Service detail will arrive shortly to take me to the White House," Andy said.

Amy Rodriguez's eyebrows slowly went up, but she remained calm. "You need to finish your last transfusion, and you still have a chest tube."

She had a Texas accent and short black hair. He estimated that she was sixteen weeks pregnant. The wedding band suggested that her husband accounted for her Hispanic name.

"Some of the nurses remember you, Dr. Carlson," she said, smiling. "They want to know if you're still shy and if you're married."

"Give my regards. I have fond memories of this hospital. Right now I need a portable suction unit to attach to the Pleurovac. And I need an extra bag of normal saline for the ride."

Nurse Rodriguez nodded.

"Unfortunately, I need these things within a few minutes," Andy said. "Don't worry. Please inform my attending physician that I'll be gone approximately one hour and that I'm responding to a request from the president of the United States. Bring me a leave of absence form and I'll sign it."

Nurse Rodriguez hurried out of the door.

The person who knocked on his door fifteen minutes later did not wait for a reply. Two gentlemen in business suits and shoulder harnesses entered the room and held their credentials to his face.

"I'm Agent Sanders and this is Agent McMahan, Dr. Carlson. We were sent by the president to accompany you to the White House. We have our own stretcher."

Sanders and McMahan appeared to have no distinguishing features, a prerequisite for a Secret Service agent. Except for their shoulder harnesses, they could have been hospital administrators.

Ms. Rodriguez returned and transferred the half-empty unit of blood and the battery-operated pump to the pole of the stretcher. Andy scooted his butt from the bed to the stretcher. Agent McMahan patted Andy down through the sheet to be sure that he had no weapons.

"This transfusion should be completed in about twenty-five minutes, Dr. Carlson," Amy said.

She connected the clear tubing from Andy's chest tube to the Pleurovac chamber now between his legs. Andy took a breath and exhaled, noting that he still had a significant leak of air bubbling through the hole in his left lung into the water chamber of the Pleurovac.

"I don't need this oxygen anymore," he said, removing his nasal cannula. I took myself off about fifteen minutes ago and my SATs are still one hundred percent. It'll simplify transport if we don't have to lug an oxygen tank along. You know how people have a way of tripping over oxygen lines."

She pulled up the side rails of the stretcher, attaching the Pleurovac unit to the left rail, and pulled the oxygen tubing away from the stretcher.

One of the most accurate determinants of the level of experience of any nurse is how long it takes her to transfer a complex patient and all of his paraphernalia from a bed to a stretcher or vice versa. Ms. Rodriguez was an experienced nurse.

Andy knew that he was no longer bleeding because nothing red was draining into the Pleurovac through the chest tube. He had seen his own chest X-ray earlier that morning and had noted his lung to be ninety-five percent expanded.

Andy rode down to the emergency department in a regular elevator. In the ED of GWMC he was rolled into another elevator. After the doors closed, Agent McMahan entered a code into a keypad on the side of the elevator and placed the palm of his right hand on a laser reader next to the keypad. The opposite side of the elevator opened, revealing another room, about the size of the great room in his farm house. This area had no windows but was loaded with security cameras.

Three elevators each had a keypad and palm reader. Two golf carts with flat beds were parked to the side. Andy's stretcher was lowered and then loaded by the two agents onto the flat bed of one of the golf carts. The wheels of his stretcher were locked into grooves on the bed of the golf cart.

The double door to the far left had a small sign next to its keypad, "White House."

McMahan entered a code into the keypad next to the White House keypad and placed his right palm on the reader. The doors opened into the tunnel. Sanders drove through the opening of the tunnel to the White House with McMahan seated next to him. Andy stared up at the ceiling. The doors closed automatically behind them.

The tunnel was wide enough for two carts to pass each other, and it was well lighted. Shortly after they entered the tunnel, he noted that the grade descended sharply for fifty yards. We must be a hundred feet in the ground, he thought, when the tunnel leveled out. The passage was monitored with security cameras pointed in both directions. Air-conditioning vents hummed overhead.

The cart continued for half a mile before beginning its ascent to the White House. Agent McMahan parked the vehicle in a flat area in front of a double door, then entered another code into a keyboard, and again placed his right palm on the reader. The doors opened toward them. He noted the four inch steel cylinders retracted into the doors.

The two agents removed his stretcher from the golf cart and adjusted it to a height of four feet.

"Would you mind raising my head almost all the way up?" Andy asked.

McMahan complied with his request.

Andy's stretcher was pushed into the basement of the White House. At the next elevators, Agent McMahan used the keypad and palm reader, with the same results. To Andy's surprise, the elevator continued up at least three floors before stopping. McMahan pressed a call button when the elevator stopped.

President Caleb Marshall came smiling to the elevator to greet Andy. "Dr. Carlson." The president extended his hand, and Andy took it.

The president directed the agents to bring Andy's stretcher into what appeared to be a living room.

"I guess I was expecting the Oval Office," Andy said.

"Well, we can talk more privately here. The first lady is visiting her mother."

With a nod he dismissed the two Secret Service agents.

The president was a tall, thin gentleman in his mid-sixties, wearing reading glasses. He had thinning salt and pepper hair and the rosy cheeks of an elderly drinker. He smiled too often, Andy recalled from his TV appearances. When he spoke at length, each version of his smile appeared a bit less sincere than the last. Andy didn't believe he would be buying what the president was shoveling today.

The president took up a comfortable chair. "The Saudi ambassador called me yesterday to say that they were cutting our share of Saudi oil, as well as cutting production. That's going to hurt us, Andy. The country is already suffering."

Andy decided to let him keep talking.

"They threatened to sell their oil to other countries if anything happened to you," he said. "I don't know why they would think we wanted to harm you. We wouldn't have known about this bomb if it hadn't been for you."

Andy looked him in the eye. The president was accomplished at lying with a straight face.

"You have prevented a disaster of monumental proportions," the president said. "A nuclear weapon on its way to the mouth of Hampton Roads. My God. It is hard to imagine the devastation we might have suffered. Tell me, I'm a little curious as to why you contacted the Saudis first."

"It was my understanding that the U.S. already knew about the bomb on the container ship," Andy replied. "I was told that the CIA was aware of the bomb and that they intended to explode it before it reached Hampton Roads."

"Does that sound reasonable to you?" the president asked. "What a preposterous idea."

"The CIA apparently wanted to place the blame for this nuclear weapon on the Saudi royal family," Andy said.

"But there's no proof for such a scheme."

"On Saturday morning, I observed two Saudi prince impersonators visiting sensitive military and civilian sites in Hampton Roads. Their behavior was alarming."

"How do you know they were impersonators?"

"The royal family flew me to Washington yesterday," Andy said. "The real Saudi princes are in their custody and they can account for their whereabouts on Saturday morning. The real princes were never involved in any nuclear terrorist plot."

"The Saudis are notorious for denying their involvement in terrorist organizations," the president said.

The president got up and poured himself a drink from a decanter. He offered one to Andy, who declined.

"During my flight to Washington yesterday afternoon," Andy said, "I had a conversation with two gentlemen from the Saudi embassy, Ambassador Salmon Akbar and Mr. Al-Zahrani. They assured me that the Saudi royal family had no involvement in this plot. They had a stack of pictures. They say that they can prove that their princes are not the same princes in the pictures at the Hampton Bay Bridge-Tunnel."

"You don't believe all this fancy footwork with cameras, do you?" the president asked.

"Sir, I was there when the pictures were taken. I can believe a lot of things today that I would have dismissed as unlikely two days ago."

"I swear to you on the graves of all the men who have lived in this White House," the president said, "the United States was not the source of that bomb."

"But you cannot swear to me on the graves of all of those dead presidents that the CIA did not plant that bomb, can you, Mr. President?"

The president did not respond.

"It is clear that someone in the U.S. government knew which ship the bomb was on, because the U.S. Navy sank it yesterday." Andy said. "According to the Washington Post the ship sank around 9:05 in the morning. I did not notify the Saudis of this conspiracy until 6:50 that morning, Mr. President. Mr. Akbar told me that King Fahd called you almost immediately."

The president puckered his lips and tilted his chin downward. He wiped his forehead with a handkerchief.

Andy continued, "The Saudis don't have any submarines or warships capable of sinking that ship. I believe that it was sunk by a United States submarine that was accompanying it across the Atlantic. And it couldn't have been sunk without your knowledge. You are the only person capable of giving such an order."

The president's complexion had turned gray. He wiped his forehead again, this time with his white shirt sleeve. "The Navy must have figured out which ship it was on."

"I've been on that ocean," Andy said. "The odds of any Navy ship being close enough by accident to identify a strange ship and determine what its cargo was within a few minutes without boarding it are zero. In short, sinking that ship was an admission that you personally could not afford for the world to see the nuclear weapon on board."

"An admission?"

"If the ship had been boarded, then the weapon's source could have been relatively easy to determine," Andy said. "I'd be willing to bet that this warhead never sees the light of day outside the U.S. Navy."

"You bring up some very difficult questions," said the president. "Like I said, the bomb was not from the United States."

"But you didn't say that the bomb was not planted by the United States," Andy said.

"Why would we plant a bomb on that ship and then blow it up?"

"The United States would stand to gain a lot from a nuclear explosion a few hundred miles east of Hampton Roads. The radiation would mostly affect northern Europe and Russia. You would have a legitimate excuse to take over the oil fields in Saudi Arabia and consolidate your strength in the Middle East."

The president walked over to a cabinet and poured himself another drink. He held the contents of the glass in his mouth for a moment, and then swallowed it all in two gulps. He sat back down.

"This may seem like a simple world to you, Carlson, but some of us have to make difficult decisions. You don't have to take the blame for six dollar a gallon gas or a sinking economy. Angry Congressmen and Senators don't call for your head every day. Americans don't curse you when you stand up to a podium."

"You've had to make some difficult decisions, President Marshall, and you still have some to make," Andy said. "You must decide whether it's more prudent to kill me and risk the wrath of the Saudis, or keep me alive and trust me not to betray you."

The president said, "You do know something about difficult choices, after all."

"If you'll level with me," Andy said, leaning toward the president, "I'll do everything that I can to support you and this country. If you'll review my military file, you'll see that I have killed many times at your direction. I wish I could believe that all of those people deserved death."

The president's face brightened. "They did. You have my word. You do have an outstanding record. I think we could come to an understanding, but I would need your assurance that you'll not share your experience over the weekend with anyone."

"I'm a Navy SEAL, Mr. President. I've been in many countries and done many things. I've never discussed any of my missions with anyone, even though I've come to doubt the morality of some of them. You have my word that I will not betray you as long as you're straight with me and I never hear about stealing Saudi oil again."

The president took off his reading glasses. "You could help us, Andy. We need to repair our relationship with the Saudis. They trust you."

"Where did the bomb come from, sir?" Andy asked.

"Since the collapse of the Soviet Union we've been in charge of dismantling hundreds of nuclear warheads of every size," he said. "We pay the Russians to allow us to destroy these weapons. We needed just one that could not be traced to the United States."

Andy nodded.

"It was a CIA operation from the start," the president said. "I really didn't want to do it, and I didn't want to know the details. I only insisted that no Americans be harmed. I felt that I had no choice but to do something about the price of gasoline. Unfortunately, when something like this goes wrong, it gets dumped back in my lap."

"At least the bomb didn't detonate," Andy said.

The president appeared to be regaining his color.

"Can you tell me if the CIA agent Lindsey Baker was told that the U.S. planted this bomb?"

"Ms. Baker believed that this warhead was a terrorist weapon placed on that ship by al Qaeda and financed by the Saudis," the president said. "She was motivated because her parents were killed in the World Trade Center and her brother was killed in Iraq. Also, she had been an emergency nurse, and she had certain physical attributes that would be attractive to you."

Andy dropped his chin and brushed his right hand over his eyes. "I guess I didn't know her as well as I thought I did."

"That's a common mistake in politics, too."

"The CIA knew that I had reported nuclear weapons in Saudi Arabia less than two years ago," Andy said. "They figured that I could recognize the implications of what the Saudi princes were doing. My story would sound very believable once a bomb exploded."

The president reached over and put his hand on Andy's shoulder. "Let's close this sad chapter. What can I do for you now?"

"I haven't been back to my farm yet, so I don't know what the CIA did to it."

"There was some damage," the president said. "Call me about your losses."

The president handed Andy a card from his desk. "These are my private numbers. It would help me if you could let the Saudis know that I was against the CIA plan. It was really a rogue operation I got stuck with."

"I'll be talking with Mr. Akbar soon."

The President smiled, but it was less convincing than the one on his face when Andy arrived in the White House.

20

Andy's neighbor, Charlie Dodd, was kind enough to pick up Andy from the George Washington Medical Center. Andy had been a patient at GW for a week. On the drive home Andy explained how he had fallen in love with Lindsey. Uncertain of his own future, Andy decided that someone he trusted should know the truth in case he didn't survive. They discussed the nuclear terrorist threat. Andy knew Charlie wouldn't lose faith in the government, because his friend didn't have any faith in the U.S. government to lose. He was a Viet Nam veteran with no use for politics or politicians. Andy outlined the president's scheme and how it had unraveled.

"Not surprised at all," Charlie said. "Most wars start with lies."

When they reached the gate of The Farm, Andy was relieved that it was closed and locked.

"I locked your gate after we picked up the John Deere you left at the airport," Charlie said. "But somebody in a big van, like a UPS truck, went in there that afternoon. I wasn't about to follow them under the circumstances. They were here for about six hours. Then they left and locked the gate."

Andy said. "Thanks for everything you did. You and Jeanne may be the only friends I've got left."

After crossing the covered bridge and riding up the hill, Andy was confronted with a huge bomb crater on the left side of his gravel road, about fifty feet into the field. There was no sign of any human remains, just dirt.

"I can bring my bulldozer over tomorrow and fill this hole in for you," Charlie said. "You know how Jeanne has been nagging me about what I paid for it. Just because I don't use it every day she thinks I wasted my money. Well, this proves her wrong. You never know when the government is going to drop a bomb on you and you're going to need your own bulldozer."

"Thanks, Charlie."

He left Andy at his front door.

The house didn't appear to be damaged on the outside. The stand of oak trees along the road had shielded it.

His head jerked from left to right. It wasn't there. His silver S-10 truck was missing.

The last time he saw it, Lindsey had driven it away from the Cow Palace towards the farmhouse. He needed that truck. He had all sorts of special equipment on that truck. Sometimes he lived out of that truck. He loved that truck. A real pattern was shaping up in his life.

Before going inside, Andy drove his Kubota RTV over to Uncle Frank's well. He found no bodies. He was uncertain what that meant.

He walked inside his home and smelled the stale air. Walking from room to room, he found no evidence that anyone had been there since the night Lindsey stabbed him. In the kitchen were the dirty plates from their spaghetti dinner, now being enjoyed by ants. On the floor in the dining room at the feet of his chair were drops of his dried blood. There was one empty bottle of wine and one unopened bottle on the counter in the kitchen.

He walked into the master bedroom. Pieces of nylon cord were still tied to each bedpost. He turned around quickly and walked back to the dining room. Avoiding the chair with the blood, he sat down with his back to the deck and punched the speed dial again for Sahar's phone. He had been calling her cell phone number regularly since he woke up in the hospital. It never rang. It was time to face facts. He no longer had any reasons to stay sober.

He took a deep swallow of the only love left in his life, Southern Comfort, which he kept handy inside the coffee table. She burned a little on the way down but always rewarded his brain quickly.

Sahar had not survived Harrison's paranoia. Lindsey had betrayed him and Sahar. Joe was dead. His parents were dead. His brothers might as well be dead, since he almost never saw them.

Not only were there no women left in his life, he had no legitimate reason to expect any. Since his brain was untrustworthy in public, he would stay at the Farm until he ran out of Southern Comfort. His heart, which he had counted on to lead him to the right woman and sobriety, was unreliable even before it was broken.

As he wandered through the house canvassing his supply of whiskey, Andy wished that he believed in Heaven, a place where his parents could be together, where he might see them and Sahar and Joe again.

Lining up all his Southern Comfort bottles on the coffee table, he considered his own longevity. The president of the United States and Harrison would eventually think of some way to have him killed without offending the Saudis. Andy didn't fear his own death. People who were afraid to die had something to lose. He took another long drink.

21

Three days later, at four o'clock in the afternoon, the only cab in Farmville pulled in front of Andy's house. Sahar had been surprised to find Andy's gate open. She took this as a bad sign.

She jumped out of the back seat with her bag and paid the driver. She was dressed like any other American teenager, in blue jeans and a faded shirt. Before leaving the driveway, she watched the cab disappear down the road to the covered bridge. The front door was wide open. She took a few tentative steps forward, until the odor smacked her in the face. She dropped her bag on the steps.

Someone had been throwing up. A lot. Someone had been drinking whiskey. A lot. She had smelled this combination before. Arabs generally don't drink, but college kids did. Andy had never had any alcohol to drink around her. She had spent several pleasant evenings with him in restaurants in Norfolk. He always ordered ice tea. The only other time she had been at the Farm, he had soft drinks.

She opened the door and surveyed the floor before entering the great room. Empty whiskey bottles decorated the coffee table. One bottle was half full. She picked up the cap and screwed it back on.

"Andy?"

There was no answer. She called again. There were dirty dishes on the dining table, along with a pistol and a box of shells. Her pulse quickened at the sight of blood splatters on the floor next to Andy's favorite chair. She backed out of the dining room, listening, looking, and dialing down the sensitivity of her nose.

Her nose advised her that most of the stench was coming from the master bedroom. She tip-toed into the room, avoiding the vomit and dirty clothes in the floor. There was a noise nearby. A breathing noise. A naked leg was protruding from the door of the master bath.

She jumped back. "Andy?"

The leg moved slightly but no one spoke. She inched forward and peeked into the bathroom. There was no doubt it was Andy. No one else had an upper body like that. At least he had his bottom underwear on, such as it was. He was lying prone. She straddled his body and looked more carefully. There were two recent wounds on the left side of his chest.

His head was wedged between the toilet and the six inch lip of the shower. His breathing appeared to be okay. She leaned closer to his face. Andy's breath matched the stuff on the floor. It appeared that he hadn't made it to the toilet, several times.

Sahar backed out of the bathroom and looked at Andy's bed. The remains of the nylon cord on the bedposts stood out. So this was how he had been injured. Someone had tied him up and tortured him. Maybe they forced him to drink all that whiskey. The whole place was a stinking mess. Andy was a stinking mess, drunker than a fraternity boy. But he was alive. She smiled. He finally needed her.

She decided not to disturb him until she cleaned up the rest of the house. Something strong would be required to overcome the awful smell. Pine-Sol, underneath the sink, would do fine. She found a garbage bag and filled it with every alcohol bottle she could find, including the half-empty bottle. She swept up the pieces of a broken coffee mug in the dining room and scrubbed the blood stains from the floor and chair. She sprayed the ants and other critters that had been feeding on the dirty dishes. Andy had an electric dishwasher, which simplified the kitchen and dining room cleanup. In an hour, that part of the house looked presentable.

There was broken glass on the floor in the bedroom, which she swept up next. She picked up her bag from the front steps and switched from blue jeans and shirt to shorts and a T-shirt. She took off her shoes and socks, pulled back the shower curtain, and looked at the size of the shower. Even he would fit in here.

She began by dragging his left leg over the shower lip. Leaning back against the shower wall, she pulled on his left arm. Bit by bit, she inched him toward the shower. She lifted his waist with the back of his shorts and moved his torso onto the lip of the shower, straining her back in the process. She gently moved his head with both hands. Using her foot against his pelvis, she pushed his right side inside the shower. He rolled over on his left side. She arranged his left arm to support his head. After pulling the shower curtain, she scrubbed the entire bathroom with Pine-Sol.

She bagged all of the dirty linens on the bed, the filthy towels in the bathroom, and the disgusting clothes scattered in the bedroom and great room. She dragged the black plastic bag to the laundry room. Soon the washing machine was humming. In the laundry room she found a pair of scissors on the shelf next to the detergents. She cut the nylon cord from Andy's bedposts so that he would never have to think about being tortured when he looked at the bed.

Returning to Andy's bedroom, she selected new linens from his closet and remade the bed. From his chest-of-drawers she selected a fresh pair of boxer shorts, a T-shirt, and a pair of cut-off blue jeans, and socks. She laid these out on the bed. From the closet she selected a clean pair of tennis shoes. These were lined up below the clothes next to the bed. Finally, she had a chance to show him how efficient she was at such duties.

There were several types of soap in the shower. She selected a liquid soap, which she applied by hand to his entire body. Since he did not respond to this, she removed his underpants. These would have to be discarded forever.

Andy would protest if he were awake. If he asked her later, she would say she never looked at his body. She stood up, satisfied with her work. She closed the lid of the toilet and placed a large folded beach towel on top. She adjusted the water temperature by directing the spray on her hand. When it was warm enough, she directed the water onto Andy and pulled the shower curtain.

She sat down on the bed and waited. Nothing happened. Peeking back inside the shower, she could see that Andy was still sleeping peacefully with the water running down his face. This SEAL needed something more obnoxious. She turned the warm water off and directed cold water over his body.

She closed the bedroom door on her way out, picked up her bag in the great room and went to the guest room on the right side of the house, where she had stayed once before. She took a quick shower and put on fresh underwear, bra, blue jeans, shirt, and tennis shoes. She brushed her hair and teeth and applied a small amount of lipstick. As she completed her makeup, she heard moans coming from Andy's side of the house. A touch of her special perfume to her sternum and she was ready. She wished her breasts were larger.

22

A ndy was acclimated to cold water--at least, he used to be. But much of acclimation is anticipation, knowing where you are and what to expect. Without opening his eyes, he felt for his diving suit. Working his way down he found that he had nothing on at all. He was shivering. He climbed up the soap dish and cut off the cold water. Holding onto the walls of the shower, he looked around.

This was his shower, in his house, in Farmville. He thought he had nothing left to despair about. This was the ultimate mistake in his hometown. He had brought some strange woman home last night. He couldn't remember a face. He couldn't remember where he found her. Blackouts were scary. The girl was probably out there waiting for a ride home. She would look like a biker's wet dream, with body piercing and tattoos. He hoped he remembered the condom.

He turned the water back on and adjusted the temperature in order to remove all of this soap he couldn't remember putting on. The fresh towel on the toilet was a nice surprise. At least she was thoughtful. He brushed his teeth and gargled some Listerine. On the bed were clean clothes. Nobody but his mother ever laid out any clothes for him. The bedroom smelled like a pine thicket in spring, and it was sparkling clean. The bed was made. He dressed hurriedly and brushed his hair. A woman this neat might not be half bad.

He stood behind the door of the bedroom to collect his bearings.

"Good morning," he said with confidence as he opened the door.

She had turned his La-Z-Boy chair around to face his door. Their eyes met. They leapt at each other like sumo wrestlers. They kissed and hugged until embarrassment set in.

She stepped back from him.

"Andy, you've been drinking," she said. "I've never seen you in such a condition."

"You've never seen me believe you were dead before," he answered. He lowered himself to the couch.

She smiled. "You got drunk for me?"

"You didn't put me in that shower, did you?"

"I was just doing my job."

"It wasn't your job. I'm so sorry for you to find me this way. It will never happen again."

"It's okay, Andy. I've taken care of sloppy men before."

"Would you please sit down? I need to ask you something very personal."

"Stop worrying. I found you unconscious. You never touched me. You never do."

"Thank you. Please forgive me. I'm ashamed that you had to clean up after me."

She laughed. "I'm not just another Arab girl you picked up in the desert, soldier. I love you."

"I need some coffee before I can respond to that," he said.

She walked into the kitchen and poured him a fresh cup. "You probably can't smell it because of all the Pine-Sol. Your house is going to smell this way for a few days. You'll have to keep the windows open."

Andy sat at the table and gulped the coffee. He extended the empty cup for a refill.

"How did you escape?" he asked.

She sat down beside him and told her story.

"A woman called me ten days ago. It was your friend, the girl who spent the weekend here. She told me that Harrison was looking for me, that he would kill me if he found me."

"What else?"

"She said that you had instructed her to call me and that you had been wounded. This made me even more scared. You look okay. I saw your wounds."

"I'm much better. Please tell me everything she said."

"She told me to take all of the cash I had, pack one bag, and run. I was lucky that you'd already given me cash to hold for emergencies. She said to leave my car, travel by bus and not to use my real name. I was supposed to disappear for at least a week, and then try to find you here."

"Hopefully her advice has brought you here undetected," he said.

"She also told me to take the battery out of my cell phone and throw the phone in the river. She said to erase the hard drive on my computer and remove any pictures or other information in my dorm room that could be used to identify me or track me."

"What did you tell your roommate?"

"The same thing that I told my counselor at ODU, that my father was sick and I had to go back to Saudi Arabia."

"I'm so proud of you," he said. "You must have been terrified."

Sahar's face brightened, but not for long. "She saved my life, didn't she?"

"Yes, and you saved mine."

"All I did was clean up."

"Seeing you alive makes me very happy. You don't know."

"Thank you for saying that, but I don't want to be indebted to her."

"You may not need to feel indebted very long," he said, "once they find out she's alive."

"Then we all have something in common."

"This is the second time that she's done something courageous to help me," Andy said.

"I saw where she cut you free after they tortured you in the bed."

"Well, it was a little more complicated than..."

"You don't need to give me details. I know all about torture. Tell me what you can do to help this woman."

It was one of the things he admired most in her. She drew her own conclusions.

Andy sipped on his second cup of coffee and frowned. "For a short period of time, I have some leverage with our president. I'll call him. It's worth a try."

"In Saudi Arabia a man can have four wives. I think I could share a man with a woman who saved my life."

"But you deserve someone for yourself, someone your own age. I know that you'll find the right man soon."

"But I love you. Men have gotten drunk to make love to me, but no man ever drank himself unconscious and lay down naked in his own vomit because he loved me. That means a lot."

Andy didn't know if this was Saudi logic or female logic, but he had no comeback.

"Can I stay with you?"

"It's just too dangerous, Sahar," he said. "Harrison will look for you here. He knows by now that you are the same girl from Prince Khalid's palace, someone who knows what weapons he has been trying to buy. And I would be constantly tempted by your wit and charm and other things."

"But who else could protect me?"

"I have a friend who can hide you. He lives in Washington, D.C. most of the time. His name is Salmon Akbar. He's the Saudi Ambassador to the United States."

"I've heard of him."

"I'll drive you as soon as I get a new vehicle. You can hide in the embassy as long as needed, and I can communicate with you. Akbar will provide new papers for you so you can go to school in Washington. This man will take your protection seriously."

"Will you forget me?"

"I'll come to visit you. I owe you so much. You've given me a reason to stay alive."

"So what will you do with your new life?"

"When I met you in the desert I was a warrior. I've never told you what my job was."

"You fought terrorists."

"My job was to cut off the heads of snakes."

"Were you good at it?"

"Too good."

"Have you much experience at cutting off the heads of weasels?"

"If it has a pulse, I've killed it."

"Then let me sharpen your sword."

Andy smiled. Sahar was a practical woman.

"This man knows that we have compared information about his arms business," he said. "He can't afford to forget about us."

"Do you have a plan?"

"Not yet. We must be cunning and patient. I need to prepare the Farm."

"How do you know he'll come here?"

"When the Farm is ready, we'll make him think you're here. He won't be able to resist such an opportunity."

"Thank you for looking out for me."

"Since I don't know how long it will be before I can get back to Washington, you shouldn't pass up any good looking guys, waiting on me."

She reached for him and held him close. He held her head against his chest. The wetness seeped through his shirt, but she didn't make a sound. She had practice.

"One more thing," he said. "Did you find any women's clothing when you cleaned up?"

She backed away and wiped her eyes with her forearm. "I can overlook one lost weekend, Andy, but I better not catch you in panties and a bra." She shook her head from side to side and walked back to the guest room.

Andy dug the president's card out of his wallet.

President Marshall picked up the phone immediately.

"Mr. President, there're some unusual things here at my farm that I was afraid to ask anyone else about."

"What kind of things?"

"Well, for one thing, my truck's missing," he said. "It's a silver-colored Chevy S-10 with an extended cab. Also, all of Lindsey Baker's clothes are missing. The two agents I left in a well were gone when I got back."

"We can certainly get you a new truck," the president said. "We did recover the bodies of four agents."

"What about the two in the well?"

"Somebody sent a telegram to the CIA about the two agents in the well," he said. "They had some broken bones, but they both lived."

"Did you find out who sent the telegram?"

"We thought it was you."

"Not me. Sir, it's clear that Ms. Baker is still alive. She took my truck with her personal gear. She sent the telegram."

"Even if that were true, why should you care? Didn't she cause your injuries?"

"She was working for you, Mr. President. She took her job serious-ly, like I did when I was a SEAL. I killed people because you ordered it or Harrison ordered it. I was more efficient than she was. I don't hold it against her."

"You're a better man than most," the president said.

"You asked what you could do for me. Ms. Baker is likely to come back to you or Harrison. She has no family. Don't kill this person who was loyal to you just to cover up your mistakes. I won't ask you for anything else."

"If we should hear from Ms. Baker, we won't harm her, Dr. Carlson," he said. "Go get yourself a new truck and send me the bill."

"Thank you, sir."

But the president had already hung up.

It wasn't true that he didn't hold anything against her. But a broken heart doesn't get mended by killing the heart-breaker.

The president picked up his private line and dialed a familiar number.

"Harrison here."

"I just spoke with Carlson. You remember. That emergency physician-ex-SEAL---the one you told me was a pathetic drunk. We need to keep him around a little while longer. The Saudis have made it clear that they're watching what we do to him. Figure out a way we can discredit him."

"Yes, sir."

"Do you recall that nuclear analyst who fouled up her assignment, Lindsey Baker?"

"Her real name was Lindsey McKee."

"Carlson says she's alive."

"The pilot said a 500-pounder landed on her head."

"If she's alive, I want her to stay that way for now," he said. "For some reason Carlson wants her alive. Gasoline went up fifty cents a gallon last week because of him. He can hurt us. Should Miss McKee contact you, tell her it wasn't her fault. And send me her file again. I don't understand why Carlson cares about some woman who stabbed him. A Marine, sure. A SEAL, not likely."

Harrison replied, "I'll let you know if the lady comes back from the dead. Carlson's attraction to Dr. McKee could explain why she suddenly became so inept."

"If she's alive, we're better off having her where we can watch her."

23

Andy agreed to work three consecutive ED night shifts weekly at Southside Community Hospital, the local hospital in Farmville. Such a schedule left open the possibility of binge drinking. Going back to DePaul was not an option. How could he possibly explain what happened to Lindsey?

He suspected that the CIA had known about his alcohol problem. They thought that his knowledge of nuclear weapons on Saudi soil and his alcoholism would make it easy for him to connect the wrong dots. Nobody counted on Sahar. Nobody counted on the attraction between himself and Lindsey. If he was lucky, nobody would count on the Farm, either. He would begin to update the natural defenses of the Farm right away.

A storm was coming, no doubt, but it was also time to move on with his personal life. Lindsey wasn't the only attractive petite woman in the universe. Farmville was a much smaller pool than Hampton Roads, but it wasn't impossible. Whatever happened to that girl he never had the courage to ask out in high school? He would start there.

In the ED at SCH Andy was surprised at how many of the local people knew his family. He had never felt this closeness at DePaul. Even people who were short of breath were anxious to tell him that they were classmates of his dad at Hampton-Sydney College, or helped his granddad pick corn, or taught one of his brothers in school.

During Andy's second night back in the pit, a thirtyish, light-skinned black man ran through the ambulance entrance with what appeared to be the lifeless body of a teenage girl.

Jasmine was known to be allergic to bee stings. She struck a bee hive in a low lying branch with her forehead while riding her bicycle, resulting in multiple stings to her face. Within a few minutes she began to itch all over. Her face, lips, and tongue began to swell. She became dizzy and nauseated. Her breathing became irregular and her airway began to close, resulting in an inspiratory noise called stridor.

The child's dad was working in the family garden in the late evening when the accident occurred. He ran to her, but she was unconscious within a few minutes. Having lived in mid-Cumberland County all of his life, her dad knew that it would take at least thirty minutes for the local rescue squad to round up a crew of volunteers to come to his house. He loaded his daughter into the back seat of the family car and raced to the hospital.

Andy was no stranger to severe allergic reactions, but this girl appeared to be dead upon arrival. He grabbed her limp body from her dad and placed her on her back in the nearest stretcher in the trauma bay. Andy had only been introduced to Alina, the Hispanic charge nurse, a few minutes before, and he had never worked with any of the other nurses on duty that evening.

One nurse applied EKG monitor pads to the girl's chest, an automatic blood pressure cuff to her left upper arm, and a pulse oximeter to a finger. Another nurse worked to find an IV site. The carotid pulse was barely palpable at thirty beats per minute. Andy grabbed a resuscitation bag and attempted to ventilate the patient with the mask and one hundred percent oxygen. But her airway was almost closed. Each squeeze of the bag brought little rise in the chest.

"Give the patient epinephrine 1:1000 0.3 milliliters subcutaneously right now and bring me a cricothyroidotomy tray and a central line kit," Andy said.

Andy knew that her mouth, lips, and tongue were so swollen that he would not be able to see the opening to her airway with a laryngoscope. To ventilate her, he would have to create a new surgical airway in her neck. This would be no easy task, since the patient's neck was already swollen from generalized hives, obscuring physical landmarks.

"I need size eight and a half surgical gloves, please," he said.

The nurse ripped open the cricothyroidotomy kit and Andy put on his gloves. He picked up the scalpel from the tray. With the index finger of his left hand he found the cricothyroid membrane, just below the Adam's apple, a small landmark in a young girl. With his right hand, he plunged the scalpel at ninety degrees to the skin, through the cricothyroid membrane, and into the trachea below the level of the swollen vocal cords. He turned the scalpel upside down and used the flat handle to dilate the opening.

"Hand me a six and a half millimeter tracheostomy tube from the crike tray," he said.

Andy forced the tube through the surgical opening and inflated the balloon cuff with air, closing the space between the tube and the inside of the tracheal wall. The respiratory therapist arrived. Andy instructed him to hyperventilate the patient with one hundred percent oxygen and to hold the tube in place manually.

The next problem was a lack of venous access to give critical medications and large amounts of fluids. The patient's body was flooded with histamine from circulating mast cells in the blood. Histamine causes blood vessels to dilate and also pokes holes in them. The result was falling blood pressure and massive swelling throughout her body. Her veins were no longer palpable or visible.

The patient's dilated veins prevented blood from getting back to her heart. Inadequate filling pressure to the heart resulted in falling cardiac output. This clinical syndrome, called anaphylactic shock, is incompatible with life unless something is done to constrict the blood vessels, stimulate the heart, and fill up the extra space in the veins with saline.

Upon arrival, the patient's blood pressure was only forty systolic. A nurse found a small vein in the hand and inserted a twenty gauge angiocath. This would not be large enough to give the massive amounts of saline required to raise the blood pressure, but it could be used to give medications.

Alina opened the central line kit for Andy and placed it on a metal stand next to him. Andy stuck the girl in the right side of her neck with an eighteen gauge hollow needle attached to a ten milliliter syringe. Dark blood appeared in the syringe. He lowered the angle of the syringe and directed the tip of the needle farther into the internal jugular vein while continuously aspirating blood. Holding the hub of the needle with his left hand, Andy unscrewed the syringe and inserted a guide wire inside the hollow needle five inches into the vein. Then he removed the needle, leaving the wire in place. Using the wire as a guide, he enlarged the track through the skin with a stiff pointed dilator advanced over the wire.

To augment volume expansion, Andy chose a "trauma line." By progressively enlarging the diameter of the track through the skin with dilators advanced over the wire into the vein, he was able to accommodate the four inch long hollow sheath of the trauma catheter. This catheter had an internal diameter of a pencil, allowing an entire liter of saline to be infused in two minutes with a pressure bag.

"Run saline wide open on a pressure bag and bring me a syringe of cardiac epinephrine from the cardiac arrest cart," he said. "Order an epinephrine drip from the pharmacy. Give this patient Solumedrol 125 milligrams intravenously."

The pulse remained at thirty beats per minute despite the subcutaneous epinephrine. The blood pressure had not budged above forty millimeters of mercury. The patient's pulse oximeter had jumped from sixty to eighty-eight percent due to the hyperventilation of the patient with one hundred percent oxygen using the tracheostomy tube and ventilation bag.

Seated on the side of the patient's bed, Andy pushed one milliliter increments of cardiac epinephrine from the syringe into the central line every thirty seconds.

Although not recommended in textbooks, Andy felt that the patient was unlikely to survive without these larger quantities of epinephrine delivered close to her heart. Permanent brain injury would result from prolonged low blood pressure.

Andy's eyes were fixed on the monitor as he injected one milliliter after another of epinephrine. The pulse climbed to sixty after six milliliters, and the BP to ninety. The nurse was already hanging the third bag of saline.

"Keep pouring in the saline," he said. "Start an epinephrine infusion at 100 milliliters per hour and titrate it to keep the systolic pressure above 100. Please put soft restraints on the patient's hands so that she will not pull her airway or central line out when she starts to wake up."

Andy remained seated on the side of the girl's bed, periodically adding another milliliter of cardiac epinephrine, until the epinephrine infusion was able to do the job on its own. The patient's vital signs improved to a heart rate of 110, blood pressure 122/68, and pulse ox 100%.

He sutured in the tracheostomy tube and central line.

Removing his gloves, he said to no one in particular, "I think she's going to be all right."

He stepped backwards and bumped into someone.

"Excuse me," he said, "I didn't see you there."

At that moment, he realized that the girl's father had been standing behind him during the resuscitation. He was glad that he did not know this until now.

He extended his hand. "I'm Dr. Carlson. I think that your daughter is going to be okay, but she will need to be in our intensive care unit for a few days. She could wake up quickly or it could take a few hours."

The gentleman took Andy's hand, but he was looking over Andy's shoulder. His daughter was struggling with the restraints, reaching out for him. He released Andy's hand and rushed to hold her.

Andy sat down and began charting.

Fifteen minutes later, Alina tapped him on the shoulder. "Dr.

Carlson, the patient's father and mother would like to talk to you. They're in the private conference room."

He took the girl's ED chart and entered the room. The parents stood up.

"My name is Ben Carlson," the father said, "and this is my wife Precious." Andy looked down at the demographic information and confirmed what he had heard. Ben was a muscular black male with a receding hairline. He appeared to be thirty-five years old. There was something familiar about his face. The scar on his left cheek was likely a childhood injury that had not been repaired. His wife was a tiny woman. She clung to her husband and fumbled with a crumpled handkerchief.

"Are you from this area?" Andy asked.

"My family has never lived anywhere else," the black man said.

"Please sit down," Andy said.

"I thought we had lost Jasmine," Precious said.

"I saw what you did in there," Ben said, "and there's no way that I can repay you. We couldn't afford to pay for medical insurance. I only work part-time here in the hospital, in central supply."

"Jasmine is going to be fine," Andy said. "I don't want you to worry any more about her." He smiled and sat down next to Ben. "Did you ever have a dog named Blue?"

"He died when I was sixteen. How did you know about Blue?"

"Do you remember coon hunting on the Carlson farm with a kid named Andy? You would have been six years old. You already had that scar on your cheek."

They stood up and embraced.

"Of course I remember," Ben said, stepping backward and looking carefully at the doctor. "You were my best friend until I was eight."

"You had a single shot .22 with your daddy's initials on the stock," Andy said.

"And you had a bow and arrow. I never saw anybody shoot one as good as you."

"Where did you go?" Andy asked.

"My dad worked for your dad. In fact, my family worked for your family for a couple of hundred years."

"I didn't understand why we had the same last name until I was a teenager. Nobody in my family talked much about slavery."

Ben looked at his shoes. "My dad got a job at Phillip Morris in Richmond when I was eight. He liked your dad, and he thought of your farm as home. But my mom had a lot of medical problems, and Phillip Morris had good medical insurance. I grew up in Richmond."

Precious said, "I grew up in Farmville. We had to move in with my parents when Ben lost his construction job. I know your old plantation house well."

"When were you there?"

"My mother helped your dad take care of your mom when she had breast cancer, and your older brothers were in Uganda. My mother stayed with her most of the last year of her life."

"We called you Pressie," he said. "Your mother is Rachael Carter."

Precious nodded.

"Then I'm indebted to your entire family many times over," Andy said. "You'll not have to worry about paying for this emergency room bill or for this hospitalization."

"You don't have to do that, Andy," Ben said.

Precious tugged on her husband's sleeve.

"In this case, I wouldn't be the one paying," Andy said. "My great-great grandfather, John Andrew Carlson, left me some money. He owes your family some back wages. From now on, if anyone in your family has a medical problem, you should call me."

Before they could reply, Andy extended his hand again to Ben. "I'm looking for an experienced construction man for my farm. This job comes with medical insurance. You can work for me when you're not working in central supply."

"I'll take that job."

"Jasmine will be out of the hospital within a week," Andy said. "Come visit me then."

"What are you building?" Ben asked.

"Something like a bomb shelter."

"You expecting trouble on your farm?"

"Yes, I am."

24

One week later Andy was sitting on the front steps of his farm-house when Ben Carlson drove up in a rusty Ford pickup.

"How's Jasmine?"

"Great. Her neck is healing fine. She's home."

Ben sat down on the steps next to Andy. "Are we starting on your bomb shelter today?"

"It's a work in progress. My dad helped me until he was killed."

"I'm sorry to hear that."

"He was helping my two older brothers with their mission work in Uganda at the time."

"Since we're building something in the ground," Ben said, "I need to come clean about the caves here."

Andy stroked his chin. "What do you know?"

"We both know that my family members were slaves on this farm long before we worked for money. Nobody in my family ever had anything bad to say about your ancestors. If Mr. Carlson had been a scoundrel, we wouldn't have taken his name. And we sure wouldn't have worked for his family for another hundred years after the Civil War if he hadn't been good to us. I'm not saying we liked being slaves. I'm just saying that we respected your secrets because we thought we were part of your family."

"I appreciate that," Andy said.

"Can you tell me a little about *my* ancestors?" Ben asked.

Andy smiled. "I'll tell you what I know. Your ancestors, a man and a woman, were purchased by Richard Carlson in 1654. Richard was an indentured servant himself when he arrived in Jamestown in 1635. He mentioned these two married slaves in his will, and left the couple to his son, who was also named Richard. Slaves were considered property."

"What's an indentured servant?"

"An indentured servant was like a slave whose contract only lasted a few years. In Richard Carlson's case, he agreed to work for three years in exchange for the money to buy passage from England."

"How do you know that these two slaves were my ancestors?"

"My family bought and sold very few slaves, although they ended up with 86 in 1860. Each slave family and their children were mentioned in the will of the patriarch, who usually divided up the slaves and his plantation among his surviving children and spouse."

"So all of those 86 slaves in 1860 were my relatives?"

"Slaves on the plantation came from several sources. They could be bought, but I couldn't find but a few ever bought in my records."

"How else did you get slaves?"

"Occasionally the patriarch would pay a neighboring plantation owner with a strong, muscular slave for temporary breeding rights. This male would be bred with young female slaves on our plantation. It sounds like raising horses, but it's the truth."

Ben didn't say anything.

"Most of the slaves on this plantation were children of other slaves," Andy said.

Ben stood up and walked around in a tight circle in front of Andy's house before speaking. "Precious has a theory," he said. "When you came to Jasmine's room every day in the hospital, she noticed something about you."

"That I'm not very good looking?"

"How do you explain the fact that you and I have the same chins and ears?" Ben asked.

Andy looked carefully at Ben. "I see what you mean. There is a resemblance."

There was an uncomfortable silence.

"I guess it's possible that you and I share a common male ancestor," Andy said.

"Have you never considered that your ancestors had children by slave women?" Ben asked.

"Yes, I have. But it's not something we ever discussed over the dinner table."

"How do you think they justified such a thing?"

Andy took a deep breath. "You're asking difficult questions, but fair ones. I wasn't there, you understand, but I think I know the answer because I know my family."

"I've waited all my life to hear this," Ben said.

"In my opinion, much of the injustice of slavery in the colonies should be laid at the feet of the churches that settled in America. I'm sure this sounds like blaming somebody else for Carlson sins, but hear me out."

Ben nodded.

"My family moved from Jamestown, to New Kent, and then to Hanover County before arriving in Cumberland in 1743. They left Hanover because they didn't want to be in the Church of England any longer. They were called dissenters. Ultimately, my family helped to start the Presbyterian Church in Virginia. There are few people today who believe every word of the Bible literally, but my ancestors did."

"The Bible was their excuse?"

"Most of God's favorite people in the Old Testament were slave owners and had children by slaves. Abraham and Jacob, for example. The Israelites had rules for owning slaves, which included the right to buy slaves from each other and to confiscate slaves from enemies. The Bible clearly gave the slave owner the right to force unmarried and unengaged female slaves to have his children. These children became his property when they were born."

"You're saying the church in colonial America adopted their slave culture from the Bible?" Ben asked.

"There's a church three miles from here that owned lots of slaves. They rented them out to the members of their congregation. I grew up in that church. The same people who demanded religious freedom for themselves could see nothing wrong with owning other people. If God prescribed it, and their own church owned slaves, it must be okay."

"I heard that most of the signers of the Declaration of Independence were slave owners," Ben said.

"That's probably true," Andy said. "What is clearly wrong in our eyes today was only recognized as evil by a few of the founders of our country. I know that my own family still carries a deep sense of guilt about their past ownership of slaves."

"You think your brothers over there in Uganda are working off their guilt?" Ben asked.

"I never had a conversation like this with my brothers, but it does seem to be quite a coincidence that they dedicated their lives to helping people with black skin."

"What about you?"

"Personally, I'm not the missionary type," Andy said. "Mission work has already taken too much from me. I prefer to help people as a doctor. I haven't made my peace with God yet. I've seen religious people kill other religious people all over the world. It hasn't been inspiring."

"I know what you mean."

"I'd like to know if you're a real relative of mine, Ben. The closest thing to a brother I had as an adult was my SEAL partner, Josiah Chambers, and he's dead. Would you be willing to take a blood test?"

"You could tell with a blood test if we were related?"

"Sure. It's a DNA study. Do you remember how all those people proved that Thomas Jefferson was their ancestor through Sally Lemming, his black housemaid?"

"I heard of that."

"I'll draw our blood and we can send it off for a definitive answer."

"Are you worried about the results, Andy?"

"I can't change what happened before I was born, but I can respond to reality. If you're my kin, I want to know it."

Andy stood up and Ben followed him toward the barn.

25

A t the door to the barn, Andy asked, "Did anybody tell you what was in the caves?"

"Granddaddy said that Mr. Carlson was always thinking about the next invasion of his farm, or the next war, or the next depression. He stored guns and ammunition."

"Sounds like a Carlson."

"Some of Mr. Carlson's guns are under your ice house, near the mansion," Ben said. "My granddaddy helped unload them."

"That's worth checking out right away." Andy said. "Let's pick up some hand tools and lights in here. We're going to need my extension ladder."

They threw the tools in the back of the Kubota RTV and turned toward the ice house.

"Why you think you need a bomb shelter?" Ben asked as they pulled up in front of the ice house, within sight of the plantation house.

Andy put his foot up on the dashboard. "Carlsons have always been paranoid about the government. My father and I started the bomb shelter before I even met the woman who got me into this mess."

"Which woman was that?"

"This was a woman who worked for the CIA. I was in love with her."

Ben nodded. "You've got an interesting life. What did the woman do?"

"She stabbed me when I found out she was planning a terrorist attack."

"Does she fly planes?"

"Not that I'm aware of."

"Then she must be one hell of a woman for you to need a bomb shelter for protection."

"The cave system here is more than a bomb shelter," Andy said, "and this girl is not the real enemy. When I exposed her scheme, I bumped into the CIA and the president of the United States. Our government has more than bombs at its disposal. But bombs don't leave much evidence, and they can always be blamed on an accident, especially out here in the country."

"I never liked that smiling fool," Ben said. "You think he would send his friends here to kill you?"

"Eventually, he will. I feel it in my gut. Right now, I have a reason for him to fear me. When his fear subsides, or he finds a way to make me look bad, he'll come after me. Politicians don't sleep well when somebody knows their secrets."

"So whatever happened to this girl?"

"She's alive. I still think about her. Crazy, isn't it? She let me get away, and she helped a friend of mine get away. I can't help feeling that she was used by the government. I bought into some of the same lies she believed."

They got out of the Kubota and looked at the sagging cabin, with its rusty tin roof and no windows. They pried open the door and looked inside. In the center of the room overhead was an ice winch, a round log with a crank. A large wooden bucket hung by a rope wound around the log. There was a closed hatch in the center of the floor below the bucket. The condition of the floor did not invite pedestrians. Individual stones were stacked up underneath the walls of the building.

"I've got an idea," Andy said. "I'm going to borrow my neighbor's bulldozer and shove this building aside. That will save us lots of time. Let me take you down to the new garage I'm building. You can look it over while I get the dozer. A mechanic's pit in the garage is already connected to the cave system. You and I are going to finish building the garage overhead."

Ben stood by while Andy shoved the remains of the wooden ice house aside with the dozer. He skillfully positioned the blade to make as much debris as possible fall away from the center of the floor. After he hooked the last wall and pulled it away, the remaining floor collapsed into a round hole ten feet in diameter. The ice pit was lined with handmade bricks.

Ben shined a flashlight into the dark depth of the pit. "It must be fifteen feet just to the part of the floor that fell in."

Andy threw a sledge hammer, two shovels, and two crowbars into the pit. They lowered the extension ladder and climbed in with a Coleman lantern. After prying the rotted boards away from the remains of the floor joists, they stacked the planks vertically on the sides of the pit. After an hour they were down to the floor joists, which splintered with the sledge hammer.

"We're now standing in packed sawdust and shavings," Andy said. "The ice was cut from shallow ponds and streams. Each layer of ice alternated with a layer of sawdust. The final layer of sawdust was about a foot thick. The insulation was so good that my family made ice cream in August."

"That ice cream was a reward for slaves," Ben said. "My granddaddy told me."

They dug through the sawdust in the center of the pit, throwing the shovelfuls toward the walls. Sure enough, after a foot the shovels hit something hard.

"Sounds like wood," Ben said. He squatted and dug with his hands.

"There's some kind of tarp covering the wood."

After clearing away a five by five foot area, Andy pulled out his pocket knife and ripped a hole in the tarp.

"Looks like a wooden crate, in good shape," Ben said, extending the rip with his hand.

Dark lettering was stamped across the top of the crate. "Browning M2HB and tripod."

Andy asked, "You ever serve in the military, Ben?"

"Desert Storm. Army sergeant. Infantry. I know this gun. This version weighs 128 pounds with the tripod. I carried it in the desert under fire."

"A .50-caliber machine gun is an awesome weapon, but it's tough to carry enough ammo unless it's mounted on something mobile," Andy said.

"Where did you learn about heavy machine guns?"

"Navy SEAL."

Ben said, "I wondered where you got those muscles."

"Let's see what else my granddaddy left for me," Andy said.

They hauled wooden and metal boxes out of the hole with ropes for the next two hours. There were three ".50-cal" heavy barrel machine guns with tripods, each packed in grease in their original crates, and forty-eight metal boxes of ammo belts marked "API."

"Armor-piercing incendiary shells can make a Roman candle out of anything with a gas tank or ammunition in it," Ben said.

"I'd like to take all this back to my shop," Andy said. "Let's take the three guns first. Normally I prefer quieter weapons, but I'll make an exception for something this sweet."

Ben said, "Since we know a lot about these guns, we can probably pick out the best defensive locations for them on the Farm."

Andy nodded.

On their way back to the shop with the guns, Andy stopped at the corner of the alfalfa field, next to the 1860 smooth bore Civil War cannon. "What do you think?"

Ben got out and looked around. "This is prime high ground. That's why the Confederate cavalry put that cannon there. From inside the tree line you could cover the field and anything that comes up the road from the covered bridge."

"This field is the only place on this side of Dry Creek open enough to land a helicopter, and that road is the only way to drive in here."

"What about that big hill on the other side of your bridge?"

"You mean Little Round Top. I understand why you'd think of it as a defensive position. From there a man could cover anything on the road, from the gate to the covered bridge."

"So after we finish the garage," Ben said, "we're going to dig a couple of holes and pour some concrete bunkers for these guns. By the time we're finished, a man could trip over one of your bunkers and not recognize it."

They were standing next to the 1860 smooth bore when Andy heard a noise from out of his past, like the sound of a large model airplane.

26

Andy ducked into a low crouch, looking overhead, and pulled Ben after him.

"Ben, drive the Kubota and follow me into the pine trees, toward that stable--and hurry. We've got to hide those guns."

Andy sprinted ahead and muscled the heavy wooden doors open. The wooden building was nearly covered with vines, with only a few patches of weathered oak planks and rusted tin roof visible.

"Turn off the lights of the Kubota and get in here as quickly as possible," Andy yelled.

Ben gunned the Kubota and pulled into the darkness of the stable.

Andy stood just inside the entrance of the stable and looked overhead as a small white airplane with a propeller in the back passed over them at a couple of hundred feet.

"Is that what I think it is?" Ben said from behind him.

"It's a drone. Last one I saw was in Bahrain. It makes an unusual sound taking off because the prop is in the back."

"Why would something like that be in Farmville?"

"It can take legible pictures of your license plate at 25,000 feet, but it has to take off from somewhere. This farm is in the path of the only runway."

"You think it's your friends?" Ben said.

"Let's find out," Andy said, pulling out his cell phone. He stepped out of the door opening while speed-dialing the airport.

The owner/manager of the airport was a high school friend of Andy's named T. Higgins." "T" explained that the Army wanted to test their new pilotless plane in a rural area. They brought the drone, along with a command module, in an eighteen-wheeler. They planned to leave it here for the next few months and rented hanger space for the trailer and the plane.

"Are there any people left on site who came with this equipment?"

"No. That's the neatest thing about it," T explained. When they want to fly it, they call and I open the hanger doors. They actually fly the plane from somewhere else."

"These are bad folks, T, not people to fool around with. The drone is here to spy on me. I can't explain it right now, but I need for you to call me every single time that drone leaves its hanger and every time it lands. Don't mention it to anyone else. I'll be glad to pay you."

"Your blocking made me an all-state running back, and got me a college scholarship. You don't owe me anything."

"Thanks T," Andy said. "You see anything else unusual, let me know."

"Then you need to know about the weird little man," T said. "He paid cash for the hanger."

"Did he have a squeaky voice and a beard?"

"You know this guy?" T asked.

"Never met him in person, but I know him. You keep a sharp eye."

Andy turned to Ben after closing his cell phone. "None of this is good news," Andy said. "That drone has been in service for at least five years. It doesn't need any test flights. Also, its range is 800 miles. It could be launched from almost anywhere. The only reason to launch it from here is that it can recon a nearby target in a moment's notice. It's cheaper than reprogramming a satellite."

"What target are you thinking of?"

"The Farm. All 3400 acres of my property are now being photographed. The CIA is desperate to find an Arab girl I've hidden, and they want to keep an eye on me. We're going to need to stay where we are for a little while. We'll have to be work on certain projects when we know the drone is grounded. And we're going to have to install some early warning signals to identify threats on the ground."

Ben looked around the large room with six stalls. "When was this used as a stable?"

"Very rarely. The stable was built on the foundation of a four-family slave cabin. More than twenty people lived here at a time, including the black overseer and the mule drivers. Yankee cannon balls hit it, and it caught on fire. Nobody got hurt. We knew they were coming."

Andy pointed toward the middle stall on the back wall. "Behind that stall is a cave entrance and tunnel that leads down to Dry Creek, about 150 yards. The families that lived here had all-weather access to water."

Ben said, "I know about the house that was here. My granddaddy told me. I've heard about the cave. The house had two chimneys, one on each end. White folks would kid Mr. Carlson about giving his slaves two chimneys. I'd like to hear more about what it was like for my family living here."

Waiting on the drone to complete its task, Andy told Ben what his father had told him about the slaves on the Farm. Ben's ancestors had been the Carlson's overseers and mule drivers for two hundred years. They were responsible for the health and productivity of all the slaves. They told the plantation owner when another slave was sick. They decided who worked as house servants, who made the clothes of homespun, who washed the clothes, and who needed shoes or a coat. Most plantations had white overseers. Some were cruel.

Each slave family had a cabin. With each cabin went a patch of ground for vegetables and chickens. The slaves ate the same food as the Carlsons. All cooking was done outdoors, by house servants, in a small building behind the plantation house. Cooking inside the mansion was thought to carry too much risk for fire. Also, there was not enough room to prepare meals for up to a hundred people at a time. The food was brought to each slave cabin in a wagon.

The agricultural economy of the South prior to the Civil War was hopelessly dependent upon slave labor. A small farmer could feed his own family without slaves, but he could not produce enough cotton, or tobacco, or peanuts to ship north or to England. There were no mechanical implements to plant, or fertilize, or harvest crops. There were no herbicides to selectively kill all the weeds and allow the crops to grow.

Slaves planted all crops by hand. They fertilized them by shoveling manure from farm animals out of a wagon pulled by a mule. They pulled the weeds by hand or chopped them with hoes. They harvested every crop by hand.

Slaves were thought to be so indispensible that whenever a plantation changed hands, either by inheritance or by sale, the slaves went with the property. Each slave was named in the sales contract. The presence of individual slave names in deeds and wills in the Old South testified to the necessity of slavery in the minds of the plantation owners.

Whether a plantation owner had no moral convictions about slavery or deemed it to be ordained by God, slavery was enormously profitable for large plantation owners. There were expenses for keeping slaves healthy and productive, but these were far outweighed by the profit from such cheap labor. A good businessman would not beat a slave. Every mark on a slave made him less valuable. The rare unproductive or difficult to manage slave would be traded to another plantation, like a troubled wide receiver for the Dallas Cowboys would be traded to another team. The slaves' knowledge that causing disruption on the plantation could result in being sold worked to keep slave families together and productive. There was no need for a whipping post on the Carlson plantation.

Next to a black foreman the most valued slaves on the plantation were the mule team drivers. First, two mules were matched in size, strength, and age. When pulling against a load they had to move straight ahead, never overpowering each other. Once such mules were identified, a slave was matched to them. This man's entire life revolved around the mules. He fed them, groomed them, and learned to get the most out of them. If necessary, he sang them to sleep. These teams pulled the plows, the cultivators, and the wagons. They dragged the logs away after trees were cut down. They yanked the stumps out of the ground. They smoothed out the soil with a wooden sled loaded with rocks.

A good mule driver was often rented out, along with his matched mules, to smaller farmers. A plantation without such teams would be as dysfunctional as a big farm today without tractors. On Sunday, the mule driver hitched the mules to a carriage and drove the owner and his family to church.

The life of a slave was hard, but slaves willing to learn were taught trades-- blacksmithing, cooking, sewing, masonry, dairyman, or animal husbandry. Andy's grandfather recalled how proud his mother had been about the number of slaves she had taught to read and write. Several adult female slaves rotated as babysitters for all of the working mothers. Many white children grew up quite attached to the house servants and black children their age. Most slaves took the surnames of their masters once they were freed, unless they had been mistreated by their masters.

Carlson slaves did not work on Sundays or Saturday afternoons. Many attended church regularly. One of Andy's relatives had a balcony built in their church for the slaves to listen to the sermons. Slaves could visit neighboring plantations in the evenings and on Sundays.

Over 600,000 dead Yankee and Confederate soldiers were required to surgically remove slavery from the South. The ruling class of the ante-bellum South did not go quietly. By 1865, plantation owners were financially exhausted, most having devoted their corn to feed Confederate soldiers and their tobacco and cotton to buy war materials. But Andy's great-great grandfather John Andrew Carlson had somewhere to hide much of his wealth from plunderers while his sons fought the Yankees. When the war was over, he could afford to pay wages to thirty of his slaves. These were the slaves who took up arms and helped him drive the Yankee cavalry off the Farm.

"How far did you say Dry Creek is from Little Round Top?" Ben asked.

"The tunnel comes out underneath a rock at the base of Little Round Top," Andy said. "My grandfather cooked his mash in a copper still at the mouth of the tunnel and used the cold water in the creek to distill the white lightning from the coil."

"Nobody ever mentioned to me that your family drank alcohol."

"We didn't drink much. Granddad did it mostly because the government said he couldn't. And it was a good cash crop during prohibition. He had a nice place to hide the fermenting barrels and the still."

Ben raised his hand. "If the tunnel connects this stable and Little Round Top, we have an invisible connection between the two most important defensive positions on the Farm. You could store unlimited amounts of ammunition in there. You could move like a ghost from a bunker here to a bunker on Little Round Top."

Andy's phone vibrated. "Go ahead, T... I see... Thanks."

"The drone just landed. That confirms that the Farm is the target," Andy said. "They weren't airborne long enough to recon anything else."

Ben said. "I believe my family felt they were part of your farm. When the Yankees showed up, they couldn't believe Mr. Carlson handed out his guns and we started shooting at them."

"We better move the guns and ammo today and explore the tunnel another day," Andy said. "I like your idea about using the tunnel for interior lines. You're expanding on an old concept here."

They walked back into the sunlight.

"Do you think that CIA girl will ever come back?" Ben asked.

"Not in a million years. The Arab girl wants to live here, but it's too dangerous. Let's move while nobody's looking."

Months passed. Andy's phone awakened him. He recognized Sahar's voice.

"Mr. Akbar has made me a secretary at the Embassy."

"I'm proud of you."

"Andy, a man came to the Embassy today asking for Mr. Akbar. He was at Prince Khalid's house when Harrison was there."

"What was his name?"

"Boris. He's a Russian arms dealer. He didn't give me his last name."

"Did he recognize you?"

"No. He never saw me without my abaya."

Andy wondered where this was going. "Did you talk to Akbar?"

"After the man left. The ambassador was very upset. He called the king right away. I hope that I've done the right thing by calling you."

"Exactly why are you telling me this?"

"I heard Akbar mention your name to the king."

"I appreciate your loyalty to me, Sahar. I don't know what this means, but thanks for the heads-up."

"I miss you," she said.

"I miss you, too."

"Thank you for not asking me about boyfriends."

"You're welcome. Keep your ears open and be careful."

"Good night."

27

Lindsey was at her desk in CIA headquarters, Langley, Virginia, eight months after the Battle of Carlson Farm, when her boss, James Harrison, called.

"Dr. McKee, could you step in my office?"

Lindsey took a seat in front of her boss. Harrison loved his role as "The Weasel." His nose already had a rodent point. He grew a beard to cultivate his image, and enjoyed shaping it to a point under his chin. He also enjoyed the concept of half-truth, as if partial truth released him from any obligation to tell the whole truth about anything. It was common knowledge that he was close to the president.

"The State Department just received a communication from King Fahd of Saudi Arabia," he said. "The king says that he has information regarding nuclear weapons already inside the United States. He says that the royal family was approached by someone who wanted to sell these weapons to him."

"Then we need to meet with King Fahd," Lindsey said.

"The problem is that the king has no confidence in the president or the State Department. He says that if we want more information, send Andy Carlson to speak with him."

Lindsey's pulse doubled. Of all the people in the world. But, of course, she knew why the king would only speak to Andy Carlson.

"Lindsey, I know that you and Carlson have a history, and that's why I'm giving you a heads-up here," Harrison said. "We intend to contact Carlson and ask him to go to Saudi Arabia. When I know more, I'll let you know. Could you review your files and see if you can come up with any possible sources of nuclear weapons that would already be inside the U. S.?"

"I will, but I can tell you right now that I know of no such weapons," Lindsey replied.

"So when Carlson gets back from Riyadh, we can interview him and go from there," Harrison said.

He must have picked up on her anxiety. "We'll bring him back here where you can sit in on the interview without his knowledge."

Her mind raced backward. When she had seen the results of her home pregnancy test, Lindsey felt her life begin to turn---as unavoidable, as relentless, and as unstoppable as an aircraft carrier. If she had not already returned to her job at the CIA, she would not have gone back to work at all. Abortion was never an option. Marriage was not an option.

Lindsey had inherited enough from her parents to be more than comfortable. The U.S. government had given her three million dollars because she was the only survivor of two World Trade Center victims. She had no intention of asking Andy's forgiveness. She didn't deserve it.

Lindsey knew that she had overlooked important details of Andy Carlson's character already. But she had been there when Andy held that emaciated child with cystic fibrosis until she died. Elizabeth Jacobs. She had seen him personally perform CPR for over an hour on a hopeless two year old that had drowned in a swimming pool. She couldn't forget the look on his face when she had touched his arm and begged him to stop. Of one thing she was sure. Andy would want to know that he was a father, even if the mother was a wretch like her.

She would notify Andy just as soon as she could find the right card. She had searched the aisles of the local Hallmark store from time to time. The store claimed to have a card for all occasions. But there was no appropriate card for a remorseful stabber who wanted to inform her victim that they had created something during the lovemaking that preceded the stabbing.

She told her colleagues that she had a steady boyfriend, but they weren't ready to get married. As the baby grew, Lindsey's need to tell Andy grew. But she could always think of a good reason not to tell him today. Hearing his name from Harrison left her panicky. What if he wanted to be there when the baby was born? He had so many reasons to be angry at her that she could not begin their next conversation with a birth announcement. If only there was a way to get close enough to him to reestablish some kind of rapport first. She needed to get a feel for his state of mind. After all, it had been almost nine months.

Lindsey got up to leave and then turned back to her boss. "You remember the trip I took to Russia several months ago to monitor the dismantling of the old Soviet nuclear arsenal?"

"I remember."

"I've been collecting photographs and diagrams of all the different types of warheads that we've been dismantling. The number of warheads still out there is gargantuan. Since missing weapons from the old Soviet empire appear to represent our greatest nuclear threat at this time, I propose that you allow me to teach a CIA task force how to diffuse all of the common types."

"Go on. I'm interested."

Lindsey explained her project in layman's terms. "While I was in Russia I got some hands-on experience with a reliable technique for rendering most Cold War era nuclear weapons unusable. It's called the *pit stuffing technique*."

Harrison leaned forward and stroked his beard to a sharper point.

"Every modern nuclear weapon has at its core a pit--a hollow sphere of plutonium or highly-enriched uranium, with a tiny tube through the wall. The design could be compared to a coconut with a small straw in it. Through this straw is introduced tritium, which supercharges the nuclear chain reaction by supplying extra neutrons. This is called boosting.

With the pit-stuffing technique, the tritium source is removed and a wire is threaded into the hole, into the center of the coconut. The wire coils up inside the plutonium core and is broken up as it is stuffed in. The result is that the weapon can't reach nuclear yield because the pit can no longer be compressed enough by the explosives surrounding it to sustain a nuclear chain reaction. The weapon is incapable of initiating a chain reaction even if the explosives outside the plutonium explode simultaneously."

"Has this technique been thoroughly tested?" the Weasel asked.

"It has," she said. "The coconut of plutonium can't be sawed in half and put back together. It's not possible to remove the wire once the pit is stuffed. There's no material that can be used to weld two halves of a plutonium coconut back together. These coconuts are very dangerous to handle and require complex machines to manufacture. I know of no technology for repairing a weapon defused like this."

"How long does it take to do a pit-stuffing?"

"Only a few minutes by someone who knows what they're doing," she said. "The tritium gas can't enter the pit until the time of detonation because the gas would corrode the plutonium. So weapons can't be stored with this boost gas in the pit. The gas stays in a reservoir."

"Removing this reservoir must be part of disarming a warhead."

"Right. To disarm a nuclear weapon, the tritium fill-tube must be accessible in the field," Lindsey continued. "So the first step is to unscrew the tritium source from the coconut and the second step is to stuff the pit with wire."

He said, "What tools would you need?"

"I want to design a kit with all of the right tools already identified, something that has a picture of each warhead type, with simple directions. Right now, there are only a few people in the U.S. capable of defusing a nuclear weapon and they are lab-oriented, not field-oriented. Do you see where I'm going?"

He nodded. "This proposal needs to be on a fast track. If there are nuclear weapons already in the U.S., it could come in handy to have more CIA personnel capable of dismantling them quickly."

"I'm glad you agree," she said.

The Weasel said. "Even those idiots in Congress can understand this kind of thing. Get it on my desk as soon as possible. By the way, where do you plan to get the parts for practice weapons?"

"I propose that we make up mock nuclear weapons that have everything but the radioactive material. Then we design a training program."

"Whatever you need."

Lindsey returned to her office. The sign on her door read, *Dr. Lindsey McKee, Nuclear Threats Analyst.*

She had to lean back in her chair, because her abdomen got in the way when she tried to sit up straight at her desk. She recalled her last conversation with Andy Carlson. He had called to warn her of the GPS tracker that was sutured under the skin in her shoulder.

She had grabbed a steak knife from the kitchen and made a slash incision over the metal. The tracker had been sewn in. There was no time to find the sutures. She had ripped the device out with her thumb and index finger as she ran toward the alfalfa field. After throwing it as far into the field as she could, she had jumped face-down into the ditch on the opposite side of the road from the field.

The blast had gone over her head, rupturing her eardrums. Thanks to Andy's truck, she was able to get away. After her eardrums healed, she decided that only the president had the power to change her status from "Terminated" to "Active."

To her surprise President Marshall had asked her to come to the White House. He even admitted that he listened to the wrong people at the CIA and regretted his approval of the Saudi operation. Lindsey had told him that she had been blinded by vengeance. She wanted to return to the job she had been trained to do---evaluating nuclear threats to the country.

The president had responded, "You certainly have the credentials for such a position. Tell me, why did an emergency nurse decide to get a Ph.D. in nuclear physics, anyway?"

"I was a nurse, but I had majored in physics at Cal Tech. My father and mother were physicists."

"You are too modest, Dr. McKee. You graduated summa cum laude after only three years at Cal Tech."

"I thought I could find some good use for my degree in the nursing profession," she had said. "Radionuclides are an important part of medicine these days, used for all sorts of diagnostic and therapeutic procedures."

"You lost both your parents in the World Trade Center, didn't you?"

"They worked for an international organization that monitored the use of nuclear technology around the globe. Their office was…"

"I'm so sorry," he had said. "And losing your brother must have been devastating."

"He was a real patriot. It was his third tour in Iraq. After he joined the Army, I decided that I wasn't doing enough as a nurse."

"That's when you joined the CIA," he had said.

"I'd been on the job as a nuclear threat analyst at the CIA for just six months when I got the news that my brother had been killed by an IED," she had said. "I knew that the Saudis were funding the resistance in that sector. The field operations people at CIA approached me with an opportunity to get even. They thought that I had all the credentials they needed. I have a lot to regret, sir. I must take responsibility for those people who died on that ship and on that farm. Dr. Carlson didn't deserve what I did to him either."

"I, too, share some of that blame," the president had said. "I've been given the chance to redeem myself before leaving this office, and Carlson was responsible for that. You also deserve a chance to redeem yourself, and I'm going to see that you get it. Your family has given a lot to this country."

He had even smiled.

28

Over eight months of sobriety had passed since Andy's life changed in one spring weekend. He and Ben had completed their construction projects. Andy had made several secret trips to the Saudi Embassy in Washington to see Sahar, who was attending George Washington University and working in the Embassy. Upon his return from one such trip, Andy noted the message light on his telephone burning brightly.

He recognized the number. He had not spoken with the president in six months.

President Marshall said, "I received a diplomatic pouch yesterday from King Fahd of Saudi Arabia. The king says that the royal family was contacted by an ex-KGB agent who has two nuclear weapons for sale. He offered these to the Saudis."

"This should have nothing to do with me, Mr. President."

"I understand your reservations, but you haven't heard me out. These weapons are supposedly already in this country, and have been here for at least thirty years, according to the ex-KGB agent."

"How could that be?"

"The king says that he will not give any more information to the United States unless you come to Riyadh and talk with him. He still doesn't trust me."

"Imagine that."

"I don't have any choice but to ask for your help. Can you be at the Farmville Municipal Airport in about one hour?"

Andy groaned. "I can try."

At the White House, President Marshall stressed his most urgent concerns to Andy—regaining the trust of the Saudis and learning as much as he could about any nuclear weapons hidden in the United States. Twenty-three hours of flight time and eight time zones later, Andy landed at the airport in Riyadh.

It was nice to arrive in Saudi Arabia's capital city in daylight, without orders to kill someone. The city was a modern oasis, populated by seven million people, mostly Sunni Muslims. The many shapes and colors of the apices of the skyscrapers reminded him of Atlanta. All of these modern buildings enjoyed air-conditioning, which was nice since the daytime temperatures could reach 120 degrees. Sandstorms were common even in the city. Scattered among the latest modern architectural triumphs were McDonald's, KFC, Pizza Hut, Burger King, Starbuck's, and Subway restaurants. The Saudis loved fountains. Almost all of the water in Saudi Arabia comes from its massive desalinization plants, the most sophisticated in the world. The airport rivaled Hartsfield in Atlanta.

He was greeted by Salmon Abdullah Akbar, whom he recognized from the mole on his left cheek. Akbar was cordial and seemed to understand Andy's discomfort in the splendor of the king's palace. He directed Andy how to sit and where to sit. He advised him to eat a little of everything brought before him.

King Fahd spoke perfect English. He was a large middle-aged man with a short dark beard. He walked with confidence. His robe was white and adorned with a red and blue rolled bandana and sash. A long gold necklace held a medallion with precious stones.

The king held in his hands a record of every mission Andy had completed in Saudi Arabia as a SEAL. He was fully aware of Andy's warning to the Saudis of Harrison's warheads at Prince Khalid's palace. He had an accurate account of Andy's role in preventing the CIA from using a faked terrorist incident to steal Saudi oil.

"Why do you help us, Dr. Carlson?" he asked.

Andy shrugged. "I don't always know what's right or wrong, but I try to do what I feel is right. Integrity shouldn't have borders. While I feel that killing terrorists and terrorist supporters results in the great-est good, I don't feel any obligation to help my country export its own terrorism. It's one thing to be invited into a country to further the cause of world peace by eliminating supporters of terrorism. It's an-other to use the soil of an ally to traffic in weapons of mass destruction."

"We are glad to know even one American with your integrity and other skills."

Over dinner the king gave the details of an unusual communication he had recently received. "An ex-KGB agent approached a member of the royal family with two nuclear weapons to sell, weapons that he claimed to have hidden inside the United States in the early 1980s. He told us that at that time, border security between Canada and Mexico was very lax and that it was easy to move these warheads, which he claimed were ten to twenty kilotons."

Andy asked, "What was the purpose of transporting nuclear weap-ons this way?"

"The motive of the Soviet Union was to have these weapons in place, near important targets, when they were ready to be used," the king said. "The Soviets did not have the sophisticated multiple in-dependent warhead ICBMs that the United States did at that time, although they pretended to have such technology. They were also spooked by Reagan's Star Wars plan to shoot down all of their missiles before they could reach America. The Soviet Union wanted to be able to have nuclear weapons already in America to bolster their missiles and submarines."

"Why do you think this is coming up now?" Andy asked.

"This KGB agent is now retired," the king said. "He intends to finish out his life in another country using the money from the sale of these nuclear weapons. He blamed all of the problems in the former Soviet Union on the Americans. It was because of America that the Soviet Union had been dissolved and dismembered. It was the Americans' fault that he had lost his job in the KGB and his apartment."

Andy tried to eat a little bit of everything brought to him, but the entrée reminded him of the water on the camels he had left in the Saudi desert. Smell did not seem to be a high priority for traditional Saudi food. He longed for a sandwich from the Subway he had seen on final approach. Not wishing to violate any protocol, he smiled and swallowed. He had a great deal of practice emptying his stomach.

"Your Highness," Andy said, "President Marshall realizes that you have good reasons not to trust him, but he gives you his word, through me, that the United States will never again be involved in a scheme to steal oil."

"And you believe him?" the king asked.

Andy's mouth was beginning to taste sweet. He wiped his forehead and willed himself not to vomit in front of the king.

"I was hoping that you would not ask me that question," Andy said, repeatedly swallowing. "I want to believe in our president, but I don't. The president didn't send me here because he likes me or even trusts me. He sent me because you insisted. He will try to kill me as soon as it is expedient. You have helped me stay alive by controlling the price of your oil."

"As you know, oil is a global market," the king said. "Eventually he can arrange to buy the same amount somewhere else. I believe that your reservations are well-founded. The ex-KGB agent who approached us bragged that your president was a client of his. He claimed that he sold more than one weapon to the CIA."

"For what purpose?"

"One of his weapons was on the container ship that was approaching Hampton Roads when it was sunk by the president."

"Then President Marshall lied to me," Andy said. "He told me that the weapon on the ship came from the old Soviet stockpile that the United States was dismantling."

"And he told others that Al Qaeda put the nuclear device on the ship and that we paid for it," the king said. "Clearly, Mr. Marshall is a liar."

"What do you suggest that I do with this information?" Andy asked.

"The ex-KGB agent gave us an e-mail address and told us how to respond in code," he said. "He would meet with a third party, if I approved of that person, in the United States. He wants the money transferred in his presence by computer before the transaction is completed."

"I can relay this message to our president, King Fahd."

"The royal family cannot afford to trust President Marshall, Dr. Carlson. We want you to be the third party. No Saudis can meet with an arms dealer on American soil. You are the only non-Saudi that we feel we can trust. Everything that you have told us has been true. If you could pose as an arms dealer who represents us, then we would feel comfortable that we would not be walking into a trap."

"This sounds dangerous for both of us."

"The royal family doesn't wish for America to be harmed by terrorists," the king said, "but we must protect ourselves. We can't give this information to anyone else. We must have your assurance that you and you alone will contact this man. Do you understand our position?"

"Unfortunately, I don't know much about international arms dealers."

King Fahd said, "You know more than you think. Harrison is such a man. Usually the seller is someone with no causes except himself and money. He doesn't care which country buys from him. He doesn't care who wins or loses. Arms sellers are absolutely untrustworthy businessmen. Never give payment until the weapons that you are buying are in front of your eyes, and you're sure that you know what you're buying. Don't be surprised if the arms dealer tries to take both the money and the weapons when he leaves."

"I believe that it's a worthwhile effort to get these two nuclear weapons out of circulation," Andy said, "but certainly not into the president's hands unless they're permanently disarmed."

"I agree," the king said. "This ex-KGB agent will identify himself as 1917 USSR. You must give me several letters or numbers that he can use to identify you, and an e-mail address. I will see that he gets them. That way he'll feel comfortable about whom he's dealing with. You must contact him within ten days. He will accept nothing less than one hundred million American dollars for both weapons."

"Where does he want to meet me?" Andy asked, feeling the nausea rise to his throat.

"He'll want to meet you at a remote location, somewhere not far from Washington, D.C.," the king said. "He'll want the longitude and latitude. There must be no military bases nearby. He'll probably fly over the site before he agrees to meet you. There must be nothing suspicious, and there must be no soldiers around. He'll have the ability to see how many people are at this location before his arrival and he'll want only you to be there."

"Then how can I protect myself?" Andy asked.

"You are a resourceful man when it comes to protecting yourself," the king said.

Andy handed the king a piece of paper with the letters "R.E.L." and an e-mail address. King Fahd nodded his head and stood up. Andy stood up.

"Dr. Carlson, we Saudis put many things on our plates for decoration. They are not to be eaten. Your willingness to eat them for my benefit is refreshing."

Andy smiled and nodded. After the king left the room, he ran to the bathroom.

Andy reviewed his trip on the return flight home. Several things were now clear. There was only one place that Andy would meet with such a man as this ex-KGB agent. President Caleb Marshall was a snake. Careful planning would be required to deal with these two enemies at the same time.

Upon arrival in Washington, Andy reported some of his conversation with the king to the president.

"You have done some good work," President Marshall said. "You have the confidence of the Saudis, which is more than I have."

"But sir, I have no experience dealing with Russian KGB agents."

"But you are believable, and capable. Let's face it, you're all that we've got."

29

Lindsey McKee was seated behind a one-way mirror when Andy Carlson entered the room next to hers at the Langley CIA headquarters. She had a digital recorder in front of her and could hear everything said in the interview room.

"It's nice to finally meet you in person, Dr. Carlson," said James Harrison, deputy director of the CIA. "The president has filled me in on certain details of your meeting with King Fahd, but I would like for you to retell the encounter for my benefit."

His voice was not much different than on the phone.

Andy recounted his conversation with King Fahd in some detail, omitting the contact information and the king's opinion of the president of the U.S.

"The royal family really does seem to trust you," the Weasel said. "I'm glad we have you in our corner."

"Mr. Harrison," Andy said, "you know that I have a history with the Saudis, with the SEALS, with nuclear weapons conspiracy, with the CIA, and with at least seven of your agents. There's no point in your blowing warm smoke up my butt."

The Weasel lowered his head.

"I would like to point out that several of your agents have tried to kill me."

"I appreciate your candor."

"With all due respect, the CIA has not shown any candor with me."

"We all regret that," the Weasel said. "We were following orders. Despite your reservations about working with us, it appears that you're our only hope of finding these warheads and permanently disarming them."

"Is that your goal, to disarm these warheads permanently?" Andy asked.

"What else would we do with them?"

"You could use them to blame some nuclear terrorist act on somebody else," Andy said. "You're asking me to believe the best from you when all I've seen is your worst side."

"What can we do for you, to get your cooperation with this project?" asked the Weasel.

"The meeting that I set up with this ex-KGB agent must take place on my farm," Andy said. "The king specifically pointed out that this man will know how many people are on the scene in advance of our meeting and that I had better not have a crowd there."

"Why do you want to use your own farm?" he asked.

"Let's just say I feel at home there."

"But we could offer you so much more protection in another location, a location that we know well and have scouted," the Weasel said.

"That's exactly what I don't want," Andy said. "The Farm has the kind of simplicity that this ex-KGB agent is looking for. The more helicopters and black sedans rolling around, the less likely anything good is going to come out of this."

"Okay, we'll go with your farm."

"I need someone who knows the Soviet weapons from the 1980s, just one person who is capable of confirming that I'm not paying one hundred million dollars of your money for two pieces of junk that couldn't hurt anybody. This person shouldn't be armed or look dangerous. He could be searched. He must be able to verify that the two warheads are worth paying for, and disarm them as soon as possible."

"Is there anything else?"

"You should monitor the movement of money in the Swiss account that you are setting up for me to use," he said. "It is possible that you can get your money back at some point after the transfer of weapons, unless it is possible that we might buy more weapons."

"An excellent suggestion," the Weasel said.

"I insist that you give this ex-KGB agent no reason to be suspicious. If he attempts to double-cross us, I only need a secure phone number with which to contact you. I'd like a fat shoebox of C4, with detonators and timers and remote triggers."

"You have my word that we won't interfere with your meeting unless you call us," he said. "The equipment you'll need will come with the nuclear weapons specialist."

"Is there anything else?" The Weasel leaned forward.

"If someone could take me back to the airport at Farmville tonight, I would appreciate it."

"Consider it done."

In the adjacent room, Lindsey stared through the mirror, wiped her eyes, and smiled.

"Mr. Harrison, I know that you're not going to like this, but I want to be the person assigned to Dr. Carlson when this ex-KGB agent is on his farm."

"We both know that you were personally involved with Carlson, and that breaks all the rules. Plus, you're --what--eight months pregnant?"

"What would be less threatening than a little woman who is eight and a half months pregnant? This ex-KGB man won't consider me a threat. Do I look like a nuclear weapons specialist?"

The Weasel protruded his chin as he stroked his beard.

"Sir, I'm the only person now in the United States with real field experience at disarming Soviet nuclear weapons from the 1980s. That trip to Russia gave me the opportunity to stuff a bunch of warheads. There's no reason to send a greenhorn when you can send a nuclear physicist with hands-on experience."

"You make good points, but you stabbed Carlson."

"That was a long time ago. We're on the same side now. I'll send him an apology card before I go."

"An apology card?"

"The good doctor isn't going to harm somebody in my condition. Of course, it's not ideal, but the positives far outweigh the negatives. I'm your most qualified agent for this assignment."

"I'll consider it."

"While you're considering you might recall that I speak Russian. I studied Russian language all three years I was at Cal Tech. That's one of the reasons I got my job here in the first place. The CIA wanted someone who could communicate with Russian scientists and had the physics background to understand them. There's one more thing that needs to be ascertained about any old Soviet warhead."

"Go ahead."

"The tritium reservoirs must be replaced on a regular schedule to keep the weapon above 90% yield, because neutrons are lost by decay over time. We will need to determine if any thirty year old weapons we buy have had their reservoirs replaced recently. The date and manufacturer is usually stamped on the reservoir in Russian. A new reservoir would also have fresh marks from the wrenches used to screw them into the threads of the plutonium core. New reservoirs might come from a new source. I don't think you've got anybody but me stateside who can disarm the weapons as well as evaluate their potential yield and the age of their tritium reservoirs."

30

The helicopter pilot set the CIA chopper down at the Farmville Municipal Airport. Wiley Pritchert was a wiry middle-aged man with a two-day beard, headphones, and a dangling cigarette.

Andy approached the helicopter and got into the back seat, next to the box of explosives and equipment. "Can you put out that cigarette, please?"

The pilot gave him a set of earphones and mashed his cigarette under his heel in the floor of the chopper.

"Dr. Carlson, this is Dr. McKee," he said. "She specializes in Soviet-made nuclear weapons. She has the rest of your equipment. We plan to fly you over to your farm with this gear."

Andy glanced at the moderately obese blonde lady in the front seat, who was wearing sunglasses. His smile was perfunctory, but his nose quickly locked in on the smell of perfume in the cockpit, distinct enough to drown the Marlboro smell. There was the clear possibility that another woman could use that fragrance. But there was only one woman in this helicopter. He stared hard at the woman in the front seat. She was wearing a wig. And she wasn't fat. She was pregnant.

Andy stared at the back of her head a few minutes. Then he took his pen out of his shirt pocket and threw it in the floor of the helicopter at Dr. McKee's feet.

"Dr. McKee, could you reach my pen?"

She leaned over. Andy grabbed the back of her pants and pulled them down hard. The tattoo was unmistakable. Lindsey jerked backwards and sat upright as the helicopter lifted off.

Andy pointed in the direction of his farm. "Mr. Pritchert, I think that you should know a little more about the people that you are working with."

"That woman sitting beside you calls herself Dr. McKee. She once told me that she loved me. And then she tried to poison me. And then she sneaked up behind me and stabbed me in the chest with a dagger. And then she stole my truck. And then she pretended that she was dead. And then she got knocked up."

"Did you say she stole your truck?" Mr. Pritchert recoiled, his mouth sagging.

"That's right. She stole my truck."

"I've been stabbed by a woman before, but she didn't steal my truck," Pritchert said. "How can the agency trust somebody like that with nuclear weapons?"

"And it had an extended cab, too."

"You can have the truck back, Dr. Carlson, and for your information," she said, "I have a Ph.D. in nuclear physics and one of my specialties is defusing nuclear weapons."

Lindsey took off the wig and sunglasses. The auburn hair spilled out.

"You can't believe anything that comes out of this woman's mouth," Andy said. "I'll bet she's also an astronaut, and a lawyer, and a movie star, too. Do you know that song, *I'd lie to you for your love, and that's the truth?*"

"Yeah. I've known a few women like that, too."

"When this is over I can explain everything," Lindsey said.

Pritchert asked, "Can we use that field over there?"

"You mean the alfalfa field where Dr. Carlson tried to drop a GPS guided bomb on me?" Lindsey asked. "Are we going back into the house where he tied me up and did things to me?"

Andy stared past her.

Wiley Pritchert set the helicopter down in the alfalfa field. "I feel really bad about leaving you two here by yourselves, with all these explosives, but that's what I was told to do."

Andy unloaded his box of explosives and other gear onto the ground. Lindsey backed out of the front seat carefully. Andy did not offer any assistance. Once on the ground, she reached back inside for an overnight bag, a yellow tool box, and a lead apron. They both ducked their heads and stepped away as the helicopter lifted off.

"I can't carry this lead apron up that hill," she said.

"Just leave your stuff on the ground," Andy said. "We can both walk up to the farmhouse and get the RTV and haul everything."

Walking up the hill to the farmhouse, Andy repeated her claim. "So you're a nuclear physics Ph.D. this week? What would you like me to call you--Dr. Strangelove?"

"Lindsey would be satisfactory," she said. "My real last name is McKee."

He stopped at the shed. "All right, Lindsey McKee. I'm trying to think of one thing that you have ever told me that I was sure was not a lie. I can't think of anything. I thought that I wanted to find you. But all of the time I was worrying about you, and wondering if you were still alive, you were cooking up another way to hurt me." He looked at her protuberant abdomen. "Your being here is a big mistake."

They reached the farmhouse. Lindsey sat on the steps of the farmhouse while Andy drove the Kubota back out into the alfalfa field to get their gear.

Andy unloaded Lindsey's gear on the steps.

"I can't go back in there with you," he said. "Make yourself at home. I'm going to store these explosives. I have somewhere else to sleep where I feel a whole lot safer. I'll meet you here in the morning at about 8:00 and we can send a message to Mr. ex-KGB. Would you do something for me?"

"If I can."

"We could be looking at the third battle on the Farm," he said. "And it could easily turn out worse than the second. Last time, a lot of people got hurt. Please don't force me to kill any more Americans."

"I volunteered for this assignment," she said.

"Unannounced, pregnant, with a new job title, at a critical time. Why did you do this to me?"

"It's important for our national security," she said.

"You don't have to be someone that you aren't for my benefit anymore," he said. "Tomorrow morning we can start over as two Americans trying to prevent a disaster."

"If that is the way you would like to approach our relationship, then I agree," she said.

"I haven't finished yet," Andy said. "On this farm, I'm Robert E. Lee. I'll decide what, when, and how we do everything that we do here. I don't care who sent you here. I have no faith in Harrison or President Marshall. When I want your opinion, I'll ask for it. If you can disarm nuclear weapons, whoopee for our side."

She turned and walked into the house. Andy drove down the farm road to the new garage.

Lindsey stood in the great room. She felt her heart accelerate. She dropped her bag on the coffee table and turned around to look at the entire room. Nothing had changed. The animals were not talking, but she felt that they were judging her. There was Robert E. Lee on the mantel. He was disappointed in her.

She walked into the dining room. There was the chair he was sitting in when she stabbed him. She looked in the kitchen, half expecting to find spaghetti on dirty dishes and empty wine glasses.

The master bedroom was neat and clean. She would not sleep in that bed. She went down the hall, past the study to the spare bedroom, where there were no memories.

He was right. It was a mistake. How could a man with so much ability to recognize subtle relationships between time and events be incapable of seeing that he was the father of her baby? *Maybe he doesn't remember the sex, or he has repressed it.* Being stabbed by a woman immediately after having sex with her could affect your memory. Traumatic experiences definitely affected memory. Mrs. Lincoln probably couldn't recall much about the play after Abe got shot.

31

A ndy slept poorly. During the night he debated the wisdom of revealing the true nature of the Farm to Lindsey. His property was a unique place to do battle. However, it offered no advantages to a person who did not know its secrets. Unfortunately, he needed Lindsey's help. She could not help him, or even protect herself, given her condition, unless she was fully aware of the terrain they now shared.

Although she had stabbed him at the onset of the last battle of the Farm, she had later saved his life by misdirecting Harrison. Once you save another person's life, you feel obligated to preserve that life. He would do anything to protect Sahar. But there was something very unusual here. Why would Lindsey put her baby in harm's way? No CIA mission should overrule her maternal instinct to protect her offspring. She must have some other reason to want to help him. Guilt? It was enough to believe that she had already made her choice between himself and Harrison. She would not betray him again, for whatever reason.

Lindsey woke early, showered, and put on a maternity dress. She hated those elastic stretcher pants that never felt comfortable in any position. The coffee was hot and aromatic by the time Andy opened the front door.

She poured him a cup and put some cream and sugar on the table. He sat down with his back to the French doors.

"Let's go over your plan, or General Lee's plan," she said.

"A plan is what you've got before things go wrong," he said. "We need more than just a plan. We need strategies and backup scenarios. I want you to assume the role of my wife."

A sip of coffee went down the wrong way. She recovered, and stared at him.

"Not my real wife," he said. "I want you to play the role of my wife here on The Farm. That will be the best explanation for your being here, and your pregnancy could work in our favor. You don't look like a threat to anyone. And let's face it, you do have talent for deception."

"Andy, please don't be hostile to me. I deserve it, but it won't help our cause."

"Okay. As long as I don't have to hear about your boyfriend. And please don't show me your latest ultrasound. Don't tell me about all the cute little outfits you already have. Don't invite me to any baby showers. We have a critical job to do here, and I don't want to be distracted."

"I understand."

"Later on today," he said, "I want you to go into Farmville and buy a couple of gold wedding bands. Here, take my class ring from Emory University to get the right size." He handed her $500. "I don't want to know why you're not wearing a wedding ring, but I hope he's not dead already."

She put the money in her purse. "He's not dead yet."

"You better check out the kitchen and buy whatever it is that wives buy for their husbands when they're expecting Russian arms dealers."

"Are we ready to discuss strategies?" she asked.

"I've written an e-mail to this ex-KGB agent, who calls himself 1917USSR. I'd like you to read it." He pulled a folded sheet of paper from his shirt pocket.

Lindsey read slowly:

To: 1917USSR
From: R.E.L.

I understand from our mutual friend that you have two items already in America that I might be interested in. If these are the size that you discussed with our mutual friend, then I would be willing to buy them for $50,000,000 each, if the tritium reservoirs were less than three years old.

I am located on a farm in a remote part of central Virginia. There are no large cities or any military bases nearby. A small airport is northwest of my farm in Cumberland County. My gate is two miles from the airport on South Airport Road and has 285 on the mailbox. I'll open it for you.

The only person besides me who would be on this farm is my wife, who is pregnant. I would like to complete this transaction before she goes into labor.

I would expect you to come with a truck and not bring more than one person with you. If you show up with a squad of soldiers, I will assume that your intentions are hostile, and I will take whatever action is necessary to protect myself and my wife. As soon as the two items are on the ground and I have inspected them, I will wire your money to any account in the world. You will have the opportunity to confirm the deposit of fifty million dollars into your account before you leave.

Awaiting your reply.

"This is good bait," she said. "Tell me about the backup."

"I'm going into my study and send this. Please don't get on your cell phone and call the CIA while I'm gone. I don't want anyone else to have his contact information. There are some biscuits in the refrigerator that we could have for breakfast."

Andy sent the e-mail and returned to his chair in the dining room. Lindsey poured him another cup of coffee.

"The biscuits will be out of the oven in ten minutes," she said.

"We will appeal to his weakness, which is greed," Andy said. "After he arrives and unloads the weapons into the garage, we'll transfer the money from the Swiss account set up by Harrison into his account. I plan to distract him by showing him one of the greatest secrets here on the Farm. While his eyes are dropping out of his head, it will be your job to disarm the two weapons. Then, even if he takes them with him, they won't do him any good. I have software on my laptop that will steal his account number and password. I'll give the CIA the information they need to get their money back when it's appropriate. We don't know if other weapons may be for sale."

"Do you think he will bring only one person?"

"I do. Probably a truck driver. If a crowd shows up, there will be a fight. But it will be my fight, not yours. How long will it take you to disarm both weapons?"

"Five to eight minutes each under good conditions."

"Walk out to the car garage next to the kitchen," he said, standing up.

She followed him from the kitchen into his two-car garage, which was empty except for a tarp in the far left corner and a freezer to the right. They stood in the center of a concrete floor.

"When they arrive I would like you to come with me and greet them in front of the house," he said. "My suggestion will be to offload the weapons in this car garage. The reason that the car garage does not have a roll back door is that it has an overhead rail system for moving heavy equipment."

He pointed up at the I-beam and the wheels at the base of each door. "I'll close these two doors after we unload the two weapons. You can work inside, underneath that tarp."

He pointed to the corner of the garage. Lindsey looked out of the small windows in each door.

"The driver may be right outside these doors," Andy said. "You could leave your tools and lead apron in the kitchen. Once you go back into the house after meeting the ex-KGB agent, take my camera and shoot a few pictures of anyone who shows up before you go through the kitchen into the car garage. You're good with a camera. You are not to show yourself again, regardless of what happens to me. I'm going to show you several places to hide after you disable the weapons."

A bell sounded in the kitchen. Lindsey went to get the biscuits out of the oven. Andy followed her through the kitchen and sat back down at the dining room table. She placed the plate of steaming biscuits on the table in front of him. He stared at the cream separator-flower pot holder. She returned to the kitchen for a couple of table knives, two small plates, and soft margarine in a plastic cup.

He scowled and began to eat.

"If something goes wrong with the exchange of money for weapons," he said, "I'll lure whoever shows up into the back swamp."

"I could help you," she said.

He put two biscuits in his shirt pockets and stood up. "I've already told you that this is not your fight. No Carlson has ever lost a fight on this ground. If you want to know some of the reasons for this, follow me."

32

Wedging herself into the right side of the bench seat in the Kubota, Lindsey said, "The baby's kicking me this morning."

"I thought we had an understanding that you were not to offer me information like that," he said. "I can't decide if I want that baby to kick harder."

He drove the quarter mile to the garage.

Lindsey looked at the building. "This looks new. When did you finish it?"

"It's not quite finished inside, but I've been working on it for several years," he said. "My dad worked on it with me before he died. A family friend named Ben has been helping me for the last six months."

Andy entered a code into the keypad next to the rollback door of the garage and the giant door rose briskly. "Tell me what you see, and look carefully."

Lindsey looked inside the room. A concrete ramp led down to the work pit below. An old tractor with a wide wheelbase straddled the far end of the pit. She looked underneath the tractor. A red tool cabinet covered the far wall underneath the tractor. To the right at floor level were a kitchenette, a bathroom, and a work area with a desk and computer. The left side of the room was filled with aisles of metal bins packed with spare parts, hoses, clamps, and fittings.

"I see a well-organized mechanic shop for farm vehicles," she said.

"Follow me." He walked briskly down the ramp, and then looked back at Lindsey. She was not moving.

"I'm sorry," he said.

He walked back up the ramp and took her hand, guiding her down the concrete slope to the bottom of the pit.

"For what it's worth, do you recall promising to keep Carlson secrets?"

"I'm not the same girl. I will keep my promise."

Andy pulled a remote keypad out of a box of oversized nuts in a bin in the cabinet and entered a series of numbers. Steel cylinders sounded in the vault door. Andy pulled the entire tool cabinet open like a door, exposing huge steel hinges on the right side of the opening. The vault door was one foot thick steel with four inch cylinders radiating from the door. He reached inside to turn on the light.

Andy led her through the opening and down another forty-five feet of concrete ramp to the floor of an underground chamber the size of a two-car garage. Lindsey could see one limestone tunnel leading to the left. Andy appeared to be walking toward the wall on the right side of the chamber. He pushed and the wall gave way. Several dark leather hides had been cleverly painted and overlapped to conceal another tunnel. Holding one of the hides aside, he flipped a switch inside and motioned for Lindsey to walk through.

Lindsey gazed at the Grand Chamber of the Confederate Cave. She was speechless.

Most of the 28,000 caves in Virginia result from a simple formula. There must be a layer of limestone fifty to 300 feet below ground level. Add a mildly acidic mixture of rain water and carbon dioxide and percolate it through the decaying vegetation in the soil for six or seven million years. The hollowing-out of the cavern is caused by the solution of carbonic acid dissolving and eroding the layer of limestone.

In the case of the Farm, seeping water eventually enlarged the first crevices and the run-off descended to the level of the Appomattox River, leaving behind huge limestone chambers and tunnels. There were never any large flowing streams, although some pools of water remained in the most dependent parts of the caverns. Most of the deposits of limestone were transported and deposited by modest amounts of water over a long period of time. A system of interconnected caves, chambers, and tunnels can only be as large as the layer of limestone from which they were formed.

As the water subsides in a limestone cave and only a slow overhead seepage remains, nature's decorating begins. The calcium carbonate solution gives up some of its carbon dioxide and allows a precipitation of lime to drip from the ceiling, forming stalactites and stalagmites. Spreading crystalline deposits of pure calcium carbonate move laterally, coating the walls and ceiling. These shimmering red, white, and blue formations are called flowstone.

"We're standing eighty feet below the grade of the garage," he said. "The garage is actually not overhead, but behind us."

An eight-inch elevated platform of wooden planks was mounted on floor joists. This platform occupied one half of the floor space of the Grand Chamber. There was a kitchen, a pantry, a bathroom, a laundry room, and a combination living room-bedroom with a propane stove. Limestone caves aren't flat, nor are they designed for people to go strolling. Twisting passages, low ceilings, and tight squeezes are the norm. Although true cavers would have been horrified by Andy's intrusions on nature, he didn't foresee any time in the future when guides would be escorting lines of tourists underneath the Farm.

Andy had leveled off many stalactites and stalagmites with a reciprocating saw to create a reasonably level floor and unobstructed overhead space. Narrow passages had been widened with a pick and shovel. The Grand Chamber was four times the size of the garage they had just walked through.

The walls of a limestone cave are mostly rusty-reddish flowstone, colored by iron oxide. Patches of shimmering white flowstone stand out like chandeliers when a light is shined in their direction. The exposed bluish limestone is a strong contrast to the general redness. The temperature is always on the cool side, but not uncomfortable in a sweater, due to the lack of wind.

From his childhood Andy had marveled at the absolute darkness of the entire cave system. If you didn't bring light with you, there was nothing but endless night. Without light, all of the majesty and wonder of nature's decorations were mute. There were no bats or rats. These creatures need an entrance to the cave system. Andy's ancestors had closed all of the other entrances to the caverns below the Farm. The recent development of 100 hour LED light-sticks had helped Andy survey much of the caverns.

"Eventually most of the floor in this chamber will be elevated to the height of the rooms I've completed," he said. "Until then you'll have to watch your step and avoid the electrical wires, the water lines, and the drain lines. All these will eventually be out of sight."

"This is all so amazing," she said.

"You haven't even started to see amazing," he said.

He took her hand and led her back through the overlapped hides into the anteroom. To the left was the ramp ascending to the garage. In front of her was another tunnel.

He said, "The Grand Chamber is where I want you to go once you've disarmed the nuclear weapons. You can enter through the fake stump outside the garage or through the vault door behind the cabinet, the way we came in. I'll give you the combination when the time comes. It will be dark and you can slip out the back door onto the deck and walk through the woods to the garage."

He led her into the second tunnel. Andy switched on a light just inside the opening and they entered a vaulted room with intact stalactites and stalagmites. Gold bars were stacked in rows and layers around these.

She blinked several times and stepped toward the gold. "Where did you get all of this?" She picked up a bar. The indented letters on top read "CSA."

Andy said, "This represents the greater part of the Confederate treasury. There was little left to buy in the South by the end of the war. My great-great grandfather, John Andrew Carlson, was in a secret society pledged to hide this gold. Four of his sons were Confederate officers. During the first week of April 1865, it had been raining hard for several days when the armies disengaged from the battle at Cumberland Church, about two miles from here.

The heavy wagons carrying this gold couldn't get across the Appomattox River at Sandy Ford because of high water and mud. The purpose of the cavalry battle fought on the Farm was to hold the Union army at bay until the wagons of gold could be unloaded and hidden.

My family stood and fought with the Confederate cavalry. Our remaining slaves fought alongside us. The Civil War was over only two days after the gold was hidden here. Appomattox Court House is twenty-five miles away. The disappearance of the Confederate treasury is well-documented. No one in the society ever gave up the secret."

"Nobody knew about the cave system here?" she asked.

"My family bought this land from King George II in 1743. No one but the Indians we drove off knew about the cave system." He pointed to his left.

"The bones and skulls in that pile are some of the remains of dead Yankees. John Andrew buried more than seventy Yankees in the caves. He also left a note about how to use this gold, but we don't have time for that. There are other caches of gold here in the cave system, according to my grandfather. The Confederate cavalry blew the entrances before retreating north on Pleasant Valley Road and Plank Road behind the infantry."

"This has got to be the farm secret you were talking about," she said.

"This is one of many secrets on the Farm," he said. "I wouldn't be showing it to you if it didn't have a critical role in my strategy with the ex-KGB agent."

"I need to sit down," Lindsey said.

Andy helped her sit on the gold. "When the gold was put in this cave it was worth about twelve dollars per ounce. There was little food or munitions left in the south to buy by 1865. Gold is now worth close to $2000 per ounce."

"So how much is it worth?" she asked.

"These bars weigh a little over 384 ounces each, or about 12 kilograms. That means each bar is worth $750,000 and these 400 bars are worth $300 million in today's currency. There's supposed to be more in other parts of the caverns. The gold really doesn't belong to me. Its sole purpose in this operation is to make a greedy man wet his pants at the thought of selling us more warheads for gold, and ultimately stealing it all."

"I believe it could work," she said.

"Hopefully, the gold will hold his attention long enough for you to disable the two bombs," Andy said. "I'll let him pick up a few bars, rub the metal with his hands, count the rows in each direction, count the number of layers, do the math in his head. I'll offer him the gold for more weapons. If he has any more weapons, he'll sell them to me. He'll realize that the gold is so well-protected that it would be near-impossible for him to steal it."

He led her out of the gold room into the anteroom. "There are two switches just inside the Grand Chamber that are wired to explosives. The one on the left will close the entrance to the gold room. The one on the right will close the entrance to the Grand Chamber. These are for a broken arrow situation."

He walked her back into the Grand Chamber and pointed out the two manual switches. "Remember, you can close the tunnels to the gold room or the Grand Chamber anytime you feel threatened."

"There are two more tunnels leaving this chamber." He pointed to a tunnel to the right of the entrance from the anteroom. "That tunnel leads to the back swamp, 125 feet down, but gradual. It ends up under water, which just happens to be good ground for an ex-SEAL. It's my own emergency entrance-exit. Outside the entrance is a homemade beaver dam. The point I want you to understand is that even if you close the vault door and blow the entrances to the gold room and the Grand Chamber, I can get back to you from the back swamp."

"Andy," she asked, "How can you waltz me in here after what I've done to you and show me this? Aren't you worried that I'll steal this gold?"

"Have you looked in the mirror lately? Just how many gold bars did you plan on walking out of here with?"

She closed her mouth tightly and tried to control the muscles in her face. Her cheeks ballooned. The corners of her mouth would not go down. She put her hand over her mouth. But laughing requires both hands on your abdomen if you are thirty-nine weeks pregnant.

"That room off the Grand Chamber leads to the medical supply room and the operating room is behind it," he said, pointing to a tunnel the size of a double front door. He helped her step up to the laundry room. "Behind this linen cabinet is a vertical three foot diameter, sixty foot aluminum culvert. It has ladder steps welded on the inside. This ladder will take you up to the inside of a homemade stump beside the garage. It's an emergency exit and also serves as a vent."

He looked at Lindsey. "When I put that culvert in, I didn't consider pregnant people. The ladder steps take up some of the room. You may not be able to get out that way unless you have your baby down here."

"Don't say anything like that," she said.

He walked her into the bathroom and pointed to the shower. "Turn the shower head from 6:00 to 9:00."

Lindsey stepped inside the lip of the shower and turned the shower head to 9:00. The wall holding the shower head and fixtures opened with a row of hinges hidden on the left side. The water connections were flexible hoses, allowing the door to open enough to walk through. Andy pulled on a cord. When the light came on, Lindsey was staring at an arsenal.

The room was a walk-in closet of guns, knives, spears, rifles, ammunition, and pistols. On a table in the rear of the room was an all-black rifle with a bipod.

"That's a Marine Corps sniper rifle, a .308 caliber with a bull barrel and a silencer." Andy unscrewed the silencer. "This extra thickness of the barrel makes the gun heavier, but it allows accurate cold bore shots at long distances."

She looked down at the ammunition boxes in the floor of the arsenal.

"I don't recommend that you use these rifles unless you have no choice," he said. "The Glock .45 or the 9 millimeter SIG Sauer are probably more effective weapons for you inside this cave. There's a bunch of pistols on the shelf. There's one in each of the fake stumps near the house. There's one inside the clock on the mantel in the dining room of the farmhouse and one in the freezer of the car garage."

"Why do you need to hide your arsenal behind the shower if it's already underground?" she asked.

"I thought I might have children some day," he said without looking at her. "The cave system on the Farm is complex. It's loaded with weapons and explosives for every purpose. I get the latest stuff whenever I can, but my personal favorites are always quiet, like my bows and arrows."

"I can verify that you're a good shot with them," she said.

"I make these stick bows in my spare time," he said. He pointed to the box of simple bows made of wound nylon string and a single sapling.

"I'm going to hide them in the back swamp with plenty of arrows. They look pretty harmless, but each bow is made exactly alike and each arrow is exactly alike. They're deadly out to thirty-five yards. No big game animal in North America has survived an arrow from one of these bows. Most of those animals were larger and more intelligent in the woods than humans."

"Don't you feel a little funny carrying around a stick bow in today's world of laser guided weapons?"

"I don't need to carry them around. I store them around the Farm.

I plan to store a bunch of these stick bows inside the beaver hutches in the back swamp. I can get to them without being seen or heard, take a shot, and disappear. Also, when people see someone running without a weapon they rarely suspect that he has weapons and explosives at his destination."

"But won't the beavers gnaw on the bow and arrows?" she asked.

"I've got a special bottle of stinky stuff that I wipe them all down with. The beavers hate the smell. It's predator urine. They'll leave the hutch until I remove the smell."

"I'm ready to go now, Andy. The baby is kicking my bladder."

He reached for her hand and led her out of the arsenal of the Grand Chamber.

They started up the ramp. Within a few steps, Andy was dragging her by her arm.

"I'm sorry," she said.

Andy put his arm around her and boosted her up the ramp, step by step.

They rode back to the farmhouse in the Kubota.

Lindsey went straight to the bathroom and Andy went straight to his computer.

33

There it was on the monitor screen:

From: 1917 USSR
To: R.E.L.
Re: Two Items for sale.

The terms of your offer are acceptable. The reservoirs are only three years old. I am not far from you. I will need to do reconnaissance before I arrive. Can we meet at 4:00 EST tomorrow morning, January 30, at your house to complete our business?
Andy clicked on Reply and typed:

Affirmative.
R.E.L.

He clicked "Send."

Andy showed Lindsey the e-mail. "We would like to complete this transaction without precipitating a fight, but a fight is coming. First we have to stir up this guy's greed."

Andy had thought that the urge to fight evil had left him. Now he was preparing to do battle again. A warrior sees his duty and does it. He doesn't choose his enemy. He doesn't believe that anyone else can do the job as well as he can.

He took her outside and demonstrated the lids to the stumps and the weapons inside. Then he wheeled open the doors to the car garage.

"Put any extra tools you decide you need in the freezer in the back corner," he said. "The freezer's not turned on. The light on the refrigerator won't come on when you open it. There's a flashlight and a SIG Sauer inside."

"I'm going to put my Geiger counter in the freezer," she said. "If you check the weapons with it, the ex-KGB agent might be impressed."

He closed the garage doors and started back toward the front door. "Would you call your buddy Pritchert and tell him to stand by in his helicopter at the Farmville Municipal Airport at 3:30 tomorrow morning?"

"Why do we need Pritchert?" she asked. "I don't think he likes me."

"Something might go wrong and we could need to track down a truckload of weapons."

"You should call him," she said.

"But he works for the CIA, and so do you. I'm the civilian here."

They walked into the great room and Lindsey picked up the phone. She punched in the number and quickly handed the phone to Andy.

After a brief pause, Pritchert came on the line.

"Mr. Pritchert, this is Andy Carlson, the guy you met in Farmville yesterday."

"I'm glad to hear that you're alive. Is she okay?"

"She's fine, but I'll tell her you asked about her. I need for you to be at the airport in Farmville at 3:30 in the morning. Be in the helicopter with your radio on. I may need you to hurry. Land in that field just below my house, the same field where you dropped us off yesterday. I have a flare that I'll use to guide you in the dark. As the crow flies it's only a mile and a half from the airport to that field. Do you have a good searchlight on that chopper?"

"I do."

"Then put your ears on at 3:30 and stand by."

"Are you bringing that truck thief along?"

34

At 4:00 the next morning, Andy heard a car cross the heavy planks of the covered bridge. He turned on the light over the car garage. Five minutes later a dark Mercedes pulled into the driveway. Andy and Lindsey came out of the house together, Lindsey wiping her hands on her apron.

The gentleman waited until they were about ten feet away before speaking. "Mr. R.E.L.?"

"I'm Robert Lee and this is my wife Hannah."

"Call me Boris."

Boris appeared to be about seventy years old. He was stocky, with a graying beard. He had vodka on his breath. He had worked hard to improve his thick accent.

They shook hands.

"You will find that I am a businessman," Boris said. "I do not care why you want the merchandise I am selling. If you are straight with me, then I will be straight with you. If you are not straight with me, then I will have to kill you and your wife."

Andy said, "I'm looking for other items like the two we are buying this morning. I'm not interested in offending a valuable resource such as you. The merchandise that you have for sale is rare. Would you like some coffee?"

"Make it black."

Andy turned to Lindsey. "Could you bring Boris a cup of black coffee and also get my laptop from the coffee table?"

Lindsey went back into the house. Once inside, she grabbed Andy's camera and shot photographs of Boris in the light from the car garage.

"As soon as I see the two devices and they are loaded into the garage,"

Andy said, "I'll transfer the money to your account right here on the hood of your car. Boris, can you tell me again how old the tritium sources are on these two items?"

"Less than three years. It's easy to move something as small as a tritium reservoir."

Lindsey returned with the coffee and the laptop and then went back into the house.

"I have my own computer," Boris said. He opened the passenger door of his car and picked up his laptop.

Andy put his laptop on the hood of Boris' car and booted it up while they sipped the coffee. He found the web page of the Swiss bank where the CIA had opened an account for him.

"If you will watch me enter my account number, you will see that the numbers in the account and the password only appear as asterisks," Andy said. "I will show you my balance."

Andy turned the screen toward Boris. The balance read $100,155,450.27 USD.

Andy clicked on the tab that said transfer and typed in "$100,000,000. Then he turned the screen toward Boris again. "If you will type your own account information and password, I will be able to transfer the money."

Boris typed in the information, again showing only asterisks on each line. "You may transfer the money."

Andy said, "I'll transfer the money when the two weapons are loaded into that garage and I'm satisfied that they are the two weapons that I ordered."

Boris pulled out his cell phone and spoke in Russian. He closed the phone. "The warheads will be here in a few minutes."

"You are no doubt concerned about inflation in the world today, which is out of control," Andy said.

"I have concerns about this, but I don't see how they impact our transaction tonight."

"Would you be interested in seeing $300 million dollars worth of gold bars?" Andy asked with a grin.

"And where would you have such a quantity of gold?" Boris asked.

"It's about a quarter of a mile down that road," Andy said.

"Why do you want to show me this gold?" he asked.

"I want you to know how I can pay for any future transactions that you can arrange."

Andy heard the sound of truck tires passing over the planks of the covered bridge.

"Let us finish the business we have started, then we can look at your gold," Boris said.

A black F-350 with a long camper and four rear wheels drove into the driveway and a stocky gentleman got out. He had Slavic features but was at least five years younger than Boris. He dyed his beard to make the port wine birthmark on his chin less obvious.

"This is Aleksi, Mr. Lee." They shook hands.

"Aleksi, would you back up to that garage and unload the two weapons inside?" Boris asked.

Aleksi got back in his truck, and Andy swung open the doors to his garage.

"I have a sliding rail hoist overhead that will make unloading easy," Andy said, pointing at the rail hoist.

Aleksi maneuvered the truck into position. When he opened the tailgate and lifted the hatchback of the camper, Andy slid the block and tackle toward him on the rail.

Aleksi hooked onto a balance chain welded onto the weapon. Andy pulled on the rope and Aleksi pushed the warhead along the rail until it was inside the garage. Andy lowered the warhead to the concrete floor.

This warhead was obviously not designed to be dropped out of an airplane. It looked like the two Andy had seen in the container at Prince Khalid's palace. He estimated that it weighed 200 pounds. A simple metal tubular frame allowed the warhead to be rocked around on the floor by two people. The balance chain allowed the warhead to be picked up by a hook without tipping the weapon over.

A forklift could move a warhead like this in a few minutes. Andy recognized a battery and a keypad. A mechanical detonator switch was coiled on top, not connected to its receptacle. The plutonium coconut, its surrounding shaped charges, and the tritium reservoir were partially covered by a separate metal housing. Hopefully, Lindsey had the right tools to remove this housing.

"If you can help me move it back a little, there will be room for the second warhead," Andy said.

Aleksi and Andy rocked the device back and forth and muscled it to the rear of the garage. Then Andy guided the block and tackle along the sliding rail back to the F-350. Aleksi jumped into the bed of the truck and hooked the balance chain of the second warhead. Andy pulled on the rope and raised the second warhead enough for Aleksi to slide it along the rail into the garage.

Andy reached in the freezer and got Lindsey's Geiger counter. As Boris watched he brought the Geiger counter close to both weapons. They hummed. Andy stretched a dark tarp over both weapons and closed the doors of the garage. With Boris watching, he clicked "Submit" on his laptop. After a few seconds he clicked on "Balance." The account showed $155,450.27.

Boris opened his own laptop and booted up. He smiled broadly as $100 million dollars appeared in his account. "You are a man of your word."

He turned to Aleksi. "You may proceed with the next transfer."

Andy and Boris got in the Kubota and drove down the path toward the garage. Andy wondered what Boris meant when he said "the next transfer."

They arrived at the garage and Andy retrieved his keypad from the box of steel nuts and opened the vault at the base of the mechanic's pit.

He turned on the light and they walked to the end of the ramp into the anteroom, where Andy turned on another light. Boris followed Andy through the short tunnel into the gold room. The light in the room glistened off of the gold. Andy could see the reflection in Boris' eyes as his pupils dilated to take in the rows and stacks of gold bars.

At the farmhouse, Lindsey was underneath the tarp in her lead apron, removing the tritium source from the first weapon. She had recognized both weapons and determined that they were at least twenty kilotons. After removing the tritium source, she began to feed the roll of wire through the hole, watching the centimeter marks as they disappeared inside. Every ten centimeters she broke off the wire; then used the next piece from the roll to push it into the center of the core. She continued until the center of the core was filled with a tangle of broken wire.

Moving to the second weapon, she again removed the tritium source, exposing the hole into the core. Soon this core was also filled with a tangle of broken wire. By this time her back was screaming and her legs were cramping. The baby did not like this kind of work. She lifted her head to stretch underneath the tarp and knocked a wrench from the top of the first warhead onto the concrete floor. The thud was not subtle.

What a stupid place to leave that wrench. She peeked out from under the tarp and watched Aleksi get out of the cab of the F-350.

Aleksi walked to the garage doors, looking to the left and right of the farm house. Then he inched up to the small window and peered inside. He watched Mr. Lee's wife doing some sort of dance. She didn't have any clothes on. He watched her do dramatic stretching exercises, then sit in the floor with her legs crossed. He smiled and walked back to his truck.

35

Lindsey remained in the floor until she heard a vehicle approaching outside. She put her clothes back on and looked outside. An ambulance was next to Aleksi's truck. *What is an ambulance doing here? I'm supposed to go out the back door of the dining room and walk to the garage. I've got to see what's happening here.*

Aleksi was talking to a young Arab male, about thirty years old, dressed as an American, with a shoulder-mounted pistol, black T-shirt, and blue jeans. She could not hear what they were saying. She returned to the kitchen and snuck across the deck and around the side of the house. From behind a bush she listened to the conversation. They were discussing a wire transfer of money, $50,000,000, and the age of the reservoir.

Apparently satisfied with the transaction, Aleksi instructed the young man to pull his ambulance forward and open the doors in the back. Aleksi got back in his truck, and backed up so that there was only one foot between the end of his tailgate and the floor of the ambulance. She watched Aleksi pull out a ramp with rollers on it and position it between the two vehicles. Both men got into the back of the F-350 and maneuvered something heavy onto the ramp.

Another thermonuclear warhead appeared on the ramp between the two vehicles, at least as large as the other two. Two more arms reached out of the back of the ambulance to pull the warhead inside.

Aleksi explained the warhead to the Arab in a thick accent. "Magdi, you can detonate this weapon in two ways. Press this button to turn the battery on. Then enter the number of minutes before detonation. Then press Enter. This is the way that I would recommend. Give yourself plenty of time to get away."

Aleccksi continued. "The second way is to attach this detonator cord to this receptacle." He handed a two foot length of electrical cord to Magdi and pointed out the receptacle on the bomb. "Once this connection is made, you can detonate the weapon by opening the safety cover on the switch at the other end of this cord. Press the yellow button three times rapidly and that will be the end of Washington, D.C. and you as well, my friend."

"I serve Allah and al Qaeda," Magdi said.

The nearest magic stump was at least twenty feet away. She would never make it without being discovered. She tried to take in as many details of the ambulance as possible. The license plate was obscured due to the position of the vehicles. On the side of the ambulance she read, "Richmond Ambulance Authority." The vehicle number was 4562. *This must be the point where the plan falls apart.*

The two men finished loading the weapon into the floor of the ambulance and Magdi shut the doors. He did not lock the ambulance doors with a key. Magdi used Boris' laptop to transfer the money and Aleksi confirmed the deposit into Boris' account. The two men shook hands, and Magdi got back into the ambulance and drove away. The transaction only took a few minutes.

Within two minutes she could hear the Kubota Diesel returning from the cave. Watching from the great room window, she could see Andy and Boris getting out of the Kubota.

Boris appeared to be in good spirits. "Aleksi, did the last transaction go well?"

"Very well, very well indeed."

"I will be in touch with you within three days regarding your proposal," Boris said to Andy. "I believe that we have at least one fifty kiloton and one 100 kiloton in our inventory. We should be able to get them rearmed with tritium within a week. But they will be expensive. $175 million dollars for both, in gold."

He shook hands with Andy, picked up his laptop and got inside the

Mercedes. Nodding to Aleksi, he drove out of the driveway. His red tail lights disappeared down the hill next to the alfalfa field.

Aleksi got back into his truck and waved to Andy. "You are a very lucky man, Mr. Lee." Then he drove away.

As the tail lights faded down the road next to the alfalfa field, Lindsey burst out of the house and ran toward Andy.

"Andy, something terrible has happened."

"With you here, I expected something terrible to happen," he said. "You're not in the Grand Chamber where you belong."

"After you left, an Arab named Magdi came in an ambulance and bought another twenty kiloton weapon from Aleksi," she said. "I stuck around the house and listened to them talk. The weapon is meant for Washington, D.C., and it can be exploded with a detonator switch mechanically."

"How long ago was this?" he asked.

"Five minutes."

"Was there another man in the back of the ambulance?"

"I could only see his arms," she said, "but there was at least one more person there."

"Call Pritchert on the phone and tell him to haul butt over here to the field," he said. "Get your yellow tool box and lead apron and miner's light and put them in the Kubota. Get the pistol from the clock on the mantel in the dining room."

Lindsey ran into the great room and Andy ran to the master bedroom closet. He stripped his clothes and put on an all-black, skin-tight diving suit. He blackened his face with camo makeup and covered his hair with a black watch cap. He strapped a ten-inch knife and black sheath to his waist and tied the end of the sheath to his left thigh. Lindsey's eyes widened when they met in the great room.

Andy picked up the flare on the coffee table. "It's time to go hunting. Pay attention. Do exactly what I say."

"I need to pee," she said. "I'm sorry."

"Maybe you can pee on the detonator switch on that warhead and short it out. Otherwise get your tools ready."

Andy hurried out the door to the Kubota. Lindsey put the yellow tool box, the lead apron, and the miner's helmet into the Kubota's bed, and pushed the Glock into what was left of the small of her back.

They drove quickly to the T where the road to the 1743 house and the road to the covered bridge met. Andy lit the flare. "Stay in the Kubota until I motion for you to come."

Running to the center of the field, he could hear the whop-whop-whop of Pritchert's helicopter. Waving the flare over his head, Andy guided the pilot to the center of the field, where he threw the flare into the alfalfa and ran back toward the Kubota.

As soon as Pritchert opened the door, Andy and Lindsey hurried over and threw their gear into the floor in the back of the chopper. Andy got in front, Lindsey in the back.

"Put your earphones on," Pritchert yelled over the rotor and engine noise. "Where to?"

"Go north to the intersection of Highway 45 and Highway 60, just west of Cumberland Courthouse," Andy said. "Land in the parking lot behind the convenience store there. By chopper it's five minutes."

They were already in the air.

"Andy, I'm going to put this pistol on the seat next to me because I can't sit back with it in my belt."

"She's got a pistol?" Pritchert asked.

"If we hurry, we will get to this intersection about four or five minutes before the ambulance does," Andy said.

"But what do you plan to do?" Lindsey asked. "If there is someone in the back of the ambulance he could already have his hand on the trigger of the device."

"What device is that?" Pritchert asked

"It's probably a twenty kiloton thermonuclear warhead," Lindsey said.

"Dr. Carlson, I got to be honest with you," he said. "This woman hasn't brought you a lot of luck."

"What do I do?" Lindsey asked Andy.

"You sit in the helicopter with Mr. Pritchert and don't move," he said. "As soon as we land, Pritchert is going to turn all the power off so that there are no lights coming from this chopper. Lindsey, what did Aleksi mean when he said to me, 'You're a lucky man, Mr. Lee'?"

"I was working underneath the tarp and I dropped a wrench on the concrete," she said. "Aleksi came over to the garage door to look in."

"So?"

"I did a few yoga exercises for him."

"Please tell me that in your condition you did not take off your clothes for that Russian and parade around nude in front of him," Andy said.

"This is the intersection you are looking for, isn't it, Dr. Carlson?" Pritchert asked.

"Set it down over there behind that store and watch out for the guy wire on that telephone pole."

Pritchert set the helicopter down smoothly and killed the engine and lights. Andy jumped out of the front seat and ran toward the intersection.

"Dr. McKee, why should Dr. Carlson care whether some Russian guy sees you without any clothes on?" Pritchert asked. "I mean, you did poison him, and stab him, and steal his truck. And you're always lying to him."

"A good question, Mr. Pritchert." She looked toward the intersection. "I don't know what kind of a girl he thinks I am. Do you see him?"

"He was over there by that big stop sign just a second ago," Pritchert said.

The stop sign was huge, mounted three feet off the ground on an eight inch by eight inch post. From their left, Lindsey spotted big headlights. The Richmond ambulance slowed to stop before making a right turn onto Highway 60.

Andy leaned back against the stop sign with his left knee pulled up to his chest. At the instant the ambulance came to a stop, he opened the narrow door on the right side of the patient compartment and entered the ambulance with his knife in his right hand.

Andy knew that this door would be open unless both paramedics were out of the ambulance getting something to eat. Anyone seated in the captain's chair behind the driver would be facing rearward and unable to see him coming. To protect the privacy of patients, the side door had no window.

When Andy opened the door, the first Arab was sitting in the captain's chair with the detonator cord in his lap. A second Arab, the driver, was visible in the small window connecting the patient compartment to the cab. Before the man in the captain's chair could process what was happening, a ten inch knife was underneath his chin. Andy pulled the blade across his neck.

He smoothly reached through the small window into the cab and pulled the knife across the neck of the driver. It was over in four seconds. Andy switched off the engine of the ambulance.

Lindsey saw Andy back out of the side door of the ambulance and wipe his knife on a sheet. He threw the sheet into the door, replaced the knife in the sheath on his leg, and walked back to the helicopter.

"You came out of nowhere," she said, getting out of the back seat of the helicopter.

"The guy in the captain's chair had a detonator in his lap. I don't know whether the driver could have detonated the warhead or not."

Pritchert got out and stood next to the helicopter, staring at the ambulance. He took several steps toward the ambulance, but came back to the helicopter.

"Lindsey, there's a warhead in the floor of that ambulance that needs your attention," Andy said. "Go in through the back of the ambulance. And don't forget your gloves and apron."

"Pritchert, call Harrison and tell him to get a crime scene truck to this location as soon as possible. Then call 911 and ask for the sheriff of Cumberland County to come to this location. Use my name."

Andy walked back to the ambulance. He opened the driver's door, put the vehicle in park, turned on the overhead lights in the back, and stepped on the parking brake. Standing at the back door of the ambulance, he shined a flashlight from the cab onto the warhead. Lindsey removed the tritium reservoir and began to feed the roll of wire into the core.

She adjusted her miner's light. "How did you know what to do?"

"I wanted to get to the ambulance before he left Cumberland Court House and before daylight. There are a few stoplights on the way to Richmond, but this is the only place they would have to come to a complete stop."

"How about using the helicopter to drop down on the ambulance?" Lindsey asked.

"Makes way too much noise. Nobody could drop down on top of that ambulance without the occupants feeling his weight. It would be difficult to get inside from the top."

"The smell in here is getting to me, and I'm done," she said, groaning. "I can take a better look at the tritium reservoir later."

Andy helped her to her feet. They walked back to the helicopter.

"You did a great job today, on three warheads," he said.

"Mr. Pritchert, did you get in touch with Harrison?" Andy asked.

"I did, and he's dispatched a truck. But he wants you to call him right away."

After several patches, the Weasel came on the line.

"Dr. Carlson," he said, "What happened?"

"We got two twenty kiloton weapons back on the Farm and Lindsey disabled them," he said. "Another buyer, an apparent al Qaeda operative named Magdi, showed up and bought a third twenty kiloton weapon that we didn't know was in the truck with the other two. He and an accomplice hauled it off in an ambulance. They were headed toward Washington. I think they intended to level the city this morning."

"What happened?" the Weasel squeaked.

"We got out in front of them at the intersection of Highway 45 North and 60 East," he said. "I was able to get inside the ambulance and take them both out. Lindsey disabled that weapon, too."

"My God." His voice descended several octaves.

"We really need somebody down here with some credentials," Andy said. "I trust the local sheriff in Cumberland, but I don't think it would be good for many people to look in that ambulance. Somebody with a badge and an impressive blue suit might help. The weapon still needs special handling. If you are going to send a truck, then come on by the Farm and pick up the other two warheads."

The Weasel said, "Then it's over."

"It's not over," Andy said. "This ex-KGB guy is coming back to my farm in about a week with two more nukes, a fifty kiloton and a 100 kiloton."

"But I don't have the money to buy any more nuclear weapons," Harrison said.

"Then I suggest you ask the president if he would rather spend $175 million getting these weapons off the street or have a couple of American cities wiped off the map."

"Are Lindsey and the baby all right?" the Weasel asked.

"Fine."

"We should have another helicopter at your location in thirty-five to forty minutes with backup. Can you stay there until it gets there?"

"Yea. Then Mr. Pritchert can take me back to get my truck at the Farmville Airport," Andy said. "Harrison, there's something you need to appreciate here, with regards to the means of transportation of the warhead."

"What's that?"

"There's a good reason that these terrorists chose an ambulance. Think about it. Once they got to the beltway around Washington they could have turned on their lights and sirens and requested a motorcade escort to George Washington University Medical Center due to an important person with a life-threatening illness or injury . No cop is going to stop such an ambulance, because he wouldn't want to be responsible for the patient's death should he pull them over for speeding. The motorcade would have taken them to less than a mile from the White House. You might want to file than information away."

"I will. I will. And a good observation."

"Were you aware that this ex-KGB agent could replace an old tritium reservoir in less than a week?"

"I'll work on that, too."

Pritchert returned from the ambulance. He was pale. "I thought you were kidding about the heads and the bomb."

The local sheriff, James Blanchard, was pulling up to the ambulance. Andy got out of the helicopter and waved at him.

Mr. Blanchard had not had his morning coffee. "Dr. Carlson, what in the world are you doing out here this time of the morning in that get-up?"

"That ambulance over there contains two dead Islamic terrorists and a thermonuclear weapon," Andy said. "The weapon is large enough to make a desert out of this county. There is a squad of CIA agents on their way here to take over the crime scene. The warhead has been disabled. It would be better for everybody if this were just written up as a flat tire on an ambulance. You don't want to get into the kind of paperwork this case could generate."

Mr. Blanchard was now wide awake. "I'm just going to walk over and peek in. I won't touch anything."

Lindsey returned to the helicopter and loaded her gear in the back. They watched Mr. Blanchard stick his head inside the side door, pull it out quickly, and grab his stomach.

"Lindsey," Andy asked, "why would Harrison be so concerned about your welfare? He seemed anxious about you and your baby."

"You don't think Mr. Harrison is the daddy, do you, doctor?" Pritchert asked.

"You filthy-minded country bumpkins," Lindsey said.

"Nothing surprises me anymore," Andy said.

After the blue suits landed, Pritchert lifted off and headed south.

"If you don't mind, you can drop me off at the airport?" Andy said. "My truck is still there."

"Is that the truck Dr. McKee stole?" Pritchert asked.

"It's a new truck to replace the one she stole," he said.

"You should go on back to Washington, or wherever you live," he said to Lindsey. "You did a good job. Harrison is coming to get the two weapons at the Farm."

"I haven't packed my stuff. And that ex-KGB guy is going to come back next week, and there could be more bombs to disable. Harrison won't want me to leave until the job's completed."

"Then I'll call you when I need you," Andy said. "I'll watch out for your stuff. You need to check in with your OB doctor. Radiation couldn't be good for that baby, whoever his daddy is."

"You mean she doesn't even know who the daddy is?" Mr. Pritchert asked.

"Yes, I do know who the father is," Lindsey said, "and I've been wearing a lead apron to protect the baby. Mr. Pritchert, you can drop me off at the airport with Dr. Carlson, or you can drop me off at the alfalfa field on the Farm. But I'm not leaving. I need to take a nap."

"She's dug her heels in now, Dr. Carlson. I'd be careful," Pritchert said.

"Just take us to the airport," Andy said.

At the gate to the Farm, Andy asked, "You keep referring to this baby like you don't know if it's a boy or a girl. Wouldn't your ultrasounds have shown the baby's sex a long time ago?"

"I haven't had any ultrasounds," she said, as they passed over the covered bridge.

"Most obstetricians would have done at least three by now."

"I haven't been to an obstetrician."

In front of the farmhouse, Andy shook his head from side to side. "It's none of my business, and I know you're a nurse, but one of the most important reasons to do an ultrasound is to determine the baby's gestational age. Using the last menstrual period can be hazardous."

"I used a different technique. I knew the exact date of conception."

A cool breeze teased the hair on the back of his neck. "That's enough pregnancy update."

36

Lindsey woke up on the couch in the great room with a blanket lying across her. She could hear Andy's part of a conversation on the telephone in his study.

"Ben, this is Andy Carlson," he said. "Did you get the box of Epi-Pens I sent to your house for emergency bee stings?...I need a favor. There's a lady here who's going to have a baby soon. No matter how much I try to avoid it, I'm going to be the only doctor around. Could you borrow an emergency delivery kit from the OR that I could keep on the farm as a standby, just in case?... Ben, the more I think about it, why don't you bring a C-section kit instead. It has everything that the delivery kit has plus some extra instruments just in case."

His next call was to Henry Schein, the medical supply house in New York. He gave them his customer number, DEA number, and Virginia license number and waited for them to confirm each. Then he dictated a list of drugs and requested that they be delivered to the Farm the next day.

President Marshall greeted Harrison with a broad smile. "I believe you have some good news for me." He handed the Weasel a drink and they clicked their glasses.

"Who would have guessed that Carlson would prevent a real nuclear terrorist disaster in the United States, especially one aimed at Washington?" Harrison asked.

"I read your report," said the president. "It's a shame that Carlson has qualities which prevent him from being our long-term ally. McKee does a good job but I think she's attached to Carlson. Have you come up with a way to discredit Carlson?"

"I think so," the Weasel said.

"Boris signed his death warrant when he sold that twenty kiloton warhead to al Qaeda," the president said. "Apparently he needed to branch out to other clients because he intended to kill us all. It now appears that we have an opportunity to get Boris and two more untraceable nuclear weapons with fresh reservoirs."

"Boris has clearly outlived his usefulness," the Weasel agreed. "I'm sorry that we're going to lose access to other weapons that he has stored here in the United States."

"Once Carlson and McKee are out of the way," the president said, "we can proceed with our original plan for the Saudis."

"We might be able to set up Iran, too," the Weasel said. "They have plenty of oil. And I know you're tired of listening to that maniac president of theirs."

"How do you propose to deal with Carlson and McKee?" the president asked.

"Boris is meeting with Dr. Carlson on his farm within a week," the Weasel said. "Carlson said the next two were fifty and 100 kilotons. If we can find out exactly when this meeting is to occur, we can kill Boris while he's there. We can eliminate the doctors at the same time."

"You must be a bit more tidy this time," the president said.

37

The president was smiling as he circled his desk, talking on his private line. "Andy, I just read Harrison's report on the job that you and Dr. McKee did for this country. We're trying to keep a lid on the publicity."

"It was Dr. McKee who disabled all three weapons."

"I want you to know that I won't forget this," he said. "I understand that you plan to meet with this ex-KGB officer again."

"I think that it's better for us to buy these weapons than to let him sell them to terrorists," Andy said. "Even if we spend the $175 million he's asking, it would be a bargain. As long as he has weapons to sell, we need to keep buying. If we try to capture him now, we lose the chance to recover all of the weapons that the Soviets buried in the United States."

The president said, "I'm going to deposit the money you need in that Swiss bank account."

Andy said, "Money is a great motivator for this man. Neither Lindsey nor I want a confrontation with him. We just want to recover and disarm those weapons before they do any harm to our country."

"Please let me know when you expect Boris at your farm."

Andy hung up the phone and turned to Lindsey. "That was a disturbing conversation with the president. Two things bother me."

She was standing in the opening between the dining room and the great room, drinking hot tea.

"The president just mentioned Boris' name to me at the end of our conversation," he said. "I never gave him the name of the arms dealer. Are you sure that you didn't give the name to Harrison or to anyone else?"

"I wouldn't do anything like that without discussing it with you first."

"Then we have confirmed that the president has been involved with Boris in the past," Andy said. "There is no reason to keep a man like Boris alive unless you are using him for something. King Fahd told me that Boris sold the CIA the nuclear weapon that was on that container ship headed to Hampton Roads. That means you were lied to from the start. That weapon was never part of any al Qaeda plot, and it was not paid for by the Saudis. The president paid for it out of some CIA slush fund. And Harrison has been in on it from the start."

She picked through her purse. Andy got up to rip off a paper towel from the roll in the kitchen. He handed it to her. She blew her nose and sat down on the couch. "I'm a fool," she said. "And you have no reason to be nice to me."

"You were used. They knew you were vulnerable because of your parents and your brother."

He sat next to her, reached over and lifted her chin to force eye contact with him. She shuddered. They both remembered the last time he had done that. "There's another fight coming," he said. "It's going to be a big one. No matter what happens, I want you to know that I'm through being angry at you."

She smiled. "You said that there were two important things wrong with your conversation with the president."

"The president wanted me to give him the time when Boris would arrive on the Farm," Andy said. "The last time that we met Boris on the Farm, he didn't ask for that information."

"Then there is some significance to his question," Lindsey said.

"The president knows that it was Boris who sold that third nuclear weapon at the Farm to al Qaeda. He knows that the two terrorists intended to incinerate Washington with it. He has a report from Harrison on the incident at the juncture of Highway 45 and Highway 60."

"Boris tried to kill the president," she said. "If I were the president,

I wouldn't want to trade money for weapons anymore. I think the president knows he must kill Boris as soon as possible. And he needs to know the exact time of Boris' arrival because he intends to have him killed here."

"There is another issue we must deal with," Andy said. "The president knows that he will get no more untraceable nuclear weapons from Boris. He'll want these two before you have a chance to disable them. Boris likely doesn't know what happened to the two al Qaeda terrorists, since we took great pains to suppress their ambulance ride."

"And Boris probably had no idea of the timing of the al Qaeda attack on Washington," she said.

"So Boris may not appreciate that the president knows of the warhead sent to kill him," Andy said. "We'll know that for sure if he sends us another email."

She said, "Boris won't abandon the gold unless he knows that the president is gunning for him."

"There's one other thing that we need to discuss," Andy said.

She straightened up and put her hand on his arm. "I was hoping that you would figure it out on your own."

She could tell her hand made him uncomfortable. She withdrew it.

Andy said, "Initially, the president thought that you were dead and no longer a risk to him. Then he kept you alive to pacify me, fearful that I might encourage the Saudis to choke America's share of Saudi oil. Granted, we both proved useful to him. But after Boris is dead and he has the warheads he wants, he'll have no use for anyone who can document his past scheme or interpret any future schemes based on faked terrorist plots. I suspect he's cooked up some way to discredit us both."

"Are you saying you think he'll try to kill us, too?" Lindsey asked. "I thought we were going to talk about the baby."

"The baby will have to wait, Lindsey. If the president plans to send a truckload of commandos onto the Farm to take Boris and his two nuclear weapons, and he has any concern for our welfare, he would include us in the plan. He intends for us to get caught in the crossfire."

"That's a nice way of saying that killing us *is* part of his plan," Lindsey said. "And us includes the baby."

"Let's go back to the piece of information that he wanted, the exact time of Boris's arrival," Andy said. "He needs to time his arrival exactly. He wants to be sure that Boris actually has the two weapons with him at the Farm. And he wants to get here before you have time to disable them."

"Doesn't Harrison monitor the account that the CIA set up for us to transfer money to Boris?" she asked.

"Correct. And a timely observation. They will wait until the transfer of the money out of that account before attacking."

"But Boris is getting paid in gold--at least, he thinks he is," she said.

"Neither the president nor Harrison know anything about the gold," Andy said. "We can manipulate the time that Harrison shows up by transferring the money from one Swiss account to another."

"What other Swiss account?" she asked.

"The one you are about to open by wire transfer from my personal account," he said. "Let's open the Keystroke program on my laptop and reconstruct Boris' bank web site, his account number, and his password. As soon as he steps on the Farm, you can clean out his account and deposit it in your new account. Then when we're ready for the arrival of the feds, you can transfer $175 million out of the feds' Swiss account into the new Swiss account."

"Where would I do this?" Lindsey asked.

"From my laptop inside the Grand Chamber of the cave after Boris arrives. Just plug it into the side of the table in the living room. A Wi-Fi antenna is on top of the garage."

"What do you plan to do with the two weapons?" she asked.

"I think that the president wants those weapons before they're disabled, and so do I," he said. "These warheads of Boris' are the most untraceable of all. They're not on any Soviet list of weapons to be dismantled. The Russians don't want to admit that they planted nuclear weapons inside our country thirty years ago. This president has no reason not to return to his original plan with the Saudis once we're dead. He's burned his bridges with King Fahd, anyway. Every Arab country with any oil has terrorists in it. He could manufacture other plots to steal oil."

"You're not suggesting keeping nuclear weapons that have not been disarmed here on the Farm?" she asked.

"You can remove the tritium reservoirs and we can store them separately in the cave. Neither of us have a use for these weapons now, but how do you know that we won't need them in the future?"

"We? You mean me and the baby?"

Andy shrugged.

"Why do we need all that money?" she asked.

"To kill future snakes like Harrison and give the rest of the country a chance against government. Also, your kid might need braces some day. I could help."

38

Lindsey and Andy were eating supper that evening when a car drove into the driveway and stopped in front of the farmhouse door. Andy went out to meet Ben, who handed him a large, flat package wrapped in blue plastic. Andy placed this package in the bed of the Kubota diesel. Later that evening the UPS truck delivered two identical cardboard boxes to the door. Andy put these boxes into the bed of the Kubota, as well.

"I need to run some supplies down to the garage," he said. "Could you check the computer and see if we have an answer yet?"

Lindsey watched through the window of the great room as Andy drove down the path toward the garage. She sat down at the computer in Andy's study and immediately spotted the message.

From: 1917 USSR
To: R.E.L.

I have a fifty KT and a 100 KT which I will trade for $175,000,000 in gold bars. The reservoirs are new. Can we meet soon? I will have to bring a heavy truck to support the weight and several friends to help with the loading. They can all be trusted. Please confirm.

When Andy returned from the garage, Lindsey pointed out the new message.

Andy sat down and clicked on "Reply."

"Can you hand me a calendar?" he asked. "There's one on the coffee table in the great room."

Andy looked at the calendar and said, "The third Saturday in February is four days away."

"Why are you interested in the third Saturday in February?" she asked.

"Things are usually really noisy around here on that day," he said. Andy typed:

From: R.E.L.
To: 1917 USSR

I can meet you at 6:00 in the morning on the third Saturday in February, four days from now. $175,000,0000 in gold is acceptable.

He clicked "Send."

Boris must have been sitting at his computer. There was a reply within two minutes.

From: 1917 USSR
To: R.E.L.

Affirmative.

Andy pulled out the card with the president's number on it.

"President Marshall, it's Andy Carlson."

"Did Boris answer?"

"The exchange is on for Saturday morning."

"I had Harrison deposit another $175 million in the Swiss account. What time did you say he would be there?"

"Six in the morning."

The president hung up immediately.

"This fight's going to get ugly," Andy said. "A crowd of snakes is gathering."

There was a good reason to choose this Saturday morning for the Second Battle of Carlson Farm. The third Saturday in February was one of two days each year that every policeman and correctional officer in three counties had to qualify at the Farmville outdoor shooting range with pistols, automatic rifles, and shotguns. The range was across the Appomattox River from Sandy Ford. Usually Andy made it a point to be out of town on this day.

Saturday would sound like the last time the Farm was invaded, in the first week of April of 1865. How appropriate. There would be no police cars screaming to the Farm to find out what all the firing was about. There was one more little touch.

He looked in the Farmville phone book and called the editor of the *Farmville Herald*, Ken Dudley.

"Ken, it's Andy Carlson. You remember every year about this time I let the Marines come over to my farm and blow up all the logjams in the river?"

"They coming anytime soon?"

"I asked them to come on Saturday because I figured the day was ruined anyway, with all that firing down at the firing range," he said. "Do you think you could get a notice into Friday's paper about the blasting along the river, so people will stay away and nobody will be upset?"

"We can do that," Ken said. "And you're right; the timing's perfect."

"You might mention that they'll probably arrive by helicopter. They want to combine their demolitions practice with an all-day war game. Why don't you just take out a big ad and charge it to me?" Andy asked.

"Something like this is a public service for us," Ken said. "We want people to know what's going on and you're just helping us do our job. The canoeists and the kayakers will be thrilled that they will finally be able to get past those spots on the river that are blocked by stumps and trees. I'll just write a brief story and advise folks to stay away from the river on Saturday and ignore the blasting and the firing. I'll call the story **Whole lotta shakin' going on Saturday.**

Before going to bed that evening, on separate ends of the house, Lindsey wanted more specifics about Saturday morning.

"Andy," she said, "you said that you wanted me to wait in the Grand Chamber and transfer Boris' money after he gets here. How are the nuclear weapons going to get into the cave?"

"I'll suggest that Boris load them onto the Kubota RTV and then use it to haul out the gold," he said. "Would the Kubota hold two weapons like a fifty kiloton and 100 kiloton?"

"I think so," she said.

"Then you should wait until the weapons are unloaded in the anteroom, and the gold is loaded into the Kubota, and the Kubota drives up the ramp and out of the building. That's when you transfer all the money from Boris' account to our new account. After that transfer, move the $175 million from the CIA Swiss account to our account."

"How will I know when to close the vault?" she asked.

"I'm going to try to get everybody out of the cave with the Kubota," he said. "If there is anyone left in the gold room, blow the gold room entrance. Lock the vault behind me. Blow the entrance to the Grand Chamber if there's anyone left in the cave. I plan to disable the Kubota before it can get too far."

"But where will you go?" she asked.

"My plan is to head for the swamp when the fireworks start," he said. "You should plan to stay in the Grand Chamber until I return. You have a wide variety of weapons to choose from."

"But what if something happens to you?" she asked.

"If I'm not back within six hours, then I'm probably dead. You should anticipate staying in the cave indefinitely. You have everything that you need there."

"What about my baby?"

"If you go into labor, call 911 from the cave and meet the ambulance in front of the house," he said. "They'll take you to Southside Community Hospital. Is this your first baby?"

"Of course it's my first baby," she said.

"Then you should have plenty of time after you go into labor."

The corners of her mouth turned down. Over the past few weeks Lindsey had come to fear that her mental faculties were declining. It was as if the baby were eating her brain cells. She imagined her brain as mush. Usually, she was sure of what to do. Now she felt tentative about everything.

The approaching birth of the baby heightened her sense of unease and insecurity. She had no nursery. There were no baby clothes or diapers. There were no expectant mother magazines back in her apartment in Washington. There had been no meticulous planning about the delivery. She didn't know whether she wanted an epidural or not. She had no obstetrician. She had requested three months leave from work. That was the extent of her planning.

Denial is the most basic form of emotional defense that a human being has. It's so easy to recognize in someone else.

One of the things that Lindsey thought would not be a problem for her was the lack of a husband. After all, she had always been self-reliant and confident. Until now.

Andy made her feel safe. He was so confident. He was a doctor. He was a fearless warrior. He was a complete idiot. It never occurred to him that her primary mission here was not to disarm nuclear weapons. Andy already had so much to worry about. She would have to wait for the right moment.

39

After breakfast on Thursday morning, Andy pointed out the urgency of their mission that day.

"There are a couple of entrances to the cave system that we need to identify before this fight," he said. "Since my dad died, I lost my enthusiasm for mapping out all the tunnels and entrances. Now we need these for interior lines."

"Then let's do it," she said. "One more biscuit for the baby."

A steady wind was blowing out of the west. To Andy, the Farm longed for the end of grey days and the color and promise of spring. They turned right out of the driveway and drove toward the plantation house in the Kubota. After 150 yards a huge Dominion power line crossed the road. Andy stopped.

"I've mapped the tunnel from the Grand Chamber as far as right here, approximately underneath this road. That's the 1743 mansion house just ahead. My family must have had an entrance to the cave system from that house."

"Why do you think that?"

"My grandmother and my mother were great canners. They put away enough stuff from our garden that we ate good vegetables year round. They seemed to produce all of this stuff out of thin air. Grandma always referred to the *root cellar* but she never showed me any root cellar. She could always come up with some special dessert if a relative showed up unannounced. I knew she had a hiding place, but I couldn't find it."

"Normally, I like treasure hunts," she said, "but I would just as soon we finished this up before the shooting starts."

The plantation house was an all-white two-story wooden mansion.

The horizontal oak siding had originally been covered with a paint made from milk, but white latex protected the petrified wood now. The window shutters, now vinyl, were painted to match the green tin roof. Four white square columns supported the central two-story portico and its gabled green tin roof.

Both the first and second stories had symmetrical picketed porches extending to the left and right of the portico columns, with three more columns on each side of the portico, allowing the porches to wrap around the front corners. Each floor had double doors facing the front and rear of the house underneath the portico. Brick chimneys towered above the apex of the green tin roof on each side of the mansion. A cupola sat astride the long axis of the roof between the chimneys and could accommodate three people.

During the Civil War a slave was stationed in the cupola, watching for the dust of approaching horses. Slaves were acutely aware that they were not immune to scavengers, who used the war as an excuse to rape, loot, and burn. This mansion was a lucky anachronism, having survived over 270 years of weather and wars.

Andy found the key to the main door of the plantation house underneath the front stoop. They walked up the five steps that led to the first floor porch and the double doors of the entrance. He opened the door on the right side with the key and stepped into the high ceiling foyer underneath the portico. Lindsey followed.

A spiral staircase ascended from the left side of the breezeway in a clockwise fashion to the second floor, where it continued a full circle to the left side of the second floor. A closet at the top of the stairs hid the steps up to the cupola. The three foot diameter crystal chandelier overhead no longer sported candles, but white candle holders with electric Christmas tree lights.

Andy took off his jacket and placed it on the "nervous bench" on the right side of the breezeway between the doors to the parlor and the dining room. On this bench sat the male suitors of Carlson girls in the eighteenth, nineteenth, and twentieth centuries. The chandelier blocked the gentleman's view of the girl's descent until she had made the turn and was facing him. The matriarch stood at the top of the stairs, assuring that the girl was appropriately attired and that the young man waited a suitable period of time. Even before he reached the "nervous bench," the young man was forced to walk the gauntlet of brothers sitting on the porch. Each brother focused his best scowl on the pretender and enjoyed every minute of it.

In the far right corner of the breezeway was an oak roll-top desk and leather chair, where the business of the plantation had been conducted. Above the desk was an oil painting of Francis Cornelius Carlson, Andy's great-grandfather. He had worn his grey Sunday suit and black string bowtie, turning his head slightly to highlight the family chin, his right hand on his hip. Andy recognized as a child that the pose was identical to the family's portrait of General R. E. Lee, which hung in the parlor.

The right front corner of the downstairs breezeway had a triangular-shaped cabinet. In the bottom drawer of this cabinet was the box of arrowheads and other Indian artifacts found by generations of Carlsons on the Farm. Whenever visiting children came, the matriarch would pull out the box of arrowheads. When it was time to go, she would say to the children, "Thank you so much for coming and would you please put all of grandma's arrowheads back?"

Long-faced children trudged out to their carriage wondering how she could possibly have known what was in their pockets.

Upstairs were four bedrooms, two on each side. Downstairs, the door to the master bedroom was at the foot of the spiral staircase. The right side of the second floor had a parlor, a large dining room, and a modern kitchen. The table in the dining room seated sixteen. There were no bathrooms in the original mansion, only chamber pots underneath each bed. Because the rooms were so large, it had been easy to add three modern bathrooms.

The round rail of the staircase had been made from only three thin ash trees. These had been soaked in the river and gradually bent into shape. This rail was supported by white pickets and continued the green theme of the shutters, roof, and doors. The floor was polished heart pine, each piece eight inches in diameter, assembled with pegs.

When Lindsey stepped into the foyer her protuberant abdomen brushed against the door frame. The sensation didn't feel quite right. She tried to find her belly button. Her uterus had a tight feeling. There was no pain. She moved her hand around the entire front of her abdomen. It felt tight all over.

"Let's move on before something happens," she said.

Andy looked at her and noted the position of her hand on her abdomen. "Are you okay?"

"I'm fine. I'm just thinking we need to find these cave openings as soon as possible."

"You're not having contractions, are you?"

"Of course not. I'm sure," she lied and removed her hand.

"What if James Carlson, the man who built this house in 1743, chose this site because there was a cave entrance here?" Andy asked. "There would be lots of reasons to build a house above the entrance to a cave. Remember that the Farm had a large Indian settlement on it when the Carlsons got here. If the cave entrance were hidden, then the family would have a great place to hide if there was an attack."

"We could have used the cave to hide from the Indians, or the British, or the Yankees, or scavengers. There would be good reason to keep it a secret. A cave would make an ideal place to store food and canned goods, since the temperature at ten feet into the ground is about fifty degrees."

"I didn't know that," she said.

They strolled into the parlor.

"Did you do all of the restoration in this house, Andy?"

"I have an industrious aunt and uncle. They did all this work," he said. "The house was built in two sections. The first part, the portico and the right side of the house, were built first. The part to the left of the breezeway was added several years later. That's an important point, I think. If there is a cave entrance it's going to be underneath the oldest part of the house, and the entrance is probably going to be on the level of the basement."

"I didn't realize that houses this old had basements," she said.

"It wasn't a basement like we build today, with concrete blocks and a concrete floor," he said. "Let's go back into the breezeway. The spiral staircase leads up to the newer part of the house on the left. The basement was really a small room underneath the breezeway, and the entrance to it is behind the staircase."

He pointed toward a small door. "Before the second part of this house was built, this staircase wasn't here, so there must have been a hole in the floor with some kind of hinges on it."

"It looks like a small closet."

"And there's nothing but a stout ladder on the other side of that door. If there's a cave entrance underneath this house, I think it's in that basement."

He opened the door. "We have one pull light overhead, but let's get some flashlights out of the kitchen."

Andy walked back into the kitchen and brought back two flashlights.

"Are you sure that I can get out of there once I get in?" she asked.

"I think so. There's two cellar doors facing the back of the house. We could unlock them if we had to."

Andy went down the ladder first and stopped at the bottom, pulling the chain on the light as he went.

"You can come on down," he said. "The ladder is made out of cedar. It'll never rot. Just hold on with your hands and back down."

The basement had a dirt floor. All of the walls were dirt and lined with ten gallon metal milk cans. Metal milk cans came into use after the Civil War. Dairymen had to transport their milk into town every day. These cans were antiques now. The narrow necks flared downward to wider bodies. The lids fit inside the necks and made good seats. Andy's cans had "Carlson" stamped on the lids.

Eight massive oak posts supported the floor joists of the breezeway. Andy and Lindsey aimed their flashlight beams around the room.

"Any entrance would have to face that way, to the north," he pointed, "because the ground slopes off toward the river, to the south. Somewhere in that wall must be a hidden entrance."

"But there isn't anything on that wall but dirt with a few milk cans in front of it," she said.

Andy stood back and stared at the wall. "If the entrance isn't in that wall, it could be in the floor in front of the wall. Hand me that spade over there in the corner. It's been there all my life."

Andy was already on his knees pushing dirt away from the center of the floor when Lindsey handed him the spade. He stood up and stepped on the blade, which came to an abrupt halt after only four inches. "We've found something."

Andy carefully shoveled the dirt from the center of the floor.

"Do you hear that sound when the spade hit bottom?" he asked. "That's the sound of wood with nothing underneath it."

Within twenty minutes Lindsey and Andy were looking at a 270-year old cedar door, three feet by four feet, with a brass ring and leather hinges.

"This hatch explains one more thing," Andy said. "Why should the door leading to this basement have a lock on the inside?" He looked up to the open door at the top of the ladder.

"Grandma always told me it was because Granddaddy didn't want us kids messing with the cream separator down here. Selling milk and cream was an important source of income for the Carlsons when I was a kid."

Andy grabbed the brass ring and the door swung up to lean against the north wall of the basement. "It's light enough for a woman to lift."

"I don't think I could get out of that trap door," she said.

"Then hold the flashlight and point it down into the opening for me."

"I see a ladder down there," she said.

He stuck his flashlight in his pocket and backed down the ladder in the hole while Lindsey shined her flashlight on the steps.

Andy looked up at the flashlight above him. "I don't know where this is going to lead, but give me thirty minutes before you panic. Try out one of my milk cans for a seat."

At the base of the ladder, Andy's flashlight found a second ladder pointed ninety degrees from the ladder he descended. Both ladders were in a short tunnel. The second ladder disappeared into the red limestone ceiling. Why were two ladders necessary?

On the opposite side of the second ladder Andy noted that steps had been chiseled into the limestone floor. He descended ten steps into a chamber the size of a one-car garage. The stalagmites and stalactites had been hacked away in this room and the remnants removed. Limestone caves don't gather dust. On the right were shelves of canned goods and jars. Some were labeled. Whiskey jars were dated from 1743 to 1956. He recognized sorghum and honey. On the left was a large bed.

Andy sat down on the bed. It was a feather mattress, covered with brown homespun. A white sheet was folded neatly at the foot of the bed. He bounced a couple of times to confirm the look of comfort. On the bedside table to the right of the bed was a pewter candle holder with a half-burned candle. He lit the candle and watched as the room came alive. The rust-colored ceiling sparkled from the reflection of the flame on the patches of white and blue limestone. He kicked a jar at his feet, a canning jar with a wide mouth, half full of clear liquid.

There was no doubt what this room was for. As a boy he had wondered where his parents disappeared at night. They reappeared smiling, saying what a nice walk they had. How many generations had pulled this on their kids? What a gig for pious Presbyterians, who refused to touch each other during the daytime.

For a moment he lay back and looked at the show. If only things were different with Lindsey. Maybe if Sahar was ten years older. No, fifteen years older. He swung his legs over the side and saw the map. The pewter candle holder was sitting on a leather map. He picked it up and moved the light over the drawings. There were several colors of ink. The map clearly identified the house, as well as connections to tunnels north of the house. The room he was in was labeled "sparkle." This map would require further evaluation in good light. He rolled it up and placed it on the bed.

Leaving "sparkle" with the candle still lit on the table, Andy proceeded north with his flashlight through another tunnel. He was able to walk upright without obstructions because someone had removed the stalactites overhead and the stalagmites on the floor. The passageway was narrow because the walls were lined with anything that needed to be kept out of sight.

Leaning against one wall were a bed stone and a grinding stone for the mill. A three foot diameter saw blade with wooden axle caught his eye. Folded next to it was the six-inch wide horse-hair belt that connected the wooden axle of the blade with the vertical axle of the grist mill in the eighteenth century or the back wheel of the Willis Overland car in the early twentieth century.

Andy looked at his watch. Fifteen minutes already. He knew he didn't have time to stroll down memory lane.

An anvil sat next to a brick mold. A long row of wooden boxes with rope handles held treasures from days gone by. The first box held the family silverware and china. Other boxes had sewing needles, bars of homemade soap, horseshoes, nails, tools, candles, serving utensils and dishes, silver pitchers, and chamber pots. Sealed glass jars held coffee, salt, and tobacco. Another box held plantation records.

It was a nineteenth century garage sale, which ended with larger items—a rocking chair, a plowshare, a copper still, a two-horse cultivator, a cast iron stove, and a spinning wheel. Even a piano and an organ had been disassembled and packed in boxes cushioned with cotton and covered with leather hides.

During the Civil War Virginia plantation owners lived in fear of raids by Union cavalry and lawless bands of deserters called scavengers. Since John Andrew Carlson had so much underground storage space, he had wisely hidden as much as he could. After the war, there was a need to look impoverished to keep carpetbaggers and beggars away. He had seen the war coming, and he was determined to hold on to what was his.

When John Andrew put his treasures in the caves, he didn't intend for them to stay there. He died two months after the war ended in 1865, his wife said from a broken heart. The Confederacy was lost. Some of his secrets went into his grave. Others went into the caves and never came out.

Andy pressed on, following the light back into time, down a rusty-colored tunnel more than fifty yards, to another chamber. He stood in the doorway and shined the light around. The room was a shrine of Carlson honor. On a walnut table were five officer swords, carefully lined up with matching gloves. The first sword belonged to James Carlson, who fought in the Revolutionary War and built the portico and right side of the plantation house. The other four belonged to John Andrew's children: James, Francis, Nathan, and Thomas. Each was engraved. All four sons were Colonels. Francis was killed at Gettysburg, under the command of General A.P. Hill, on the third day. Nathan died at Saylor's Creek, less than a week before the end of the war and only a few miles from his home in Cumberland County. Their swords were sent home.

James and Thomas were Confederate Colonels, commanding regiments under General Joseph E. Johnston, who was their neighbor in

Farmville before the War. Johnston had been several years ahead of the Carlson brothers at West Point, but they knew each other well. General R. E. Lee had surrendered the Army of Northern Virginia on the ninth of April at Appomattox Court House, twenty-five miles from the Farm. Johnston surrendered in North Carolina on April 26, 1865. When surrounded on that day, the two Carlson Colonels refused to surrender their swords. They proposed to the Union general that they be allowed to fight any Yankee of any rank to the death. The Union general decided that such men should not die for a lost cause. He accepted their pistols instead.

A separate table was dedicated to Carlson warriors in WWI, WWII, and Viet Nam. His family seemed to have missed the Korean War. Andy's great-grandfather Francis had served as an artillery officer in General Pershing's Expeditionary Force of WWI. His grandfather Charles was an Army Ranger who landed on Omaha Beach on June 6, 1944.

Andy's father George had left his knife and his Special Forces Green Beret uniform from his two tours in Viet Nam. Andy knew about the purple heart, but he had never seen his dad's Bronze Star or Silver Star. Each table had pictures, uniforms, hats, medals, helmets, pistols, and knives. No Carlson left a record of battles won or lost. Neither his father nor his grandfather ever talked to him about their wars, but they would talk about their ancestor's wars.

Andy realized that he could spend hours studying these things. He looked at his watch. He had been gone thirty minutes already. He hurried to the next chamber, where he found at least two hundred 1860 Enfield rifles, rubbed down with vegetable oil, stacked and ready to go. There were boxes of Civil War paper cartridges, antiques now.

Another tunnel beckoned him, but the air was getting stale. After twenty yards the chamber opened up to his flashlight. Andy was accustomed to seeing stacks of gold bars by now. He counted the number of bars in each row, the number of rows, the number of layers. 200 bars.

John Andrew had spread the Confederate Gold around. But who could have carried all this to this chamber? There must be another entrance nearby, away from the house. Lindsey would be worried by now.

He hurried back, thinking about the last days of the Civil War. Over 1000 rifles had been found on the Carlson plantation the day after General Lee retreated from Cumberland Church, across the Farm, and on to Appomattox. Most of these guns were not accompanied by a dead soldier. They had been abandoned by starving, barefoot, exhausted Confederate soldiers, who knew the war was lost. The sight of the swollen Appomattox River prompted many a lonesome war-weary country boy to slip into the woods and head for home.

Andy's grandfather had complained that as a boy he had been given the job of driving a team of mules and a wagon around the plantation to pick up all the half-buried rifles, bayonets, and knives. Too many laborers were getting hurt. He had told Andy that he couldn't plow fifty feet without running into the sharp edge of some weapon.

Eight hundred of these rifles were buried behind the plantation house in a shallow grave. The rest went into the cave. During WWII the United States needed all the metal it could find. So grandpa got to dig up all those rifles again. They were melted down and used for modern weapons. Not exactly beating swords into plowshares. At that time there were so many Civil War relics in Virginia, nobody thought they held any value.

When he reached the "sparkle" room, Andy's flashlight caught a wooden box underneath the bed. He pulled it out. Something precious was wrapped in homespun. He unwound the cloth and there it was—the violin that Martha Carlson had played for George Washington and Lafayette in this house, on more than one occasion. Martha's husband James had been a captain and an aide to General Washington. Because Martha spoke French, Lafayette enjoyed visiting the plantation during the lull in fighting during the winters.

Martha was the most requested violinist at the weddings of prominent

Virginians. When James' daughter Suzannah married, Lafayette had wiped his eyes after Martha's performance. She was accompanied by a young slave girl, whom she had taught to play the piano and organ.

None of this was surprising to Andy, or all that remarkable. If your family had lived in Virginia since 1635, you probably knew anybody who had two shillings to rub together. James Madison and Patrick Henry were the neighbors of James Carlson on the south side of Sandy Ford and Peter Francisco his neighbor to the north of the plantation. He replaced the violin and picked up the map on the bed.

When he reached the ladders, Andy heard voices overhead.

40

Lindsey felt her belly. The tightness had gone. She looked at her watch. Andy had been in the cave entrance for twenty-five minutes. The top of the metal milk can she was sitting on didn't provide quite enough room for her current circumstances.

She startled at the creaking of the pine heart floor above her. Someone was walking across the breezeway. She couldn't cry out. She couldn't climb into the hole. Andy hadn't unlocked the cellar doors facing the rear of the house. Her mush brain had convinced her not to carry a weapon. Whoever was above her would find the open door if he looked behind the spiral staircase. The only tool available to her was the shovel. She eased herself to a standing position and reached for it.

"Andy," a pleasant voice called.

She didn't respond.

"Andy, it's Ben. I got your message."

A drop of something dripped off her nose or out of it as she sat back down and wiped her face with her sleeve. "We're down here, Ben."

A middle-aged, light-skinned black male stuck his head around the corner of the doorway and looked at her, then the open hatch in the floor.

"Andy in that hole?"

"Yes, he is. He should be back any minute."

"Do you mind if I come down?" he asked.

"Not at all. Andy's told me about you. You're the man who helped him build Fortress Farmville."

"Your name wouldn't be Lindsey, would it?"

"Yes, it is. Pardon my manners."

Ben backed down the stairs and extended his hand to Lindsey, who smiled and reached for it.

"A million years sure went by fast," he said.

Lindsey decided to pass on the remark.

Ben sat down on the dirt floor, turned one of the milk cans on its side, and stuck it behind his back against the wall.

"Andy never mentioned that you were the pregnant lady here."

"He didn't know about the pregnancy until a short time ago."

Be careful, she thought.

Ben nodded. There was something about his face.

"He still doesn't know he's the father," she said.

Shut up, you idiot.

"Paternity issues run in his family, ma'am."

What could he mean by that?

They heard a noise above them. Andy was standing in the doorway.

"Cousin Ben," Andy said. "How are you?"

"I'm fine. I was gettin' to know Lindsey while you were down there."

"Thanks for coming over on such short notice."

"How'd you get up there anyway?" Ben asked.

"There's another stairway from the tunnel that comes out in an armoire in the master bedroom. Why don't you close that hatch and spread some dirt over it while I pull Lindsey up this ladder?"

My mush brain thought he called Ben his cousin.

Seated on the steps in front of the plantation house, Andy spread out the leather map on the porch.

"This is a map of the entire cave system on the Farm," Andy said. "I recognize the parts that I've already surveyed. Many of my ancestors have apparently added information to the map, since there's several ink colors. The chambers are named."

He put his index finger on the map. "This is the plantation house."

Ben and Lindsey twisted their heads around.

He turned the map to face them. "Let's orient the map toward my house, which is northwest of the mansion. Look at this other building, about a hundred yards from where we're sitting."

"It's that old barn. I can see from here," Lindsey said. "It has a big G on the map."

"And there are two more Gs," Andy said. "This one is in the gold room next to the Grand Chamber. I've never been in this tunnel to the east, but it has a G on it."

Ben pointed. "Here's the tunnel from the old slave quarters to Dry Creek and Little Round Top. We already knew it didn't connect with any other part of the cave system."

The elevations were recorded on the map, indicating that some tunnels were as shallow as fifty feet below ground level while others were as deep as 300 feet, to the level of the Appomattox River. The height of each chamber and tunnel was recorded. Some were only a few feet high. The map maker apparently turned around when a tunnel was too shallow, or there wasn't enough good air to breathe. He marked these tunnels with an X.

"This map is priceless," Lindsey said.

"It is to us," Andy said. "Imagine moving unseen in the battle to come."

"You expecting company," Ben asked.

"This Saturday we're hosting mercenaries and arms dealers. Neither party wants to see us survive the weekend."

"Where do you want me?" Ben asked.

"That's mighty gracious of you, buddy, but you've already helped me get ready. We knew this was coming. It's not your fight. You've got a wife and a family. I don't."

Is now the time?

"I left a package and some papers for you on the table in my house," Andy said. "You can pick them up on your way out. I wanted to be sure that you and your family enjoyed a nice piece of this Farm forever, and had the money to build a house. You'd mess up my plans if you got killed."

Ben looked at Lindsey and back at Andy. "If that's what you want. Let me know if you change your mind. And good luck."

They shook hands.

As he drove away, Lindsey said, "We could have used his help."

"He'll be here."

"But you just told him not to come."

"Didn't you see how easily he gave up? He knows I'd never ask him to risk his life for me."

"How will you coordinate your movements?" she asked.

"We won't need to. He's an expert with a .50 cal. heavy machine gun. Ben will hold his fire until he can hurt our enemies the most. Let's get back to the house and see how we can use the new information we have."

Before they could get into the RTV Andy's cell phone rang.

"Andy, it's T. That plane is about to take off."

"Thanks, buddy."

"There's a drone coming over those trees to the northwest in about half a minute," Andy said.

"Should we hide?"

"Let's walk out in the yard so they can get a good look at us."

The small plane appeared on cue.

"I'd like you to call your boss Harrison tonight," Andy said. "Tell him everything is set up for Saturday. You and I are tolerating each other. You'll let him know when the warheads are disarmed. This will give him one more chance to show his intentions."

As they watched the plane make a wide turn along the river, Andy said, "I really would like for the Weasel to be here himself on Saturday. I'm going into town and call Sahar from a pay phone. I'll ask her to call me at my house tonight and say she's coming for a visit this weekend."

Lindsey casually felt her belly again. The tightness was back. "You don't want her here with all this going on?"

"Of course not. Harrison is probably listening to every phone call to the farmhouse. He wants Sahar. I'll give her a script to read tonight from another pay phone. She's a great actress. And she has her own reasons to hate him. If Harrison thinks she's coming Friday night, he'll want to be here on Saturday."

41

Spreading the leather map out on the dining room table next to his own survey, Andy smiled. "I was right about the Indian settlement, the one that has all of those burial mounds in rows just above Sandy Ford," he said.

Lindsey watched him study the map as she walked around the room. Walking didn't seem to affect the tightness. The contractions didn't seem to be getting stronger, or lasting longer, or coming more frequently than every twenty minutes. But they were terrifying. What if she delivered her baby and wasn't even here to help Andy on Saturday?

"Let's name the main north-south tunnel that runs from the garage and the Grand Chamber all the way south to the plantation house Interstate 95. So if I said go north on I-95, you would know what I meant."

Lindsey sat down, nodded, and felt her belly under the table. No contraction.

"Then let's call this tunnel that runs east-west to the Indian settlement Interstate 40," he said. "The western entrance to I-40 must be in one of those Indian mounds. The Indians got smooth rocks from the Appomattox River next to their settlement and piled them on top of their graves. If we can locate this entrance, either from the tunnel side or from the outside, we would have an important advantage against the two groups coming here to kill us."

"We need to make up for our lack of numbers somehow," she said.

"I'm working on that," Andy said. "First we need to go to Wal-Mart. I want to pick up one of those bullhorns operated by compressed air, the kind that city folks are supposed to take in their backpacks in case they get lost."

They talked on the drive to Wal-Mart.

"Tomorrow we ride to the Indian settlement and the Indian burial mounds just above Sandy Ford, on the Appomattox River, to find the western entrance to I-40."

"How would you use it?"

"It's disorienting to your enemy when you pop up behind his lines with silent weapons. It's even more terrifying to have your flanks assaulted by someone you can't see or hear. We could create panic."

Andy reviewed his shopping list. "I'd like to get several miner's lights from sporting goods. They have them with LEDs now, for blood tracking at night. And I want a box of those LED flares that last a hundred hours, and a bullhorn."

They pulled into the Farmville Wal-Mart Supercenter. "While we're here," Andy said, "Why don't you pick up some Pampers, baby wipes, simple baby clothes, and some other baby stuff?"

"I thought that you didn't want to think about this baby."

"I don't, but you've made that baby my responsibility until this fight is over."

42

Early Friday morning Andy drove the Kubota down the hill to the covered bridge. Once inside, he uncovered the weapons. Standing in the bed of the RTV, he slid these across the rafters, where they would not be seen by satellites or drones. It was thirty degrees and clear, with little wind. To his northwest, Willis Mountain was a leafless mass of gray humps. The hardwoods offered little cover for men or animals in February. In addition to the lack of cover in stands of oak, the dead leaves were too noisy to walk in.

Andy planned to follow the lead of the deer during winter, moving like ghosts through the fallen pine needles. But there was work to be done this chilly morning in the hardwoods on either side of the road leading from the gate to the covered bridge. He pushed a hammer stapler into his jacket pocket and dragged two pieces of cardboard at a time into the woods.

After orienting each cardboard figure properly, he stapled them to a tree. Moving across an area he called the Briar Patch, to the left of the covered bridge, he created a small army of cardboard figures. Each figure was partially obscured by another tree, a bush, or a rock. Satisfied with the dozen new volunteers, he returned to the Kubota front seat for the trip wires and C4 charges.

Walking back into the woods of the Brier Patch, Andy turned uphill and located a spot where the figures looked like real Andy Carlsons, complete with automatic weapons. Here he attached the charges at knee height onto six trees, all connected by clear monofilament nylon. One person running through the Briar Patch would trip all six charges.

On the right side of the road to the covered bridge, at the base of

Little Round Top, Andy arranged the same cardboard figures of himself. He did not use C4 charges.

The next stop was the back swamp, a fifty acre wildlife refuge which accompanied the Appomattox River and protected the left flank of the Farm. He stood in thigh-deep water with a backpack on. Only SEALS and beavers were acclimated for this kind of work. He walked back and forth from a box of C4 charges wedged in the fork of an alder tree, tying explosive charges underwater to the trunks of small trees. The trip wires ran underwater across openings to another tree. All trip lines ran east-west between openings, but each had to be tripped individually.

He planted twenty charges, then walked into the center of the swamp and took off his shirt and jacket. He arranged them on a bush about fifty yards past the first line of charges. The deer and beaver would likely smell the shirt and stay out of the area. Humans would be shooting at the jacket.

Two grenades were left in each of six beaver hutches, along with a stick bow and four arrows. Diving underwater into the artificial beaver hutch at the mouth of the tunnel up to the anteroom, Andy left a miner's helmet, two grenades, an LED flare, and a loaded SIG Sauer.

Walking up the grade out of the swamp and toward the garage, he reviewed the path he would take running into the swamp. He would use the same combination of ditches and cedar trees that he always used while bow hunting. Someone might get a glimpse of him if he wanted them to, but not in time to hit him with anything. He was satisfied that the back swamp was ready.

As he worked, he became more aware of his unease that Lindsey was here. She did insist on it. He had given her opportunities to leave. He could use her help. What was it that gave him pause at this late hour? It was that extra life that he was using as a prop. Once he had fully absorbed her condition, he had tuned out images of possible fathers, just as he had learned to tune out pain, or weather, or grief when necessary. Men are just as susceptible to denial as women.

He returned to the farmhouse, then loaded the Kubota with the leather map, a shovel, a box of grenades, a box of LED flares, a couple of pistols, a miner's hat, and the bullhorn. Lindsey climbed into the Kubota with some difficulty, and they drove down behind his farm house to the power line, turned west and followed the well-worn path up and down the hills to Sandy Ford. The Indian settlement was seventy-five yards north of Sandy Ford. The piles of river rocks were in rows so straight they appeared to have been laid out by a surveyor.

"At the bottom of all those round rock piles are hatchet heads, arrowheads, and spear heads that would be needed in the afterlife," he said. Unrolling the leather map on the bed of the Kubota, he pointed out to Lindsey the most likely mounds. He took her by the hand and led her to the most promising mound.

"Just sit here and rest," he said.

"Give me at least thirty minutes before you start in with that bullhorn," he called back at her. "Then blow it only about once every sixty seconds. Wait an hour before you give up and drive the Kubota back to the farmhouse. I'll meet you there if you don't see me crawl out of the ground."

"How will you keep from getting lost?" she asked.

"A compass works fine underground, but GPS devices are useless," he said.

Andy left the Kubota on the power line seventy-five yards from Lindsey, jogged back to the farmhouse, and drove his golf cart to the garage. Starting at the tunnel from the Grand Chamber, Andy followed I-95 South, placing LED flares every 100 yards. After fifteen minutes he reached the intersection of I-95 with I-40 and turned west. He left a flare and three grenades at the juncture and hurried down the tunnel, which descended over 150 feet in 200 yards.

As he moved along with his miner's light, Andy became aware of his air hunger. There wasn't much oxygen in the tunnel. He had to be close to Sandy Ford, to the Indian mounds. He checked his watch. In ten minutes, Lindsey should start blowing the horn. The tunnel came to an abrupt end in a small chamber.

The chamber floor was littered with Yankee bones, belt buckles, metal buttons, old swords, rotting and rusting Enfields, and bayonets. He kicked them out of the way. The river rocks were packed tightly. He shined the flashlight up. Drawings were on the ceiling and walls of the chamber. He recognized a drawing of a man with a spear. He was close.

One at a time, he pulled the melon-sized rocks from the soil and threw them behind him. He had displaced about forty rocks when the bullhorn blast knocked him backwards.

"Lindsey," he called.

No answer. *She must be almost on top of me.*

He dug furiously. His breathing improved. He could feel a breeze of fresh air being sucked into the tunnel. Three more rocks and he saw light.

"Lindsey," he yelled.

There was Lindsey's face, about twelve inches from his. They dug toward each other. Within twenty minutes there was an opening large enough for him to crawl out. When he stood up, covered with dirt, Andy put his arms around her and bumped against her protuberant abdomen.

"I'm sorry", he said. "I was just glad to see you."

"You're forgiven," she said.

"I want to cover up this opening," he said, "until I need it on Saturday."

He walked up the slope and found a three-inch cedar sapling. He pushed it to the side with his left foot, then opened his pocketknife and sawed the sapling off with the saw blade. Then he walked back to the cave entrance and pushed the trunk of the cedar tree into the mouth of the cave until its branches covered the opening.

"That cedar tree will stay green for another two weeks and will allow me to locate the entrance," he said. "It's the only cedar tree growing sideways on this hillside. This shaft will give great ventilation to the tunnel system this time of year. The cool air will be drawn in around the cedar tree like a warm chimney will draw air through a fireplace. Eventually, I'll put a disguised ventilation pipe at the intersection of I-40 and I-95, but no time for that now."

He walked back to the Kubota and got two C4 charges and two remote detonators, which he stuffed in behind the branches of the cedar tree. Andy held Lindsey's hand as she picked her way across the side of the hill to the power line, where the Kubota was parked.

As he got back inside the RTV, Andy said, "I'm going to wire a long trip wire between two trees on this hillside before tomorrow, but I need to make some special charges first. In the cave arsenal is a cardboard box of steel ball bearings. I'll pack these around two bouncing betty mines. When a person steps on the trigger for a bouncing betty, a charge blows the mine into the air, about chest high, where the main charge detonates."

"Sounds unpleasant," she said. The contractions were back.

"By mounting these charges on trees facing each other and connecting them with a trip wire, all of the metal fragments in the betty and all of the ball bearings will be directed between the trees. It's the equivalent of a double canister charge from two Civil War cannon at a range of twenty yards--two giant shotguns. Anything between the trees will be shredded, just like the Confederates who reached the stone wall at Pickett's charge on the third day of the battle at Gettysburg."

She felt her belly again.

"All the great battles have already been fought," Andy said. "We're just changing a few details. We were lucky to find that map. It'll help us complete our own battle plan. The Union Army won the battle of Gettysburg because they occupied the most strategic ground, which happened to be high ground. The mercenaries and soldiers I expect on Saturday know nothing about the terrain here, above ground or below."

"You're as audacious as General Lee. I'll give you that."

"General Lee lost the Battle of Gettysburg," Andy said. "He didn't know the ground he was fighting on. Let's drive over to the tobacco barn and see if we can locate its connection to I-95. I was almost under it yesterday. That's where I found the other two hundred bars of gold. It would give us an unseen position in the rear of the battlefield. We're almost ready."

"The thing that bothers me the most is the number of soldiers we have, even if Ben shows up," she said.

It was another lie. The thing that bothered her most was contracting again.

43

They drove until the power line met the road to the mansion, turned right, and stopped the Kubota after twenty yards. The tobacco barn was fifty yards east of the road.

Andy picked up the shovel from the back of the Kubota and began to pick his way through the fifteen year old pine trees around the two-story barn. Lindsey could not move gracefully, but she was not going to be left behind.

"This barn has been rebuilt several times," he said as they walked. "I haven't been in here for a couple of years, but when I was here I wasn't looking for the right things."

There were two doors which sagged on each side. Andy had to lift each door to slide it open. The door hinges screeched.

Tobacco sticks were still hanging from the rafters.

He pointed up. "All of my childhood I only saw that block and tackle used a couple of times. It was supposed to be used to get heavy objects out of a wagon. You would drive in and pick a piece of machinery up and then drive the wagon out from under it, out the other side of the building."

"Two years ago I used it to change a wheel on the smoothbore cannon at the top of the alfalfa field, so the current ropes are good," he said. "Putting on that cannon wheel is the only time I've ever seen that block and tackle used."

Andy untied the rope from a post and fed the rope upwards. The weight of the cast iron hook carried the rope from the block and tackle down to a spot in the center of the dirt floor. With the shovel, Andy began to dig next to the hook. After six inches he heard the same hollow sound he had heard the previous day in the basement of the mansion.

"It's here," he said.

A brass ring was below the hook. Andy cleared away the majority of the dirt on top of the door, then attached the hook from the block and tackle to the ring. Using the mechanical advantage of the block and tackle, he brought the large cedar door up to seventy-five degrees.

He tied the rope to one of the poles in the barn. They shined their flashlights down into the hole at stone steps which descended into another tunnel. The stacked stones had been chipped to fit each other, leading gently down in the direction of the plantation house.

Andy stepped in and started down. He reached for Lindsey's hand. Together they descended twenty steps, brushing off the cobwebs. At the base of the steps was another stash of Enfield rifles, probably still loaded, and four wooden boxes of paper cartridges and caps.

She shined her flashlight back toward the mansion. "There's the gold."

"More Enfields are another twenty yards on the left," Andy said. "Remember. That tunnel to the south goes to the mansion, and that other tunnel is I-95 north. I-95 runs from the mansion, past my farmhouse, to the Grand Chamber underneath the new garage. About a hundred yards north of here on I-95 is the junction with I-40, which descends to the Indian mounds at Sandy Ford."

"I've got it," she said. "Why do you think that there are stone steps here, instead of a ladder?"

"With these steps a man could walk underneath that heavy door and lift it with his back. It would be nearly impossible to lift from a ladder. A man could hold the door open while his kids crawled out. This was an escape hatch from the plantation house. I wonder how many times it was used."

"How do you plan to use this entrance to the cave system tomorrow?"

"Not sure yet," he said. "It's likely that Boris' men will attempt to protect the gold and align themselves across a front facing south, with the garage to their backs. That means that Harrison's men will likely be facing north. I may be able to pick off a good number from both lines without either one of them even knowing that I'm there."

"Another job for bows and arrows?" she asked.

"Maybe my .308 with the silencer and the subsonic rounds will work best from this location. I could climb up into those rafters and have a grand view of the battle. Do you see the square hole at the crest of the roof?" He pointed. "I may be able to make five or six clean shots before Harrison's men get so disoriented that they run. No one would even hear me firing."

"You've done it. I see how you can move all over the west side of Dry Creek in the cave system," she said. "I'll bet there're a lot of interesting places down there to hide stuff. But I'm hungry now."

She didn't mention the contractions that were occurring every twenty minutes.

"Thanks for the company," he said as they got back into the Kubota.

44

At the farmhouse, Lindsey prepared lunch. "It sounds like you plan to attack from several directions."

"Attack may be the wrong word," he said. "My advantages of concealment and mobility can best be exploited by stealth. I won't be charging any squad of soldiers with an AK-47. The only time that I want them to see me is when they're being lured into a trap of some sort. Have you ever heard of the Spartans?"

"The Spartans were fierce warriors a long time ago."

"Their insight could be useful to us tomorrow. On one occasion a Persian warrior bragged, 'Our archers are so numerous that the flight of their arrows darkens the sun.' The Spartan warrior Dienekes replied, 'So much the better. For we shall fight them in the shade.'

Andy explained, "In those days archers didn't shoot at individual targets. Thousands fired high, arching shots at the same time from hundreds of yards away. The arrows would descend on an advancing army. One arrow could kill a horse at 250 yards. What Dienekes was saying is that archers would be useless if the fight occurred among trees, which would block the descent of the arrows. This is one of our strategies, to fight them where their weapons are of little value."

"You have almost convinced me that we have a chance," she said.

"Tomorrow, we must be flexible," he said. "We'll create disorder and confusion among our two enemies, who will be fighting each other already. Then I'll strike."

"How will you know when that moment is?" she asked.

"I'll recognize it when I see it," Andy answered. "If you threw a snake into a barnyard, could you predict where each chicken would run?"

"No."

"Then I won't try to predict what the enemy will do at every turn," he said.

"What about your explosives? They make noise," she said.

"No one can tell who put them there," he said. "Each of our enemies will think that the other accounts for the explosions. And the town will think the explosions come from the Marines blowing log-jams out of the river. Hopefully neither of our enemies will know that I'm on the battlefield until it's too late."

"The idea of Harrison coming here to try to take Boris down and us down at the same time is foolhardy," Andy added. "Three is a crowd in a firefight. The president and the Weasel don't consider us worthy adversaries. We're only afterthoughts to kill in the cleanup."

"Boris will have problems, too," Lindsey said. "He must fight you and Harrison, while being distracted by the nuclear weapons and the gold."

"So we're not in such bad shape after all," Andy said.

"I hate to bring this up now, but tomorrow is my due date," she said.

"Tomorrow, the day of the battle, is your due date?" Andy asked, jumping out of his chair. "Just a minute."

He ran into his office and scanned the room. Since emergency physicians don't generally make house calls, Andy rarely used his black doctor's bag. He did keep several pocket reference books and a pregnancy wheel in it.

A pregnancy wheel is a twelve month calendar in a hand-sized circle. A second, smaller wheel in the center of the calendar has several arrows. Dialing the red arrow to the date of the first day of the last menstrual period, or the blue arrow to the date of conception, the green arrow pointed to the due date. In this case, Andy placed the green arrow on tomorrow's date. His eyes tracked counterclockwise to the blue arrow. His right hand moved slowly toward the scar in his left chest wall.

He steadied himself in the doorway of his office, rapidly developing a powerful thirst. A chill ran through his body. He was a fool. It was so obvious. If only he had approached the situation analytically. No wonder she wouldn't leave. No wonder she wanted to talk about the baby. The weight of this revelation was staggering. Powerful people wanted to kill his baby before it was even born. And the mother of his child wouldn't leave even if he ordered her to go.

Lindsey had never seen such a look of bewilderment on Andy's face before. He had been as unwavering in command as Stonewall Jackson. Now, as he returned to the dining room, his face was ashen. He slumped into a chair and stared at the floor.

She reached over and touched his shoulder. "It could be anytime in the next week or so, not necessarily tomorrow. I feel fine. I think I'm having Braxton Hicks contractions every now and then. Nothing to get excited about. It's not real labor."

"For the next twenty-four hours, I want you to sit on the couch in the Grand Chamber and squeeze your legs together."

"That's never been very useful in the past at delaying childbirth."

"It's all I can come up with on short notice. Your pregnancy is just part of the battlefield that I don't have control over," he said. "So I'll be even more flexible, ready to react, but hopeful that you can keep a lid on it for twenty-four hours."

"Keep a lid on it?"

"I did eliminate one possibility of disaster," he said, with more composure. "The equipment we got from Harrison. I figured that it was too risky to use."

"You know that his nickname is the Weasel, don't you?" she asked.

"I've appreciated the resemblance in both his facial features and his behavior," Andy said. "It's time to destroy the cell phone he sent us, and the radios. I'm going to take those radios apart and remove their power supplies. They could have GPS trackers."

"That's a really bad word."

"I have my own radios and my own C4 and detonators and timers."

"Where do you get stuff like that?"

"In the country you meet people who know how to get stuff and are willing to trade for it," he said. "At every military base in America there are folks from the level of private all the way up to General who will gladly trade government secrets and weapons for cash. That's just one of the reasons we should keep our options open with the last two warheads Boris will bring."

"How do you know where to contact people for all the stuff you have?"

"That's the catch," he said. "You can't tell anybody, or the whole system breaks down. I can tell you that if I wanted an Abrams tank, I could get one in Buckingham County. But helicopters and tanks and armored personnel carriers would be a liability on the Farm. In the cave system here I have shoulder-fired rockets that can make toast out of any of those weapon systems. I hope that we don't need them in the fight tomorrow."

"Me, too."

"I have a request to make." He cleared his throat and exhaled audibly. His color was returning. "We really need to stay focused. Would it be okay if we waited until after this fight to discuss the baby further?"

Lindsey picked up her plate and tea cup and pushed away from the table. "That's fine with me," she said, smiling at the kitchen.

"Lindsey, I'm sorry about all the things I said to you when you got here."

"Actually, it was a pretty reasonable response to a woman who claimed she loved you, but stabbed you. Whatever happens, I do care about you and I'm sorry for what I did."

"We're moving into another area we need to discuss later, but I accept your apology."

45

At 11:15 Friday night Andy and Lindsey were checking equipment in the great room.

Andy sat down on the couch. "Lindsey, one of the most useful exercises before any battle is to spend some time thinking of the goals of your enemy and how he is likely to try to implement them."

"I'm listening."

"We know that Boris' primary interest is the gold. We know the president wants to kill Boris, and us, and walk away with two warheads for his personal use."

"Sounds right."

"With so much at stake, each side will want reconnaissance," Andy said. "This could be done by air tonight using infrared cameras. The purpose would be to see how many people were outside and where they were positioned. King Fahd told me that Boris always did this."

"I haven't heard any drones today," she said.

"Me either, but a flyover will be of limited value to Boris because of all the deer. With infrared, a deer lying down might look like a soldier lying down. He would probably have to take pictures at low altitude to be sure of what he was looking at. That would attract attention."

"What would you do tonight if you were Harrison?"

"If I were Harrison, I would send in a recon team and have them set up an observation post. To be useful in the morning, they would have to take up position tonight. They would need to be at a high point on the Farm, close enough to see my farmhouse. They would need to see the alfalfa field because it's the only place close by where a helicopter could land."

"The cupola of the plantation house would be ideal," she said, "because it's on the highest ground. They would have a view down the road to the farmhouse, to your barn, shop, shed, and garage."

"And they could see anything that landed in the field. They would be able to see any vehicle driving up from the covered bridge."

Lindsey sat down beside him. "What would they bring?"

"Night vision goggles, binoculars, sophisticated radios. They would need one sniper who might also bring a laser target designator. I wouldn't send but three people. The sniper needs the spotter. They need a radio man. You're correct, their best position would be in the cupola."

"Andy, you'll have to show yourself at some point tomorrow. These three would be a threat to you, too."

"I agree. A night stroll down I-95 is in order. I'll come out in the basement of the mansion, where we were yesterday. I'll stop at the tobacco barn and use my own night vision binoculars to look at the windows upstairs and into the cupola."

She said, "The gate's locked. How would they get in?"

"Swim the river behind the house. It's a 300 foot climb up the hill behind the house, but the strategic nature of the view from the cupola would be obvious even to an amateur like Harrison."

"An amateur? He's got to be pretty smart to be deputy director of the CIA."

"You only rise in organizations like the CIA if you're comfortable lying for a living and sending other men to do your dirty work. He's never had to kill anybody himself. If he comes tomorrow, he'll have a squad of bodyguards and body armor."

"I hope you're reading him right. He enjoys being sneaky."

"But so do I," Andy said. "And I have incentives that he can't possibly understand. Whoever comes to the plantation house tonight is here to kill and to make killing easier for Harrison. None of these people can claim innocence. I can't afford a spotter or a sniper or a radioman. There can't be anyone behind me tomorrow."

He stood up and began to gather his gear.

"Be careful."

"I know every squeak in the floor of that house and every room in the dark."

Andy put on his black diving outfit, black boots, and black watch cap. Lindsey watched him smear on black face paint. He picked up the .45 semi-automatic pistol from behind the clock on the mantel, screwed on the silencer, and checked the magazine. Thirteen rounds in the magazine in the Glock's handle and one in the chamber.

Picking up the hinged top of the coffee table, he pulled out a black shoulder holster, strapped it under his left arm and inserted the pistol. His ten-inch knife went on the left thigh, supported by a thin black belt with the tip of the sheath tied around his left leg. His night vision binoculars had a complex elastic strap. He inserted each of his arms into a different hole in the strap. When he pulled the last strap over his head the binoculars were held tightly to his chest, easily reached but never flopping around or interfering with shooting. His favorite hunting bow had eight arrows in its quiver.

"I wouldn't want to be one of your enemies tonight," she said.

"You're not my enemy, day or night. Somebody has to be good at eliminating the bad guys in the real world. The job chose me. I don't have the same guilt feelings about doing it defending you on this Farm as I did in other countries."

"You would rather kill Americans?"

"Here I get to decide. I learned the hard way to be skeptical about the reasons military intelligence gave us for killing people. I believe that every man deserves the right to defend himself in his own home, and to defend his family, especially from the government. Thomas Jefferson believed the same thing."

"How do you plan to get to the plantation house tonight?"

"Someday I plan to connect I-95 with the gun closet of this farmhouse, but tonight I have to go through the woods back to the garage and the Grand Chamber."

"Before you go, I've got one more question," she said. "So what if you do kill all of Boris' men, wipe out his bank account, grab the two warheads, and kill Harrison and all of his mercenaries? The president is still the president. He has infinite resources. You could win this battle, but lose the war."

"I have a plan for Mr. Marshall, should we prevail tomorrow. It would be best if you didn't know, in case you get caught alive."

Andy left fresh 24-hour LED flares along the tunnel of I-95 South and stopped at the stone steps underneath the tobacco barn. He slowly lifted the door with his back and crawled out. Looking through the six inch opening at the barn door he remembered the loud squeak the door made.

The plantation house looked dark. He saw no one in the windows or the cupola. Andy recalled that at age fourteen he had rolled round Civil War cannon balls at metal milk cans in the grass in front of the mansion on Sunday afternoons. At the time he had a crush on his cousin Patsy. She couldn't figure out why she always won. He looked at his watch. 12:30 Saturday morning.

When he was older, his brothers had rolled old tires with targets of cardboard inside down this same hill in front of the plantation house. That was his introduction to shooting arrows and throwing hatchets and knives at moving targets.

After watching for half an hour, he slipped back underneath the door in the floor of the tobacco barn into the tunnel. He put his bow and quiver back over his head. In the last hundred yards to the plantation house he lit and dropped several more LED flares. Silently he dodged the remains of stalagmites and stalactites, moving past the gold, the Enfield rifles, the farm implements and treasures, the kegs of gunpowder, and the sparkle room.

Arriving in the breezeway, he stopped again and listened. Whatever happened tonight, he didn't want to do any long-term damage to the old mansion. The scouting party would have to break in somewhere. The rear doors of the breezeway were purposefully high. There were no steps to them and no door knobs outside. They would probably choose to break in the front door because it had windows within reach of the door knob on the inside. But they would still have to pick the deadbolt. Shooting a deadbolt with a silencer would still make a significant noise from the shattering metal.

The other possibility was the kitchen door on the right side, past the wrap-around porches. It had a storm door that was locked, as well as a heavy door with a deadbolt. His aunt and uncle had used this new kitchen as their main entrance and exit because there was much less distance to carry groceries to the kitchen than coming through the front door.

From the cupola, he looked down through the trees toward the river with his night vision binoculars. Three men were trudging up the steep hill toward the house. His ancestors would not have left those trees there. They would have wanted to monitor traffic on the Appomattox River, which was the highway for commerce for centuries.

The proximity of the plantation to the river had given the Carlsons an advantage with regard to shipping their tobacco and cotton overseas. Huge bales were loaded onto narrow boats on the Appomattox River, directly behind the mansion, at the very point where intruders now climbed the bank.

The packed narrow boats floated down the Appomattox River to the James River, and on to Hampton Roads. The Carlson family had a cousin in the shipping business in Norfolk. They didn't have to wait for their money. Most of their cotton and tobacco went to England, but some was shipped north to Baltimore. Until the Civil War, this connection had made the Carlson plantation a money-making machine.

One intruder carried a rifle and another carried the Laser Target Designator. The third had the satellite radio high on his back to keep it dry. Two carried pistols at the waist. They were wearing night vision goggles. These were definitely black ops soldiers of Harrison, ex-military mercenaries. Since they came to kill, they were fair game the moment they set foot on the Farm. He could not allow any spotters, snipers, or laser target designators to see the morning.

The water was at least four feet deep at the point they crossed, Andy surmised. Either they rigged a line and pulled their equipment across on a pulley or they crossed in a small boat. Soldiers don't like to wear body armor in water.

Andy exited the front door of the house and locked the deadbolt with the key he kept in the corner cabinet of the breezeway. He walked to the right front of the house where he could see both the front door and the side door.

A large magnolia tree at this location gave him a good shot across the lower front porch of the plantation house, as well as to the kitchen door. His black SEAL diving suit absorbed light. Night vision goggles have one notorious deficiency—they allow no peripheral vision. The wearer can only see what is directly in front of him.

Andy's weapon of choice was the bow and arrow. With a traditional bow, there are no sights. Only enough ambient light is needed to get an outline of the target. The traditional archer does not need to make mental calculations about range. He sees the arching flight of the arrow in his mind and automatically knows how high to hold his bow. Andy did not hunt deer at night because it gave him too much of an advantage.

They would be coming around one side of the house soon. He kneeled and nocked an arrow, then pushed two more arrows gently into the ground next to his knee. The three walked directly toward him from the right side, stopped to try the kitchen door, then continued past him to the front porch and its steps.

They stood on the porch and examined the door.

One reached into his shirt pocket. "You guys look for an easier entrance while I try to pick this lock."

They split up. After the man with the LTD walked past him again and turned toward the kitchen door, Andy drew his bow. He waited until the soldier was almost at the steps before releasing. The soldier at the front door looked up quickly at the sound of someone tripping over a bush.

Andy pulled another arrow from the ground and nocked it. The soldier with the rifle on the porch was leaning over with his face almost touching the deadbolt. The arrow entered his chest underneath his extended right arm. His night vision goggles were dragged off his face as he slid down the door and collapsed into a grasshopper position.

The radio man would require a frontal shot because of the satellite radio on his back. He came around to the right side from the rear of the house and stopped to look at his buddy lying on the porch. He stepped forward to investigate. The arrow caught him in the throat and severed his spinal cord.

Andy checked each body. He left all their weapons under the magnolia tree. He removed the GPS trackers and man-to-man radios pinned to their shoulders and their ear mikes, and then pulled the satellite phone off of the radioman. All of these were carried inside the mansion.

He left all three GPS trackers in the cupola but took one of the shirt radios and the satellite radio with him back down I-95 North to the Grand Chamber. He wouldn't be talking tomorrow morning, but it might be helpful to listen. The GPS tracker in the satellite phone would not work in the cave.

Andy felt neither pride nor elation with the night's work. He had set up scores of ambushes as a SEAL and been ambushed several times himself. The only fear he had tonight was that tomorrow could bring some harm to Lindsey and their child.

Lindsey heard the front door of the farmhouse open at 2:10. Her heart raced.

"Andy?" She was sitting on the couch.

"It's me."

"What happened?"

"Nothing much. Let's get some sleep."

They turned in opposite directions.

46

The Second Battle at Carlson's Farm began with precision, like most disasters. Boris arrived promptly at 6:00 in the morning at the farmhouse with twelve men in camo fatigues, half wearing body armor and helmets. Lindsey was at her station in the Grand Chamber.

They appeared to be native European, aged thirty to forty. In their eyes Andy saw confidence in a quick kill and a big payday. He felt his pulse quicken.

Andy did not see Aleksi. He greeted Boris warmly and suggested that they transport the two nuclear weapons in the Kubota down to the cave and use the Kubota to transport the gold back to the truck. Four of Boris' men lifted the weapons into the bed of the Kubota, which was a bit back-heavy until Andy and Boris sat on the bench seat in the front. Boris' men followed along behind the Kubota.

Opening the vault in the garage pit was Lindsey's signal to transfer all the money in Boris' account and the $175 million from Harrison's CIA account to the new Swiss bank account.

The weapons were off-loaded into the back of the anteroom. Boris' men carried the first fifty bars of gold out of the tunnel from the gold room and placed them in the bed of the Kubota.

Just before two of Boris' soldiers drove the Kubota out of the cave and up the ramp, Andy reached over and turned on the floor heater. "You men will be more comfortable in this nippy weather with this heater."

They smiled in gratitude. Andy let the Kubota move well ahead and then started through the vault door up the ramp. Boris followed. They walked out of the garage and moved another forty yards ahead before an explosion shook the ground behind them. Boris looked back at the garage and Andy ran down the hill to his right toward the back swamp. Boris rushed back into the garage, ran down the ramp, and discovered that the vault door was closed.

Boris' face resembled an oversized beet. Blood vessels popped in the whites of his eyes. He ran back up the ramp and called for his men to pursue Andy, pointing down the wooded hill toward the swamp. The C4 underneath the seat of the Kubota abruptly exploded, hurling the two occupants through the roof of the RTV and lifting the front end of the vehicle into the air. The charge had been shaped to go straight up through the seat, leaving the gold in the bed of the RTV intact.

Andy had almost reached the swamp when he heard a third explosion, underground and from the direction of the garage. This was not in the plan. Had one or more of Boris' men remained in the cave and survived the first explosion? Was Lindsey all right?

He would go back when he could, but the battle was underway. Reaching four-foot water, Andy dove to the bottom of the swamp and found the opening underneath the first beaver dam. Standing in the cold water, he could see between the branches above water. He painted his face black with mud. He checked the location of the grenades and the stick bow and arrows in the hutch.

Within three minutes a swarm of soldiers entered the swamp. They looked across the forty-six acres of water, stumps, bushes, beaver dams, alders, cedars, and swamp grass. The squad leader decided they should form a skirmish line to move from north to south through the swamp. He obviously felt that Andy could not remain concealed during such a grid search. After seven men had spread out fifty yards apart, they began to churn towards the south, paralleling the river.

The swamp erupted like the fireworks display at the airport every fourth of July. The mangled bodies of four soldiers were hurled into the air by explosions before the rest stopped to reconnoiter.

The remaining three apparently realized that they were in an underwater mine field. Two more bodies were lifted skyward as they tried to move at an angle back toward Andy. Only one soldier made it back to the starting point, where he was greeted in the chest with a simple wooden arrow from a stick bow.

Firing broke out from the firing range across from Sandy Ford. Throwing down the stick bow, Andy rushed east to the man-made beaver dam which covered the tunnel from the swamp to the ante-room of the cave. He dove underwater and swam mightily to reach the underwater opening. Once inside the tunnel, Andy could see an LED flare far above him. He lit a new flare and hurried with his head down, trying to avoid the remaining stalagmites and stalactites. As he neared the level of the Grand Chamber he heard the sound of gunfire above ground. The battle between Boris and the Weasel was joined. What had happened to Lindsey?

47

The floor of the anteroom was littered with rubble. The two warheads looked untouched. The vault door was locked. The entrance to the gold room was partially sealed. Most of the overlapping hides that hid the opening of the Grand Chamber were gone. The floor of the tunnel leading to the Grand Chamber was also covered with rubble.

Sprinting over the rocks into the Grand Chamber, Andy saw an injured soldier struggling to get out of the chair in the living room. As he stood on his good leg and attempted to pick up his AK-47 on the table, Andy reached across his own body with his right hand, pulled his knife from its left hip holster, and threw it like a Frisbee into the abdomen of the soldier.

Lindsey's right leg was protruding from a pile of rocks. The leg was angulated laterally at the knee. Her right wrist was deformed. He hurried to remove the rocks from her body. Her chest was still moving. She was unconscious, but her airway was open. A hematoma and laceration extended from her mid-forehead into her auburn hair. He palpated the laceration to its base, but found no deformity in the skull. The scalp bleeding had stopped. He reached for her carotid pulse. It was rapid and shallow. For the first time today, Andy was afraid.

The battle above ground would have to proceed without him. Lindsey really shouldn't be moved without immobilization on a spinal board with a rigid cervical collar. She could have a neck or back injury and moving her could paralyze her.

But he could not resuscitate her in a pile of rocks and debris. He would have to take some risks. He palpated the cervical spine and found no abnormalities. He carried her through the medical supply room into the operating room. He placed her on the table and turned on the light. Then he saw the blood that stained her stretch pants. It had run down his pants legs as he carried her.

Andy opened the top drawer of his Craftsman tool box and grabbed a large pair of bandage scissors. Starting at the ankles, he cut the pants all the way to her waist on both sides. Then he cut the blue panties and saw the bright red blood trickling from her vagina. *Not the baby. His baby*. He hurriedly cut through her shirt and bra and sweater, until he could watch her chest move with each breath.

There did not appear to be any significant chest wall bruises. But there were bruises to the abdomen. The diagnosis was traumatic abruptio placenta, a condition where bleeding from the injured placenta separates it from the wall of the uterus. Andy knew that if his child were not delivered immediately, it would suffocate from lack of blood flow and oxygen through the umbilical cord.

He ran into the supply room to get two bags of normal saline. Using the angiocaths from the Craftsman tool box, he started two IVs in the left arm, avoiding the right arm due to its deformity and swelling. He taped both saline locks in place. After spiking the two saline bags and draining them down to the end of the tubing, he attached a large needle to each five foot length of tubing and inserted the needles into the saline locks. He opened the clamp on each line, and then confirmed wide open flow from each. The bags of intravenous fluid were hung on a metal tree overhead.

A vaginal delivery was unacceptable under these circumstances. Massive bleeding could be precipitated even by a manual vaginal exam. Lindsey needed a Cesarean section. But Andy was not an obstetrician. And he had no blood to replace her losses. He had scrubbed in on only four C-sections back in medical school and during his internship, a lifetime ago. And in only one of these did he actually get to pull the baby out of the uterus. He had never performed any of the surgical part of an emergency C-section.

Every seasoned emergency physician has begun a few hopeless re-suscitations, only to be surprised that the patients responded to his efforts, jumped up and grabbed the brass ring of life, and survived despite all odds. Such moments were the crack cocaine of the emergency physician.

Emergency surgery on a stranger who appeared to be dying was enough to cause anxiety even in a seasoned physician. But the hands that were steady enough to make a head shot at 1000 yards were now trembling. It's okay to shake, he thought. Just don't freeze. He was going to do whatever was necessary to deliver his child and to insure that mother and child survived.

Andy picked up the C-section/delivery kit that he had borrowed from Ben Carlson from the shelf in the OR. He opened the outside of the kit and placed it on the stainless steel table next to the OR table where Lindsey lay unconscious. On the shelf above the operating table he found the nasal cannula for oxygen. He placed the two prongs in her nose, wrapped the tubing around her ears, and connected the end of the tubing to a green tank of oxygen in the floor at the left corner of the table. He adjusted the oxygen flow to three liters per minute.

Using a disposable scalpel from the Craftsman tool box, Andy opened the cardboard boxes from Henry Shein. He placed the drugs he would need on the top of the tool box. He opened the second drawer of the tool box to collect the needles and syringes he would need to draw up the drugs. He tore strips of one inch adhesive tape to make labels.

Lindsey moaned.

Andy said, "Lindsey, I'm here."

"I hurt...My leg...My arm...My stomach...Is my baby all right?"

"Your baby's going to be fine," he said with more assurance than he felt, "now that your blood pressure is coming up. I'm going to need your help here. I know you're hurting, but we need to get that baby out. I want your permission to do a C-section. It's the only safe way for the baby. You're bleeding from an abruption. The bleeding between your placenta and the uterine wall will suffocate the baby if we don't do it now. I want to do a spinal anesthetic on you so that I can take the pain away from both your abdomen and your leg. Is that O.K.?"

"Do whatever you have to do."

"I'm going to have to roll you over onto your left side for a minute," he said. "I'll try to be careful moving your right leg, but it's going to hurt. We can't stop to splint your knee."

She said. "I can't tell you what hurts most- the leg or my stomach or my arm."

As gently as he could, Andy rolled Lindsey onto her left side. He put on sterile gloves and opened the spinal/epidural tray. After scrubbing a spot over the third and fourth lumbar vertebrae with Betadine, Andy drew up an injection of Duramorph, 200 micrograms of morphine, and mixed it with bupivicaine, a long-acting local anesthetic. He anesthetized the skin between the third and fourth vertebrae with lidocaine, using a one inch needle.

The three-inch spinal needle had to be inserted using the fingers only. He guided the needle between the bodies of these two lumbar vertebrae to the lining of the spinal canal, where he felt resistance.

"Hold on, and try not to move," he said.

She was moaning softly. He punched through the lining of the spinal canal and removed the stylet in the center of the spinal needle. Spinal fluid dripped out of the hub of the needle. Andy injected the Duramorph and Bupivicaine combination into the spinal canal, and withdrew the needle.

He lowered Lindsey onto her back and winced at the sight of her dangling right lower leg.

Emergency resuscitations are all about priorities. The baby had to be delivered first. Even a patient with twenty injuries must be approached in a logical fashion, addressing the most life-threatening problems first. He was grateful that she had a pulse in her right foot, but her leg was way down his list of priorities.

Lindsey stopped moaning. He looked at her face.

"With the exception of my wrist, I'm ready to go dancing," she said.

"The Duramorph will last for twenty-four hours, but the bupivicaine only lasts about two hours," he explained.

"Andy, most of the pain in my belly and leg is gone now."

"I want to get something underneath your chest and shoulders, so that all that medication won't go in the wrong direction."

"Did you say this was going to take two hours?"

"I hope it's closer to a few minutes to get the baby out," he said. "Repairing you will take a little longer, but we're talking minutes here." *If things go well.*

Andy checked the IV bags, which were empty. He returned from the supply room with two more bags. After hanging these, he rolled up two blankets to prop up Lindsey's chest and head.

"Is this so that I can watch?" she asked.

"This is so you won't stop breathing," he said. "If you lie down too flat the medication I gave you in the spinal canal will go toward your brain instead of toward your lower abdomen and legs."

"I remember that now. I never worked much in the OR or in OB."

Andy prepared an antibiotic solution. He squirted Cefoxitin into a sterile bowl of normal saline. Then he injected more Cefoxitin into the saline bag infusing into Lindsey's arm. The entire abdomen was prepped with Betadine-soaked sponges.

"I need to put in a Foley catheter," he said.

"Why?"

"Your bladder must be empty when I make the incision across your lower abdomen. It would be embarrassing if I cut into your distended bladder instead of your uterus."

"Please don't embarrass yourself in front of the crowd in here."

Andy could hear explosions overhead, but he paid no attention. He filled the cuff of the Foley catheter with 10 milliliters of saline and tossed the bag into the floor. "I'll also need for you to hold a retractor during the C-section."

"Are you sure I can do that?" she asked.

"I'm going to put this surgical glove on your good left hand. I want you to leave your hand lying on this sterile towel until I hand you the retractor. In fact, I'm going to put the retractor in myself. It's shaped like an L. I'll bring your hand down to it when the time comes."

"I'm sorry," she said. "What am I retracting?"

"You will be holding back the upper part of your horizontal incision so that I can see to open up your uterus and take the baby out," he said. "I plan to use a weighted retractor to hold down the lower part of your incision."

It would not be helpful to tell her that he had never done any of this before. Andy picked up the surgical knife and said, "This is called a bikini incision because the incision is horizontal at the bikini line."

He made a six inch horizontal incision across her lower abdomen in one stroke, trying to guess the size of the baby's head. Multiple sites of bleeding appeared in the wound margins. The squirters had to be buzzed with the battery cautery, a loop of hot wire on the end of a flashlight-shaped handle. The hot wire fried the cut ends of small bleeding vessels, resulting in an unusual smell which neither of them commented on. He continued his incision with the scalpel down to the fascia, the fibrous tissue covering the vertical rectus muscles in her lower abdomen.

The rectus muscles were dissected with blunt scissors until he could identify the peritoneum, the lining of the inside of the abdomen. He picked up the peritoneum with a clamp and tented it. Blunt scissors were used to enter the peritoneal cavity through the tent. Continuing to hold the lining of the abdominal cavity in the shape of a tent, Andy was able to advance the incision horizontally in both directions with the blunt scissors. The uterus was exposed throughout the entire length of the skin incision.

"It's time for you to retract." Andy inserted the metal L-shaped retractor underneath the upper margin of the incision so that Lindsey could keep the uterus visible. He led Lindsey's hand to the retractor. "Pull. A little higher. That's right. Hold it right there."

Andy placed another retractor underneath the lower margin of the horizontal surgical wound and let its weighted end hang between her legs.

To enter the uterus, Andy used the same technique he had used to enter the peritoneum. Using a clamp in his left hand, he grasped the wall of the uterus and pulled it up into the shape of a tent. He cut through the tent with the blunt scissors and extended his horizontal incision in the uterus to the left and right.

Normally, the next thing an obstetrician would like to see is a transparent amniotic sac, with an infant clearly visible. However, due to the bleeding inside of the uterus, the anatomy was obscure, and the amniotic fluid was bloody. It was time to be bold.

Andy inserted his right hand through the bloody soup of amniotic fluid, clots, umbilical cord and separated placenta until he found the baby's head. Placing both hands inside the uterus, he gently guided the baby's head into the surgical opening in the uterus and lifted the infant onto Lindsey's upper abdomen, next to her retractor.

He suctioned the baby's nose and mouth with a bulb aspirator. The child's color was poor, but it was making respiratory efforts. He vigorously wiped the blood, desquamated skin, and amniotic fluid from the baby's face with a sterile surgical towel and clamped the umbilical cord with a plastic clamp.

"It's a boy," Andy said. "He's a little scrawny."

She heard the first weak cry and struggled to lift her head without dropping the retractor. The crying became more vigorous and the infant's color began to improve. Andy cut the umbilical cord on the mother's side of the clamp.

"He's all right, but we need to lay him on your bare chest so that he won't get cold," Andy said. "I'll cover him with a blanket. You need to hold that clamp a little while longer."

"Is it okay for him to cry like that?" she asked.

"It's the best thing for him," he said. "He's learning how to use his lungs, and he's drying them out."

Andy reached back into the uterus to deliver as much of the placenta as possible in one piece.

"There's a problem here," he said. "It's related to the ultrasounds you didn't have."

"Please don't scare me any more than I already am."

"Hold on a minute and I can give you some more information."

He guided the second head through the bloody placental debris and clots and placed this infant next to the boy. He suctioned the child's nose and mouth and wiped away the blood and dead skin with a sterile towel.

"Is there an echo in here?" Lindsey asked.

Andy clamped the umbilical cord twice and cut between the clamps. "No echo. Your baby girl just joined the choir. She's a runt, too."

Lindsey strained to support her upper body on her left elbow. Her eyes darted from one wailing infant to the other. "I don't know what to say."

"Don't let go of the clamp yet. Congratulations. They look like survivors."

"What are their Apgar scores?" she asked.

"I've forgotten how to calculate an Apgar score," he said. "But we don't need it. Any kid who can scream like that is gonna make it. And so are you."

A wave of euphoria swept over him, a feeling so wonderful that he thought of God for the first time in years. Today he had been blessed.

"I'm sorry about the timing," she said.

"The timing is yesterday's news. I'd like to make a couple of random observations, though. Even a one-armed paper hanger has two legs, and he only has to work with one piece of wallpaper at a time."

Lindsey looked at the deformities in her right leg and right wrist. "What am I going to do?"

"Look on the bright side. You've got two breasts."

When your doctor starts joking, it's a good sign for the patient.

Andy removed the remains of the placentas and clots from the uterus. He injected twenty units of pitocin into the IV in Lindsey's left forearm and adjusted the flow rate downward. This drug would help the uterus clamp down and stop bleeding. After changing surgical gloves, he returned to the uterus and suctioned it clean. Using an absorbable suture, he repaired the horizontal incision in the uterus with individual sutures.

When the uterus was repaired, Andy suctioned the extra blood and amniotic fluid from the abdominal cavity and began to massage the uterine wall. Massaging the uterine wall would cause the muscle to contract, limiting bleeding. He poured the solution of Cefoxitin into the abdomen and then suctioned the inside of the peritoneal cavity clear again.

"You can let go of the retractor now," he said.

He removed the retractor from her hand. "Now you can put your one arm around your twins."

Their crying seemed to diminish shortly after Lindsey touched them.

Andy changed his surgical gloves again to repair the lining of the abdomen. This was done with individual sutures. The fascia over the rectus muscle was repaired in the same fashion.

Interrupted sutures are tied individually, as opposed to a running stitch. If a running stitch breaks at any point, the entire incision falls apart.

The last stitches went in the abdominal skin and subcutaneous tissue. These were nylon and interrupted.

Andy wiped the incision site with Betadine and allowed it to dry before placing a thick, long dressing over the incision. He taped the margins of the dressing with paper tape. "I'm done with my first C-section and delivered my first set of twins."

"What?"

"I hope I didn't sew the wrong things together or leave anything in there that I'm going to need later today."

"You did great, I'm sure," she said.

"Then where's my watch?"

She laughed. "I think the twins are looking for my nipples."

"Then don't hold out on them. Let me help."

Andy arranged the twins close to her nipples. "You control the left side and I'll make sure nobody falls off the right side. He guided their mouths. The girl latched on first.

"I can see how this could be fun," Andy said, "but there is a battle above ground."

"My arm hurts so bad I can't feed even one of them by myself."

Andy felt her radial pulse and looked at the deformity in her right wrist. "Since the babies are out, there isn't any reason why you couldn't have a little intravenous morphine for your wrist. If we keep doing it, eventually it would get in the breast milk."

He looked around the limestone walls of the operating room. "The Henry Schein boxes. They're just the right size. I can pad them and then wrap the babies in blankets."

"When do I get off this table?"

He injected the morphine into Lindsey's IV in two milligram increments and stopped at eight milligrams. "This morphine would have depressed your babies' respiratory drive if we had used it while they were still inside you."

Lindsey appeared to be more comfortable.

He carried her into the Grand Chamber with the Foley bag on top of her stomach. He was pleased to see that Lindsey was producing a steady urine flow into the bag, indicating good perfusion of her organs. He stepped over the dead Russian and placed Lindsey on a blanket on the couch. "You'll be fairly comfortable for the next couple of hours."

Andy dragged the Russian by the feet into the anteroom. Returning to the OR, he picked up the cardboard boxes with the sleeping babies and placed them in the floor next to the couch.

"Andy, I need to explain a few things to you."

48

"First tell me what happened in the Grand Chamber after the load of gold left," Andy said.

"I heard somebody in the gold room, so I detonated the tunnel between the anteroom and the gold room," she said. "I went to close the vault door. There was an explosion outside, which I thought was the Kubota."

"It was," he said.

"I locked the vault and went back inside the Grand Chamber. The gold tunnel blast blew most of the hides away that were covering the entrance to the Grand Chamber. One of Boris' men stayed in the gold room and survived the tunnel blast. He climbed over the rocks after I went back in and threw a grenade. I don't remember anything after that. But that's not what I want to talk about."

"I should warn you that people say things when they get morphine that they don't mean."

"Ask me anything you want," she said.

"I already know, Lindsey. I know I'm dense. One of the good things about a C-section is that the baby avoids the head and facial trauma of passing through the birth canal. When I wiped that boy's face off, I saw a Carlson chin. When the girl opened her eyes, I saw my mother's eyes."

She raised her head to the maximum height possible on one good elbow and looked down.

"These babies are miracles," she said.

"Weren't you on birth control pills?"

"I had been taking antibiotics for a sinus infection, and they interfered with my birth control pills."

"I now have three more reasons to be careful up there. I hope that our children will be smarter than we are."

"Me too," she said. "I've already got a list of stuff that they're never going to do."

49

"**I** 'd like to work on your arm and leg, but there're people out there who want to kill us," he said. "Now that your vital signs are good and the babies look good, I think I should address these people before they find a way in here."

"What can you do now?" she asked. "A lot could have happened while you were operating on me."

"One of Stonewall Jackson's officers asked him the same question during the Battle of Fredericksburg. A group of Confederate officers were looking out over the carnage of Union troops on the plain in front of the stone wall below Maury's Heights. This officer said, 'They just keep coming. What can we do?'

General Jackson said, 'We can kill them all, every last one.'"

"I guess that's some kind of plan."

"And do you want to know something else? A short time later his wife delivered their firstborn child."

"That's a beautiful story," she slurred through the cotton mouth of narcotics.

"The Weasel and his men will never stop trying to kill us on their own," Andy said. "They won't leave without the nuclear weapons. Boris and his men will never give up on the gold."

He paused for a moment. "I now have an infant son and daughter to protect. Their mother needs blood transfusions that I can't provide until these invaders are dead. Nothing that has happened between us in the past matters. I will be back for you. All of you. This century has not seen the terrible power of the Farm to protect its own."

The babies were sleeping peacefully in their cardboard Henry

Schein boxes. They did not stir when Andy kissed them on the foreheads.

He adjusted Lindsey's pitocin drip. Her eyes were already closed. She would not remember their first kiss in nine months.

Before leaving the Grand Chamber Andy looked up at his painting of Robert E. Lee, which he had moved from the farmhouse to the cave the previous day. He read the inscription engraved on the frame, as he had many times. "Blessed be the Lord God, who teaches my hands to war and my fingers to fight."

Today these words grabbed him. The problem had never been that he did not believe in God. He had lost his trust in God when his mother and father had been taken. But God had been preparing him to do battle on this day. He had already given him Ben and Lindsey and the twins. Somehow, He would allow him to keep his promise to Lindsey.

Andy applied more black face paint and put on his black watch cap. He strapped on his knife and put his arm and head through the sling of the quiver of arrows. He picked up his bow, then walked into the laundry room and unsnapped the linen closet. The cabinet swung open, revealing the welded steps inside the sixty foot vertical culvert that led to the magic stump next to the garage.

When he reached the top of the ladder Andy could see through several round one eighth-inch holes in the sides of the stump. Boris had eight men with their backs to the garage, firing their automatic rifles from behind trees, protecting the gold. Most were within range of an arrow, but the timing of his shots would be critical. Boris was not in sight. Harrison had ten or twelve men at least fifty yards past Boris' line, firing from behind trees and rocks. They were positioned as he had predicted. He could hear background firing from the range across the River.

Andy pushed up on the lid of the stump. He slid the lid back behind the stump and let it fall to the ground. The firing was so intense that he was not concerned about his own noise. All of Boris' men were firing toward the farmhouse, away from him. The squad leader was the obvious first target at thirty-six yards. He wore no body armor. Standing on the top rail with his head still below sight, Andy waited until all of Boris' men were engaged. Then he brought his bow to full draw. Rising until his knees were locked, Andy lined up the string with the squad leader's heart. The arrow passed through his chest as Andy ducked back out of sight.

The two men who noticed their squad leader go down apparently thought that he had been shot from the front. The rest of the squad had body armor vests. He nocked a second arrow and waited.

Body armor is effective at stopping conventional bullets precisely because most people aim for the center of the chest. The neck was deemed too small a target to be worth covering. Besides, neck armor is uncomfortable.

Andy aimed his next arrow at the third cervical vertebrae of a bulky man kneeling forty-five yards away. The man lurched forward. Instantaneous quadriplegia, but the fletching of the arrow now pointed to the sky. The three Russians who saw the arrow sticking out of the back of the neck of the soldier in their firing line looked anxiously back over their shoulders. They had been flanked by an unknown force of unknown size, from an uncertain century. These three broke and ran to their left, seeking the shelter of a ditch. The remaining three continued to fire at Harrison's men.

A wiry fellow crawled out of the ditch and moved in Andy's direction on his stomach, holding his AK-47 across his forearms. He used his elbows to pull and his legs to push. He apparently planned to shimmy over to a stump and use it for cover until he could determine where the arrow came from. When he lifted his head above the stump, Andy inserted his knife just above the man's Adam's apple. It was a painless death.

Andy studied the body armor of the three men who had not seen the arrow sticking out of the back of the neck of their comrade. When each man raised his automatic rifle to the firing position, he exposed a three inch diameter area in his left armpit. That was the chink. The next arrow found this chink and penetrated through the chest of the next soldier to be halted by the armor on the opposite side.

It would be unwise to further weaken Boris' force at this point. He pulled the lid back on the stump and descended the welded steps back to the level of the linen closet.

50

L indsey and the babies were still sleeping. Andy laid his bow on the couch, took off his quiver, and picked up his camo binoculars and a pouch of timed C4 charges. He hurried south on I-95. Moving swiftly through the tunnel, dodging stalagmites and stalactites, he completed a subterranean envelopment of Harrison's line in eight minutes, guided by the LED flares left the previous day.

Lifting the heavy door of the tobacco barn with his back, he crawled out onto the dirt floor. Since he had weapons hidden throughout the cave system, Andy carried only the pouch of timed explosive charges around his waist and his knife. Turning east through the thick stand of pine trees, he ran downhill to the covered bridge. As expected, Harrison's men had stopped in front of the bridge in order to avoid the noise of driving over the heavy planks. No one was guarding their truck.

Andy looked into the back of the truck. Cardboard boxes were stacked in rows, filling half the space inside. He jumped up into the bed and cut open one of the boxes. The box held four one-kilogram bags of white powder. He stuck a bag and tasted the powder on the tip of his knife. Heroin. He stabbed several other boxes. There were millions of dollars of street narcotics. Of course. This was how he was to be discredited after he was killed. The Saudis would have trouble justifying retaliation against the United States over the death of an international drug dealer.

Crawling underneath the truck, he found the gas tank. It was not made of steel, but the bands that held it up were. He attached a C4 charge with a magnetic strip to the band that supported the center of the tank. He set the digital timer for twenty minutes and pulled the activating safety strip. Rolling out from under the truck, he re-crossed the covered bridge and moved uphill through the pine trees toward the alfalfa field.

The firefight continued from the top of the hill between the farm-house and the garage. Circling the wooded side of the alfalfa field, Andy crossed the main road and used the ditches to remain invisible as he made his way to the rear of his farmhouse. The policemen and correctional officers were firing away behind him at the practice range on the opposite side of Sandy Ford.

Boris had left his truck at the edge of the farmhouse driveway. He had the foresight to turn it around to face his only exit. Andy moved from tree to tree in his dark wet suit and watch cap, reaching his shed undetected. The truck blocked the main road toward the covered bridge. Andy moved cautiously through the machinery and tractors to the truck. Creeping up to the right side, he confirmed that the cab was empty. He rolled underneath and attached his second C4 charge to the gas tank. He set the timer for ten minutes and pulled the safety strip out. Then he retraced his path through the shed, stopping every few yards to look for movement.

Inside the fake stump in the front yard of the farmhouse was the black Savage Model 10 .308 sniper rifle with the silencer, loaded with subsonic rounds. A BB gun made more noise than this rifle. The stump had been placed in the trees to cover the main road, the front of the house, and the path between the farmhouse and the new garage. He removed the top to his magic stump and climbed in, pulling the lid back over his head.

Harrison's truck near the covered bridge exploded, sending a fire-ball up above the trees. Andy looked at his watch and held his hands over his ears. Boris's truck rocketed fifteen feet into the air. Andy re-moved the plugs from the four vertical firing holes inside the stump.

Using his binoculars, Andy determined that Harrison's men had Boris' dwindling force encircled halfway between the garage and the house. Each of Harrison's men had body armor and helmets. Sitting with the rifle on his left knee and his back against the inside of the hollow stump, Andy located six easy targets. The stump was large enough to hide the entire barrel of the .308. Harrison's soldiers began to drop silently, one by one, from shots to the bases of their necks.

Since each of Harrison's men had his attention focused toward Boris' men, firing continuously and reloading, the last man alive didn't know that he was the last man alive. Boris's men thought that they must be winning, since the level of firing at them had gradually diminished to zero. They crawled forward to investigate, moving from tree to tree, directly toward Andy. He shot them all in the forehead, one by one, without making a sound.

Andy studied the landscape from his firing slots. As he prepared to get out of the stump, he heard a helicopter approaching. It circled over the covered bridge and descended toward the center of the alfalfa field. It was a modified Army-green helicopter like the one that the CIA team had landed at the intersection of Highway 45 and Highway 60. Six more agents in full gear jumped out of the chopper and ran across the alfalfa field toward him.

He turned the .308 to meet them, holding fire until they were well out in the open. A wiry little man with a pointed beard sprinted from behind the farmhouse toward these soldiers and their helicopter. It was the Weasel, making his escape.

He, too, had body armor. Apparently they didn't make a helmet to fit his small head. Andy flipped the lid off of the stump and rested the bipod of the .308 rifle on the stump's rim. He placed the crosshairs of the rifle scope on the door of the helicopter and waited for the Weasel to step into view.

The Weasel's head exploded. The only noise came from the acceleration of the chopper blades, anticipating liftoff. The glare of the sun on the windshield of the helicopter made the pilot obscure to Andy. He shot through the cab where the pilot should be, but the chopper lifted off anyway. He ejected the shell and shot again. The chopper reached a height of fifty feet, keeled left, dug its blade into the alfalfa, and exploded. The chopper blade went spinning end over end across the field as a mushroom of fire carried pieces of debris overhead. Only twisted pieces of metal remained in the dark circle of scorched ground.

Andy left the sniper rifle inside the hollow stump and put the lid back on. The six new agents had hit the dirt when the helicopter blew up. They were slowly getting up. Andy surmised that they were hearing impaired and stunned from the helicopter explosion behind them.

Andy removed his black watch cap to reveal his sandy hair and sprinted around the side of his farmhouse. Looking over his shoulder, he could see that all six had taken the bait. The race was on to the Indian settlement just above Sandy Ford. Since Andy was not carrying any weapon but a knife, and he knew where to run, he easily kept ahead of the men chasing him. Fifty yards before reaching the Indian mound entrance of the cave, he jumped the two-foot high clear monofilament nylon trip wire that ran for forty yards between two sycamore trees. Taped to each tree and facing each other were the two homemade bouncing Betties, their explosive charges wrapped with one inch steel ball bearings.

Andy stopped at the cave entrance and pulled out the cedar bush. He picked up the remote detonator in the mouth of the cave, kneeled, and ducked his head. The agents came into view, running and scanning the terrain, their M-16s out front. Andy watched until a group of four were visible between the sycamore trees, then raised his head. Before any one of them could get off a shot, he ducked into the entrance of I-40.

Safely inside the entrance, he felt the trembling ground underneath his knees and heard the terrible sounds of ball bearings striking trees, rocks, dirt, and human flesh.

He reached for the C4 charge wedged in the rocks above the cave entrance. Moving up the grade in the tunnel, he stopped at the point where he lost line-of-sight to the entrance. Small creatures were running past him toward the light. Rats had already moved into the cave.

Holding the transmitter in his hand, he concentrated on the light in the entrance. There were apparently two men left. They were debating whether they should enter the cave or throw a grenade in.

"If we blow the entrance we won't know if he's dead," one said. "Harrison said to make sure he was dead."

"Harrison isn't in charge any longer," the other said.

"Let's just use our flashlights and pistols," the first one said. "We would be small targets lying down. He's caught like a bear in a cave. Where could he possibly go?"

Andy waited until both were inside, then flattened himself behind a stalagmite. He pressed the switch of the radio transmitter. The tunnel went black and debris flew over his head. After hearing no movement or voices, he moved farther up the cave until he came to a narrow area with a low ceiling. Here he placed another charge. Moving forty more yards up I-40, he again lay down behind a stalagmite and listened. Nothing. He pressed the remote radio transmitter. The blast sealed off a section of I-40 West, snarling rat traffic for a long time.

But there was at least one large rat not yet accounted for.

51

A ndy hurried up the grade on I-40, moving east until he could see the LED flare at the junction of I-95. He turned left and continued north toward the Grand Chamber. Entering the chamber, he found Lindsey staring down at the two infants in their boxes.

"Thank God you're back. We've been so worried. And I think they're both hungry."

"What if I rotate them to the chow line?" he asked, picking up the boy. Roll over on your left side a little and support the head with your good arm. I'll plug him in."

They watched him latch on to Lindsey's left breast.

"I was afraid that I wouldn't be large enough to do this."

"He takes after his dad. I've always been partial to small breasts," Andy said. "Did you know that my mother's name was Ava?"

"No, I didn't, but I like it. My brother's name was Jack," she said. "Jack and Ava sound nice together."

"They would sound better with a last name."

"Is that a casual observation, or did you have a specific name in mind?"

"How about Carlson?"

"I'll consider it."

"Wouldn't it be best for these twins to grow up with their real dad?"

"That's probably true," she said.

"I could offer free medical advice and treatment to them throughout their childhood."

"Those are certainly valid arguments, but I need to hear one more thing."

"I love you," he said.

"I knew it already."

"We need to move on this idea right away," he said. "You would be dragging one leg down the aisle already, not to mention the cast on your wrist. We don't want to wait until the kids are old enough to start asking questions. And I think a wedding picture with a crippled bride holding two babies is likely to spark inquiries for a long time."

"Those are certainly reasonable considerations," she said. "Have you thought about the financial implications of our getting married?"

Andy wrinkled his brow. "Now that you mention it," he said. "I've already paid for wedding rings. If I have to take them back, the jeweler might not give me my money. I would be stuck with two wedding rings and no wedding."

"You're being very persuasive, I must admit."

"I foresee an awful lot of diapers and bottles for a single mom with one arm and one leg in a cast. Social Services might come knocking on your door, asking questions."

"Okay, I'll marry you," she said. "But the real reason is that I don't want anyone else to do these chow line rotations."

"While you're topping off Jack, I'm going to start on your wrist."

Andy left Ava in her Henry Schein box and placed the box on the floor to the left of the couch. He located the fiberglass splint material in the supply room, the two percent lidocaine, a syringe and a needle. After putting on sterile gloves, he cleansed the deformed wrist with Betadine, painting it burgundy.

"This is going to hurt for a few seconds going in," he said, "but then you'll feel much better."

He palpated the ends of the fractured distal radius and ulna at the wrist and inserted the needle at ninety degrees to the skin, directing the needle to the pocket of blood at the fracture site. "This is a fracture block. You've probably seen the orthopedist do one in the ED."

Aspirating blood to confirm that the needle was between the

fragments of bone, he slowly injected ten milliliters of two percent lidocaine.

"The pain is easing," she said.

"I'm glad," he said. "We shouldn't give you any more morphine."

He withdrew the needle and began to prepare the splint.

"I'm going to wet this fiberglass in the sink while that fracture block takes hold," he said. "I'll need to pull on your hand to align the bones in your wrist again. You have a bad Colles fracture, but it should heal nicely."

After the fiberglass was soaked in the OR sink, he brought it back in the Grand Chamber and spread it out on the table next to the couch, pressing excess water out of the mesh. He opened two Ace bandages. Holding her forearm at the elbow, Andy pulled on her right hand and pressed downward with his thumb until he felt the bones below his thumb click back in place.

Resting her forearm and hand on the table, he applied a sugar tong splint. The first wet splint was wrapped horizontally around the elbow and extended to the fingertips on either side of the hand, with the elbow held at ninety degrees. The second U-shaped splint of wet fiberglass was applied vertically at the elbow, with half the splint extending on either side of the upper arm toward the armpit, overlapping the first U-shaped splint at the elbow. Both splints were wrapped with Ace bandages. Then the fiberglass material was molded to Lindsey's forearm, wrist, and hand by squeezing the mesh.

The mesh would harden within five minutes. Such a splint offers excellent stabilization, but allows swelling in the first twenty-four hours after the injury.

The result was that Lindsey had use of her shoulder but was unable to move her elbow out of the ninety degree position or rotate her forearm or wrist. The procedure was topped off with an arm sling, which supported the double cast. Once a wrist fracture is reduced and stabilized with a fiberglass splint, the pain diminishes quickly.

Andy returned to the supply room to find a Velcro knee immobilizer.

"I suspect that you have a lateral plateau fracture of your tibia at the knee, because of the way your lower leg was angulated when I found you. The best treatment until we get an X-ray will be to splint it so that the fractured bones don't rub against each other."

"We're talking more surgery, aren't we?" she asked.

"It's just a T-shaped plate with some screws, usually."

"When did you say this spinal block will wear off?"

"The spinal block will provide you with pain relief until I can get you to the hospital," he said. "We've got morphine backup and baby formula in bottles for emergencies."

"Is everybody dead up there?"

"I haven't seen Boris dead yet," Andy replied. "It's time for me to check out things upstairs. Don't be lulled into thinking this battle is over. Someone is watching the battle by satellite or drone. We're dealing with fools here. They'll likely continue to do the same things, expecting a different result."

He stuffed the Glock in his belt and put the black watch cap back on his head. From the linen cabinet he climbed the welded steps to the lookout in the stump. There was no sign of life.

Andy advanced in the trees paralleling the path toward his farmhouse. There were plenty of bodies, but no sign of life. The front end of the Kubota Diesel was missing, but so was the gold. A bad sign. If anyone got away with gold bars, they would be back.

52

The whop-whop-whop of another helicopter came from the north, apparently headed for the alfalfa field that already held the remains of one helicopter. As it passed overhead, Andy noted that it was a small, black model, a two-seater. It hovered, apparently reconnoitering.

The purpose of the helicopter was soon apparent. Boris stomped on the pedal of the golf cart behind the shed and urged it forward with his head, like a kid listening to music with a nice beat. It was not hard to figure why the cart was sluggish.

Andy ran to the magic stump to retrieve the .308 Savage rifle with the silencer. He reloaded the magazine with five standard .308 rounds kept inside the stump and exchanged scopes using the quick-disconnect mounts.

Boris forced the golf cart further into the field. Fortunately for him, the journey was downhill. The black chopper came down vertically and the pilot killed the engine.

Andy kneeled next to the stump and rested the bipod on the rim. He estimated 250 yards to the helicopter. The pilot would have landed closer to the farmhouse except for the wreckage of the other helicopter already in the alfalfa field. Andy chose the vertical rear rotor as the most vulnerable target. He waited for the chopper to land. One shot shattered the rear rotor blades.

Neither the pilot nor Boris even looked at the tail of the chopper. With standard hypersonic rounds and a silencer a person can hear an echo--that is, if he is not the target--but he can't determine from what direction the noise originates. The powder charge is still muffled by the silencer. The difference in range is that the full powder charge is accurate enough for a head shot at 1000 meters in the hands of a marksman like Andy. The chopper could not be controlled with the rear rotor damaged.

Andy determined that this small helicopter, like the golf cart, was inadequate for Boris' needs. The gold bars weighed at least a thousand pounds.

Boris opened the passenger door of the chopper and shot the pilot in the face with a pistol. Evidently he also recognized the weight problem. He walked around to the pilot's door, unfastened the seatbelt, and pulled the pilot's body to the ground.

Returning to the passenger side of the helicopter, Boris reached for the first bar of gold. The .308 bullet, traveling at over 3,000 feet per second, qualified Boris for the leading role in the Russian version of "The Headless Horseman."

Andy walked out into the field. He checked the pilot and Boris' shoulders. He counted the gold bars. They were all there. He drove the golf cart farther downhill to the gravel road, where he reversed directions. The golf cart would have an easier time getting back up the hill on the road.

Bodies littered his front yard and the farm road. Some of these combatants killed each other over gold or warheads, but most of them died because they underestimated the Farm. They would receive the same measure of remorse that John Andrew had for the seventy Yankees he buried here.

Andy drove the golf cart with the gold to the garage and opened the vault with the keypad. After dragging the dead Russian out of the garage, he cleared the rubble to make space for the golf cart in the anteroom, next to the two warheads.

He walked back up the ramp toward the house, checking each body. There were no soldiers left alive.

Entering the farmhouse carefully, Glock drawn, he checked each room. Counting the two pilots, all of Boris and Harrison's first assault force, the six commandoes from the second helicopter, Boris, and Harrison, there would be twenty-eight more long-term guests at the Farm to keep the Yankees company. Andy wasn't proud of this number. He just needed to know how deep to dig the hole or how much tunnel space would be needed.

Andy's largest tractor had a seven foot bush hog mower attached in the rear. He backed the tractor and mower out of the shed and returned to the garage. After raising the mower eighteen inches with the rear hydraulics, he adjusted the top-link to make the mower housing level with the ground. At the garage Andy turned the tractor around and backed the mower up to the door.

"It's time to get you and the babies to the hospital," he said to Lindsey. "I'm going to give you a ride to the gate on my bush hog. We can call 911 from there."

He took the mattress off the bed in the cave and dragged it out to the mower. Then he picked Lindsey up and carried her out to the mattress.

He returned to the Grand Chamber to pick up the babies in their cardboard boxes.

"I want you to take Ava and hold her on your chest, so we only have to worry about Jack in the box."

She laughed. "I hope he doesn't spring out, like my breasts. Even if I had buttons left on this blouse and a functional bra, I couldn't fasten them."

"If you're going to hang them out, you may as well use them."

"You think it's all right for Ava to nurse while we ride along?" she asked.

"I often take a drink with me when I'm on the tractor," Andy said.

He placed Jack's box on the mattress next to Lindsey, covered Lindsey and Ava with another blanket, and stuffed two pillows under Lindsey's head.

After closing the vault door, he locked the door to the garage and got on the tractor. Looking back over his shoulder, he drove to the farmhouse.

In front of the farmhouse he shut down the tractor engine. "The only bad guy left is in the White House."

"You can't go shoot the president."

"Probably not, but I don't think he's through shooting at us," he said, opening his cell phone.

53

"**D**r. Carlson," President Marshall said.

Andy could hear irregular breathing.

Neither party said anything for a moment.

The president struggled to find his press conference voice. "Uh. I understand from Harrison that his men and Boris' men are having quite a shootout on your farm. We were wondering where you were."

"Harrison was not supposed to be at the Farm today, Mr. President. You lied to me. You endangered my life and Dr. McKee's life."

"Who are you to tell the President of the United States what to do, Carlson? This is a national security matter. I make the rules. I'm sending enough Rangers down there to straighten things out."

"Then their blood will be on your hands, sir."

"You may have been good in the desert once upon a time, Carlson, but Army Rangers will create a new exit for your gastrointestinal tract if you get in my way. Tell Dr. McKee that if she wants to see her baby born, she'll keep her hands off the warheads until the CIA weapons people get there."

The line went dead.

"President Marshall is sending Rangers to the Farm," Andy said. "My guess would be a jolly green or a Black Hawk is en route."

"But we're not in any condition to take on that kind of firepower."

"We're on our way to the hospital," he said, restarting the engine. "I want to get to the bridge before they get here."

"We trust you."

Andy drove past Boris' demolished truck and turned left toward the covered bridge. The first helicopter in the field was not recognizable.

The small black helicopter left plenty of space in the field for a larger aircraft.

"We can't get caught in the open," he yelled back to Lindsey. "Hold on."

He hurried into third gear, looking overhead, behind, and ahead as they raced toward the bridge. The sound of the planks on the covered bridge was reassuring.

He positioned the tractor and bush hog inside the covered bridge and lowered the mower to ground level. Before shutting down the engine, he turned the steel front-end loader bucket upside down and lowered it to the planks of the bridge.

Seated on the tractor, he flipped open his phone and called Charlie Dodd.

"It's Andy. I'm expecting two types of unwelcome company within the next twenty minutes. Could you sit on your porch and be a spotter for me?"

"What you looking for?"

"A large helicopter coming from the north or east."

"There's already been two helicopters land on your place today," Charlie said. "I couldn't tell whether the Army was blowing trees and stumps in the river or you were having your own air show."

"With all that firing down at the range, I may not hear this chopper soon enough," Andy said. "I need to know when it's close."

"What else you looking for?"

"I think some vehicles will try to break through my gate."

"They'll be easy to spot from the porch. I'll get my binoculars and call you back when I see something."

Standing on the seat of the tractor, Andy reached into the rafters of the bridge to a shelf that had been made by nailing planks across the horizontal beams of the trusses.

He lowered two different tubular weapons to the top of the tractor, then the .50-cal without the tripod, wrapped with a long belt of ammo. Reaching farther on the shelf, he retrieved a remote detonator.

"I recognize the machine gun. What are those tubes?" she asked.

"The AT4 CS is a recoilless rifle. This one came from Fort Bragg. It'll take out an armored vehicle. It can safely be fired within a confined space. You've probably heard of the other tube—the Stinger surface-to-air missile. The government tried to buy back all of the Stingers from the Mujahedeen guerrillas after the Russians left Afghanistan, but a few of them got misplaced in Buckingham County. My grandfather left me the .50-cal."

"It's hard to believe that a person can buy Stinger missiles locally."

"Anyone with enough money can buy these weapons today," he said, jumping off the tractor. "Some people collect stamps. My family has always collected weapons. Somebody has to be prepared to protect the rest of us from our government. That's what the cave is for. You're marrying one of those nuts you read about who hordes guns and ammo."

"Jack is getting fussy," Lindsey said.

Andy picked up the Henry Schein box and sniffed. "No plumbing problems here. He could be nervous about being in his first firefight."

"Maybe he's just hungry. Can we rotate again while you're waiting on the next phase of this campaign?"

"Which one has the freshest milk?"

"Go for the right side."

Andy picked Jack up out of the box and switched him with Ava. He sniffed Ava.

"I don't usually carry Pampers on the tractor."

He placed Ava in the box and slid it underneath the rear wheels of the tractor, two feet from Lindsey's head. "That front-end loader provides two sloped steel armor plates between us and anyone that comes down the road from the gate. I can rest the AT4 and the machine gun on the bucket without exposing myself."

He unrolled the belt on the .50 cal and slid the machine gun underneath the tractor.

He pushed the AT4 between the front wheels.

The cell phone rang.

"Bad news, Andy. There're two helicopters, both UH-60L Black Hawks with Army camo. They're hugging the river from the northwest, two miles away."

"Helicopters are almost here," he said to Lindsey, closing his phone.

Andy picked the Stinger off the top of the tractor and placed it on his right shoulder. He walked thirty yards up the gravel road toward the alfalfa field and dropped to one knee. Since the field was surrounded by mature oak trees and pines, the choppers would have to climb up before landing. There should be a clear sight window up the road. He wouldn't shoot the first chopper. Even if he had more than one stinger at the bridge, the second helicopter wouldn't hang around if he shot the first one. Ben would know what to do.

The chopper blades churned louder and louder. Like a bird of prey, the first UH-60 appeared over the top of the trees. It descended out of view into the field. The second Black Hawk appeared immediately. At the moment the infrared sensor locked on the target, he fired. The missile was approaching Mach two as it slammed into the helicopter. The western sky filled with fire, debris, and secondary explosions from the weapons onboard.

When the sound of these explosions diminished, Andy heard a sound like no other. This was the second time he had been saved by that sound, sweeter than a violin. The first time was in Iraq. He had been trapped that day in a street blocked off by insurgents. Three wounded men lay behind him. He had been down to his last ammo clip.

The music was the steady, controlled bursts of an experienced .50-cal operator. From the bunker inside the tree line at the top of the alfalfa field, Ben was methodically chewing on the first Black Hawk and anyone unfortunate enough to have been in it. The heavy rounds ricocheted through the trees to his northwest. The bursts were abruptly drowned out when an incendiary shell hit the gas tank of the chopper. No one outside a bunker could survive the series of secondary explosions that followed.

Andy walked back underneath the roof of the bridge. "What a waste of fine soldiers. In battle there can be no mercy until your enemy is dead or has surrendered. I can only make President Marshall pay for this."

He tossed the Stinger tube out of the window of the bridge into the creek.

"I had in mind a quieter nursery," Lindsey said, "but I'm not complaining."

"It's a good thing," he said, "because it's not over. The next assault will likely come down that road."

He pointed up the hill from the bridge toward the gate. "Cars and trucks couldn't get here as quickly as that chopper. These vehicles will have the nuclear weapons experts, the morgue crew, and the CIA team. One of their primary goals is to kill you."

He picked up the remote detonator from the top of the tractor and held its two buttons down at the same time. A green light came on. "There is an anti-tank mine in the road, part way down the hill. I'm hoping it will stack up the vehicles long enough for me to work them over with my .50-cal." He crawled under the tractor and looked down at Ava in the box.

"I'm going to wrap her head better to protect her ears. Do what you can to protect Jack."

"Do you have any idea how many are coming?" Lindsey asked.

"No. I'm hoping the guys driving in here expect the Rangers to have everything under control. Since that hill is sloped toward us, I should be able to shoot into the windshield of each vehicle when they get stacked up. Maybe they won't see us until the first vehicle hits the mine."

"What's the bow for?"

"Quiet deaths."

"Jack and Ava will appreciate that."

54

They waited underneath the tractor on the covered bridge.

"The Carlsons have been improving on the defense of this property for over 250 years," Andy said. "So far our enemies have used predictable battle plans."

The cell phone rang again.

"Your buddies are at the gate. They're cutting the chain now. I see three vehicles. The first two are shaped like UPS trucks painted black. The last vehicle is a dark sedan."

"I don't think they're Jehovah's Witnesses," Andy said, closing the phone.

Andy took his position underneath the tractor and rested the .50-cal on the bucket of the front end loader. He pulled earplugs out of his pocket and pushed them in place.

The SWAT truck rounded the turn in the gravel farm road from the gate and started down the hill. Before it reached the mine, it stopped.

"They see the tractor," he said.

Andy set the machine gun down and picked up the AT4 CS recoilless rifle. The range was forty-five meters. The shot hoisted the first van into the air, igniting secondary explosions. The second van began to back up.

He picked up the .50-cal again. The heavy barrel rested on the bottom of the front-end loader bucket as he fired. The bullets painted ragged lines back and forth across the windshield and body of the second van. It stopped moving.

Since there was little debris left from the first van to obscure his view, Andy concentrated his incendiary bullets on the undercarriage of the second van. He found the gas tank.

Andy strained to see the dark sedan through the mangled metal and flaming debris ascending from the second van. Small pieces of the vehicle rained on the tin roof overhead.

Small arms fire struck the front-end loader and splintered the wooden posts at the entrance to the bridge. Andy found the source. Three men were behind the sedan.

"I'll be back," Andy said. He laid the machine gun down on the planks of the bridge underneath his tractor and picked up his bow and quiver. Sprinting from the front of the bridge to the woody hill to his right, he watched the three men in suits turn their pistols from the bridge toward him.

The ground at Little Round Top strongly favored those on high ground, just like the hill by the same name favored the Yankees on the second day of the Battle of Gettysburg. Andy disappeared into the woods at the base of the hill. The three suits would recognize the strategic nature of the high ground. They would run into the woods and climb that hill.

Andy ran unobserved on level ground along Dry Creek. By the time the three men crested the hill, he was in position on their left flank, halfway down the back side of the hill, in a turkey blind.

He stuck two arrows into the ground and nocked a third. The three began firing at the twelve life-sized cardboard Fathead Andy Carlson targets facing them at the bottom of Little Round Top.

The suits moved from tree to tree as they fired. They were unaware of the arrows coming toward them from their left, only twenty to thirty yards away. Andy shot the last man in line first, just like he had learned to shoot the last turkey in line as a boy.

He crawled out of the blind and checked each body on his way back to the bridge.

"Lindsey?"

"The feeling is coming back in my legs and stomach," she said. "How are you?"

"Ready to get you to the hospital."

The cell phone rang again.

"More bad news, Andy. They just keep coming. Two Humvees with four soldiers in each, followed by a tractor-trailer pulling a low boy."

"What's on the low boy?

"A CAT nine bulldozer."

"A grave digger."

"You need help?"

"I need you more as my spotter."

"There's a .50-cal mounted on the second Humvee," Charlie said.

Andy looked at the ammo belt of his .50 cal. Forty rounds at most. "Lindsey, I'm going to need to conserve ammo. This belt, my knife, and my bow are all we've got. I have three arrows left."

The first Humvee stopped at the empty sedan and looked at the wreckage of the two SWAT trucks in the road. The driver turned off the road to his right to skirt the obstruction.

"They don't see us yet," Andy said.

Just as the Humvee re-entered the road half way down the hill, it hit the mine. The vehicle was launched twenty yards up Little Round Top. The bridge vibrated. Andy ducked as more pieces of metal bounced off the front-end loader bucket and the roof of the bridge. Humvees have a well-deserved reputation for leaving no survivors, regardless of what explosive device they drive over.

Three of the soldiers in the second Humvee dismounted and ran into the thick woods to Andy's left, the Briar Patch. They appeared to be carrying M16s.

While these three attempted their flanking maneuver, the other two in the vehicle jumped behind the metal plate guarding their .50 cal. As they turned the heavy barrel toward the bridge, Andy burned a path across the protective plate with his .50 cal. Both men dived out of the Humvee, apparently uninjured. They hid behind their vehicle with .45 caliber pistols, where they were joined by the driver of the low boy and another soldier. These two carried M16s.

The soldiers behind the Humvee realized that the plate that protected the operator of their .50-cal could not withstand the armor piercing incendiary shells coming their way. This shield was designed to deflect NATO rounds and other small arms. It had a vertical aiming slot which also left the operator vulnerable. The four behind the second Humvee concentrated their fire on the tractor, where Andy held his fire behind the front end loader.

Two explosions from the Briar Patch shook the bridge again.

"What was that?"Lindsey asked.

"Fathead targets along the creek. They're pretty good shots. Hope they got 'em all."

One of the soldiers behind the remaining Humvee ran back to the low-boy. He kept his head low. Andy had no shot.

The Cat nine dozer fired up. Andy recognized the significance. The driver would elevate the four–inch thick steel blade and the three soldiers would fall in behind. He would be unable to stop them from his position, even with .50 cal. armor piercing shells. They would drive up into his face and toss a grenade. He looked overhead in the rafters of the bridge. He had no weapon to compete with this tactic. He had twenty rounds left in the belt of his .50 cal.

The dozer backed off the low boy trailer and slowly advanced to the Humvee, where the three soldiers fell in behind. With the blade elevated, it may as well have been a tank. The giant yellow grave digger marched relentlessly toward the bridge. The best Andy could do was fire an occasional round to keep the three pinned down behind the dozer.

Surrender was not an option. The president didn't want to take Andy or Lindsey into custody. He wanted to make their children orphans. If the three men behind the dozer had grenades, the twins would not survive.

The dozer was almost within grenade range. The three soldiers had stopped firing. They would be pulling the pins of their grenades soon. Andy clutched the .50-cal with a handful of shells in its ammo belt and sprinted around the left side of the blade.

55

The staccato fire of a .50-cal from the bunker on top of Little Round Top took out the driver of the dozer, which stopped fifteen yards from the bridge. One of the soldiers broke toward Andy. He received Andy's last rounds. The other two soldiers were cut down by Ben as they ran toward the tree line of the Briar Patch. The battlefield fell silent except for the distant shooting from the practice range across the river.

Andy walked out from behind the bulldozer and waved toward the bunker. He held both hands up with his palms toward Ben, signaling him to remain in position and cover his withdrawal.

"Lindsey, is everybody okay?"

"We're ready to go. My pain is really coming back, and Ava needs a change."

He backed the dozer up and off the gravel road, and then killed the engine.

He opened his cell phone and dialed 911, requesting two Advanced Life Support ambulances.

Pulling Ava's box out from underneath the tractor, Andy kissed her forehead and said, "Remind me about your Pampers the next time we go for a drive."

Andy started his tractor, picked up the front end loader and turned it right–side up. He raised the mower with the rear hydraulics. It was a winding path through the smoldering tangle of metal toward the gate, carrying one mattress, one mother and two bundles of joy on the mower.

At the gate, Andy turned the tractor around so that the mower housing faced South Airport Road and blocked the entrance. When he turned off the engine, he could hear the first ambulance wailing.

Andy knew both the EMTs in the ambulance well. They were a couple, affectionately known as Jack Sprat and his wife. He explained to skinny Jack that one of the charges set off by the Marines had ruptured a propane line near his house and that Lindsey had been injured in an explosion.

"Do we need to call the Farmville Fire Department?" asked his rotund wife, who served as the driver.

"Everything's okay now," Andy said. "I got the propane turned off."

"We heard the Marines blowing all those logjams out of the river," Mr. Sprat said. "It sounds like they're really enjoying the war games."

"My brother-in-law is in that mob qualifying down at the practice range," his wife said.

Andy pointed to the low boy. "The Marines even brought their own bulldozer to push up the debris."

Andy introduced Lindsey to the EMTS. "This is Charlie and Jeanne Dodd's daughter from Colorado. She has a broken arm and a broken right leg. She suffered a concussion today. Then she had an emergency C-section. She needs to be transfused and evaluated by the obstetrician. The orthopedist on call needs to evaluate Lindsey's fractures. She needs pain medication. Her parents will be along soon and supply insurance information. I want the twins to go in the second unit."

"Brian and Tim are on their way," skinny Jack said. He wrote furiously on the EMS run sheet.

Andy said, "The boy's name is Jack. The girl's name is Ava."

While the EMTs loaded Lindsey into the back of the ambulance, Andy stood next to the rear doors and called Charlie Dodd again.

"Need another favor."

"You think it's over?" Charlie asked.

"The burial squad is usually the last actor on the battlefield, but I wouldn't count chickens yet."

"What started all this?"

"My girlfriend came back."

"Trouble seems to follow that girl."

"Some of it wasn't her fault."

"She's the same one that stabbed you?"

"We're over that. She got hurt pretty bad today. I just sent her to the hospital in an ambulance."

"I see them. She going to be all right?"

"I think so. She also had twins today."

"Slow down a minute."

"I'm the father."

"For crying out loud," Charlie said. "You need to give me a program with a diagram and all the players on it so I can keep up. I didn't even know you were expecting."

"I didn't know, either, until a short time ago."

"So what can I do?"

"The president and the CIA may still want to kill her."

"You think they would come to the hospital?"

"That's why I need your help. Could you go to the hospital and act like Lindsey is your daughter? Take Jeanne with you. Say she's visiting from Colorado. Her name would be Lindsey Dodd."

"You getting married?"

"She said 'yes' today."

"Should I take my gun with me?"

"Wear a coat to cover it up."

"I'm protecting Lindsey from the feds?"

"Sit outside the door and stop anybody you don't recognize. Congratulate Jeanne on being a grandmother again."

"I'll do that."

"If you do a good job, I'll let you walk her down the aisle some day. Her real dad's dead."

"Let's get this straight," Charlie said. "She stabbed you on an off day. Now she's had two of your babies. She got beat up real bad. The feds are trying to kill her. I'm going to be her bodyguard. I'm giving her away?"

"Something like that. She's really a nice girl who needs another line of work."

Andy leaned in and said, "Lindsey, you're going to need a few days in the hospital. I'll catch up with you later tonight."

She asked, "Lindsey Dodd?"

"We can't use your name yet."

The return of gunfire from the road behind him was a bad sign. It sounded like two .50-cals.

56

"Put the babies in your unit with their mom and go now," Andy yelled. He saw Brian's ambulance approaching from the intersection of South Airport Road and Plank Road. "Tell Brian to wait here at the gate."

Andy picked up his bow and quiver from the mower and ran toward the gunfire. As he reached the crest of the road, Andy saw Ben drop the .50-cal in his hands and collapse behind a rock. He was not moving.

A survivor from the Briar Patch had waited until Ben was out in the open to fire the .50-cal from the Humvee. This soldier's back was toward Andy. He kept firing at the rock Ben had fallen behind.

Andy dropped to one knee, nocked an arrow, and smoothly brought his bow to full draw. The arrow arched seventy-five yards before slicing through the upper back of the soldier, who collapsed.

Andy looked behind him. Brian and Tim had stopped at the gate. He motioned for them to follow him and ran toward Ben.

Andy knelt next to his cousin. Ben was pale but conscious. Blood gurgled from his mouth. The front of his battle fatigue shirt was already saturated in blood.

"I'm sorry," Ben gasped. "Take care of Precious and my kids."

He lapsed into unconsciousness with agonal respirations.

"If there is a just God," Andy said, "He would not bless me and curse me on the same day. He didn't give me a chance to save Josiah in the desert. I never had a chance to save my mother. Today He is giving me that chance."

Andy ripped Ben's battle fatigue shirt apart and looked at the wound. A golf ball-sized hole had replaced his left nipple. He felt behind him without turning him over. The exit wound was at the tip of Ben's left scapula, the wing-shaped bone in the back of the shoulder.

Brian and Tim pulled up next to Andy and jumped out.

"Bring the stretcher over here. Gunshot wound to the chest."

Brian and Andy picked Ben up by the armpits and legs and placed him on the stretcher. He was now unconscious. They shoved the stretcher into the back of the ambulance. Andy sat down in the captain's chair behind Ben's head.

"I need both of you to help me before we move. He needs an airway and IVs now. You guys start two intraosseous lines in the legs while I try to get some oxygen in him."

Andy attempted to ventilate Ben using the resuscitation mask attached to the oxygen line in the ambulance.

Brian drilled a hole into the shin of both lower legs, using a small Craftsman drill. When the drill hit its plastic stop, he removed the center of each bit, leaving a large bore hollow needle firmly inside the bone marrow of each tibia. The bone marrow of the tibia communicates directly with the large veins in the thigh. These intraosseous lines don't fall out and provide reliable access to the venous circulation when most peripheral veins are collapsed due to blood loss.

Tim spiked two bags of normal saline and attached the tubing to the intraosseous lines.

"Open them wide and put both on a pressure bag," Andy said.

Ventilation was not going well. When Andy squeezed the resuscitation bag with a tight mask over Ben's face, he heard bubbles. The chest was not moving. The oxygenated air was taking the path of least resistance, passing through the large hole in Ben's lung and out the holes in his chest wall. If the chest wall is not moving, oxygen is not getting to the blood from the heart.

"Put an occlusive dressing over both wounds," Andy said.

Brian tore open a square bandage covered with petroleum jelly and slapped it over the wound in front and the wound in Ben's back.

"Tim, tape down three sides of the wound in front. Brian, keep trying to ventilate while I get ready to intubate him."

Andy assembled the laryngoscope, an endotracheal tube, and a stylet to make the tube rigid. He bent the end of the tube to the shape of a hockey stick in order to make it easier to insert. He attached a syringe to the pilot tube that ran along the side of the endotracheal tube to the air cuff at the end of the tube.

"He's still got a carotid pulse," Brian said.

"I need a stiff suction catheter for my right hand," Andy said. "And get him on the monitors."

Andy opened Ben's mouth with his right thumb and forefinger, pushing the lower teeth down with the thumb and the upper teeth up with the index finger, holding the endotracheal tube like a cigarette between his index and middle fingers.

"We won't need a sedative or a paralytic agent," he said, suctioning blood from the mouth and throat.

Holding the laryngoscope in his left hand and the endotracheal tube in his right hand, he inserted the blade of the laryngoscope along the right side of the tongue. Lifting up, he searched for airway landmarks in the blood. He inserted the blade a bit deeper.

"Crike pressure please," he said.

Brian pressed on the cricothyroid cartilage in the neck. The epiglottis popped into view. Lifting just a little more with the laryngoscope blade, he saw the vocal cords, the entrance to the upper airway. He inserted the tube between the vocal cords, inflated the cuff, and held the tube in place.

"I'm at twenty-three centimeters at the corner of the mouth," Andy said. He removed the mask from the ventilation bag and attached the bag to the end of the endotracheal tube.

"Hold this tube where it is while I see if I can ventilate him," he said to Tim.

The chest still did not move. Each squeeze of the bag only resulted in gurgling from the left chest.

"Let's try something," Andy said. "I know this tube is not in the esophagus. Give me the syringe for the pilot tube cuff."

He aspirated the air from the cuff, forced the entire endotracheal tube another four centimeters into the airway, and re-inflated the cuff.

When he squeezed the bag, the right side of the chest rose easily.

Brian understood. "You pushed the tube into the right main stem bronchus, isolating the right lung. Now we can at least ventilate him with one lung."

"Roll him over onto his right side," Andy said. "Stuff pillows underneath to keep his left side up."

When they turned Ben onto his right side, blood poured out the exit wound in his left posterior chest, soaking the stretcher and puddling in the floor of the ambulance.

"Why are you turning him?" Tim asked.

"It matches the best ventilation with the best perfusion," Brian said. "His right lung is all we have to work with. Gravity and resistance from the collapsed left lung will cause what blood he has to favor the right lung, where all of the oxygen is now going."

"But we still have to stop the bleeding," Andy said. "Tape this tube in where it is and hyperventilate him with one hundred percent oxygen."

Andy yanked off the occlusive dressing and looked at the wound again. "My hand won't go though that hole. Give me some eight and a half gloves and the scalpel from the crike tray."

He glanced up at the monitors. Heart rate 144/minute. BP forty systolic. Ben's lips were blue from the unoxygenated blood in his body.

Andy stuck the scalpel in the wound and cut the muscles between Ben's fifth and sixth ribs from the wound toward his left armpit.

"His fourth rib is shattered," he said. "We can take advantage of that to make a larger hole."

He made an L-shaped incision on the left side of the sternum, resulting in a free flap of anterior chest wall.

Brian's eyes widened as Andy wiggled his right hand into Ben's chest. "What are you doing?"

"I'm going to wrap my fist around his left hilum. That includes the left main stem bronchus, his left pulmonary artery, and left pulmonary vein. It's just plugging the hole in the dike until we can get him to the ED."

"Are we ready to roll?" Tim asked.

"Brian, you drive. Call the ED and tell them what we've got. I want eight units of O negative blood in the ED when we get there. I need a thoracotomy tray and a chest tube tray. Ask them to page the thoracic surgeon and notify the OR and anesthesia."

"Tim, hang two more bags of saline and then take over the resuscitation bag. Give him twenty breaths per minute. Now that I have the blood supply and the air supply for his left lung in my right fist, we won't be losing much ground until we get to the hospital. I can hold this."

Brian slammed the ambulance doors closed. He spit gravel behind them until they returned to the gate and turned right on South Airport Road. Most folks don't know that you can lay rubber on asphalt with an ambulance. They reached Plank Road, where Brian turned right again. The hospital was six minutes away. He floored the accelerator again and turned on the lights and siren.

Alina, the charge nurse, met them at the ambulance entrance. "Take him to Trauma One. All of your trays are out."

"Start a unit of blood in each leg," Andy said.

They picked Ben up with the bloody sheet on the stretcher and transferred him to the trauma stretcher, still on his right side. The respiratory therapist took over ventilation.

Three nurses stopped what they were doing and rushed to the bedside.

"Everybody look for two more IV sites in his arms. I can't start a central line with my hand in his chest. Put this stretcher in head-down position to encourage blood flow to his heart and brain."

"I'm going to need five units of fresh frozen plasma thawed out," Andy said. "Somebody take notes. I want as much saline and blood in him as we can possibly pump for now. Nuke a couple of blankets in the microwave so he won't get hypothermic. Is the thoracic surgeon coming?"

"We haven't found him yet," Alina said.

"Then I have a job for you. Put on surgical gloves and step over here."

"Me?"

"You have the smallest hands in the department and you're left handed."

"What does that mean?"

"Stand on the left side of this stretcher and slip your left hand next to mine into his chest."

"But..."

"No time to practice. Slide your hand in and follow my forearm down until you can feel my fist. Blood is a good lubricant. Just force your way in."

Her hand disappeared into Ben's chest next to Andy's forearm.

"Is that your hand I'm on top of?" she asked.

"As far as I know, we're the only people visiting this man's chest today," Andy said. "You're doing great. Move your hand past my fist until you can encircle the same structures that I'm squeezing. I'll tell you when you've got it right."

"I've got a good line in his right arm," Brian said.

"Great work. Draw his labs first, and then start saline in that line, wide open on a pressure bag."

"Dr. Carlson, I think I've got everything in my fist that you have," Alina said.

Andy replied, "It feels right. Squeeze tight and don't let go until I give the word."

Andy looked up at the monitors as he wiggled his hand out of the wound. Blood pressure 70 systolic. Heart rate 130.

"Give me a trauma line for the left femoral vein," Andy said. "I think I can still get it in with him on his right side. Somebody put in a Foley catheter and a nasogastric tube."

Andy scrubbed the left groin and inserted the central line into Ben's left femoral vein. "This line is for saline only, wide open, one after another, on a pump. Keep blood going in both intraosseous lines, one unit of O negative after another. Keep score."

The nursing supervisor arrived at the foot of the bed. Her mouth opened so wide that her denture adhesive failed. She reached for her mouth.

Andy looked up. "I need the OR crew immediately for an emergency thoracotomy. Try to get at least three OR nurses. If you can't find anybody, then you can be an OR nurse."

"Has the thoracic surgeon answered his page?" the supervisor asked, readjusting her dentures.

"Not yet," answered the unit coordinator.

The nursing supervisor ran down the hall, punching numbers into her cell phone.

"Send a police car to Dr. Nase's office," Alina said. "He's not on call, but he'll always help."

"Good thinking," Andy said. He nodded at the unit coordinator, who was standing on her tiptoes trying to follow the action. She ran back to her phone.

Andy looked down at the Foley catheter, which was in Ben's bladder. Only a trickle of urine was coming through the tubing. "Now we have another way to monitor perfusion," Andy said. "I want a report on urine output every fifteen minutes."

"How are you holding out, Alina?"

"I'm hanging in there, but my hand is cramping."

Andy looked at her position. He lowered the bed with his foot and pushed a rolling stool behind her.

"Sit down and make yourself as comfortable as you can. You may have to hold what you've got until a surgeon gets here."

The unit coordinator yelled, "The police are at Dr. Nase's office. He went to lunch without his beeper."

Andy and Alina looked at each other.

"Ask them to go looking for him," Alina yelled. "His staff might know where he went. Keep trying Dr. Jones. He's really the one on call."

"Roll the patient onto his back long enough to get a chest X-ray while Alina holds what she's got," Andy said.

"Alina, may I take an X-ray of your hand inside this man's chest?" he asked. "I'll get you a copy for your bedroom wall."

"It's okay; I'm not pregnant."

"If we can get this patient into the OR and cross clamp the left pulmonary vessels and the left main stem bronchus," Andy said, "Dr. Jones or Dr. Nase can take their time figuring out how much of the left lung can be saved."

Andy watched the blood and saline pour in from four IVs. "The blood pressure and heart rate are about the same. I wonder how bad we're leaking. I want a blood gas, and a repeat CBC."

Andy looked again at the Foley bag. Urine output was still meager.

"He's bled a ton," Andy said to Alina. "I need to know what's happening inside the chest. Let's suction the left side and see how much blood is leaking into the left pleural space."

Andy inserted a stiff twelve inch catheter next to Alina's hand and turned on the wall suction. Two hundred milliliters came out immediately. He waited several minutes then suctioned again. Fifty more milliliters were aspirated.

"Blood is getting past your grip, Alina," he said.

"I'm doing the best I can," she said.

"You're doing fantastic," he said. "But since we can't seem to locate Dr. Jones or Dr. Nase, I think that I should widen our opening in the chest and cross clamp the blood vessels and airway to his left lung."

"I've never seen anyone do anything like that in the ED," Alina said.

"Push the thoracotomy tray closer. I'll take the heat." There was no turning back now.

The portable chest X-ray was taken.

"Now roll him over on his right side again," Andy said. "And somebody get me an OR gown, a cap, and another pair of surgical gloves, size eight and a half."

Andy checked the patient's pupils, which were sluggishly reactive to light.

"He's not getting enough blood flow to his head to be awake, but I would like to give him a dose of Etomidate for sedation just before I make my incision. Draw up 24 milligrams. I also want ten milligrams of Norcuron to paralyze him. Neither should affect his blood pressure."

A nurse helped Andy into his gown and surgical gloves. He found the clamps he needed on the tray.

"Get me two hand-held battery cautery units and a number ten surgical scalpel," he said.

Andy scrubbed the chest wall around the hole that Alina had her arm in. "Give the Etomidate and Norcuron IV now."

As soon as the drugs were in, Andy began at the corner of the wound, next to Alina's hand, and extended the incision with the scalpel, following the intercostal space between the fifth and sixth ribs to the left mid-axillary line, below the armpit. New bleeders appeared, which he fried with the battery cautery. His second pass with the scalpel penetrated to the pleura, the inside lining of the chest.

"Rib cutters," he ordered.

Rib cutters are reminiscent of loppers used to prune trees. Andy snapped the fourth and fifth ribs in the mid-axillary line. Almost everyone in the trauma room groaned.

"Rib spreaders," he ordered.

A rib spreader functions like a small car jack with a base of five to six inches on each end. These bases are shaped like a gutter to accommodate a rib above and below. Once a spreader is wedged between two ribs, a crank is turned. This opens up the intercostal space, or space between two ribs.

If a single rib is cut in two places seven to eight centimeters apart, and one base of the rib spreader is placed against this loose section of rib, the chest opening will be much wider when the crank is turned. In this case, the .50 caliber slug had demolished the medial fourth and fifth ribs near their attachment to the sternum, or breast bone. The rib cutters had cut the fourth and fifth ribs laterally in the mid-axillary line. Andy clamped and tied the intercostal blood vessels medially and laterally.

Bending the free segment of the fourth and fifth ribs back like an awning over a window, Andy wedged the rib spreader between the reflected segment of the fourth and fifth ribs above and the sixth rib below.

As he turned the crank the opening into the left chest became rectangular shaped, the size of a paperback novel. This opening was large enough for his over-sized right hand in addition to Alina's slim hand and forearm. Andy adjusted the overhead surgical light into the wound and aspirated as much blood as he could see. He saw no injury to the heart.

Andy felt the left ventricular wall bump against his hand with every beat. The segments of the pulmonary artery and vein that Alina held were torn. If these vessels had been entirely avulsed by the .50 caliber slug, Ben would already be dead.

Andy chose a vascular clamp from the thorocotomy tray. These clamps have soft protective jaws that prevent damage to the structures they compress. He suctioned around Alina's hand until he recognized the left main pulmonary artery. It was the large vessel that vibrated with each heartbeat.

Using his fingers, he bluntly dissected the fibrous tissue around the vessel in order to allow both jaws of the clamp around the pulmonary artery. He inserted the clamp and adjusted the jaws around the vessel.

He directed the thumb and finger loops of the clamp to lie flat before squeezing the jaws and locking them.

"Hold on, Alina. Not much longer," he said.

Andy aspirated another twenty-five milliliters of blood and clamped the left main pulmonary vein, again adjusting the clamp to lie flat against the first clamp when the jaws were locked.

"One more, Alina, "he said. "I know your hand is aching."

The left main stem bronchus was easy to identify, since it had no blood flowing in it and cartilaginous rings to keep it open. Andy carefully clamped the bronchus next to Alina's fist. He suctioned the floor of the left chest and watched for any signs of further bleeding. There were none.

"Open your hand, Alina, and pull it out," he said.

The surgical field remained dry. Andy noted that most of the damage was to the upper lobe of the left lung.

He looked up at the monitors. The blood pressure was 105, the heart rate 111.

Urine was steadily dripping out of the Foley tube into the bag.

"I want another X-ray," he said, "and a clean pair of shorts."

Alina nudged him and smiled.

"You saved two butts tonight, Alina," he said. "Incredible job. It's a lot easier to fill a bucket if you plug up the hole in the bottom first. Let's pour in all the blood we have now and keep the saline wide open."

Dr. Jones strode into the trauma room and looked at the patient's open chest. His pupils dilated to take in what he was seeing.

"Uh. What's going on here?" he asked.

"Hi Bill," Andy said. "This is a thirty-five year old male with a .50 caliber gunshot wound to the left chest. The left pulmonary artery, the left pulmonary vein, and the left main stem bronchus are all clamped. We now have good control of bleeding. There's no air leak. We've given him eleven liters of saline and six units of O negative. That's the best set of vital signs so far." He pointed to the monitors.

The unit coordinator yelled, "The OR says they're ready. The anesthesiologist is here."

"I'll go scrub," Dr. Jones said. "Take the patient to the OR. Do you have an op permit?"

Andy said, "No time, but I'll call his wife. I know her personally. The patient is Ben Carlson. He's a hospital employee. He accidentally got shot in the war games on my farm."

Andy had learned early in his career that most ED doctors and nurses would rather not know who their critical patients are. If no one on the staff recognizes the patient, it's better to keep it that way until the patient is stabilized or dead. When a trauma patient arrives unconscious with tubes in every orifice of his face, he is often unrecognizable. Such patients are processed by numbers, like "Trauma Patient 1234," until they are identified by a relative.

Andy went to the private conference room and made the call.

"Precious, this is Andy. Ben was injured today, but he's in the hospital now and he's going to be okay. I'll send out a Farmville police officer to get you. Ask someone to page me when you get to the emergency room. Please ask Jasmine to babysit as a favor to me. One more thing, I can't explain it now, but Ben became an uncle today."

Before leaving the hospital, Andy checked on the twins. They were doing well, although they preferred momma's breasts to bottles held by strangers. Lindsey's right wrist fracture was adequately treated, but she required a prolonged surgical procedure to reassemble the bones in her left lower leg. She was sleeping when Andy left.

By 9:00 in the evening, Andy was back at home. There was one very large snake that needed surgery. He hit the speed dial for the president's private number.

"President Marshall, this is Andy Carlson."

The president coughed.

"Harrison and all his men are dead," Andy said. "Boris and all his men are dead. Your two Black Hawks collided over my farm during a training mission. Harrison's chopper crashed in the same alfalfa field. Lindsey took care of Boris's two warheads. Your CIA and cleanup crews are dead. If you still think that you can win on this ground, you should know that I have about two dozen guys just like me out in the woods right now. They're all former SEALS."

The president did not speak.

"Let me take care of the burial arrangements for all these dead people," Andy said. "You can start working on the lies you're going to tell the families of the men you wasted here today."

The president hung up.

Andy's first e-mail went to the Chairman of the House Committee on the Judiciary, responsible for initiating impeachment proceedings. He included enough facts about the president's recent activities to ignite a fire. He attached a digital audio recording of the president's first conversation with him in the White House, while he was recovering from his own chest wound. He had taped the recorder to the one place he knew the Secret Service would not grab when they patted him down prior to leaving his room at George Washington University Medical Center.

Andy considered that this was the only intelligent thing that he had ever done with this organ. Thinking of the twins, he changed his mind.

The Washington Post might like a copy of this material, he thought. He clicked "Forward."

Tomorrow morning the president would probably be too busy answering questions to cause more trouble for the Carlson family.

57

Lindsey required two weeks in the hospital, but the babies were discharged in twenty-four hours. Ben's recovery was much quicker than Lindsey's. He lost half of the upper lobe of his left lung, but he was alert and talking two days later. His chest tube was out in seven days. He was anxious to get started on his new house. Andy took a leave of absence from the ED.

Andy asked Precious to bring Ben and the rest of her family to Andy's farmhouse until Lindsey got her casts off in six weeks. He pointed out that she would be closer to her husband, who probably needed advice about their new home.

In between visits to the hospital, feedings, and changing diapers, Andy restocked the cave system on the Farm and cleaned up the mess. Using his new Army bulldozer, he enlarged a crater in the alfalfa field and buried the soldiers, along with the debris.

The president took Andy's advice and sent no more soldiers or agents. Serious questions about a presidential and CIA scheme to use nuclear weapons to frame Arab countries were now being raised in the newspapers. Hearings were scheduled before the House Judiciary Committee.

After six weeks, Lindsey was walking again and able to take over childcare. Andy gave Precious what he called a "furniture bonus."

As the first hearing got underway, Andy moved his family into the Confederate cave. Charlie Dodd kept an eye on the gate across South Airport Road from his horse ranch. Ben kept his cell phone close as he dug the foundation for his house with a new backhoe, a gift from Andy.

One evening after they poured the concrete footings to Ben's new house, Andy said, "Being neighbors now, and relatives, and depending on each other, it's time I showed you everything."

He took Ben into the Grand Chamber for the first time. They reviewed the leather map.

Ben stared at the map. "Do you see this tunnel that goes east to my new property?"

"The map indicates that the overhead clearance is only a foot here," Andy said, pointing.

"But it continues all the way to my property. We could enlarge that opening. I could build a barn over it, like your tobacco barn."

"Now you're thinking like me," Andy said. "You want to see the gold?"

"I suspected that was what the G meant on your map," Ben said, looking over the stacks and rows of gold bars. "My granddaddy didn't believe it was there, but his daddy said it was."

"We're going to do some good things with this gold, Ben, but they won't be selfish things. You're going to be my partner."

Each evening Andy and Lindsey watched the impeachment process unfold on their television.

"Congress takes a month to make instant coffee," Lindsey said. She held an infant in each arm and limped through the tunnel from the Grand Chamber to the anteroom.

She stopped at the tunnel entrance to the anteroom and turned to Andy. "Sahar called today while you were out with Ben. She has a new boyfriend, a diplomat who lives in D.C."

"Oh Thank God."

"I've never heard you use that expression."

"I've made my peace with God, Lindsey. When you and the twins and Ben survived, I got down on my knees and asked forgiveness. I thanked Him for the blessings in my life. God always had a plan for me, but I wouldn't accept it."

"What does that have to do with Sahar?" she asked.

"The last time I talked to God, I threw in a request for a boyfriend for Sahar. Thanks for passing on His answer."

Lindsey smiled and continued walking into the anteroom. "And here are two nuclear warheads that I do not want you to play with. Daddy instructed me to remove the tritium reservoirs and cover the warheads with lead panels for your protection. A man named Uncle Boris donated $254 million to help you get started in life. And over here in this tunnel is $300 million in gold for your college fund. Even the president of the United States sent you $175 million to celebrate your birth. And when you get older, you're going to have the same kind of passion for everything you do that your daddy has. In no time at all you'll be running around with nothing but a loincloth and a spear. Your daddy has a whole lot of secrets to tell you someday, and you're gonna love the Farm."

CPSIA information can be obtained at www.ICGtesting.com
Printed in the USA
BVOW01*0255040414

349695BV00002B/12/P